ROSE RIVERS lives in a beautiful big London house with her artist father, querulous mother, six siblings and seven servants – and finds her life stifling. She loves to study and longs to go to boarding school like her twin brother, but Victorian young ladies are supposed to be content staying at home.

She misses her brother very much. But then she makes two new friends, though neither are considered suitable: the new nursery maid, Clover Moon, and her father's bohemian protégé, Paris Walker. Rose suddenly finds her life turned upside down . . .

JACQUELINE WILSON wrote her first novel when she was nine years old, and she has been writing ever since. She is now one of Britain's bestselling and most beloved children's authors. She has written over 100 books and is the creator of characters such as Tracy Beaker and Hetty Feather. More than forty million copies of her books have been sold.

As well as winning many awards for her books, including the Children's Book of the Year, Jacqueline is a former Children's Laureate, and in 2008 she was appointed a Dame.

Jacqueline is also a great reader, and has amassed over twenty thousand books, along with her famous collection of silver rings.

Find out more about Jacqueline and her books at www.jacquelinewilson.co.uk

Jacqueline Wilson

Illustrated by Nick Sharratt

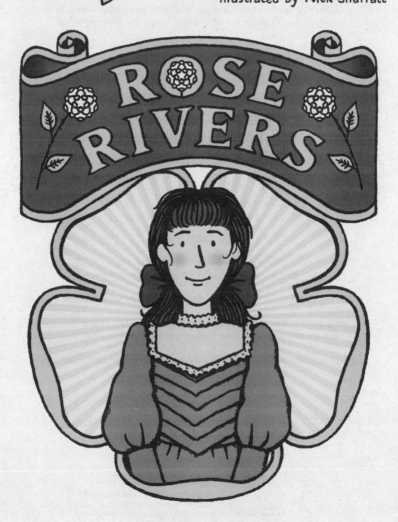

ROSE RIVERS

CORGI YEARLING

CORGI YEARLING

UK | USA | Canada | Ireland | Australia
India | New Zealand | South Africa

Corgi Yearling is part of the Penguin Random House group of companies
whose addresses can be found at global.penguinrandomhouse.com.

www.penguin.co.uk
www.puffin.co.uk
www.ladybird.co.uk

First published by Doubleday 2018
This edition published 2019

001

Text copyright © Jaqueline Wilson, 2018
Illustrations copyright © Nick Sharratt, 2018

The moral right of the author and illustrator has been asserted

Set in 12/17pt New Century Schoolbook by Jouve (UK), Milton Keynes
Printed and bound in Great Britain by Clays Ltd, Elcograf S.p.A.

A CIP catalogue record for this book is available from the British Library

ISBN: 978-0-440-87166-8

All correspondence to:
Corgi Yearling
Penguin Random House Children's
80 Strand, London WC2R 0RL

To Cate and Nash of Much Ado Books

1

'**I HAVE A LITTLE** present for you, Rose,' said Papa.

He handed me a rectangular package tied with string that looked promisingly like a book. I love reading more than anything else, especially the books in Papa's studio. He doesn't know that I borrow them secretly. I don't bother with Mama's books in the cabinet in the drawing room as they are silly romantic tosh.

I opened my package eagerly, though I feared it would be a Mrs Molesworth or a Miss Yonge, the sort of authors considered suitable for a girl of thirteen.

But it wasn't a novel at all, for children or adults. It was a sketchbook, every page blank.

'I thought this would be a good time for you to start sketching seriously, sweetheart. I know you've been feeling rather mopey since Rupert left for school,' said Papa.

I didn't know what to say. He was trying so hard to cheer me up. And it's not as if I don't like drawing. I've spent half my childhood drawing witches and dragons and mermaids and tigers and goblins. Goblins are fun because I give them the faces of people I particularly detest. When my brother Algie crayoned all over the pages of my book of Tennyson's poetry, I created an entire community of grotesque goblins with his features.

I also like drawing girls. Not pretty girls with long brushed hair and demure dresses. Wild girls who have cut off their curls and tucked up their skirts or borrowed boy's breeches. They climb trees and leap streams and teeter on the very edge of cliffs. Sometimes I draw them being chastised. They are sent away in disgrace. They don't care!

Mama always tuts when she sees my drawings. She doesn't approve of them at all. Papa laughs and thinks them funny, but he says that I should start drawing seriously now. He is hoping that I have true artistic ability. It's not just because he is an indulgent father (though he is!). He'd like at least one of his children to have inherited his talent. Rupert is the eldest but has never had the patience or indeed any natural ability

2

at art. I am his twin and only fifteen minutes younger, so now Papa is pinning his hopes on me.

'I love your drawings, Rose. They're very lively and amusing, but I think it's time for you to learn to sketch properly. You should draw from life,' he said now, unusually serious.

'Not *still* life, Papa?' I groaned.

Our governess, Miss Rayner, sometimes arranges odds and ends that she feels are 'artistic' for us to paint with our shared box of Winsor & Newton watercolours. Last time she gathered a blue and white striped milk jug from the kitchen, a garish china couple won at a fairground, a bowl of fruit and a posy of violets in a pink pot. I tried reasonably hard, but the milk jug tilted alarmingly, the china couple looked drunk, the bowl of fruit wouldn't stay circular and the posy wilted before I could finish it.

'I know you find still-life compositions boring, Rose, but they teach you observation and perspective and shading. They will bring your sketches to life, so that they seem realistic representations.'

'I don't care for real life, Papa. I prefer living in my imagination,' I said.

He laughed at this. He doesn't mind if we argue with him, so long as we do it politely. He actively encourages us to discuss and dispute.

'I do sympathize, Rose,' he chuckled. 'But sometimes we have to do things we don't care for. I spent my first year at art school copying plaster casts. It was deadly boring but it taught me a great deal.'

3

'Then send *me* to art school, Papa!' I said.

He laughed again. 'Perhaps, when you are eighteen or so, I might send you to Paris to be properly trained, though I know Mama will object!'

'Mama always objects,' I said. 'In fact, one *could* say that Mama is objectionable!'

'That's enough, Rose,' Papa said firmly. He lets me argue with him, but he will never allow me to criticize Mama.

'How can I wait five whole years anyway?' I said instead. 'Couldn't I go to a boarding school where they have a good art teacher?'

I'd read about girls' boarding schools. I longed to go to one. I imagined charismatic teachers and intelligent girls having lively discussions in classrooms. I saw myself strolling through rose gardens, arm in arm with bookish girls, sipping cocoa together in our nightgowns, confiding secrets.

I knew I was wishing for the moon. This was another tired old argument, and one that involved further criticism of Mama. She had no qualms about sending my brother Rupert away to school, but she refused to even consider *my* education. I have to make do with Miss Rayner in the nursery schoolroom.

Sometimes I find it very hard indeed to like Mama. However, I love Papa and I will try to learn to sketch properly for his sake.

'May I sketch *you*, Papa?' I asked.

'Certainly! And I will sketch *you* simultaneously, Rose!' he said, very pleased.

It was companionable sitting in Papa's studio. We had a delightful conversation about artists too. They seem to live the most interesting and unconventional lives. I would very much like to be an artist – but I don't really like doing art. I tried so hard to do a good sketch of Papa, but it was a complete failure. He went lopsided like the milk jug, and I made him look incredibly fierce when he's the most amiable man I've ever met. Not that I've met many men. I sometimes think a nun in a convent has a better social life than me. If only I could go to school. Rupert is so LUCKY!

When I'd finished sketching, Papa wanted to see my portrait, but I wouldn't let him. I didn't want him to see what a failure I was. He is always hopeful that one of us will show artistic talent. He does his best to be encouraging. He praises Algie's scribbles even when they're in inappropriate places like the whitewashed nursery cupboards or the hall skirting board.

Papa's praise obviously means a great deal, because he is the painter Edward Rivers, well known in artistic circles. He is a follower of the great Pre-Raphaelite painters, and when he was a young man he was considered equal to them in talent. He was also wild and bohemian. He even had a pet wombat, just like his hero, Rossetti.

How I wish he had a wombat now! Our pets are nowhere near as exotic. We have Mistletoe, a large white cat who sleeps all day on his rocking chair by the kitchen range, and Alphonse, Mama's tiny Mexican dog, who snaps a great deal, and shivers when Mr Hodgson takes him for his daily walk.

Alphonse will be tucked up with Mama on the chaise longue in the drawing room, both of them staring into space with their beady eyes. How strange that it is called the *drawing* room when no one ever draws there, not even Papa. Now that I'm in my teens and considered a young lady I'm allowed to sit in the drawing room. Not that I want to! It's not at all comfortable, though the chairs and sofas are cushioned and well sprung. Even Papa seems out of his element there, though he sits dutifully beside Mama for half an hour every day, resolutely keeping her company.

Mama suffers from ill health. She's been poorly ever since my youngest sister, Phoebe, was born, and is forever resting. Phoebe is a delightful baby sister, the roundest, rosiest little dumpling. She has such a sunny nature, all chuckles and smiles. By contrast Mama looks pale and unappetizing nowadays, like Cook's vanilla shape. She has grown much fatter since Phoebe, and has had to order a dozen new gowns, though I'm sure she could simply have had her old ones altered. Mama cares terribly about clothes. It irritates her enormously that I don't give a fig about my appearance.

'You dress like a hoyden, Rose! How can you wander around barefoot, like a ragamuffin off the streets? Have you even brushed your hair this morning? Stop frowning at me like that! Your forehead creases in such an ugly fashion. It's because you always have your head in a book! You will end up having to wear spectacles like a frumpy old spinster.'

I rather fancy wearing spectacles. I think they might make me look scholarly. I cannot see why being a spinster is so scorned anyway. Miss Rayner is a spinster and she seems perfectly content, humming hymns and sucking fruit drops and tapping her foot merrily when the little ones pipe on their penny whistles. She doesn't appear to mind that she only has three frocks and they're all patched and darned, even her best black silk. She seems a happy soul.

Mama is the lady of the house and has a distinguished artist husband and seven children and a beautiful home in London and a wardrobe full of new gowns, and yet she's as miserable as sin.

She makes everyone else miserable too, even Papa, though he tries to ignore her complaints.

'For pity's sake, Edward, I wish you'd stop doing these sordid urban sketches. Who on earth wants to see pallid drawings of street children? I wish you'd never agreed to do the illustrations for Sarah Smith's wretched little books. I know she does charity work for destitute girls, but I really don't see why you have to be involved. Why don't you do proper oil paintings again?'

'I don't feel inclined,' Papa said stiffly.

'Because you've lost your famous muse,' said Mama, with an edge to her voice. Papa used to do portraits of the Honourable Louisa Mayhorne. His most famous is the one where she's wearing a low-cut evening dress with one black strap slipping off her pearly shoulder. It caused a scandal, but everyone agreed that it was a wonderful painting. Perhaps Louisa didn't care for the attention, because she doesn't pose for Papa any more. I wish she did. She always winked at me and called me Chickie, and once gave me a little box of rose creams.

'Why won't you take on respectable commissions for portraits? If you're tired of London Society, perhaps you should try in Scotland. You know very well that my father would be delighted to introduce you to the members of the Caledonian Club,' Mama needled him.

'I'm afraid I'm not inspired by whiskery old gentlemen with bulging waistcoats and tartan trews,' Papa said.

'I dare say those waistcoats are bulging with purses of gold coins,' Mama responded tartly. 'It would be a great help if you cared to contribute to the household finances.'

Poor Papa. That is the trouble. He really *is* poor. He makes very little money from his art, especially nowadays. We live in The Lion House, one of the grandest houses in Kensington, but it's actually Mama's, not his. Well, Mama didn't contribute the money herself. She's never done a stroke of work in her life, but my grandparents are very rich. They disapproved of my father but, when it became plain that Mama was determined to marry him, they couldn't bear the thought of their only child living in some ramshackle artist's garret. They gritted their teeth and provided the couple with a house.

Then Rupert and I were born, and the grandparents were delighted, in spite of everything. They were especially pleased to have a grandson to inherit their business.

We travel up to their huge country house near Dundee every New Year's Eve. They call it Hogmanay and it is a very grand occasion, with dinner and dancing and drinking – a great deal of drinking. When twelve o'clock strikes, Grandpapa sets off fireworks in the garden. We wake up and watch from our bedroom windows, though Sebastian puts his hands over his ears and poor Beth cowers in her bed.

Last year Rupert was allowed to stay up and help Grandpapa light the fireworks. I am exactly the same age bar fifteen minutes, but I'm not allowed anywhere near a match. Grandpapa quotes the poem about Pauline from that silly nursery book *Struwwelpeter*. He relishes reciting: 'Her apron burns, her arms, her hair; she burns all over everywhere.' Grandmama frowns and wags her finger in warning. She is even stricter than Mama.

Grandmama always looks as if she is sucking a lemon. She smells of citrus too, because she douses herself liberally in lemon verbena. Rupert and I have a theory about this. Grandpapa likes to behave like landed gentry but he's actually made his money from trade. He owns the biggest jute mill in Dundee. We were once taken there as a special treat. The mill was quite extraordinary. It was the noisiest place in the entire world, with the machines setting up such a clatter that everyone has to gesture, proper conversation quite impossible. But it wasn't the noise that was most memorable. It was the *smell*.

Jute is a plant grown in India. We have many plants in our back garden, and some of them smell, but sweetly, especially the honeysuckle and jasmine. I don't know what jute smells like in its native state (neither does Miss Rayner, because she's not very well informed, even though she's a governess), but when jute's being manufactured for sacks and carpet backing, it smells utterly disgusting. It's a sour, rancid, cloying smell, so astonishingly strong that, a full day after our visit to the mill, Rupert and I still reeked of it.

I thought of the workforce toiling away for twelve hours a day in this nauseating stench. Some are girls my age. It makes me feel ashamed. Our grandmother once worked in this very mill. Not as a mill girl, but in the accounts office, filling little brown envelopes with wages for Friday payday.

She didn't tell us this, of course. While Grandpapa was sorting out some problem with a mill hand, the foreman took Rupert and me for a cup of tea and a slice of Keiller's Dundee cake. He asked after our grandmama and told us that he'd known her when she was 'a wee lassie working here'. We boggled at the thought, but neither of us quite dared question Grandmama about this later. Rupert suggested that she wears such strong perfume now because she's determined to smell sweet.

Oh, I *do* miss Rupert. He is by far my favourite brother. We are not at all alike even though we are twins (Rupert is very good-looking and I am not), but when we were little Papa called us Tweedledee and Tweedledum. We went everywhere together and frequently spoke in unison. We weren't interested in our sister Beth when she was born. We couldn't be bothered with any other playmate. We were an entity unto ourselves.

Everything started changing this past year. Rupert has suddenly grown much taller than me and has become rather a dandy, growing his hair a little longer than usual, and he's particular about his clothes. He's very proud of his brocade waistcoat, and is desperate for a pocket watch and chain to wear with it. He's had a pair of boots specially made to wear at school, fine leather with jet buttons.

Papa suggested that the cobbler should add special steel caps to the toes. 'That way they'll be all the better for kicking,' he said. 'They will be Rupert's secret weapon when it comes to fighting.'

'There won't be any fights!' said Mama. 'This is a school for young gentlemen!'

'Which means that fights are a certainty,' said Papa.

He spoke with authority because he'd been sent to Kilbourne himself when he was a boy. He didn't want Rupert to follow in his footsteps, even in his steel-capped boots.

'Public schools are dire and degrading, worse than any prison,' he said. He knows about prisons too, because when he was young he was rather wild, and after an evening of drinking and tomfoolery he'd once spent the night in a prison cell. That is meant to be a deadly secret, but I'm actually rather proud to have a father who was once a criminal.

Mama hadn't minded Papa's wild ways when, as a youth, he travelled up to Scotland to paint the mountains and lochs, paying his way by doing portraits of aristocratic lairds or rich industrialists. He painted Grandpapa, and then he painted Mama, who was his only child, a young girl of seventeen. And during those sittings they fell passionately in love.

That portrait of Mama is in the drawing room now. It is a shock comparing that soft rosy girl with shining eyes and dimples in her cheeks to the wan and irritable invalid on the chaise longue.

She wouldn't listen to Papa, and insisted that her sons had to be properly educated, which meant sending them to Kilbourne. Grandpapa insisted too, though he didn't go to public school himself. Grandpapa generally has the final say, because he is the provider. Papa calls him the Great Provider. He doesn't say it in a very Christian way.

The day before Rupert left for school Grandpapa sent him his own gold watch. I loved that watch. When Grandpapa was in a good mood he let me play with the chain and listen to the steady tick. I had always hoped he might one day give it to me.

I expect I will inherit Grandmama's pearls and her jet locket and her collection of Cairngorm brooches. I'm afraid I think they're all hideous. Perhaps she will leave them to Beth or Clarrie or little Phoebe instead. I'd much prefer the gold watch.

I hoped it might be thought too precious for Rupert to take to school. I planned to sneak into his room and dangle the watch by my ear, listening to its *tick, tick, tick*. But Rupert begged to take the watch with him.

'Don't be ridiculous, Rupe,' said Papa. 'It's an enormously expensive timepiece with any number of jewels, according to your grandfather. It will get broken in the hurly-burly of Kilbourne.'

'But Rupert loves it so, don't you, darling,' said Mama. 'He must take the watch! My father gave it to him because he *wanted* him to take it to school. I'm sure the other boys will be impressed.'

'The other boys will think Rupe a show-off,' said Papa. 'Why will no one in this family listen to me when I'm the only member with previous experience of public school?'

'Now who's being a show-off?' said Mama, her cheeks going pink.

Papa looked stung. When it comes to boasting about his background he's the precise opposite of a show-off. Grandmama and Grandpapa had looked down on him at first, but they'd had no inkling that he came from an aristocratic family. I think his cousins might even be lords and ladies. His parents have a huge country house as big as a palace. When I was little, I imagined it like the pictures in my books of fairy tales: high on a hill, all gothic towers, with attics full of servant girls spinning straw into gold, and underground tunnels chock-a-block with goblins mining for jewels. For all I know it really might be like that. I've never been there, never met a single one of Papa's relatives. He fell out with them long ago because of his dissolute conduct with his art-school friends.

Anyway, last week Rupert went off to school with his trunk and tuck box – and the gold watch on a chain in his brocade waistcoat pocket. Once again Papa tried to persuade him that this wasn't a good idea, but Rupert still wouldn't listen.

'What's the point of having a splendid watch if I can't wear it, Pa?' he said.

'Look, Rupe, I just want you to fit in at school.'

'I don't see why you're getting in such a fuss about it. I've never had any problems fitting in with any of the chaps round here.'

It was true. All the boys in the streets around us want to be Rupert's friends. The girls too, actually. When we play cricket in Kensington Gardens, everyone wants to be on Rupert's team. He is always the captain. I have always been so proud that he is my brother.

I miss him so. I've written to him every single day, but he hasn't written back to me once. He has simply sent a short note to Mama and Papa, with a tiny afterthought to me: *P.S. Say hello to Rose and the others.*

You see, not even my own message! I have to share it with my brothers and sisters. I felt like bursting into tears.

'Don't pull that face, dear,' said Mama. 'You can't expect Rupert to write you great long letters. He'll be terrifically busy with his lessons and his sporting activities and his new friends.'

Papa took me to one side. 'I'm sure Mama is right,' he said quietly. 'But I remember writing letters home when I was at Kilbourne. We were crammed into the common room and there was no privacy whatsoever. We were all required to send a brief letter home to the parents, but any boy writing to his sister would have been mocked and ridiculed. Boys can be very harsh with each other, especially when they're feeling lost and unhappy.'

'Do you think *Rupert* will be feeling lost and unhappy?' I asked.

'Of course he will. He'll be missing home desperately. And I know he'll be missing you especially, Rose, because you matter so much to him,' said Papa.

'Oh!' I said. 'Do you really think so?'

So I wrote Rupert an even longer letter telling him how much I missed him. In fact, on the back of it I attempted a comical picture of our entire family assembled in the garden. It was quite a struggle fitting everyone in. I put Mama reclining on a garden chair with Alphonse on her lap at one end, and Papa at the other end, sketching. I assembled us children in age order, leaving a little gap beside me where Rupert belongs. I drew me waving, Beth clutching her favourite doll, Sebastian holding up his pet mouse, Algie sticking out his tongue, Clarrie making a daisy chain, and Nurse cradling baby Phoebe. I drew the servants standing in a row behind: Mr Hodgson the butler, Mrs Harrison the cook, Edie the parlourmaid, Maggie the housemaid, Jack the boot boy, and little Mary-Jane, the general skivvy. I even put Mistletoe the cat up a tree.

Halfway through my hand started aching terribly, but I carried on as a labour of love. Then I begged an envelope from Papa – a large one so my picture wouldn't get creased. I addressed it to Rupert at Kilbourne and wrote in capitals on the back *STRICTLY PRIVATE AND PERSONAL* so that no boys would look at the contents and mock or ridicule him.

2

I'M NOT MAKING ANY progress with my sketching. I carry the drawing book around with me so it looks as if I'm applying myself, but the pages remain blank.

Papa saw me with it and smiled. 'How are you getting on, my dear?' he asked eagerly.

'Very well thank you, Papa,' I said. I couldn't bear to disappoint him.

'Can I see?' he asked, holding out his hand for the book.

'I'd sooner not show you,' I mumbled.

'Don't worry. I understand perfectly. In fact, *I* like to keep my own sketches to myself,' said Papa. 'Still, is it stopping you missing Rupert so much?'

I shrugged. 'A little.'

Of course, it is having no effect whatsoever. I'm still missing Rupert terribly. I suppose it's not surprising. In thirteen whole years we've never spent a day apart.

'I wish you wouldn't fret so, Miss Rose,' said Nurse. 'It's silly moping after Master Rupert. Anyone would think he was your sweetheart, not your brother.'

Nurse had once had a sweetheart – the under-butler from a grand house. He came courting every Sunday, very red in the face, as if he'd scrubbed himself vigorously with carbolic soap. But Papa's mama had put a stop to Nurse's outings because little-boy Papa ran away when the housemaid took him to the park and he wasn't found until after dark. In those days Nurse was the only one who could control him.

Nurse is long past finding a sweetheart now – if she ever truly had one. She rambles a lot, and sometimes I think she makes things up, though the scrubbed red face sounds convincing enough. Poor old Nurse. She certainly won't be up to looking after *our* children when we're grown up. So what will happen to her?

I asked her if she had any savings, and she said, 'That's none of your business, Miss Rose. Ladies never discuss money matters, in any case. Now why don't you please your papa and do some sketching?'

'I'd sketch Rupert if he were here,' I said, sighing.

'Why don't you sketch one of your other brothers?'

'Sketch *me!*' Algie demanded.

'No thank you,' I said. 'Who would want to draw an ugly little goblin like you?'

Then he kicked me, and I smacked him, and he roared and then bit me. He ended up in the nursery corner and I was sent to my room in disgrace, which infuriated me.

I lay on my bed in a sulk until I heard a whispery little voice in the corridor going, 'Montmorency! Come here, Montmorency! Where *are* you, Montmorency?'

I opened my door. My middle brother, Sebastian, was creeping along the corridor, his long pale hair in his eyes as he peered at the floor.

'Have you let Montmorency Mouse out again?' I asked.

'He was squeaking so in his cage, wanting to be petted,' said Sebastian. 'I told him I wasn't allowed to let him out any more, but he wouldn't listen. I asked him to be a good boy and not try to escape, and I thought he promised, but when I opened his cage he just *darted* out of my hands and ran out through the door before I could catch him. I'm so worried that Mistletoe will see him and not understand that he's part of the family.'

'Mistletoe hardly ever comes upstairs. And he's too fat and lazy to bother with Montmorency,' I said, hoping I was right.

I joined Sebastian on his mouse hunt. Luckily Montmorency hadn't got far. We found him hiding behind the thick velvet curtains at the landing window. I grabbed him quickly and we got him safely back in his cage.

'You are a true heroine,' said Sebastian. 'We are so grateful, aren't we, Montmorency?'

'Grateful enough to keep very still while I sketch you?' I asked.

'Well, I can try,' said Sebastian, adopting a pose.

I tried too, but it didn't work. Sebastian looked more like my sister than my brother. Still, I suppose he does in real life too.

I knew that Papa would find my portrayal of Sebastian upsetting, even though I hadn't drawn him lopsided and his limbs looked the right length. Papa prides himself on being open-minded and unconventional, and he doesn't give a hoot that his family disapprove of him, but he still has rigid ideas where his children are concerned.

'I want you to be free to express yourself, my chicks!' he says, but in practice this simply means letting Algie and Clarrie romp about. It doesn't mean letting Sebastian wear a ribbon in his hair or dress up in Clarrie's frilly pinafores, as I suspect he would like to. And it certainly doesn't mean letting me stride about in breeches and boots or go to a proper school like Rupert.

'Don't you *want* me to be educated, Papa?' I asked him last night, exasperated.

'Of course I do! That's why we employ the redoubtable Miss Rayner,' he said.

I sighed. When I was Clarrie's age, Miss Rayner had seemed a sparkling diamond mine of information. I learned all about wild beasts in Africa, and Queen Elizabeth, and caterpillars turning into butterflies.

I thrilled at the stories of Noah's Ark and Moses and the Burning Bush and Daniel in the Lions' Den. I wrote my own little stories about 'A Day in the Life of a Penny' and 'A Robin's Nest' and 'The Naughty Little Puppy' (Miss Rayner supplied the titles). I added and subtracted and multiplied and divided, and gloried in the ticks and stars on each page of my exercise book.

Miss Rayner praised me unstintingly, which must have been irritating for my siblings, especially Rupert. He's very clever, but he's quick and careless and often makes mistakes. I wonder how he's managing at school. He will badly want to be top of his form.

I am top of Miss Rayner's class, but there is no competition now that Rupert is away. Sebastian and Algie and Clarrie are much younger than me. And Beth doesn't attend to lessons at all. She generally sits in a corner and counts, in her own little world.

Poor Beth. I don't know how to describe my sister. *I* think she is quite clever, but Mama says she is backward.

Papa hates her using that word. 'Beth is simply her own splendid, remarkable self,' he insists.

He tries so hard to make her happy, reading to her and plying her with presents. Beth still cries a great deal. She frequently has tantrums, even though she is a great girl of ten. Nurse has given up trying to chastise her, because Beth just flings herself on the floor and screams and kicks.

I can never make up my mind whether Beth is deliberately naughty or simply can't help it. I don't really *know* her properly, not like my other siblings. I know what she looks like, of course, and I know what sets her off, and I know the few things she likes (dolls, sparkly things, counting, rocking, repeating what we say) and all the things she doesn't (too many to list). But I don't know what she's like *inside*. She has such a pretty face, with big blue eyes and long shining dark hair, and when she's still and silent she looks beautiful. But she is usually shouting and struggling or crouching in a corner, head bent, eyes closed, refusing to communicate at all.

Papa is her favourite. She dislikes Mama. I'm afraid she dislikes Nurse too. Beth doesn't seem to think much of her brothers and sisters either, not even little Phoebe. Rupert can occasionally charm her. She won't allow any of us to touch her, but she will let Rupert play Round and Round the Garden with her, and when he tickles her she creases up, squirming and spluttering. It's the only time she ever laughs.

I wondered if she was missing Rupert as much as me and went to see if she felt like talking about him. When I opened the nursery door, she looked up at once, clapping her hands.

'It's just me, Rose,' I said, sure that she had hoped I was Rupert.

'Rose. Rose, Rose, Rose!'

'Oh my, someone's getting a fancy welcome,' said Nurse. 'There now, pet, don't get over-excited.'

She smiled at Beth anxiously. Nurse has always prided herself on being able to control us. She can usually even bring Algie to heel. But Beth defeats her.

'I've never known such a child,' she complains. 'There's no reasoning with her. I never thought I'd be struggling with such a difficult little girl at my age. She brings shame on my nursery. I hardly dare take her out in case she has one of her turns in public.'

Beth has frequent turns in the nursery. She refuses to share and doesn't play properly. She commandeers all the bricks and won't build a castle or a row of houses or a fort – she wants to balance them one on top of the other, placing them with exaggerated care, muttering, *'One, two, three, four, five, six, seven, eight, nine, ten.'* She makes such a performance of this that I can understand why Algie is often tempted to knock her bricks flying.

She likes building towers with books, though she's strictly forbidden to do this now because when they fall down, the spines break and the pages scatter. But Beth doesn't just like building with books, she likes to read them too. I used to think she was only pretending she could read. Miss Rayner gave up trying to teach her because she was so disruptive in the classroom. But when I wandered into the night nursery one day, I discovered Beth sitting cross-legged on the floor reading *Pilgrim's Progress*. She was truly reading it, muttering passages to herself while pointing along the lines, so engrossed that she didn't hear me coming in.

I was amazed. I have been reading fluently since I was four and a half and can tackle most adult books now, but I find *Pilgrim's Progress* very heavy going. I can never read more than a page or two at a time, though I like the strange illustrations and I've pored over the maps of Christian's journey.

I marvelled that my strange sister could master the story. Perhaps she liked the sound of a City of Destruction. She's the source of much destruction in our own house, and she's certainly often stuck in a Slough of Despond.

I knelt down beside her on the rag rug.

'I was wondering, Beth. Are you missing Rupert?' I asked her.

'Rupert,' said Beth, looking miserable.

'I'm missing him terribly too. Do you remember – he's at school now,' I said.

'At school now,' Beth agreed.

'I wish *I* could go to school,' I said.

'Go to school,' Beth said, as if she wanted to go too.

'It's not fair. We can't help being girls, can we?'

'Can we,' Beth echoed.

'I wonder if you really understand or whether you're simply copying me,' I said, reaching out and gently pulling her long shiny hair.

I didn't realize that Beth would count this as touching and start moaning and shuddering.

'Oh no! I'm sorry. Please don't start. You mustn't have a turn because Nurse will get cross,' I said.

'Nurse will get cross,' said Beth mournfully.

'But it's your fault, Beth. Why do you always have to make such a fuss?'

'Make such a fuss.' She stared down at her hands and then started licking her fingers, counting them under her breath. I tried to work out what she was doing.

'Are you licking yourself clean like Mistletoe?'

'Like Mistletoe,' said Beth. She got up and went over to her row of dolls, which were carefully arranged on the windowsill, and started licking their china fingers too. They sat in size order, from the tiniest thumb-size doll's-house doll up to big Marianne, who had once been mine. I was long past playing with dolls, but when I looked at Marianne's blonde curls and blue eyes I felt nostalgic. I used to like lying her down so that her eyes shut with a little click and then sitting her up so that they opened and she smiled at me.

'Dear old Marianne,' I said, going over to the windowsill too. I remembered when she'd been nearly as big as me. I'd had to drag her around, her toes trailing on the floor. Now I could lift her up and hold her in my arms comfortably.

'No!' said Beth, getting agitated because I'd moved Marianne. 'No, no, no!' It was the only word she ever initiated.

'Don't get her started, Miss Rose,' said Nurse.

I ignored her. I felt I was getting on famously with Beth today. 'I think Marianne's horribly stiff from sitting on that hard windowsill day after day. She wants to have a little walk around,' I said, demonstrating by moving the doll's legs. I hoped it would amuse Beth, but it made her even more upset.

'No, no, no!' she shouted, trying to wrestle the doll away from me.

'For goodness' sake, Beth!' I said, struggling with her. 'Careful! Watch out or—'

And then it happened. Marianne fell on the floor and banged her head hard – and her eyes *disappeared*. They fell right into the depths of her china head and rattled there, leaving two dark scary holes in her face.

Beth screamed. She went on screaming and I couldn't calm her. Neither could Nurse or Edie or Maggie. Mama couldn't be disturbed because she was entertaining Lady Mirabelle Robson. She's an interfering, whiskery old woman with the yellow eyes of a goat, but Mama likes her simply because she's a Lady.

They sent for Papa instead. He thrust Marianne into a cupboard where Beth couldn't see her, and then tried to comfort her, but she squirmed and kicked, her eyes closed and her mouth square.

'Dear, oh dear, what a to-do!' Nurse said. 'Really, Miss Beth, you're going to be the death of me. I'm too old for your tricks. Please stop that screaming, for pity's sake.'

Beth didn't seem to have any pity. The more Nurse and Papa and I tried to placate her, the harder she screamed. Edie came back in to say that Mama wanted to see me in the drawing room. Lady Robson had departed rapidly. Mama had the curtains drawn and was lying on her chaise longue, a cologne-soaked handkerchief clutched to her forehead. I could barely make her out in the gloom, but there was no mistaking the anger on her face.

'Edie told me what happened. How could you upset Beth in such a manner? You've ruined that beautiful French doll with your carelessness!' she said.

'I didn't *intend* to upset Beth. We were having a lovely time until I started to play with her doll. I wanted to amuse her but it just went wrong. I'm terribly sad about Marianne – she was my doll too, and I used to love her enormously. Perhaps we can put a bandage round her eyes, and then she can be like Mr Watts's painting, the one he calls *Hope*,' I said. Papa had taken me to see it and I had secretly thought it rather dreary, but pretended to admire it all the same. 'Please don't get so upset, Mama.' I was trying to be reassuring, but everything I said only seemed to infuriate her.

'Don't speak to me in that patronizing manner, Rose! I wish you'd learn your lesson and keep away from Beth – you always upset her. It was particularly embarrassing this afternoon, with Lady Robson visiting. I was hoping she'd invite you to tea with her granddaughter. You really must start making some proper friends, Rose. We were getting along splendidly until Beth started that terrible shrieking. I didn't know where to look. "What is that banshee wailing?" she said. Those were her exact words. And now I'm sure Lady Robson will tell all her society friends about the incident, and they will think me a

terrible mother for having such an uncontrollable child,'
Mama said, mopping her forehead.

'Well, what do we care about an old nanny goat like
Lady Robson!' I said without thinking.

I got sent to bed, though I was too old for childish
punishments and it was only halfway through the
afternoon. I decided I didn't care in the slightest. I read
for a long time, until my head started aching too, and
then I studied Papa's book on the great masterpieces of
art. *Master*pieces. Why are there no *Mistress*pieces?

I wasn't even allowed to go down for dinner. Nurse
brought me a bowl of bread and milk instead – nursery
punishment food. She tutted at me too.

'Poor Beth!' she said. 'She was in such a state! I was
worried she'd start fitting. I'm not sure she's out of the
woods yet.'

I lay worrying until, at long last, it was dark and Papa
came in to say goodnight.

'I didn't mean to upset Beth, Papa,' I said miserably.

'I know you didn't, my pet,' he said.

'She will be all right, won't she, Papa?'

'Of course she will, silly girl.'

'Mama was so hurtful. She said I always upset her.'

'Your mama isn't very well at the moment.'

'You always stand up for her, Papa.'

'That's my job. I am an English gentleman,' said Papa,
standing up straight and thumping himself on the chest.
'I stand up for my wife and children.' He clicked his heels
together.

'Oh, Papa. You're always joking,' I said.

He held my chin very gently. 'Perhaps you should try to joke too, Rose. You take life so seriously. I wish you were a little happier.'

'I am happy sometimes! I'm just missing Rupert so.'

'I think we all are.'

'Beth's missing him too. Oh, Papa, promise she's not going to start fitting.'

'Of course she won't.'

'She's so sad about poor Marianne. We'd better keep her in that cupboard now she looks so upsetting.'

'I'm going to take her to a doll's hospital tomorrow,' said Papa.

'Is there truly such a thing, or is that another joke?' I asked.

'There is, truly, and I have a hunch they'll be able to help Marianne make a full recovery. If she has to stay in hospital for a long time, I might see if I can find another pretty doll to keep Beth company in the meantime.'

'You spoil Beth, Papa. In fact you spoil us all.' I looked at him. I couldn't see properly by candlelight, but he seemed particularly tired and careworn. I thought of all the tales of Papa's youth. 'Do you ever wish you were still single, free to paint as long as you like without a care in the world?'

Papa smiled wistfully. 'And what should I do with you and all your siblings? Put you in the cupboard with Marianne? Go to sleep now, dear.'

'I think I'll go and kiss Beth goodnight and tell her I'm sorry,' I said.

Papa hesitated. 'Better not. You don't want to wake her up if Nurse has got her to sleep at last.'

'I suppose not,' I said. I tried to settle, but I kept thinking about Beth. Long after Papa and Mama had gone up to bed I crept out of my room and tiptoed along the corridor to the night nursery, where Nurse was snoring, and Sebastian and Algie and Clarrie were tucked into their little brass cots. At the end was the bed occupied by Beth.

I hovered over her, peering at her in the dark. Her head was deeply buried in her pillow, her hair in a long plait coiled like a snake about her shoulders. I held my breath because she was such a light sleeper. I listened to her breathing. It was soft and regular, such a great relief.

I reached out and very lightly patted Beth's shoulder. It was the only time I could actually touch her. She stirred and I bit my lip, but she didn't wake.

'Sleep well,' I whispered. Beth murmured something indistinctly, as if she were wishing me the same.

3

BETH HAS A NEW nurse. She comes on Lady Robson's recommendation.

'My daughter-in-law had a little trouble with my third grandchild, Marmaduke. He was so strong-willed I thought we'd never break his spirit. But I took it upon myself to hire this magnificent trained nurse and, in a matter of weeks, we saw such a difference in the little boy. He became so tranquil, so obedient. I highly recommend Nurse Budd, Mrs Rivers. She will make all the difference to your troubled daughter, I promise you. She comes with the very best refcrences,' she told Mama.

'A simple recommendation from you is all the reference she needs, Lady Robson,' said Mama sycophantically.

She was given Nurse Budd's particulars, who came straight away. I don't like her one jot. I feel so guilty because it's all my fault for upsetting Beth when Lady Robson was here. Nurse Budd is as narrow and rigid as a drainpipe, though she pretends to be a soft, simple creature who loves all children. She refers to her charge as 'my dear little Beth'. I don't think Beth is fooled. Neither is Nurse.

'I don't care for that Nurse Budd, for all she's got a special nursing certificate. I don't like this talk of "training". I won't let her beat my Beth. I won't stand for any child in my nursery being whipped.'

As far as we can tell, Nurse Budd has never raised a finger against Beth. She doesn't raise her voice either. But Beth's behaviour *has* started to improve. I don't know how she's done it. Nurse Budd insists on having special quarters for her and her charge, so now they share the big green guest room. Nurse Budd says they need privacy to work on Beth's training.

I hate not being able to see Beth whenever I want. Nurse Budd scolded me when I burst into their new room without knocking.

'Now now, Miss Rose. I don't want you disturbing my Miss Beth,' she said in a silly, syrupy voice. 'She's having a little lie-in. Off you pop now.'

I refused to pop. I was worried about Beth. She scarcely stirred when I talked to her. Her eyelids fluttered and she murmured something, but she wasn't properly awake.

'I think you tired her out yesterday, Nurse Budd,' I said accusingly.

'Sleep is nature's remedy, Miss Rose. Miss Beth needs to rest as much as possible. Half her trouble is simply that she's *over*tired. Now run along and stop trying to teach me my job. I am a trained nurse, you know.' She nodded at the certificate she'd pinned up on the wall.

I didn't know what to do. I went to consult Nurse.

'There you are, Miss Rose! Dear goodness, you haven't even brushed your hair yet. Miss Rayner's in the schoolroom already. Hurry up now. And look at those muddy boots! You didn't put them out for young Jack to clean.'

'Who cares about my stupid boots! Nurse, Beth's still asleep and Nurse Budd doesn't want to wake her up. Don't you think she should?' I asked.

'I've always taken pride in having my lambs up and washed and dressed by eight,' said Nurse. 'But that stuck-up Madam Budd clearly has other ideas. Can't be bothered, most like. And there she is telling me Lady Robson's daughters have much better-run nurseries.'

'Come with me to wake Beth up please, Nurse,' I said.

'Well, I'll try,' she said. 'But Nurse Budd won't thank me for interfering.'

We went together, Nurse carrying baby Phoebe on her hip.

'Oh my goodness, more visitors!' said Nurse Budd, frowning. 'Keep quiet now! I don't want my little patient to wake up before she's ready. She needs her beauty sleep.'

'Let me have a look at my Beth,' said Nurse, refusing to be intimidated. She tried to shake Beth awake. Beth moaned sleepily.

'For goodness' sake, don't wake her like that!' said Nurse Budd.

'She looks very flushed,' said Nurse. She put out her hand and touched Beth's forehead. 'She could be feverish.'

Phoebe started whimpering, wanting her milk.

'Nonsense. She's simply warm from being tucked up in bed,' said Nurse Budd. 'I'd attend to your own charge if I were you. Miss Beth is no longer your responsibility. You couldn't handle her, could you?'

Beth moaned and drew up her knees as if sensing their hostility in her sleep.

'Please don't squabble – you're upsetting Beth,' I said.

That made them both pick on me instead, suggesting I should mind my own business. I was sent off to the schoolroom with a flea in my ear.

Miss Rayner's morning lessons seemed more tedious than ever. She asked me to write a story called 'Tales of a Bunny Rabbit' and then to work my way through two pages of long division.

'A *bunny rabbit*?' I said. 'I'm thirteen years old, Miss Rayner! And I mastered long division when I was eight.'

She blinked at me nervously, but she didn't tell me off for my outburst. 'You're right, Rose,' she said. 'I'm sorry, dear. I'll set you some more appropriate work.'

She suggested an essay on 'A Young Lady's Duties' and then asked me to add up invented pages of 'Housekeeping Accounts'. Both tasks were extremely boring. Perhaps the tale of the bunny rabbit would have been preferable.

I'm afraid I didn't take my new work very seriously. I suggested that, with such tiresome duties, all the young ladies should cast aside their frocks and pinafores forthwith, clothe themselves in sturdy breeches, tie up their treasures in a red spotted handkerchief and stride off to seek their fortunes instead. I scored through poor Miss Rayner's copperplate accounts of two and three quarter yards of blue ribbon priced at five pence a yard and a dozen and a half yellow roses at a ha'pence a bloom, and suggested that fancy ribbon was superfluous, and buttercups were prettier than roses and could be picked in any meadow for nothing at all.

Miss Rayner sighed. 'You're not being very cooperative this morning, dear,' she said reproachfully.

'I'm sorry. I don't mean to be horrid to you, Miss Rayner. It's just that I'm so wretched now that Rupert's at school and I'm not. I feel so left behind. I'm going to be stuck at home like this for ever and ever,' I said. I had a lump in my throat and was on the brink of tears.

'I do understand how you feel, Rose,' said Miss Rayner. She glanced at the little ones, who were now working on a bunny-rabbit frieze for the nursery wall. Sebastian's mouse was sitting on his shoulder, daintily nibbling on a chunk of cheese filched from Cook in the kitchen. Seeing that they were all occupied, Miss Rayner sank onto the sofa and patted the cushion next to her.

I sat beside her, though it was a very uncomfortable sofa, demoted from the drawing room. It sagged rather because Algie bounced up and down on it so often.

Miss Rayner patted my hand. 'There now, Rose. Of course you're missing Rupert. We all are, he's such a dear boy. But you mustn't think that your life is over! My goodness, it's just beginning! When you're a year or two older, your mama and papa will find a tutor to teach you a foreign language and give you proper singing and piano lessons so that you become even more accomplished. Before you know it you'll be seventeen and presented at Court and then, my word, won't you have a wonderful time going to balls in pretty gowns and meeting dashing young gentlemen.' Her eyes shone at the thought in a wholly generous manner.

I wondered if Miss Rayner had ever longed for balls and young gentlemen herself. Of course, that would never have been possible. Miss Rayner had been poor, with elderly parents, and when they both died she'd had to scrape a living as a governess. I wouldn't want to swap places with her. How terrible having to cope with Algie every day! Clarrie can be difficult too, and Sebastian is challenging in his own demure way. And of course I'm a trial nowadays, moping about the house and rebelling in my half-hearted fashion.

'I'm sorry, Miss Rayner,' I said. 'I know I must seem very selfish and spoiled.'

'Not at all, dear,' she insisted sweetly. 'You're understandably lonely just now. The little ones are so much younger than you, and poor Beth isn't really able to be a companion to you, even though you're closer in age.'

'I worry so about Beth, Miss Rayner,' I confided.

'I do too, ever so,' she said. 'I feel so inadequate, not being able to teach her any more. But I simply couldn't control the poor girl. Thank goodness she's having proper expert care now.'

'I don't consider Nurse Budd very proper at all, and I don't think she's an expert either,' I said. 'Anyone would think she was Florence Nightingale herself.' I'd read about Miss Nightingale's splendid work during the Crimean War. *There* was a woman who didn't droop at home and fill her empty life with fancy frocks and balls! 'Miss Rayner, do you think I have the makings of a pioneering nurse? Or maybe even a doctor?'

'Oh goodness, dear, I'm not sure your mama would approve of that idea!'

'Papa might agree – though he wants me to be an artist. However, I'm not sure I have the talent or the inclination. I don't think I'd enjoy being stuck in a studio doing portraits all day long, though it would be wonderful to paint like Lady Butler.'

'And who is that, dear? One of your mama's friends?'

'No, no, she's a true artist. Papa took me to see her magnificent painting in the Royal Academy. It was an incredibly large picture of soldiers on horses. It looked as if the horses were going to gallop right out of the painting and trample us! Lady Butler specializes in military battles. I'd love to do that. It would be so exciting!' I cried.

'I don't think that's a very good idea,' said Miss Rayner. 'It doesn't sound suitable subject matter for a lady artist.'

I took no notice of her. She's a dear, but she's not very well-informed, especially when it comes to art. I spent the rest of the morning attempting to draw a soldier on a horse. It was a waste of time. I can't draw convincing soldiers. I give them moustaches and broad shoulders, but they still look very girly. And I'm hopeless at horses. They have such strange legs for a start. It must be so confusing having four. How do they stop them cantering in different directions? I'm pretty sure the back legs have knees that go the wrong way, but I'm not sure *how*. Papa is right. I *do* need to sketch from real life.

So I asked Nurse if we could go to Hyde Park after the children had had their afternoon nap. 'I want to go to Rotten Row and watch the people riding their horses. The children would love it and I could sketch,' I explained.

'You must be joking, Miss Rose. That's much too far, especially for Miss Clarrie. I dare say Master Sebastian would find it a challenge too – that child has no stamina at all. And I'm the poor soul who would have to push Miss Phoebe all that way in the perambulator, and my bunions are playing up today,' said Nurse.

'I could push the perambulator – I don't mind a bit. In fact, you don't even need to come, Nursie darling. I'll take charge of the children and you can put your feet up and have a nice rest. The walk will do Sebastian good – it might put some colour in his cheeks. If Clarrie tires, I can sit her on the end of the pram and give her a lift too. And we both know that Algie never, ever tires. He really needs more exercise, he's getting very chubby,' I said, trying my hardest to persuade her.

But Nurse insisted we had to go on our usual walk along the streets, through the rose gardens, round the pond and back again. I've been on that same walk thousands of times. I could find my way blindfold.

So Nurse set off with the little ones and I stayed at home, hunched up on the window seat by the stairwell, sketchbook on my lap, pencils in my pocket. Papa was out, Mama was in her drawing room, Nurse Budd was upstairs with Beth. The servants were down in the basement. The house seemed very silent, the only sound the ticking of the grandfather clock in the hall.

I listened to it, trying to time my breaths to the ticks. It seemed to be speaking to me. *Set off! Run fast! Go now!*

So I did! I didn't even stop to put on a coat or hat. I simply clutched my sketchbook to my chest, walked across the patterned carpet of the hall, turned the handle of the front door and went out. I patted the heads of our stone lions for luck, first one, then the other. Then I set off.

I'd been out by myself before. Occasionally Papa sends me to post a letter in the scarlet pillar box at the end of the road. I lead such a restricted life that even that tiny trip is an adventure. Trekking to Hyde Park unaccompanied seemed like a trip up the Amazon.

At first I walked very fast, but when I turned the corner I started running. I held my arms out as if I were flying, intoxicated with this new freedom. I couldn't believe how easy it was to escape the dark confines of the house. Why ever hadn't I done this before? I could slip out by myself any afternoon!

When I reached Kensington High Street I calmed down a little because a few ladies were staring at me, and one fierce soul in black bombazine caught hold of me and asked if I was running away from my nurse.

'I am too old to have a nurse,' I said, and wriggled away from her.

After that I walked more decorously, not wanting to draw further attention. I enjoyed looking in the shop windows, though I didn't care for any of the clothes on display. I hate the way ladies' costumes are so rigid. If I stay as thin and flat as I am now, perhaps I won't need to wear a corset and all those other hideous underpinnings. I'll wear a loose dress of some beautiful soft patterned silk – maybe a kimono? Papa very much admires Oriental art and has a fine set of Japanese prints in his studio.

Perhaps, if I sketch assiduously every day, I can become a great lady artist and have my own studio. When I'm painting I will wear a voluminous smock and wipe my brushes on it as I fancy. Papa is frequently paint-stained, and his hands are either rainbow coloured with chalk or black with charcoal. Perhaps that's why Mama cringes when he puts his arms around her.

I walked on and at long, long last, reached Hyde Park. I flopped down beside Rotten Row and started drawing men on horseback. I couldn't be bothered with the fine ladies because they looked so lopsided riding side-saddle, and no lady ever fought in a military battle anyway, as far as I was aware.

I sketched brown horses, black horses and grey horses – magnificent sleek beasts which looked like a different species to the milkman's old nag or the coalman's massive carthorse. I learned how their necks arched and which way their knees bent. And yet they *still* didn't look right.

I tried hard, but eventually I had to give up. Besides, I soon grew very cold and cramped sitting on the damp grass. I wasn't too sure of the time either. I had to get back or there might be trouble when I returned home.

There *was* trouble. Apparently I'd been missing for a full hour after Nurse and the children arrived back from their afternoon stroll. Time for the servants to scour the house for me, for Nurse to tell Mama, and for Maggie to be sent off to fetch a policeman because they thought I might have been kidnapped!

I stood squirming in the drawing room while Mama lectured me. She spoke lying down, a scented handkerchief on her forehead, because my disappearance had given her another sick headache.

'Shame on you, Miss Rose,' said Edie. 'How could you be so thoughtless! Your poor mama's been beside herself.'

'I'm sorry, Mama. I didn't mean to worry you so. I simply thought I'd take a little stroll by myself,' I said.

She reacted as if I'd taken it into my head to march around Kensington like Lady Godiva, clothed only in my hair.

'You must surely understand that children of thirteen do not wander around London by themselves!'

'Rupert does, quite often,' I retorted. 'Don't you remember the day he spent his pocket money on a cab to Buckingham Palace so that he could see the soldiers in their scarlet uniform?'

'I do indeed, the little scamp!' said Mama, shaking her head fondly. Rupert can do no wrong in her eyes. 'Rupert is a young man with a very independent spirit. He is able to look after himself. Boys aren't subject to the sort of dangers girls are. There are all sorts of evil men who prey upon young girls!'

She hissed the last sentence dramatically, as if she believed a thousand crazed cut-throats lurked in the sleepy streets of Kensington, ready to attack any young girl who came skipping past. I smirked at the idea, which infuriated her.

'How dare you snigger like that, you insolent girl! You seem to think you know best!'

I felt I *did* know better than Mama, but I knew it would be fatal to say so. I stayed silent, staring at my feet. My white satin indoor shoes looked a little the worse for wear after their long walk. I thought of the thrilling fairy story of the red shoes. Perhaps I would never remove my white satin shoes now. They would take me further and further away, until I'd danced the length and breadth of Britain, and I'd end up dying of exhaustion climbing a Scottish mountain or tumbling down some Welsh waterfall. (My geography was too hazy to name specific places.)

'Rose! Don't ignore me!' Mama said sharply. 'Where did you go? Tell me at once!'

'I went to Hyde Park,' I said flatly.

'Don't lie to me,' Mama warned.

'I did, Mama, truly. You can ask Nurse. I begged her to take us there, but she said it was too far for the little ones.'

'Of course it is. So why did you want to go to Hyde Park? Children go to Kensington Gardens,' said Mama.

'I didn't want to look at children. I see enough of them at home. I wanted to go and look at the riders in Rotten Row.'

'You're interested in riding?' Mama asked. She sounded a little less hostile. 'Well, why on earth didn't you say so before?'

4

I DID MY BEST TO tell Mama that I didn't want
to ride. When I was little I didn't even want a rocking
horse. Mounting a huge creature with flaring nostrils,
sharp teeth, steel-capped hoofs and an unpredictable
nature seemed a terrible idea. Mama spoke about her
friend Mrs Feynsham-Jones, whose daughters were all
magnificent horsewomen. She wondered if they might
allow me to ride with them.

'I don't *want* to ride, Mama,' I said yet again. 'And I
can't bear those Feynsham-Jones girls. They're ghastly,
all three of them.'

'Don't be so difficult, Rose! The Feynsham-Jones girls are lovely young ladies,' Mama declared.

They aren't official Ladies, but Mama feels that double-barrelled names are the next best thing, and with the middle Feynsham-Jones girl you got two for the price of one. Lucinda-May is my age, and the dullest creature ever, even worse than her silly big sister, Pamela, and her whining younger sister, Cecily. They came to tea this summer and it wasn't a success.

Mama made Nurse keep Beth upstairs in the nursery with baby Phoebe so that she shouldn't disgrace us. She insisted that Clarrie and I wear our best organdie party frocks, and Sebastian and Algie had to wear their cream summer suits. Rupert chose to wear his striped boating blazer and cricketing flannels instead, but looked so charming that Mama let him get away with it.

He was the only one who didn't end up in disgrace. He played an elaborate game of Charming Pamela, sitting next to her and asking her questions as if he really wanted to know the answer, then plying her with cups of tea and little raspberry sponge cakes in a wondrous parody of gentlemanly behaviour. She simpered and tossed her long curls and giggled at his jokes, her pale face turning as pink as the icing on her cake. She thought Rupert was really smitten with her, the silly girl, though whenever she bent her head over cake or cup he rolled his eyes at me or openly yawned. It was hard not to snort with laughter.

I was supposed to be entertaining Lucinda-May, but it was an uphill task. I don't know how to make small talk or indeed *any* kind of talk. I asked her what games she liked, and she said she had just learned to play Bezique and was very fond of it. She offered to show me, and asked me to fetch two packs of cards. It turned out that Bezique was an incredibly boring card game. I had meant a *real* game of Pirates or Savages or Damsels in Distress, the sort of games I used to play with Rupert – but when I explained she looked appalled.

'I don't play those sorts of rough, childish games any more,' she said, looking at me as if I were very strange indeed.

So then I asked her which books she enjoyed, thinking this safe territory.

'I don't really care to read much nowadays, though I used to like fairy stories,' she said.

How can she bear not to read? I read when I wake up, when I go to bed, when I have my bath, when I have nursery tea, when I'm sent out into the garden for fresh air, and I read for hours and hours and hours whenever I sit on the window seat halfway up the stairs.

'Perhaps you don't have any very exciting books,' I said. 'You could borrow some of mine, if you like. I read anything I fancy – all kinds of grown-up novels, though *I* still like fairy tales too. Which are your favourites? I like the Jack stories: "Jack and the Beanstalk" and "Jack the Giant Killer".'

Lucinda-May looked puzzled. 'I never cared for stories about boys, especially not ones with giants in them. I liked stories about pretty fairies.'

Oh dear. *Those* kinds of fairy stories. Pwetty lickle fairy-wairy stories. I gave up trying to entertain Lucinda-May, made some excuse about using the facilities, left the room and didn't come back. I couldn't go to my usual window seat because Nurse and Edie always found me there. I went right up to the attics, using the narrow servants' stairs. They'd never think of looking for me there.

I peeped into the maids' bedroom, curious to find out more about them. I was startled to see how bare it was: just an iron bed, a washstand with a jug and basin, and two hooks on the door for their clothes. The bed wasn't very big, but they obviously had to share it. They've tried to make their room pretty, with a rag rug on the floor, a patchwork quilt on the bed, and fairground china spaniels on the windowsill. I wonder if either has a gentleman admirer who won the spaniels at a coconut shy.

The other attic rooms were used to store old furniture and cast-offs. Most had buckets on the floor, because the roof leaked. It was just as well that Nurse shared the night nursery with the little children, and Nurse Budd slept with Beth.

The rest of the staff slept down in the basement. Mr Hodgson had a proper chamber, and Mrs Harrison shared her room with young Mary-Jane, who had to squeeze herself in beside Cook's big bulk. Little Jack Boots had to do without any kind of bed, curling up on a rug under the kitchen table. He isn't Jack who climbed a magic beanstalk, Jack who killed giants. He is Jack who cleans our dirty boots, though his own are worn through, with the soles flapping comically when he walks. No, it isn't comical at all.

Were Jack and Mary-Jane close, like Rupert and me? Did they have little private jokes? Did they talk about us? Do they like us or despise us?

I was forced back downstairs because someone had started shrieking. I thought at first it must be Beth, though the screams were unusually high-pitched and I found that it was Lucinda-May! She was standing on the velvet sofa in the drawing room, screaming at the top of her lungs.

I stared at her in astonishment, delighted that such a dull girl was now behaving so badly, throwing a tantrum of Beth-like proportions. However, it turned out that she was screaming with terror, not temper. Sebastian had been carrying Montmorency Mouse inside his shirt, and Montmorency had woken up, nose twitching at the smell of cake crumbs, wriggled out between Sebastian's buttons, run across his chest, over his tummy and down his leg to the carpet.

Sebastian tried to catch him while Algie and Clarrie laughed, but all three Feynsham-Jones girls had reacted ridiculously. Cecily jumped onto her mother's lap, spilling her tea. Pamela clutched hold of Rupert, practically climbing onto *his* lap. Lucinda-May had no one to cling to, so jumped up on the sofa and screeched. She couldn't have made more fuss if a man-eating tiger were prowling our drawing room.

Poor little Montmorency was terrified by all the noise and darted under the sofa. Sebastian had to wriggle right underneath, and emerged with little bits of fluff sticking to his cream suit, because Maggie isn't very thorough when she sweeps.

After the Feynsham-Joneses had departed Mama was furious. She told Sebastian that if he let Montmorency loose again she would give his mouse to Mistletoe. I don't think she meant it, but Sebastian burst into tears and declared that *he* would have to live in a cage too, because he couldn't bear to be parted from Montmorency. Algie and Clarrie and I were delighted by the turn of events, because we'd found Lucinda-May and little sissy Cecily hard going.

'Aren't you glad that terrible Pamela has gone, Rupert?' I asked.

'Of course!' he said.

'I don't know how you stood it when she held you so tightly!' I laughed.

'Yes, it was frightful,' Rupert agreed.

For once we were all united in scorn for the Feynsham-Jones girls. I'm pretty certain they detested us too. They surely won't want me to go riding with them, no matter how hard Mama tries to ingratiate herself.

Remembering the disastrous tea party made me think about Mary-Jane and Jack again. I'd been full of good intentions to try to make their life less bleak, but I'd been so intent on making the most of Rupert during his last weeks at home that I'd done nothing.

I decided to try now. I wasn't quite sure how to go about it. I couldn't just march down to the basement and announce that I wanted to be their friend. It would sound so peculiar. But then I hit on the idea of drawing them. Papa sketches humbly born children for Sarah Smith's books, so why shouldn't I?

Cook and Mr Hodgson were very suspicious when I asked if Mary-Jane and Jack could come upstairs with me for half an hour.

'What do you want with my Mary-Jane? She's busy peeling my veg for dinner. I know she's a bit heavy-handed, but she's a good girl really. You aren't going to tell your ma on her, are you, Miss Rose?' Cook fussed, while Mary-Jane hid behind her, biting her lip.

'Is young Jack in trouble?' asked Mr Hodgson. 'Tell me what he's done and I'll sort it out, Miss Rose. He makes a nice job of all the boots. You can practically see your face in them. We might make a footman of him yet, though he's got to be trained up right. He's still a bit rough and ready round the edges, but he's a good lad for all that.' He cuffed Jack about the head even so, but there was such concern on his face it was almost like a caress.

'They haven't done anything. I'm sure they're both splendid at their jobs. I simply want to draw them, if that's all right with you,' I said.

'*Draw* them?' they said in unison. It clearly wasn't all right, but they let them come upstairs with me. I suppose they had to. I'm the eldest daughter of the house. They are servants. It seems so strange that I can tell adults what to do even when they're old enough to be my grandparents.

Mary-Jane and Jack trailed after me nervously. I didn't quite know where to take them. We usually entertained guests in the drawing room, but that didn't seem sensible, especially with Mama reclining on her chaise longue. I wondered about taking them up to my bedroom, but it was my own private space and I hated anyone invading it, even my own brothers and sisters. Especially Algie.

The nursery wasn't suitable either. Nurse would disapprove of the kitchen staff marching into her territory. Papa was out doing his own sketching. I made a bold decision: I would use his studio.

I felt anxious all the same. Papa lets me come in, but only when he's there. I have to keep very still and not disturb him. He doesn't mind me looking at his current work, but I'm not allowed to touch his pastels and paints, or fiddle with the props scattered about the studio. I knew that Algie and Clarrie would create havoc there, and Sebastian would be unable to resist dressing up in the draperies. What would I do if Jack and Mary-Jane behaved like my siblings?

But Jack and Mary-Jane didn't behave like ordinary children. They stood stock-still just inside the doorway, staring at Papa's paintings. They seemed particularly disconcerted by the abandoned nude study of the Honourable Louisa propped in one corner. Well, she wasn't *completely* nude. She had a filmy strip of gauze about her hips, and her chest was half hidden by her long auburn hair, but she was still pretty bare.

'It's all right. Don't look so shocked. She isn't rude, she's *art*,' I said.

They glanced at me as if I were mad. Perhaps I was. I was pretending to be blasé and sophisticated, but I found that portrait shocking too. It seemed extraordinary that she had taken off her clothes – shoes, stockings, dress, petticoats, drawers, even her corset – and stood there in front of Papa, seemingly quite at ease. Her eyes were very blue and bright, her mouth half open as if she were chatting to him. It implied that they were on very intimate terms.

I wondered if Mama had seen the portrait. Perhaps that was why Papa hadn't finished it and Louisa didn't come to the house any more. Artists had been painting nudes throughout the centuries. I had looked at engravings in Papa's art books and had seen Greek and Roman statues, pale Flemish ladies, rounded Renaissance beauties. But they were women in history and I didn't know them. Louisa was real, and I'd seen her as she ran lightly up and down our stairs in her blue velvet coat, her glorious hair piled high and held in place by tortoiseshell combs.

I covered her portrait with an old sheet. Jack and Mary-Jane stared anxiously at me.

'Now, let's begin,' I said brightly.

'Do you want us to tidy this room, miss?' Mary-Jane asked huskily.

It certainly needed tidying. Papa never allowed Maggie to dust and sweep in his studio because he said she'd get everything in a muddle. It was in a fine old muddle already, canvas and cloth and paint and brushes spilling everywhere.

'No, I don't want you to tidy, Mary-Jane. I want to sketch you. And you too, Jack,' I said.

They blinked at me.

'How do you mean *sketch*, miss?' Jack asked, scratching his head.

'I want to draw you,' I said, holding out my sketchpad and pencil.

He looked horrified. So did Mary-Jane.

'I'm not taking my clothes off, miss!' said Jack.

'I'm not either. I'm a good girl,' said Mary-Jane.

'I don't want you to pose nude for me!' I told them. 'I simply want to draw you as you are. Don't look so worried! It won't hurt. Look, go and stand under the skylight. Then I'll sit here and draw you.'

I tried to arrange them as if they were having a natural conversation – maybe even playing a game. It was impossible. It was like trying to breathe life into a pair of broomsticks. They stuck their arms and legs out at the oddest of angles and scarcely breathed, grimacing as if I were about to throw a bucket of water over them.

'Couldn't you just relax a bit?' I begged them. 'How about jiggling your arms and legs about, maybe running around a little, and *then* standing still?'

They didn't manage this either. Mary-Jane waved her arms limply, and Jack ran very slowly, as if through treacle. Then they both stopped in exaggerated poses, as if playing Statues.

'Oh goodness, children, this isn't working,' I said despairingly.

'We aren't children, miss,' said Jack, offended.

'We're ser-vants,' said Mary-Jane, enunciating slowly to try to make me understand.

'But you're children too! That's what's so queer about it. Don't you mind working for us?' I asked. 'Wouldn't you like a different sort of life?'

They gave each other a quick glance and then looked back at me warily.

'You're not going to dismiss us, are you, miss? Because I ain't got nowhere else to go, and Mr Hodgson says I'm a good lad and I buff up the boots so's I can see my face in them,' Jack insisted.

'Well, Cook sometimes calls me a bad girl and I knows I'm a bit careless, but I'm learning, honest I am, and I've got a home to go to but I can't go back because Ma says I've got to earn my own living, and she'll wallop me if I get dismissed,' said Mary-Jane, starting to cry.

'Oh, please don't get so upset! Of course you're not being dismissed! I promise you I just want to draw you, and maybe get to know you a bit better. To be a kind friend to you,' I said earnestly. 'Look, I tell you what. If you'll let me sketch you for half an hour, I'll pay you. Like wages. Would that make it easier for you?'

'Pay us how much, miss?' Jack asked.

I calculated. I wasn't very good at saving pocket money, but I reckoned my piggy-bank pennies might add up to half a crown.

'How about a shilling each?' I suggested. I was worried that it wasn't enough, but Jack and Mary-Jane looked dumbstruck at the thought of such riches.

'Right, miss. It's a deal. You can draw us any way you want. Stand up, Mary-Jane, and close your mouth – you look gormless,' said Jack.

'Don't you lord it over me, Jack Boots. I bin here longer than you,' said Mary-Jane, giving him a push.

At last they'd started behaving like real children, squabbling like Algie and Clarrie. They still weren't posing properly, but I managed to do a rough outline. As I drew, I asked them questions, trying to find out more about them. They were more confiding now because they'd started to trust me. Or maybe they were spurred on by the thought of the shilling.

I was taken aback by what they'd said. I'd had no idea what their life was like. I'd vaguely understood that they came from poor backgrounds but hadn't imagined any of the grim details. Jack didn't know who his family were or even his exact age.

'They said my ma came knocking at the workhouse when she was expecting me, see. And then she had me but she was frail and she died. So I was brought up in the workhouse nursery,' he said.

'Oh, Jack, how sad!' I said. 'You must miss your mother so much.'

He gave me a sideways look. 'Well, I didn't know her, did I?'

'And what about your father? Did he come and visit you?'

'Ain't got a father, not that I know of. There's just me,' said Jack.

'So who looked after you in the workhouse?' I asked.

'No one much. We had to fend for ourselves,' he said. 'If you didn't gobble your grub the second it was put in front of you, some other pig stole it. If you didn't sidle out the way of the matrons quick, they strapped you just for the fun of it.'

'And did they get really angry if you asked for more gruel?' I asked. I'd read *Oliver Twist* and wept.

'You'd have to be a fool to ask for more. It was always burned and tasted blimming horrible,' said Jack.

'Ssh, you shouldn't say that word in front of Miss,' said Mary-Jane primly.

'So what about you, Mary-Jane? You grew up with a proper family, didn't you?'

She told me a few bare facts about them. They didn't sound proper at all.

'There's eleven of us – well, nine now, because Johnnie got trampled by a horse and Maisie ran off and Ma says she's gone to the bad,' Mary-Jane said. 'Maisie used to help look after the little ones, but now it's our Jen's job. I haven't got a proper job at home, so when Ma heard from her pal who's Cook's sister that she was wanting a kitchen maid to train up, Ma said I had to go for it.'

My head was reeling as I compared their lives with mine. I was often sorry for myself and felt my life was unfair. How would I have coped with Jack's life or Mary-Jane's?

'I can see you've both had a very hard start. But it's better for you now, isn't it? I mean, you have good food to eat and you're well cared for,' I said. My voice reminded me of someone. Oh dear Lord, it was *Mama*.

'You're both happy here, aren't you?' I added pleadingly.

I wanted them to reassure me that they were very happy, that this was a good home and Mama and Papa were kind employers, but they were looking at me dumbly.

'Happy, miss?' Jack said at last.

'Don't rightly know what to say, miss,' said Mary-Jane.

I tried to pretend that they simply couldn't express themselves properly, but I knew this was nonsense. I wanted to think that they *liked* being servants. But of course they weren't happy working all day long with no love and no play. Try as I might, I could never be their friend because I was the daughter of the house and they were the servants, and it didn't matter a hoot to anyone that we were all children.

5

PAPA CAME HOME LATE, when we were halfway through dinner. Now that I've turned thirteen I am allowed to join the grown-ups, but it's not much fun without Rupert. Mama complains and Papa pacifies and I spoon my soup, and Mr Hodgson and Edie wait on us and say nothing.

I'd sooner be back in the hurly-burly of the nursery, with Sebastian hiding morsels of food in his pocket for Montmorency, and Algie encouraging his toy soldier to climb the Everest of his mashed potato, and Clarrie hiding crusts under her plate. And of course Phoebe has joined us now, which is a delight, though it's not advisable to sit too near her, as rusks and bottles are hurled without warning.

I asked Mama whether I could have my meals in the nursery again so that I could help Nurse with Phoebe. It sounded a sensible and sisterly suggestion, but Mama wouldn't hear of it.

'You're not a nurserymaid, Rose! It's time you learned how to be a young lady,' she said.

So I have to change for dinner, which is an awful bore. Mama thinks it's time to have a couple of grown-up dresses made for me. They will have tight waists, and that will mean a dreaded corset.

'I can't wear such an awful garment. I wouldn't even be able to lace it up,' I protested.

'I will ask Edie to help you,' said Mama.

I hated that idea. I can't bear the idea of her seeing me in my chemise and drawers. She is always so superior. She makes me feel less guilty about having servants because she acts in such a condescending manner and is never remotely servile, even with Mama.

Mama and I bickered over my clothes while we sipped Brown Windsor soup, and when we were served our cutlets Mama started talking about riding lessons. She said she was going to call on Mrs Feynsham-Jones to discuss the matter, though I begged her not to.

As soon as Papa appeared in the dining room, hastily thrusting his arms into his velvet jacket, I appealed to him.

'There you are at last, Papa! Mama is desperate for me to go riding with those terrible Feynsham-Jones girls and I can't bear the idea,' I cried.

'Rose! Let your father sit down and eat before you start plaguing him. Though why you are so late I cannot understand, Edward. It's not very considerate, either to me or to the servants,' Mama whined.

'I am sorry, my dear. I've been rushing around all over London. My dear novelist friend Sarah Smith told me about a special hospital, so I bundled Marianne up in a shawl and carried her all the way there. I spent the rest of the afternoon on a shopping quest, but it took longer than I'd bargained for.'

'Who on earth is Marianne?' Mama asked. 'One of those little street children?'

'I'm referring to Beth's doll,' said Papa patiently. 'I've found a special *doll's* hospital, and they say they can conduct an operation and restore her sight – isn't that good news!'

'For goodness' sake, Edward, I wish you wouldn't be so whimsical,' said Mama.

'I love it when Papa is whimsical,' I said. 'He is capital at make-believe.'

'Nobody asked your opinion, Rose,' Mama said dismissively.

'However, there have been several dolly casualties in the area and I'm afraid the hospital has a long waiting list. Marianne will have to wait weeks for her operation,' said Papa.

'*Weeks!* Oh, poor Beth!' I said.

'It's all your fault, Rose. You would interfere. You have to learn the consequence of your actions,' said Mama. She gave Papa a sharp look.

'You don't need to lecture me, Mama. I feel badly enough about it. And now we're saddled with Nurse Budd, which is a *dreadful* consequence.'

'Don't be ridiculous. Beth's had a very peaceful day, thank goodness. No tears or tantrums. Nurse Budd is working her magic already, and yet I don't think she's so much as laid a finger on her,' said Mama.

'No child of mine is ever going to be physically chastised,' said Papa. His voice was quiet and even, and for once he wasn't joking. 'I'm not as thrilled as you are with Nurse Budd. I'm not sure I agree with her concept of training a child. Beth isn't a performing dog.'

'I so agree with you, Papa,' I said.

'You're both talking nonsense,' said Mama. 'Nurse Budd is a marvellous find and we're very lucky to get her at short notice. Lady Robson said—'

'Do you know something, Jeannie?' Papa interrupted. 'I am not the slightest bit interested in what Lady Robson says. She strikes me as an exceptionally foolish and interfering old woman.'

Mama breathed in deeply, glancing at Mr Hodgson and Edie, who were standing like statues at either end of the long table. There was a long silence while we ate our cutlets. I couldn't finish mine, and neither could Mama. Papa ate determinedly but without appetite.

When Edie had taken our plates and Papa had asked Mr Hodgson to fetch another bottle of wine from the cellar, Mama hissed, 'I'll thank you not to insult me in front of the servants, Edward.'

'I wasn't aware that I was insulting you, Jeannie. I was insulting Lady Robson.' Papa looked at me. 'Thank your lucky stars your mama doesn't want you to go riding with any of Lady Robson's granddaughters. If they take after her, you really *would* have something to complain about.'

'After Beth's histrionics I'm sure Lady Robson would never allow any of her family near a child of mine,' Mama said bitterly. 'Indeed, I very much doubt whether Mrs Feynsham-Jones will permit Rose to ride with Pamela and Lucinda-May and Cecily, though I shall call on her tomorrow and suggest it.'

'But why would you do that, when Rose is adamant that she doesn't *wish* to learn to ride, especially in the company of those particular girls?' Papa enquired.

'This afternoon Rose ran away, walking all the way to Rotten Row in Hyde Park, simply to see the horses,' said Mama.

'Did you, Rose?' Papa asked. 'Why this sudden interest?'

Mr Hodgson had returned and was pouring Papa a glass of wine, while Edie served us with blackberry trifle. I waited while they did so, feeling a little foolish. When they'd resumed their positions, I mumbled, 'I wanted to see the horses' legs.'

'The *legs*?' said Mama.

'They bend backwards, and yet they looked so strange when I tried to draw them. So I thought I should take a look at some real ones,' I said.

'Excellent!' said Papa. 'Well done!'

'Don't praise the child for running away! She had the whole house in uproar. Anything could have happened to her, walking all that way unaccompanied,' said Mama.

'Yes, I dare say. You must never do it again, Rose,' said Papa, but he winked at me.

Mama waited until Mr Hodgson and Edie had bustled out with our dishes. She'd only had two mouthfuls of her trifle, complaining that the blackberries weren't sweet enough. Mama looked as if she needed sweetening herself.

'I think it's very unfair of you to encourage Rose, Edward. I'm simply trying to be a responsible parent. She is becoming very wayward and unladylike. She has no accomplishments to speak of. And no friends at all,' said Mama.

'I do have friends,' I said, stung. 'Rupert is my best friend.'

'Rupert doesn't count. He is your brother, and now he is away at school.'

'Boys are so lucky to be sent to school,' I said, sighing.

'I'd like you to make friends with other girls. I simply want you to be *normal*,' said Mama. 'Is that too much to ask? Why are all you children so *contrary*?'

She stood up as Mr Hodgson and Edie came back in, dabbing her eyes with her napkin, and then hurried out of the room so quickly that Mr Hodgson didn't have time to open the door for her.

There was another uncomfortable silence.

Papa hesitated. 'Should you perhaps go after your mother?' he asked me.

'I think she's better left to herself,' I said.

It wasn't very nice of me when Mama was so distressed, but I enjoyed being with Papa. He let me have a little coffee while he had more wine, and we both nibbled delicious chocolates.

'I bought a box as a little treat for your mother, but I don't think she'd appreciate them right now,' said Papa. 'You help yourself, darling. Try the rose cream!'

'Oh, they're my favourites! Louisa once gave me a little box of them!'

Papa frowned and dismissed Mr Hodgson and Edie. There was a little silence while I savoured my chocolate.

'It's truly delicious, Papa! You do spoil Mama,' I said. 'She doesn't deserve such a kind, thoughtful husband.'

Papa frowned. 'Nonsense,' he said firmly. 'I'm not at all kind or thoughtful. Your poor mother has a lot to put up with.'

'I know she finds *me* a trial,' I said. 'Papa, I don't have to be friends with those beastly Feynsham-Jones girls, do I?'

'I think your mother has set her heart on it. She wants you to make some new friends now that Rupert is at school.'

'But those sisters are so niminy-piminy, especially Lucinda-May,' I protested. 'We have nothing to say to each other. She doesn't even like reading!'

'She does sound a little dull. I wish I could find a jolly girl to be chums with you,' said Papa.

'But *I* am not a jolly girl,' I said.

'Perhaps not always. But I still think you're perfect.'

'Oh, Papa! You're only saying that because I'm your daughter.'

'Yes, I think *all* my children are perfect.'

'You think *Algie* perfect?'

Papa laughed. 'Of course I do. He is a delightful scamp who frequently makes me roar with laughter. Clarrie is a mischievous little monkey too, but so good natured. Sebastian is extraordinarily sensitive, and very loving and caring. Phoebe is an utter delight. I love hearing her chuckle!'

'And Beth?' I asked softly.

'Poor darling, troubled Beth,' said Papa.

'She will miss Marianne so. You know how she hates any kind of change.'

'But I have found her a substitute while Marianne is convalescing!' Papa said excitedly. 'Shall I show you?'

He rushed out to the hall, where he'd stowed a big parcel against the coat stand.

'Oh, Papa! A new doll?' I asked.

'Wait till you see her! After Marianne was admitted to hospital I spent the afternoon rushing from one toy shop to the next, but none had the perfect doll. They were all dressed up in fussy bonnets and elaborate dresses and parasols. They weren't dolls you could hug and play with properly. I knew Beth would hate them.

'But then someone mentioned a little doll-maker in Hoxton, of all places, so I took a cab there. It's a shame you're too grown up for dolls yourself, Rose. It's the most magical shop, run by a sweet old gentleman, rather crippled but still spry. He has a delightful little girl for his assistant, very bright and perky, with a tangle of dark hair and big green eyes. She pays the most particular attention to all the dolls and helped me select this special one.' Papa knelt down and started struggling with the string around the package.

'Would you like me to assist you, sir?' Mr Hodgson was hovering. He bent down to help, his old bones cracking.

'No, no, Hodgson, I'll manage. That's half the pleasure of parcels, the battle to get them open! You go and have your supper, old chap,' said Papa.

I loved the way he talked to the servants as if they were friends. Mama was much more brusque. She said Papa didn't know how to treat the staff – though Papa's family had had a great flock of servants for many generations, while Mama's family had probably once, not so long ago, been servants themselves.

Papa didn't mind me helping though. Between us we prised off the string and opened up the box. It was carefully stuffed with packing straw, and when we burrowed through that to find the doll, we discovered that her face had been carefully protected with scraps of material, and she had another large piece folded around her as if she were tucked up in bed.

'That's the work of little Miss Clover Moon, the doll-maker's assistant,' said Papa fondly. 'Well, what do you think of her, Rose?'

I eased the doll out of the box and held her at arm's length. 'She's a beauty!' I said, marvelling at her dark red curls and the dimples in her smooth china cheeks. 'She looks so smiley too!'

'That's why I chose her. I thought she might make Beth smile back,' Papa said eagerly. 'Do you think Beth will like her?'

'I'm sure she will,' I said.

'Shall we go and see?' said Papa, taking the doll from me.

I hesitated. 'I don't think Nurse Budd will want us to disturb her, Papa, not after supper. She can be very fierce.'

'Are you scared of Nurse Budd, Rose?'

'Not exactly. I'm wary of her.'

'Do you think Beth is scared of her?'

It was so difficult to work out what was going on in Beth's head. She seemed scared of everybody.

I shrugged my shoulders. 'I don't *think* so.'

'Anyway, *I'm* not scared of her, so let us introduce Beth to her new doll right this minute,' said Papa.

We went up the stairs to the second floor. There were whispers and giggles coming from the children's night nursery, and the soft sound of Nurse soothing Phoebe. There was only silence coming from the green guest room.

Papa had said he wasn't the slightest bit afraid of Nurse Budd, but he hesitated outside the door and took a deep breath before he knocked. There was a long pause and then we heard footsteps. The door opened a crack.

'What is it now?' Nurse Budd hissed at me – and then saw Papa by my side. 'I'm sorry, sir. I didn't realize you were there. Is it urgent? I don't really want Miss Beth disturbed.'

'Is she asleep?' Papa asked.

'Resting, sir,' Nurse Budd said firmly.

We heard regular tapping noises behind her. Beth often rocked herself to and fro in bed, so that the headboard banged against the wall.

'Beth?' I called hopefully.

'Ssh! Don't agitate her, dear.'

'Come, Nurse Budd, Beth enjoys seeing her sister. And we have a surprise for her,' said Papa, indicating the doll.

'I don't think children like dear little Miss Beth cope well with surprises, sir,' said Nurse Budd, but she let us in.

Beth was in bed, rocking, wide awake. She looked pale in the dim lamplight, but her eyes were bright and she made soft humming noises that sounded welcoming.

'Hello, my little humming bird,' said Papa. 'Rose and I have brought you a new friend. Do you like her? I was told at the doll-maker's that her name is Marigold. Say how do you do.' He held Marigold out towards Beth. The doll's arms were outstretched, as if she were greeting her. Beth hunched up small, looking uncertain, but when Papa balanced Marigold at the end of her bed she propped herself up on one elbow to look at her.

'How do you do?' she whispered.

'That's right, my darling. How very polite of you,' Papa said.

I took Marigold and made her give Beth a little bob. 'How do you do, Beth?' I said, in a squeaky little doll voice. 'I am delighted to make your acquaintance. May I come and live with you? I hear you're missing Marianne.'

'Marianne?' said Beth.

'I've taken poor Marianne to a special doll's hospital. They've promised me they will make her as right as rain. Meanwhile you have Marigold to keep you company. I'm sure Marianne will get on splendidly with her when she comes home,' said Papa.

'Oh, sir, what a lovely dolly!' said Nurse Budd.

'What a lovely dolly,' said Beth, and she took Marigold and hugged her hard.

'Careful now. You don't want to crush her pretty silk dress, do you, dear,' said Nurse Budd.

'She may crush it all she pleases,' said Papa. 'Marigold isn't going to be one of those only-for-best dolls, and kept in a cupboard. Beth may play with her all she likes, and undress her and tangle her hair and let her paddle in the bathtub for all I care. She can sleep in Beth's arms all night long and keep her company at all times. Is that clear?' He said this pleasantly, but there was a firmness about his tone.

'Yes, sir. Certainly, sir,' said Nurse Budd.

'Then we will leave you both in peace. Come along, Rose. Kiss your sister goodnight,' said Papa.

I bent over Beth and very lightly kissed her soft cheek. She smelled of warm little girl and laundered nightgown.

'Night, Beth,' I whispered.

Beth held Marigold up so that I could kiss her too.

'Goodnight, my darling,' said Papa. 'Goodnight, Nurse Budd.'

'Goodnight, sir. Goodnight, Miss Rose,' said Nurse Budd.

When we were out on the landing, Papa gave me a big hug. 'There now! Marigold has worked wonders,' he said. 'I think she's made Beth happy, don't you?'

'Definitely, Papa.'

'So how can I make *you* happy, Rose?'

'Promise you'll thwart Mama's plans for me to go riding with the Feynsham-Joneses?'

'I'll do my best,' said Papa.

6

PAPA'S BEST WASN'T GOOD enough. Mama called on Mrs Feynsham-Jones. I expect she said I was gauche and friendless and asked if her daughters might take pity on me. I burned at the thought. I imagined the Feynsham-Jones girls protesting:

'Oh, Mama, do we *have* to take Rose riding with us?'

'She's pathetic, Mama, so strange, with no idea how to make proper conversation.'

'She won't be any good at riding, Mama. Imagine, she's never even been on a horse. We've all been riding since we were tots.'

But it's all fixed. I have a riding lesson at four on Saturday afternoon. Mr Hodgson was told to accompany me to the Feynsham-Joneses' at half past three so that I could borrow a riding skirt.

I felt sick with dread after lunch. I sat on the window seat trying to distract myself by sketching the stuffed peacock perched on the newel post at the bottom of the staircase. I was aware of howling upstairs. Perhaps Nurse Budd's training wasn't quite as effective as she boasted.

Then Algie came charging down the stairs and snatched my sketchbook before I knew what was happening.

'Silly old book! Silly old Rose. Silly old Nurse! Pooh to the lot of you!' Algie yelled, and ran away before I could catch him.

Nurse came puffing down the stairs in pursuit, wielding a hairbrush. 'That little varmint!' she panted. 'Just wait till I catch him! You should see what he's done to poor Miss Clarrie! She said she wished she looked like Snow White, with hair as black as ebony, so Algie tipped a tin of black treacle over her head! Can you imagine! It will take me all day to wash it out. Poor Clarrie is in floods of tears in the bath but Algie isn't the slightest bit sorry. He just doubled up laughing. *I'll* give him a laugh!' She brandished the hairbrush.

I've had several encounters with the bristle end in the past. No wonder Algie was running. He dived down the hall, along the passageway and through the green baize door to the servants' quarters.

Nurse slowed down, panting, clutching her side. 'I've got such a stitch!' she said.

I knew she was reluctant to go barging into Cook's territory. They've been working here since I was born and are officially great friends, but they are both hot-tempered women and have frequent fallings-out. Last week there was a very fierce argument after Nurse complained that the nursery blancmange was lumpy. They haven't spoken since.

'I'll go and find him for you,' I offered.

Nurse nodded gratefully. We could hear Phoebe starting to wail, accompanying Clarrie's dismal bellowing. Nurse trudged back up the main stairs. Mama happened to be coming down in her afternoon frock and frowned. Nurse tried to flatten herself against the wall.

'Really, Nurse!' Mama scolded. 'Please use the servants' stairs unless you are accompanying the children.'

'Yes, madam,' Nurse murmured. 'I'm sorry, madam.'

It was painful seeing Mama tick her off as if she were a chit of a girl instead of an old lady. I thought about trying to explain the circumstances to Mama, but I knew she wouldn't listen. I sidled away because I knew that Nurse would hate to lose face in front of me.

I went into the servants' quarters. Jack was squatting on the floor, his hands in a pair of boots, idly marching them up and down the stone flags. He jumped when he saw me and did his best to squeeze himself into a dark corner.

'Mr Hodgson says I don't have to let you do that sketching thing again, not if I don't want to,' he said huskily.

'Don't you be cheeky, lad,' said Mr Hodgson, giving him a cuff, though he'd probably said exactly that. 'Please excuse him, Miss Rose. He wasn't brought up well so he hasn't any manners. But he's learning as best he can.'

'I think you're doing a grand job with him, Mr Hodgson,' I said.

'So how can I help you, Miss Rose? It's too early to set off for your riding lesson,' he said.

'That's right, Mr Hodgson. But you don't need to trouble yourself, not if you're busy. I couldn't possibly get lost simply going up the road and round the corner. Why, I walked all the way to Hyde Park the other day,' I said.

'I know you did, Miss Rose, and you caused quite a panic. Your mama has charged me with the responsibility of taking you and indeed collecting you too. But I shall do it as unobtrusively as possible if you object to my company,' he said, a little huffily.

'Oh no, Mr Hodgson, I don't object to your company at all. It's simply that I'd like some independence. It's very frustrating having to be accompanied everywhere,' I said. 'You've no idea how tiresome it is being a girl.'

'I dare say, Miss Rose. So how can we help you?'

'I've come to collect Algie. I think he barged his way in here . . .'

'Indeed he did, Miss Rose. I think he's cosying up to Cook,' said Mr Hodgson.

I found Algie sitting on the kitchen table, with Cook scrubbing at his treacly hands, distracting him by feeding him apple peelings and sultanas.

'Oh, Cook, you shouldn't spoil him so! He's been very naughty,' I said, glaring at Algie.

'This little lamb?' she said, giving Algie's snub nose a gentle pinch. He gave her a cherubic smile.

'He's more of a black sheep than a little lamb,' I said tartly, snatching my sketchbook from him and clutching it to my chest.

It's so irritating. All the servants love Algie and let him get away with murder. They laugh at him and pet him and play with him. They've never been like that with me, even when I was his age.

He's smudged my peacock sketch with treacle, so my bird resembles a very large crow with a trailing tail. I tore it out of my sketchbook and went up to the nursery, wondering it I might have more luck sketching my siblings. I tried Phoebe first but she was too wriggly, so I started drawing Clarrie. She was still woebegone, her hair sticky even after a good wash.

'Don't draw me, I'm too ugly,' she protested, frowning at me. 'Draw me Snow White.'

So I gave up sketching from life and drew Clarrie as a chubby Snow White with long black hair. Then I drew a Wicked Stepmother. She looked disconcertingly like Mama.

'And now draw all the dwarfs!' Clarrie demanded.

I started on them, but had only managed one (the spit of Algie) when Maggie came looking for me.

'Mr Hodgson is waiting for you, Miss Rose,' she said.

He foisted me upon the Feynsham-Joneses – and it was all just as terrible as I'd feared. There was a great to-do over the wretched riding skirt. I am nearest Lucinda-May in age, but she is shorter than me and her old riding skirt only reached my knees. I had to wear Pamela's instead. The waistband dug into me so I could scarcely breathe. I am thinner than Pamela, but she wears a corset so her waist is minute, with embarrassing curves above and below. I am as straight as a ruler, and I intend to stay that way.

'Don't worry,' said Pamela smugly, seeing me staring at myself in the looking glass. 'I'm sure you will start developing soon.'

I felt like slapping her. She looked splendid in her new riding outfit. She'd tied her long curls back into a neat bun and seemed much older than fourteen. Her exposed neck looked very white and graceful against the black of her riding jacket. She sported a delightful top hat.

'Do you think I could borrow a hat too?' I asked hopefully, but she said she didn't have a spare one.

Lucinda-May set hers off with a long plait which she tossed from side to side. Even chubby little Cecily looked stylish in her riding clothes, and marched up and down showing off her shiny riding boots.

They led me down the garden and through the gate to the stables in the mews. I thought there would be one pony for us all to take turns on, but Pamela and Lucinda-May and Cecily each had their own, and greeted them with great cries and kisses, as if they hadn't seen them for weeks.

I looked warily at Blue Boy and Cocoa. Even Cecily's Shetland pony, Jingle, looked alarming. There were several jolly grooms who helped the girls mount, but I was stuck with a terrifying little woman called Miss Havers, who looked like a whippet.

'I am going to teach you to ride,' she said. She frowned at my long hair, my blouse, my kid boots. 'Why aren't you dressed in proper riding clothes?'

'I don't think her mama realized she needed special clothes,' said Lucinda-May pityingly.

Miss Havers sighed. 'You must have been on a pony though,' she said.

'No, I've never done any riding,' I told her.

'Didn't you have a Shetland when you were little?' she asked.

I shook my head.

'Well, you must have ridden donkeys at the seaside,' she persisted.

The beaches I'd been to in Scotland were chilly places with no amusements, and certainly no donkeys. I shook my head again.

'Good heavens,' said Miss Havers. 'How strange.'

Lucinda-May edged closer to her. She attempted a whisper but I heard every word. 'Mama says we must make allowances because the Rivers family are *bohemian*.' She said the last word as if it were very shameful.

I flushed. 'My father is a famous artist,' I said haughtily.

'And Mr Rivers comes from a very distinguished family, so you're talking rot, Lucinda-May,' said Pamela. She raised her eyebrows to me. 'Take no notice, Rose.'

I was amazed. Why on earth was stuck-up, simpering Pamela defending me? Lucinda-May looked astonished too.

'Now then, girls, enough of the chit-chat,' Miss Havers snapped. She glared at me. 'I can see I'm going to have my work cut out! What sort of a girl are you?'

I stared at her. 'I dare say you could call me a *bohemian* girl,' I said, with a nod at Lucinda-May.

Miss Havers sighed impatiently. 'Are you spirited and plucky – or a little timid mouse?' she asked.

'Spirited and plucky,' I said at once.

It was the worst answer I could have given. If I'd said I was a mouse, she might have put me on a fat, meek little pony like Cecily's Jingle. Instead she put me on huge cob called Marker. He had a contemptuous expression, and blew down his nostrils at me.

'Isn't he rather big?' I asked, all my so-called spirit and pluck deserting me.

'He's on the small side for a cob, and as docile as they come. He'll suit you down to the ground,' said Miss Havers.

'As long as he doesn't *throw* me to the ground,' I said.

Miss Havers frowned. She clearly had no sense of humour. 'If you listen to my instructions you won't fall off,' she said coldly.

I listened for all I was worth, but I couldn't make sense of anything she said. She gave me a long lecture about stirrups and girths and bits and martingales, but she might just as well have been talking Greek. Then she led Marker to the mounting block and told me to get on his back.

It seemed impossible. I felt as if I were climbing Everest. Pamela and Lucinda-May and Cecily tittered at my undignified efforts. Even the grooms were sniggering. Only Miss Havers stayed stern.

'For pity's sake, don't haul yourself up by clutching the poor pony like that! He's made of fine flesh and blood. Spring lightly! *Lightly!*'

When I was at last seated, damp with embarrassment, she twisted me about cruelly so that my right leg was hooked over the pommel and dangling down on Marker's left side, without even a stirrup to support it. Girls cannot be mounted sensibly, a leg on either side of the horse – they have to ride side-saddle.

Marker sensed my terror and discomfort and whinnied irritably, dancing from side to side. I clung onto the reins, sure I was about to be tipped off.

'Hold them *loosely*! No clutching. Dear goodness, a babe in arms has more feel for riding than you, girl!'

Miss Havers continued abusing me while walking Marker and me round and round the small yard. I clenched my buttocks as hard as I could to stay in contact with the slippery leather of the saddle. Miss Havers told me to try to feel at one with the horse. I slumped low and tried to think horse thoughts, and she admonished me for looking like a sack of potatoes.

The other girls had trotted off to the grounds of Holland House, but Miss Havers didn't feel I was safe to go out in public yet. Marker jiggled and fretted, clearly annoyed that he wasn't getting any exercise. Then a flock of sparrows that had been pecking at a pile of something unmentionable suddenly flew up, straight towards us. Marker was startled and reared up on his hind legs.

'Keep your seat!' Miss Havers shouted.

I didn't know how. I went flying and fell flat on the yard floor. It was a terrible shock. I hurt so much I lay still, my eyes shut.

'Oh my Lord!' Miss Havers gasped, slapping at my face.

'You've done it now, miss,' a stable lad muttered. 'She looks like a goner to me.'

'Shut your mouth, boy, and go and attend to the pony,' Miss Havers said curtly.

I kept my eyes closed and lay limp and unresponsive, my heart pounding with shock and shame. Would Miss Havers make me get on again? I felt I would die if I had to go through the whole miserable business a second time. I stayed there until a couple of grooms hauled me up and started carrying me back through the garden. My borrowed riding skirt was caught up and I feared I was showing all my underwear. I opened my eyes and groaned a little, while surreptitiously trying to pull the skirt down.

'Keep still, girl! How are you feeling? Which part of you hurts?' Miss Havers demanded.

'My right leg,' I mumbled. It was cramping badly after being forced into such an unnatural position.

'She'll have crushed it,' said the stable lad, running along beside us. 'It'll dangle uselessly for the rest of her life, poor soul.'

'I'll dangle *you* in a minute,' said Miss Havers. 'The leg will be fine. I expect it's simply bruised. Girls fall off horses through their own stupid fault every day of the week.'

'Yes, but not *this* girl – a friend of Miss Pamela and Lucinda-May and Cecily,' he insisted. 'What's Mrs Feynsham-Jones going to say, eh?'

Mrs Feynsham-Jones said quite a lot. She sent the stable boy running for her doctor and had me carried up to Pamela's room and laid on her bed.

'You poor dear soul, try to bear up,' she said, holding my hand.

'Will I send for her mother, madam?' asked a maid.

'I think the doctor had better examine her first. We will have to tell poor Rose's mama very sensitively. She's rather an invalid and suffers from nerves,' said Mrs Feynsham-Jones.

I felt very apprehensive about the doctor's visit. I remembered the time Algie played at being a tightrope walker along the top of a wall and over-estimated his balancing skills. He dislocated his shoulder and screamed blue murder when the doctor put it back into place. I didn't want my leg to be manipulated in such a brutal way. The cramp had faded anyway.

I knew I should tell Mrs Feynsham-Jones that I was perfectly all right, just a little bumped and bruised. However, the doctor arrived surprisingly quickly, before I could manufacture a miraculous recovery. I told him that I was feeling much better now, but he prodded and pressed me all over anyway. Thank goodness he didn't decide anything needed to be manipulated.

'Keep her lying down for half an hour, and tell her nurse to keep an eye on her during the night to make sure there's no relapse. But she should be as right as rain,' he told Mrs Feynsham-Jones. Then he nodded at me. 'Don't worry, my dear, I'm sure they'll make a horsewoman of you yet.'

I was determined never to go near a horse again. I realized I hadn't even studied the construction of Marker's legs. I had just looked at them warily in case they started kicking out at me.

'Stay here quietly, Rose,' said Mrs Feynsham-Jones. 'The girls will be back from their ride before long.'

I soon got bored. I sat up gingerly, and then eased myself off the bed. I could walk perfectly well, thank goodness. I didn't even have a limp. I gave a great sigh of relief and wandered around Pamela's room, peering at her belongings. She seemed to care for reading more than vacant Lucinda-May: she actually had a bookcase, though she didn't have many proper books, just a pristine leather-bound set of Mr Dickens's novels. It didn't look as if she'd read any of them. I wondered if she would let me borrow one or two. After all, she'd let me borrow her riding skirt, and seemed surprisingly fond of me all of a sudden.

I bent down to examine the bottom shelf. It was mostly dreary fashion journals, but she also had some big bound volumes of the *Girl's Own Paper*. They have proper stories in them, and I like reading the advice columns because the girls have such trivial problems and the adviser is so sharp with them.

I picked out last year's volume, and perched carefully on the end of Pamela's bed with it. I usually sat cross-legged, but my right leg was still throbbing. I started flicking through the pages for the first column of tart answers.

IRISH GIRL: We cannot decipher your letter because your handwriting is appalling.

KEEN TO PROSPER: It is unattractive for a young girl to seek to earn a great deal of money.

DESIREE: If you want to know how to make an Apple Charlotte, you should obtain a recipe in the cheapest cookery book published.

LOVELORN: We do not approve of hankering after such an unsuitable gentleman. You cannot be a well-brought-up girl. Do try to curb your romantic nature.

There were dried flowers inserted between several of the pages. Pamela definitely had a romantic nature. Then a letter slithered from between the pages. I stared at the dashing black copperplate. I knew that handwriting!

I turned the letter over to see the signature, hoping I was somehow mistaken ... But no, there it was, plain for all to see, with the distinctive flourish of the *t* at the end. *Rupert*.

7

I READ THE LETTER AND returned it to the
annual, which I thrust onto the bookshelf. I lay back
on the bed, wrapping my arms around me, rocking to
and fro to distract myself. Beth rocks in exactly the same
way. I never understood why before.

I can't remember the letter word for word, but the
beginning and end are seared on my heart.

My dear Pamela. And then: *Your loving friend, Rupert.*
LOVING, LOVING, LOVING, LOVING, LOVING.

It wasn't exactly a love letter. Rupert didn't wax lyrical
about the arch of her eyebrow, the long line of her neck,

the curl of her blonde hair. Rupert wrote about himself, not Pamela. There was a long paragraph about the other boys in his form. He dismissed most as swots or saps, but said there were two capital fellows called Hardy and Martin, and the three of them got up to all sorts of japes.

He mentioned one of the prefects, Mackinley, who seemed a lordly sort of fellow. It was apparently Rupert's job to cook sausages for his breakfast. There was a great deal about food – the beefsteak pudding at lunch and then herrings for Mackinley's tea, though Rupert and the capital fellows had to make do with bread and jam.

There were complaints about the hardness of his school bed and the thinness of his blankets, and a passage about his charwoman and her adenoids. It was supposed to be comical, but it sounded unpleasantly mocking.

The last sentence was the worst:

School is all right, I suppose, but this first half seems endless because I'm missing you.

I cannot bear it. Rupert isn't missing *me* at all. He hasn't even bothered to write to me. He's written to Pamela instead. He's missing *her*, though he hardly knows her.

There was a great fuss when I got home. Mama insisted I spend the night in the green guest room so that Nurse Budd could keep an eye on me. I hated this idea, but at least I would get to see how she treated Beth. There was an argument about whether Beth could take Marigold to bed with her.

'It would be such a shame to spoil her hair and her lovely silk frock,' said Nurse Budd.

'Papa said that Beth should be allowed to take her to bed,' I said.

Nurse Budd sighed. 'Well, Miss Rose, we must do as your papa says – though I think he'll regret it when this lovely doll is ruined,' she said.

'Ruined?' said Beth anxiously.

'Now now, Miss Beth, no need to get worked up,' said Nurse Budd. 'I think it's dosing time, my dear.'

She went over to the washstand and unlocked a small leather case with black bottles neatly stacked inside. 'Open wide for your nice medicine, Miss Beth.'

'Nice medicine,' said Beth, her mouth gaping like a baby bird's.

I was astonished. Whenever Nurse tried to dose Beth with castor oil she screamed blue murder and spat it straight out. Now Beth swallowed this dark sticky potion eagerly and even licked the spoon.

'What is that medicine?' I asked. 'And why are you giving it to her? She isn't ill.'

'It's only Godfrey's Cordial, Miss Rose. Lovely and soothing – and look at the label: it's so safe it's recommended for little babies,' said Nurse Budd, showing me. She even pulled out the cork so that I could have a sniff. It smelled strongly of treacle.

'I should keep it well away from Algie if I were you,' I said.

I settled down to sleep. I dreaded Nurse Budd peering at me during the night, but she was soon snoring steadily. So was Beth. I stayed wide awake, thinking about Rupert and Pamela. I needed soothing too. I felt like taking a swig of Godfrey's Cordial myself.

Your loving friend.

The phrase seemed to be scrawled on the insides of my eyelids so that I could see it awake or asleep.

Why did Rupert think so much of Pamela? She was more than a year older than him and deadly dull. When we were forced to take tea with the Feynsham-Joneses, Rupert had talked to her, but kept rolling his eyes at me to show how bored he was.

He couldn't be bothered to write to me, his twin sister, his closest companion, his best friend since birth, but he wrote to Pamela. Had they been secretly meeting during the summer? When he came home for his first half holiday, would he want to see *her*? What about Christmas? Would he go skating on the Round Pond and select a Christmas tree from the market and build a snowman with *her*?

Dear GIRL'S OWN ANNUAL,

I am writing this by candlelight, feeling desperate. My beloved twin brother Rupert has gone away to school and I am missing him terribly, but now I've found out that he isn't thinking of me at all — he

88

is writing ridiculous letters to a dull acquaintance
of ours, a girl not remotely worthy of him. What
shall I do?

Yours sincerely
ANGUISHED SISTER.

ANGUISHED SISTER: Your handwriting is so appalling
we can scarcely decipher it. Writing by candlelight is no
excuse! We feel you are making a ridiculous fuss about
nothing. Your brother is free to write to whomever he
wishes, as long as his letters are perfectly proper. Jealousy
is not a becoming trait in a young lady.

They didn't really write this – I was just imagining
it. I *knew* I was being ridiculous. I've always known that
Rupert would one day become interested in girls, though
he always claimed that they irritated him, especially
the niminy-piminy ones. I'd thought *I* was the only girl he
cared for.

He'd said so the morning he left for school. He
swaggered about in his new smart clothes, and seemed
very lively at breakfast, but I noticed he ate very little.
Half an hour later I heard him being sick in the
downstairs water closet.

'If you're ill, then maybe you shouldn't travel today,' I
said.

'Of course I'm not ill,' said Rupert fiercely. 'Never felt
better.'

His face was very white, and when I took his hand I found it was icy.

'Oh, Rupert, you poor thing,' I said.

He snatched his hand away. 'Stop fussing,' he said.

When it was time for him to go to the railway station with Papa, he gave us all a big hug. I was last. He whispered, 'I shall miss you most of all, Rose.'

But not as much as Pamela Feynsham-Jones!

When she came back from her ride I couldn't bear to confront her about the letter. I barely spoke to her or her sisters. They thought I was too groggy from my fall to hold a proper conversation. In all the confusion I failed to return Pamela's riding skirt and reclaim my own, but I vowed I was never going back there. Or sitting on a horse ever again.

I exaggerated the details of my fall so that Mama wouldn't keep pressing me to go riding. I described Marker as a vicious beast totally out of control.

She shook her head at me. 'Mrs Feynsham-Jones assured me that the stables had selected a steady horse with an amiable nature, suitable for a beginner,' she said. 'I wish you wouldn't tell such dreadful lies, Rose.'

But Papa was worried about me, and the next morning, after my long sleepless night, called in his own doctor.

'I've already seen a doctor, Papa. I'm fine, truly,' I said, though I winced when he took hold of my elbow.

He rolled up my nightgown sleeve and we both stared at the bruises that had blossomed on my arm like purple flowers.

'You don't look fine, sweetheart,' said Papa.

'They're only bruises.'

'You're also deathly pale, with dark circles under your eyes. We're definitely calling the doctor.'

'It's a waste of time and money, Edward,' Mama fussed from the doorway. 'She's simply had a little fall. Mrs Feynsham-Jones says she's lost count of the number of times her daughters have fallen off their ponies, and they've never made a fuss. Why, Pamela once twisted her ankle when she was thrown, but she simply bound it up with a handkerchief and got on again.'

I screwed up my face at the sound of Pamela's name.

Papa was watching me. 'Does it hurt very much, Rose?' he asked gently.

I shook my head, feeling guilty. I had to endure the second doctor's examination with Nurse Budd in attendance.

'I feel that the child's father is overly concerned, sir, but of course it's none of my business,' she told him, 'even though I am a trained nurse.'

'I tend to agree with you, Nurse. This young girl will be as right as rain when her bruises fade,' said the doctor, patting me brusquely. Then he peered across at Beth, who was huddled in her own bed, her hands clasped over her head, Marigold hidden under her sheets. Beth hates it when strangers come to the house.

'I fear for this poor imbecile though.' The doctor made no attempt to lower his voice. Many people ignored the fact that Beth has ears and a perfectly normal understanding, even though she's troubled. 'You're doing a grand job controlling her, Nurse, but poor souls like her are incapable of improvement. I don't know why the family don't put her in an asylum and be done with it. The child is scarcely aware of her surroundings – she would do better in an institution.'

'No she wouldn't!' I said, shocked. 'And she's not an imbecile! You shouldn't say such dreadful things.'

'Now now, Miss Rose, don't take that tone with the doctor!' said Nurse Budd. She shook her head at him. 'You see what I have to deal with.'

He nodded at her sympathetically and gave me a tight smile. 'I don't really think it's seemly for little girls to lecture professional gentlemen,' he said. 'Now, you may get up and go about your daily tasks and stop worrying your poor papa.'

I was happy to do so. I joined Miss Rayner and the little ones in the schoolroom, and started the dreary task of copying out 'The Angel in the House' by Coventry Patmore. I love poetry, Tennyson above all, but I think Mr Patmore should be *sent* to Coventry for writing such tedious verse. But then, wonderfully, Papa put his head round the door.

'Excuse me, Miss Rayner, but I wonder if I could borrow Rose for the morning. The doctor assures me that she is more or less unharmed, but she still looks very pale. I think a little stroll in the fresh air would be beneficial.'

'I'm sure I'm pale as well, Pa. Can *I* come for a stroll?' Algie asked eagerly.

'Your cheeks are as rosy as apples, my son. We will have our own outing another day. But this morning belongs to Rose,' said Papa.

He bundled me up in my new purple jacket. Mama had ordered it from her dressmaker. I hated the design and the elaborate trimmings, and had refused to wear it.

'It's too hot. I'm absolutely roasting,' I said.

'Nonsense, it's quite crisp this morning. I can't have you getting a chill in your weakened state,' said Papa.

I pulled a face.

'I'm joking, silly. But the new jacket is very splendid. You look quite the young lady,' he said.

'Exactly. I don't *want* to look like a lady,' I said.

'I'm so sorry. I didn't realize you wanted to look like a young man,' said Papa. 'Seriously, it really becomes you, Rose.'

'Oh well, I suppose the purple matches my bruises,' I said grumpily.

'Are you bruised all over, sweetheart?'

Papa looked so genuinely concerned that I felt it would be mean to pretend.

'Not really,' I admitted. Only my arms were bruised, though my right leg ached and my knee was grazed.

'That's a relief. Although I think we'll tell your mama that you're rather badly injured. That should put an end to the riding lessons,' said Papa.

'Oh, that's a good plan!' I said, cheering up a little as we set off up the street.

'Is it the riding itself you don't care for, or those Feynsham-Jones girls?' Papa asked.

'A combination,' I said. 'I'm scared of horses – and I detest the Feynsham-Joneses.'

'Oh dear,' said Papa. 'Little Cecily is rather too fond of herself. I've never seen a child so frilled and beribboned! Thank the Lord our Clarrie is happy with a single ribbon and a plain pinafore. I felt sorry for you, stuck with Lucinda-May because she does seem to be an exceptionally vacant girl, though perfectly pleasant. Pamela's more lively. Rupert seemed to find her tolerable.'

'More than tolerable,' I said – and I burst into tears.

It was a great shock to both of us. I never cry, especially not out in the street in broad daylight.

Papa looked at me in concern. 'Oh, my darling, you *are* unwell! Let's get you back home immediately!'

'No, please don't make me go home. There's nothing the matter, I promise. I'm just feeling miserable,' I sobbed.

'Then we must try to cheer you up,' said Papa.

He put his arm round me and steered me all the way along Kensington High Street towards a big hotel opposite the Gardens. We went through the imposing front door and stood under the glass chandelier, where he consulted his pocket watch.

'Would you like a late breakfast or an early lunch, Rose? I find that eating always cheers me up when I'm down in the dumps,' said Papa. 'In fact, why don't we have *both*?'

'I'm very sorry, sir,' said the man behind the reception desk. 'Our restaurant is in the process of being refurbished.

But we would be delighted to serve you light refreshments in our new downstairs sitting room.'

The sitting room was very modern and pretty, with comfortable chairs we could sink into.

'I love a chair that allows a chap to sprawl,' said Papa, doing just that.

'I wish I could sprawl too,' I said, perching decorously. I looked around the room. There were no little tables covered in knick-knacks, no display cabinets and desks, no dreary brown landscapes crowding the wall, no dark wallpaper with overblown roses like red cabbages. It was all fresh and pale and sparse, with screens showing golden herons flying across a pale sky, and Japanese prints of the sea on the walls. I knew Papa very much admires the Japanese style. He once painted a portrait of Louisa wearing a kimono, her arms raised as she fixed a decorative comb in her hair.

'Isn't it beautiful here?' I said.

'It is indeed,' said Papa wistfully.

'I wish we had a sitting room like this.'

'I'm afraid it's not to your mama's taste, sweetheart.'

'Yes, but you're the artist,' I insisted. 'You're the one who knows about such things. You should be able to have the house exactly as you want!'

'It's not quite as simple as that,' said Papa. 'When you're grown up you'll find you can't always do exactly what you want.'

At first I thought he meant that Mama and the Scottish relations were in charge of the purse strings, and an entire overhaul of the house might not be possible on his own paltry earnings. But then I saw that he kept glancing at the Japanese prints and I wondered if he were thinking of Louisa too.

Papa sighed, but then beckoned the waiter over. 'We will have plum cake,' he told him. 'And what would you like to drink, Rose? Shall we share a pot of tea? And I think I would like a glass of champagne, even though it's only mid-morning. My spirits need lifting.'

'I wish I could have champagne,' I said.

'Well, why not? We'll have two glasses of champagne, please.'

'Papa! Really?' I said, thrilled.

I wasn't sure if he was serious until the champagne arrived.

'I wish you health and happiness, my darling,' said Papa, raising his glass to me.

I took a cautious sip. I wondered if the champagne would turn out to be syrupy and disgusting. I had once secretly tried a gulp of sherry from the decanter in the drawing room and disliked it intensely. Champagne was entirely different. It was light and bubbly, and so delicious that I took several mouthfuls and then choked.

'Careful,' said Papa, passing me his napkin. 'Maybe you'd better stick to tea! But have a slice of cake. Mmm, it looks excellent.'

I merely nibbled half-heartedly at first, but it was such a very fine plum cake that I ended up finishing my slice and eating half another. I wanted to save the other half for Beth, who never goes out for treats in case she has one of her turns. Papa had the waiter pack it up in a little white box for me. They even tied a ribbon round it.

I couldn't parcel up my champagne so I took a few more sips.

'Careful now,' said Papa. 'Imagine what Mama would say if you came home tipsy.'

'I rather wish I *could* get tipsy,' I said. 'Isn't alcohol meant to drown your sorrows?'

'Oh dear, do you really feel so sorrowful, Rose?' asked Papa.

'Well, the cake and champagne have helped a lot,' I said gratefully. 'But I still feel pretty wretched.'

Papa put his hand over mine. 'Still missing Rupert terribly?' he asked.

'Yes, I am. I'm so miserable that he hasn't written to me,' I confessed.

'But, darling, I've tried to explain what it's like when you're away at school. A chap doesn't write to his sister, no matter how much he might secretly want to.'

'The chap still writes to his sweetheart though,' I said bitterly.

'Rupert has a *sweetheart*?' said Papa, choking on his champagne. 'You can't be serious, Rose!'

'I am deadly serious,' I said mournfully. 'I read the letter, even though I know it's very sneaky to read another person's correspondence.'

'So who is the young lady in question?' Papa asked, all agog.

'It's Pamela Feynsham-Jones,' I said, spitting the words out.

'Oh goodness – Pamela?'

'I just don't understand it,' I said. 'Those Feynsham-Jones girls are so boring. Rupert and I have always joked about them. Yet now he seems to be positively yearning for her.'

'Take comfort from the fact that thirteen-year-old boys are notoriously fickle. I dare say that by Christmas he'll have stopped yearning after the redoubtable Pamela, and will probably declare himself passionately in love with some other young lady entirely,' said Papa, chuckling.

'It's not funny, Papa! It's ridiculous! Rupert has always despised all girls apart from me.' I had such a lump in my throat I could barely swallow.

I expected Papa to continue joking, but he squeezed my hand.

'Poor Rose,' he said softly.

'I know I'm behaving like a fool,' I said.

'Not at all. You and Rupert have always been very close. You were so sweet when you were little. You insisted on doing everything together. You must feel very lonely without him – and now you've been betrayed into the bargain! But I promise you'll find a special friend of your own soon, Rose.'

'Please don't let Mama inflict any more girls like the Feynsham-Joneses on me,' I begged.

'I'll do my best,' said Papa. 'Right, my darling. Shall we go and have a stroll in the Gardens now?'

I felt a little wobbly when I stood up, though Papa had ended up drinking most of my champagne. I needed to use the ladies' cloakroom, so Papa escorted me there. On the way we went past the restaurant. The door was open and we peeped in. There, halfway up a ladder, was a young man in a smock, painting an elaborate picture on the wall. It was a Japanese scene, with lots of ladies hiding behind fans and sipping tea and painting scrolls in a very decorous manner.

'I say, that looks splendid!' said Papa.

The young man turned round. He had a smear of black paint on one cheek and his long curly hair needed a good brush, but he still looked incredibly handsome.

'Oh my goodness! Edward Rivers!' he cried, and then he leaped down off his ladder and rushed to embrace Papa.

'Paris!' Papa declared, and hugged him back. Then he turned to me. 'Rose, this is Mr Walker, my dear friend from art-school days.'

I shook the artist's hand. I discovered later that he'd left black paint on my palm. Mr Paris Walker had literally made an impression on me.

I **LONG TO GO TO** Paris! Papa lived there for a while after leaving art school. I think it's a wonderful name. I felt very shy when Papa introduced me. I grew up meeting artists, but they were always old Pre-Raphaelites, grey-haired and wrinkled. Mr Walker seemed extraordinarily young, perhaps half Papa's age. I couldn't understand how they could have been at art school together. It turned out that Mr Walker had been Papa's pupil when he taught at the Academy.

'Not that Paris needed any tuition. He's so talented he started at the Academy when he was only fifteen,' said Papa, clapping his friend on the back.

'So talented that I can't sell a single one of my paintings and have to earn my living decorating fancy hotels!' said Mr Walker, laughing.

'Well, you're making a magnificent job of it, I must say,' said Papa. 'Don't you think so, Rose? My daughter is rather artistic herself, Paris.'

I felt myself blushing. 'I'm not at all. Papa is obviously prejudiced,' I mumbled.

'I'm encouraging her to sketch from life,' Papa said. 'She has a head full of amusing fancies, but no idea whether horses' legs should go backwards or forwards.'

They both laughed and I felt very silly. I kept silent while they reminisced about their time at the Academy.

'I'd have thought you'd be exhibiting there by now,' said Papa.

Mr Walker shrugged. 'So did I!' he said ruefully. 'Still, I keep in touch and always attend the exhibitions.'

'I dare say you find the art there stuffy and old-fashioned,' said Papa.

'No one could call your portrait of the lady in the black dress stuffy and old-fashioned,' Mr Walker replied.

I looked at Papa. Now he was the one who was blushing.

'Of course, you had a stunning model,' Mr Walker went on. 'Is she still your special muse?'

'Good heavens, no,' Papa said, with false heartiness. 'I believe she's a married lady now, and is no doubt getting rather dull and stout.'

I don't think she's any such thing. It was just Papa pretending. Adults tell just as many lies as children and are forever twisting the truth.

'Marriage has obvious benefits for you, Edward,' said Mr Walker, smiling at me.

'Very much so,' said Papa. 'I have seven splendid children into the bargain. You must come to tea and meet them all!'

'I should like that enormously,' said Mr Walker.

I decided that I should like it enormously too. I do hope he comes. When we said goodbye he shook my hand warmly and said that it was a delight to meet me.

'It's a delight to meet you too, Mr Walker,' I said.

He smiled and I hoped I was looking my best, but when I went to the ladies' cloakroom I was mortified to see my reflection. My eyes were red with crying and there was a large crumb at the corner of my mouth. I hoped he hadn't noticed.

I didn't feel like going home at all – and then in the afternoon Mrs Feynsham-Jones called round, accompanied by Pamela, with my skirt neatly folded in a parcel.

'She's been so concerned about you, Rose dear,' said Mrs Feynsham-Jones. 'Well, of course we've *all* been worried. I feel personally responsible, Mrs Rivers.'

'Oh, Mrs Feynsham-Jones, I'm sure it was all Rose's fault. She's such a reckless girl,' said Mama. 'I dare say she dug in her heels and set off at a gallop.'

'Hardly!' said Pamela, smirking. 'Poor Rose seems very nervous on horseback. Still, I suppose it must be unsettling learning so late in life. We were all riding by the time we were four, weren't we, Mama?'

I could have slapped her! I sat there silently on the uncomfortable gilt chair, feeling my cheeks flush scarlet.

'I'm sure Rose will prove a quick learner all the same,' said Mama. 'Once she's had a few more lessons she'll be trotting around very capably.'

'I'm not going to have any more lessons,' I mumbled.

'Of course you are! Mrs Feynsham-Jones has been kind enough to invite you to ride once a week,' said Mama.

'But it's pointless. I have no aptitude whatsoever,' I insisted.

'Don't be so silly, Rose dear. All you have to do is sit on the animal and not fall off,' said Mama shortly. She has never been on a horse in her life, but clearly considers herself an expert.

'I'm inclined to agree with Rose,' said Mrs Feynsham-Jones. 'I had a word with Miss Havers at the stables. She says that Rose has no feel for the horse at all. Of course we can persevere, but I'm afraid we'll never make a proper horsewoman of her.'

'Oh dear,' said Mama, her hopes dashed.

'But of course we'd still like Rose to come to tea. She's already struck up quite a friendship with Pamela,' said Mrs Feynsham-Jones.

'Really? Ah, perhaps you'd like to give Pamela back her riding skirt, Rose? Take her up to your bedroom. I'm sure you two would like to play while we ladies chat.'

'Play?' said Pamela when we had left the drawing room. On the landing we came across Algie and Clarrie and Sebastian playing Circus. Sebastian was being a lion tamer, with a piece of string glued to his upper lip so that he could twirl his 'moustache'. Clarrie was his assistant, and wore last year's fairy costume, which was alarmingly tight. Algie was the lion, roaring loudly through the banisters.

'Do *you* play Circus too, Rose?' Pamela asked.

'Of course not,' I said shortly.

'But I dare say you used to, with Rupert.'

I can't stand the way Pamela says his name. She drags out the first syllable with a sentimental 'ooooh' sound, sounding like a demented dove.

'We always played together,' I said.

'You are so lucky to have brothers,' said Pamela. Sebastian was using his dressing-gown cord as a whip, and Algie was red in the face with roaring. It was clear that she didn't mean them. 'What games did you and Rooooopert play?'

Oh, we had so many. We played Treasure Island, with the nursery table upturned and the big stuffed peacock from the hall pinned to Rupert's shoulder. We played Tyger Tyger Burning Bright, and trekked through the jungle stalking the tigerskin in Papa's smoking room. We played Mountaineering up and down the stairs, muffled up in Mama's old fur coats. We played Murder, taking it in turns to creep up and strangle each other.

Beth sometimes played with us then, but she was never any good at games. She screamed when we made the stuffed peacock fly through the air. She cowered when Rupert made the tigerskin rear up. She fell down the stairs when we climbed up, and yelled her head off when it was her turn to be strangled.

We didn't understand then that Beth couldn't help being difficult. We just thought her a hopeless duffer and teased her. I feel so ashamed when I think of it now. I was so happy to be the tomboy twin who was good at pretending. If Rupert started to get bored, I could always invent an entirely new game.

'*I* know, Rupe,' I'd cry, and turn myself into a vagabond or a hyena or an African queen, and Rupert would laugh and join in the game with renewed enthusiasm.

Of course, we were much too old for pretend games now, but this summer I'd suggested we create our own newspaper. Rupert was editor and chief correspondent, reporting on all household affairs and adding his own commentaries on real news events filched from Papa's copies of *The Times*. I illustrated each item and wrote a serial about an artistic community where everyone drank and schemed and took lovers.

Papa read our newspaper and found it hilarious, but Mama was so shocked by my story that she tore it up.

'Tell me about your games, Rose,' Pamela wheedled, putting her arm round me.

'Oh, they were very silly,' I muttered, not wanting to elaborate for her.

At the top of the stairs I pretended to stumble so that I could duck away from her arm.

'I'll give you back your riding skirt,' I said, hurrying along the corridor.

The nursery door was open, and we could see Nurse walking wearily up and down with Phoebe, who was grizzling.

'Oh, I forgot about the *baby*! You're so lucky, Rose!' said Pamela, as if a small infant were as amazing and rare as a unicorn. 'I *have* to see her!'

She went marching into the nursery as if she owned it, and gave Nurse the briefest of nods. 'Let me hold the little lamb!' she commanded, as if Nurse were her servant.

I supposed Nurse was technically *my* servant, but she'd given me too many shakes and smacks and spoonfuls of foul castor oil for me to think of ordering her about now. Even Papa still knocked on the door before coming in to play with the little ones. But Pamela took hold of Phoebe as if she were her mother and clutched her to her impressive chest.

'She's adorable! But why's she crying, Nurse? Is she hungry? Why don't you feed her?' Pamela asked.

'She's already been fed, miss,' Nurse replied indignantly. 'She's just got a bit of wind. I wouldn't hold her like that or she'll bring up her milk all over you.'

I hoped that Phoebe would, but she simply gave a big hiccup and then, in surprise, stopped crying.

'There! That's better, isn't it, darling? Oh, see how she's smiling at me! She likes me, don't you, baby dear?' Pamela said.

Nurse and I stared at her sourly. Phoebe smiled and smiled.

'Oh, the perfect pet!' Pamela buried her nose in the sweet warmth of Phoebe's neck. It probably tickled, because Phoebe started giggling.

'Now don't get her too excited, miss. She has to go down for her nap,' said Nurse.

'You don't want to have a boring old nap, do you, baby girl? You want to play with your new friend Pamela,' said Pamela, tickling Phoebe's tummy so that she wriggled and gurgled in delight.

Pamela suddenly held her at arm's length. 'Oh dear, she's starting to feel very damp,' she said. 'Perhaps you'd better take her back now, Nurse.'

Nurse snorted irritably and did as she was told.

'My room's this way,' I said, setting off again.

'What colour is it?' Pamela asked, as if it were a matter of tremendous importance.

'It's pink and blue and white,' I said.

'Oh, how pretty!'

Mama had had it decorated with a pink rosebud wallpaper. Peter Jones had made up rose velvet curtains with a coverlet to match, and there was a dark rose carpet on the floor.

I suppose it *is* pretty, though it looks like a florist's shop. It even smells like one, because there's a large blue bowl of rose pot pourri which scents the air in a sickly fashion. Still, I have done my best to imprint my own personality on the room. Papa had a carpenter make me bookshelves, and now my books add a scholarly air, and the rich reds and blues and browns of the leather bindings soothe the eye.

Pamela admired my room, and exclaimed over the prettiness of the curtains and the softness of the carpet.

'But what a shame to spoil the look with those fusty old books,' she declared. 'Couldn't you store them away in a cupboard?'

How could my brother *like* her? I began to wonder if I'd made a silly mistake. Perhaps Rupert hadn't written that letter after all. I'd seen the signature with its loving message, but perhaps Pamela had somehow written the letter herself, copying Rupert's handwriting. It sounded far-fetched, but no more so than the idea that Rupert cared about her more than he did about his own sister.

I handed Pamela her horrid riding skirt and tried to interest her in my favourite books, but she didn't seem remotely interested. She roamed restlessly round and round my rose carpet, as if intent on wearing a groove in the pile.

'Do you all have your own bedrooms?' she asked. 'I suppose those little ones playing the wild game on the stairs must sleep with your nurse.'

'Yes, Sebastian and Algie and Clarrie sleep in the nursery,' I said.

'And what about ... ?' Pamela paused delicately. I could see her lips pursing, ready to make the Rooo sound, but she lost courage at the last moment. 'Your sister?' she murmured in an undertone.

'Baby Phoebe?' I said, deliberately misunderstanding. 'Well, of course she sleeps in her cot beside Nurse. In the night nursery.'

'I actually meant your *other* sister. You know – the unfortunate one.'

I kept my face blank, forcing her to continue.

'The cretin,' Pamela whispered.

'My sister Beth is *not* a cretin,' I said furiously. 'She is highly intelligent.'

When she was four, Beth had joined Rupert and me in the schoolroom, and within weeks she could read simple words and add and subtract. Miss Rayner was overjoyed. Papa declared that Beth's fretfulness and tantrums must have been simple frustration because she was bored. Now that she could use her brain she would calm down and develop a sunny nature.

But Beth remained resolutely stormy, fussing over the slightest thing, frightened of change, liable to throw herself full length on the floor and kick and scream. She took against poor Miss Rayner, and often had to be forcibly removed from the schoolroom, until her lessons were abandoned altogether.

I know that Beth can read, but she is not generally allowed books because she tore pages out of a valuable collection of Tennyson's poems with Pre-Raphaelite illustrations. She's not allowed to write either, ever since she threw a bottle of ink and ruined the old Persian rug.

It must be so boring to be Beth. No wonder she is attached to her dolls. I'm so pleased that she likes her new doll so much.

Pamela must have seen my face soften. 'I'm sorry,' she said, sounding genuine. 'I didn't realize. I've never seen your sister Beth. I've just heard silly rumours, that's all. I think she must be your favourite sister . . .'

'Yes, she is very dear to me,' I said.

I wondered if I dared take Pamela to meet Beth. I have to admit that Beth has been much calmer since Nurse Budd joined the household. However, she still finds it disturbing to meet new people. I decided not to risk it.

'Do you have a favourite brother?' Pamela asked.

'Yes, I do,' I said, looking her straight in the eye. 'My brother Rupert. I dare say you know he is away at school at the moment.'

She went a little pink, but stared back at me serenely. 'Yes, at Kilbourne. It's a very good school. My papa went there.'

'Mine did too,' I said.

'Rupert sounds as if he's settling in well, doesn't he?'

I swallowed. 'Yes, he does.'

'Did he tell you about the trick they played on Jenkins Minor?' Pamela asked. 'Those boys!'

'What trick?' I asked, in agony.

'Didn't he tell you about it? It was in his first letter to me.'

First letter. So there have been at least two. Maybe more.

'You don't mind that Rupert writes to me too, do you?' Pamela asked.

'Of course not,' I muttered. 'Though I didn't realize you were such good friends.'

Pamela smiled. 'Well, we only became close this summer. We met by chance in the High Street. Rupert was taking a stroll while Mama and my sisters and I were shopping in the arcade, so we invited him to have an ice cream at the little Italian parlour. Then we met up at the Serpentine – and of course there was that trip Rupert and I took on the Kensington omnibus. It was such a hoot, though I didn't dare tell Mama! Did Rupert mention it?'

'I believe he said something about it,' I bluffed. I was stunned. Rupert had been seeing Pamela all summer, and he'd never said a word to me about it.

I'd been puzzled when he sometimes went off for a stroll by himself. He had seemed a little moody and distant, but I thought he was probably just worrying about going to school.

It was difficult to hide my hurt from Pamela, especially when she put her arm round me again.

'Dear Rose,' she said. 'I do hope *we* can become good friends too.'

I'm never, ever going to be any kind of friends with Pamela Feynsham-Jones. Rupert is still my brother, but he's no longer my best friend. He has betrayed me. I will never get over it.

I HAVE CHANGED MY mind. I couldn't give two pins about Rupert and his pash on Pamela Feynsham-Jones.

I have a pash myself.

Mr Walker came calling last Thursday! I was on the window seat, reading, when I heard the front doorbell jangle. I assumed it would be someone calling on Mama. I tucked up my feet and huddled behind the velvet curtain, not wanting to be seen. I feared it might be the Feynsham-Joneses.

Edie went flouncing to the door, her freshly starched white apron crackling. 'Yes, sir?' she said, sounding a little surprised.

I heard someone announcing themselves. I wasn't sure who it could be. Edie didn't sound as if she knew him. She ushered him into the hall, but no further.

'Please wait here a moment, sir. I'll see if the mistress is at home,' she said.

'Very well – though it's actually your master I've come to see,' he replied.

I thought I recognized that voice. I slid off the window seat and peered down the stairwell. Yes, it was Paris Walker! He saw me peeping and waved up at me.

'Hello!' he said.

'I'm Rose,' I said shyly. 'We met before at the hotel.'

'Of course we did. You're Miss Rose Rivers, the artist. Are you at home, Miss Rivers? I have come calling on you specially.' He swept me a very grand bow.

'How delightful,' I said, joining in the game by curtsying.

'And I dare say I'd better have a word or two with your dear father while I'm at it. Is he in his studio?'

'I expect so,' I said.

'Then shall I simply scoot upstairs without bothering your maid any further?' he said. 'You'll show me the way, won't you, Miss Rivers?'

'Of course I will,' I said. 'This way.'

But he'd only climbed three steps when Edie came scurrying back.

'Sir! Come back! What are you doing?' she demanded.

'I said Mr Walker could come upstairs, Edie,' I said.

'Have you taken leave of your senses, Miss Rose?' she said. 'Please come down this minute, sir, or I'll be forced to call Mr Hodgson. I'm afraid you'll have to leave. Mrs Rivers is not at home today – and we don't recognize your name as an acquaintance.'

'Oh my Lord,' said Mr Walker, shrugging his shoulders and pulling a face at me. 'I'd better go then, Miss Rivers.'

'No! Please stay! This is all a stupid mistake. How could you treat our guest like this, Edie!'

Though perhaps it wasn't entirely Edie's fault. Mr Walker's hair was in a tangle, he had smears of blue paint all over his ancient cord jacket, and his trousers were frayed at the hem. If you hadn't known he was an artist, you might have thought him a vagabond or beggar. Heaven knows how Edie described him to Mama. She took no notice of my protests and stood there with her chin up, making flicking gestures to indicate that Mr Walker should make himself scarce immediately.

I didn't waste time arguing with her. I didn't rush to Mama in the drawing room – I knew *she* wouldn't listen. I had to summon Papa. I didn't have time to clatter all the way up to his studio. I opened my mouth and yelled at the top of my voice, *'Papa! Come immediately! Mr Paris Walker is being turned out of our house!'*

Well, that caused pandemonium! Edie actually shook me. Nurse came running, Phoebe on her hip, petticoats trailing. Beth heard my shout and wailed. Sebastian and Algie and Clarrie all started shouting. Mama came to the door of the drawing room, quivering with rage. But, wonderfully, Papa came flying down the stairs two at a time, a delighted smile on his face.

'My goodness, Rose, what a clarion call! All my children seem to have excellent lungs! Paris, my dear chap, how splendid to see you. Edie, run and tell Cook to prepare tea for us, with at least two types of cake, possibly three. Jeannie, my sweet, allow me to introduce my marvellous erstwhile protégé and now dear friend Mr Paris Walker, artist extraordinaire.'

Dearest Papa sorted everything out, though Mama looked appalled at the idea of Mr Walker joining us for tea. I got invited too! Sebastian and Algie and Clarrie had to have bread and butter and plain sponge up in the nursery under Nurse's supervision. Beth had hers with Nurse Budd hovering over her like a hawk. *I* got to sit in the drawing room and eat cucumber sandwiches, iced sponge layered with jam and cream, and apple puffs. I ate enthusiastically, though I dabbed my lips after every bite just in case there was a crumb there. Mama kept frowning at me because it's not ladylike to have a voracious appetite.

When I reached for a second apple puff she murmured, 'I think you've had more than enough, Rose, dear.'

I wasn't to be deterred. Apple puffs are my absolute favourite. We never get them at teatime. Cook must have made them for dinner, when you rarely get a chance of second helpings. Before Mama could stop me I'd taken a great bite out of the second puff. I thought I might have gone too far, but she simply sighed. She didn't lecture me – she was in too good a mood.

It was truly amazing. For the first five minutes she'd been icy cold, sitting ramrod straight, her lips pinched, a sharp line between her eyebrows. She scarcely uttered a word, leaving Papa to chat merrily to Mr Walker. Papa seemed oblivious to her mood. Perhaps he simply chose to ignore it. I can never tell if he's insensitive or devious. He plied Mr Walker with questions, wanting to know all about his travels since leaving the Academy. He sighed when Mr Walker spoke about his time in his namesake French city, and listened enviously when he spoke of Florence and Rome and Venice. Papa had never been to Italy.

'What a fool I was to make a journey north to Scotland when I could have gone south to sunny Italy and seen such wonders,' he said.

Mama sniffed, clenching her hands so hard that the handle of her teacup was in danger of snapping. Was Papa implying that he wished he'd never gone to Scotland because then he wouldn't have met her? Or was he simply denigrating her country? This time Papa couldn't ignore her reaction.

'Come, Jeannie, you can hardly call the bleak city of Dundee picturesque. Even the most patriotic Scot would hesitate to call it bonnie,' he said.

'It has the silvery Tay river, and we have Broughty Ferry and a wealth of beauty spots in the nearby countryside,' Mama said coldly.

'I should love to see Scotland for myself, Mrs Rivers,' said Mr Walker. 'I've always had a great longing to see the mountains, glens and lochs. Where would you recommend?'

Mama unbent slightly, and became a Baedeker guide to Scotland. Mr Walker listened and asked questions and marvelled at the answers, leaning forward eagerly, even complimenting Mama on her Scottish accent.

'I'm afraid it's not very attractive,' she said. 'I know English society feels any accent is unrefined.'

'My dear Mrs Rivers, Queen Victoria herself is entranced by Scotland and its lilting tongue,' said Mr Walker. 'As soon as I've finished this wretched mural at the Palace Hotel I shall be off there like a shot. I might even change my tattered trousers for a kilt. You are being very tolerant about my appearance. I really must apologize. I'm afraid I'm nowhere near as successful as Edward. I am rather embarrassed financially at the moment, and the hotel management refuse to pay me a farthing until the work is completed.'

'Tell me about your work, Mr Walker,' asked Mama.

This made me blink. Mama rarely shows any interest in Papa's work. There's a scrapbook hidden in a corner of his studio bulging with newspaper cuttings, along with a comical picture from *Punch* showing a cluster of society folk pushing and shoving to get a proper view of the Louisa portrait. I don't think Mama went to any of the exhibitions. There were celebrations, and I remember waking up late at night and hearing Papa singing in a very jolly way, but Mama never accompanied him.

I remember a new acquaintance once asking Mama, 'Isn't your husband the painter responsible for those notorious portraits of that stunning society girl?'

Mama had frozen. She could have been a painting herself. For several seconds she had sat utterly motionless and silent, then cleared her throat and started talking about the weather.

But here she was with Mr Paris Walker, pressing him for details of his work, wanting to know the design and colour scheme of the hotel mural.

'Japanese style!' she said, as if it were an entirely new and delightful idea, though she wouldn't hear of it when Papa suggested refurbishing the house in that manner.

'Perhaps we could go and dine there when Mr Walker's mural is finished,' I suggested hopefully, because the plum cake had been so delicious.

'I don't think luxury hotels cater for children,' said Mama. 'Try not to interrupt when we're talking, Rose, dear.'

My age is elastic as far as she is concerned. She is forever nagging at me to grow up and act like a young lady, and yet whenever I get an opportunity to practise she wants me back in the nursery. She turned her back on me and carried on talking to Mr Walker about art. He spoke of his admiration for the Italian masters.

'Oh yes, I agree, I love the Italians too,' said Mama. She reeled off a few names in a flamboyant manner, as if she spoke fluent Italian and they were old acquaintances.

Papa caught my eye and we both struggled to keep a straight face.

Mama flushed. 'Of course, I'm well aware that I am no artist myself,' she said huffily. 'But I don't see why I cannot have an opinion on art.'

'I can see that you're a woman of great taste and discrimination, Mrs Rivers,' said Mr Walker. He looked utterly sincere, but I wondered if he were teasing her.

'Mama's dressmaker always compliments her on her eye for fashion,' I said, which was true enough. 'I'm afraid I haven't inherited it.' I tugged at my crumpled dress and wrinkled stockings.

'Oh, Rose,' said Mama.

'I think you have your own natural style, Miss Rivers,' said Mr Walker. 'I wouldn't have you change it for the world.'

I don't think he was sincere, but I was delighted all the same.

'Maybe I should paint a portrait of you, Rose, before your natural style wears off and you turn into an everyday demure young lady,' Papa said.

'I wish you would paint portraits of all the children,' said Mama. 'Though I'd prefer them all to be properly dressed, with well-brushed hair. I certainly don't want them looking like the little street ragamuffins you've taken to sketching, Edward. A waste of time, if you ask me.'

'But I'm not asking you, my dear,' said Papa. His tone was perfectly pleasant and the 'my dear' sounded affectionate, but there was an edge to his voice.

'Of course, Edward is renowned for his portraits,' said Mr Walker.

Mama flinched.

'Edward must have painted *you* many times, Mrs Rivers,' he went on hurriedly. 'Isn't that a sumptuous portrait of you in a blue satin gown over there?'

'Why, yes, Edward painted it long ago, on our honeymoon,' said Mama. 'I believe the shine on the blue satin was much admired when it was first exhibited.'

'And the shine in your blue eyes,' said Mr Walker.

'Oh, come, Mr Walker, stop this nonsense,' said Mama.

'Edward, why aren't you painting another portrait of Mrs Rivers?' Mr Walker demanded.

'I think I have given up portraiture for now,' said Papa.

'And I'm hardly the young girl in the blue satin portrait any more.' Mama looked down at herself disparagingly. 'No woman can bear seven children and keep a girlish figure.'

'Really, Jeannie, stop fishing for compliments!' said Papa.

'I think you are simply stating the truth as you see it, Mrs Rivers,' said Mr Walker, looking straight into her eyes. 'I'm sure Edward won't mind if I insist that you are a beautiful woman now, no longer an insipid young girl. It's criminal not to record that beauty. If Edward is no longer a portrait painter, please would you let *me* paint you?'

Mama flushed rose pink. Somehow she *did* suddenly look beautiful.

'You're very gallant, Mr Walker,' she murmured, 'but I don't think you can possibly be serious. And I'm sure my husband will not think it appropriate.'

'On the contrary, I think it's an excellent idea,' said Papa, though he looked surprised. 'Yes, of course you must paint Jeannie's portrait, Paris. I'm sure you'll make a marvellous job of it.'

'I will set to work as soon as my mural is finished – it'll only take a couple of weeks if I hurry. What kind of portrait would you like, Mrs Rivers? Full length? A sitting pose? Head and shoulders? Would you like me to include your lovely little dog?' Mr Walker glanced at Alphonse, who was slumped on his cushion snoring like a small yellow piglet.

'I'm not really sure. Perhaps *you* should decide, Mr Walker. You're the artist after all,' said Mama.

'There's just one small problem,' he said. 'I'm embarrassed to say I don't have my own studio. I'm currently living in one dank room in a dubious lodging house. I cannot possibly invite a lady to such quarters.'

'You must use my studio,' said Papa. 'I'm not working on any painting in particular at the moment – and if inspiration strikes, there's plenty of room for two. What do you say, old chap?'

'I say it sounds a capital idea. But what do *you* think, Mrs Rivers? Would you truly be happy to sit for your portrait? It would mean a regular commitment, possibly for weeks. I know how busy you are,' said Mr Walker.

Mama busy! Most of the day she lies on her chaise longue. You'd think her dress was stitched to the upholstery. She gives orders to Cook and Edie and Maggie, and languidly strokes her dog, but that is all.

She sees more of Alphonse than she does of any of her children, even baby Phoebe.

At five o'clock Nurse brings the baby to see her, along with Sebastian, Algie and Clarrie. It is a performance getting every child ready. Sebastian generally stays spotless – he hates getting dirty – but Algie and Clarrie are usually in a very sticky state, and Phoebe leaks copiously at either end. They all have to be thoroughly washed and brushed, and then dressed up in their best cream silks. Sebastian loves his silk suit. He doesn't even mind the lace collar. Algie and Clarrie protest bitterly every single day, and Phoebe generally howls when Nurse stuffs her into her petticoats and her long smocked baby gown, then kicks hard to rid herself of the woolly booties constricting her toes.

After all this elaborate preparation Mama takes little interest in her children. It is supposed to be the children's *hour*, but she listlessly supervises games of Spillikins for half an hour at most before suggesting that Nurse return her tribe to the nursery. When Algie is being particularly boisterous, Mama has been known to cut the visit to ten minutes!

Beth has started to come too, though she was banned from the drawing room after she tried to play with the Meissen figurines on the mantelpiece, taking a fancy to the china shepherdesses. When Nurse stopped her, Beth flew into a temper and swept them all to the floor.

Mama has thick carpets, but nearly all the Meissen broke beyond repair. She was devastated, though Papa didn't seem to mind: he said he'd always thought the Meissen repellent, and joked that Beth was simply expressing her artistic contempt for them. Mama grew angrier than ever, and they had such a serious row that Papa went to stay at his club that night.

Mama permits Beth to come down to the drawing room nowadays, but has Edie remove the best china, just in case.

Beth is better behaved now. She is at her best in the afternoon, quiet and docile, and can sometimes be persuaded to sing. She's always repeated snatches of songs – nursery ditties like 'Twinkle, Twinkle, Little Star', and music-hall favourites like 'The Boy I Love Is Up in the Gallery', which Maggie sings while she dusts. But Nurse Budd has been teaching her hymns, and Beth looks like an angel when she clasps her hands and sings about Jesus.

'I certainly am kept very busy running the house and bringing up my seven children,' Mama said now. 'But I'm sure I could make time to sit for my portrait, Mr Walker.'

10

MR WALKER COMES EVERY weekday morning and works in Papa's studio. Mama sits like Patience on a monument, a little smile on her face, her pretty hands clasped, while he dabs at his canvas and keeps up a stream of chatter.

I sit nearby, acting as a child chaperone, because Papa is mostly out sketching street children to illustrate a new children's book written by his writer friend, Miss Sarah Smith. Papa says it is a perfect opportunity for me to practise drawing. I am supposed to be drawing Mama. I have made several cursory attempts, but most of the time

I am secretly sketching Mr Walker! I can't get his features right. I shall keep on trying until I get a true likeness.

I've never spent so much time with Mama. She is so very tedious. While Mr Walker works, she prattles on and on. When she starts gesturing, her bracelets tinkle. Sometimes he gently reminds her not to move, but mostly he simply murmurs responses. I don't think he actually listens to her. He just says yes and no at the appropriate places.

She talks and talks and talks, yet she doesn't say *anything*. It's all society gossip. She mentions Lord and Lady this and that as if she actually knows them. She talks of their balls and parties as if she's attended every one. She confides details of their family births and marriages and deaths, and asks Mr Walker if he's acquainted with any of the younger men. Mr Walker says no.

She chatters about the latest fashions, discussing the merits of ruching and lace trimming, wondering whether a certain colour would be right for her complexion. Mr Walker says yes.

She fusses about the servants, complaining that Edie isn't respectful enough and Mr Hodgson is becoming doddery and Jack Boots too clumsy. She asks Mr Walker his opinion, and he murmurs that the house seems very well run all the same.

She talks about us children, saying what a happy little soul Phoebe is, and isn't Clarrie a special sweetheart, and Algie such a lively youngster, and Sebastian remarkably sensitive, and Mr Walker says yes and yes and yes and yes. She barely mentions Beth, briefly referring to the 'poor dear child', and he murmurs another sympathetic yes.

Of course, she sighs over me and wishes I were more ladylike and less wayward, and you'll never, ever guess what happened today! Mr Walker didn't answer with a monosyllable. He said, 'I think Rose is splendid just as she is. Edward says she has promising artistic talent!'

Mama sniffed. 'I'm not so sure about that. Artistic talent is wasted on a girl anyway. You don't get lady artists.'

'Oh yes you do, Mama! What about Lady Butler, who paints all those military scenes!' I said.

'Hardly a ladylike subject!'

'And the French artist Rosa Bonheur.'

'Do stop interrupting, child. And anyway, she's *French*,' said Mama, as if this meant she couldn't possibly be respectable.

'I think Rosa Bonheur's very good at painting horses,' said Mr Walker.

'Well, I hardly think horses are Rose's ideal subject matter. She fell off the very first time she went riding and now won't go back to the stables,' said Mama. 'And the Feynsham-Joneses have been so kind too, offering us the use of their ponies. Perhaps Rupert will care to go riding when he comes home for his half-term break. He gets on so well with those sweet Feynsham-Jones girls.'

That shut me up. I sat silently while Mama boasted endlessly about dear Rupert – top of his form, excelling at sport, the most popular boy in his year.

Mr Walker didn't comment.

'Where did you go to school, Mr Walker?' Mama asked.

'I'm afraid I attended several schools and detested them all,' he said.

'Why didn't you like school?' I burst out. 'I'd give anything to be able to go! I'd love to learn Latin and Greek and find out about the world.'

'Oh, the lessons weren't too bad, though I wasn't really interested in anything but painting,' said Mr Walker. 'It was the rest of it I couldn't bear – the rules, the heartiness, the cruelty, the tedium.'

'Papa didn't like school either,' I said. 'So did you break the rules, Mr Walker?'

'Rose, I don't think poor Mr Walker wants to be plagued with all your questions,' Mama said.

'I don't mind a bit, Mrs Rivers. I'm afraid I did break the rules, Miss Rivers, and consequently had to leave some of the schools prematurely.'

'You mean you were *expelled*?' I asked.

'Rose! Hold your tongue!' said Mama sharply. 'Of course Mr Walker meant no such thing.'

He kept quiet, but when I glanced at him he nodded and winked. I longed to ask what he'd done, but I knew Mama would send me away if I continued. I pressed my lips together and drew her, though I found myself digging the point of my pencil into each of her curves and her little pursed mouth. Then I turned the page and drew Mr Walker instead – but *not* a sketch from life.

I tried to imagine what he might have done to get expelled from school. I drew comical alternatives: he played tricks on teachers, painted on walls, climbed the topmost tower.

At the end of the morning Mama looked at her portrait as usual and beamed. 'Yes, it's really coming on now. Excellent! Would you like to stay for luncheon, Mr Walker?' She'd invited him before but he'd always said no. However, today he agreed and said it would be lovely. Mama went bustling off to confer with Cook, wanting to serve something special.

I went to peer at Mr Walker's half-finished portrait myself.

'What do you think?' he asked.

'I think it's a very fine painting,' I said.

'But I sense a little hesitation?'

'No, I think it's wonderful – the colour, the brushwork, the whole composition. I think you're a marvellous painter, Mr Walker, even better than Papa,' I told him.

'You're still not sure though, are you?' he said, looking amused. 'Don't you think I've captured a good likeness of your mother?'

I took a deep breath. 'Not exactly,' I said. 'Your portrait looks remarkably like Mama, but somehow she's too pretty. And young.'

Mr Walker smiled at me. 'Don't you think that's the way your mother would like to be seen?'

'Oh yes. So I suppose that makes you a very *artful* artist.'

'You're a very perceptive girl, Rose.'

Is Mr Walker painting such a flattering portrait because he simply likes to please? Or is it because Mama is a wealthy woman and will pay him handsomely, and introduce him to the Feynsham-Joneses and Lady Robson. I'm sure they'd all appreciate flattering portraits too. Years ago Mama persuaded Papa to offer a portrait as a prize for the Christmas Charity Bazaar in aid of Orphan Girls, and the Honourable Mrs Helmsley drew the winning ticket.

Mrs Helmsley is enormous. Even the strongest whalebone corset can't control her rolls of fat. Once, when she was taking tea with us, she leaned forward to grab the biggest slice of cake and split her seams. Rupert and I didn't dare glance at each other because we knew we'd start spluttering.

Papa kept his side of the bargain and painted her. It was a fine portrait, like Mrs Helmsley in every way. *Too* like. Every single roll of fat was highlighted. Mrs Helmsley was mortified. She didn't make a scene as we expected. She didn't reject the painting. She simply asked if the servants could wrap it up in brown paper, and then she took it away with her. I don't know what she did with it. I'm sure she didn't hang it on the wall. Perhaps spiders are spinning cobwebs over her curves in the attic.

Mama never asked Papa to do a portrait for the bazaar again. Perhaps that was the point. He can be very wily.

I think Mr Walker is too. He likes Papa. Has he made Mama a gentle beauty in his painting to please him?

Of course, Mr Walker may simply like Mama and want to please *her*.

He *can't*, can he? Mama *is* still quite pretty when she makes an effort. Her black hair is glossy, her eyes a deep blue, her figure plump but pleasing. Her voice, with its Scottish lilt, is attractive. But the things she *says* are so trivial. She is actually very ignorant, yet she declares things with such authority, as if she is the fount of all knowledge.

I trembled at the thought of all the silly things she might say at lunch. I made a great effort, washed all the pencil smudges off my hands, and remembered to brush my hair and tie a ribbon in it. I changed my favourite forest-green velvet dress (too short for me now, but it makes me feel like Robin Hood) for the cream silk I wear on Sundays.

I went skipping down the stairs, but as I approached the dining-room door Mama stopped me.

'Where are you going, child?'

'To have lunch!' I said, astonished.

'You don't take your luncheon in the dining room,' said Mama.

This was true enough normally. Mama doesn't use the dining room unless Papa is around either. She has her lunch on a tray in the drawing room, while I have lunch upstairs with the little ones.

'But Mr Walker is here!' I said.

'We will have a quiet lunch together,' said Mama. 'I am sure we have both had enough of your chatter, dear. Go and join the other children in the nursery.'

I felt stung. I hated the way Mama said the word 'dear'. I am not her dear. I am her least favourite child. She prefers Beth at her most trying, Algie at his most destructive. I would be her least favourite child if I were an *only* child.

It was useless to argue with her. I stomped off to the nursery and joined Nurse and my siblings for boiled plaice and semolina pudding, two pale, pimply dishes that turned my stomach.

I took only a mouthful of each, even though Nurse nagged at me.

'I don't know what to do with you nowadays, Miss Rose,' she said. She put a spoonful of white slop in Phoebe's mouth. 'You used to be a dear soul like Baby here. Whatever happened to that good little girl?'

'I sometimes wish I was little and good again, Nurse. Or completely grown up and able to do as I wish. I hate being stuck like this, neither one thing nor the other. It's so *mean* of Mama not to let me have lunch with her and Mr Walker when she lets me dine with the grown-ups now,' I said heatedly.

Nurse sniffed. 'I don't know why your mama's taken it into her head to have that scruffy young man come to the house every day. He looks like a tramp. I'm sure he's not a gentleman.'

'Oh, Nurse, don't be so narrow-minded. Mr Walker is an *artist*, like Papa,' I said.

Nurse turned to Algie. 'Master Algie, don't you go helping yourself to more jam! You've got more jam than semolina now!'

'Good! It's the only way to get it down. It looks like Phoebe's sick,' said Algie, licking his spoonful of raspberry jam with relish.

'Do you have to be so revolting, Algie?' I snapped.

He waggled his jammy tongue at me. 'Oh, Nurse, Mr Walker is an *artist*,' he said, clasping his hands together and speaking in a silly high-pitched voice.

I didn't think he sounded at all like me, but Clarrie and Sebastian burst out laughing, and even Nurse couldn't help smirking, though she told Algie not to be ridiculous.

'It's Rose who's ridiculous, going all swoony over Mr Walker when he's a man and she's just a little girl,' he said. 'She's in love!'

'Stop being such a stupid little boy,' I said angrily, and swept out of the nursery, though Nurse remonstrated with me, insisting I should come back and ask permission to leave the table like a nicely brought-up young lady.

Out on the landing I heard Beth crying. She seems determined to resist the rules too. We're not supposed to go into her room at meal times because Nurse Budd says it distracts her. But Beth is my *sister*, and she sounded so very distressed. I barged in without even bothering to knock.

Nurse Budd was holding her by the shoulder, trying to feed her. Beth couldn't get free because there was a belt tying her to the chair. She clamped her mouth shut when Nurse Budd thrust the spoon towards her, and it clanked against her teeth.

'Stop it! How dare you! You're hurting her!' I cried, trying to stop Nurse Budd.

'For goodness' sake, Miss Rose, calm down,' she said. 'I'm simply giving the child her lunch.'

'You're torturing her! You've got her tied up like a prisoner!' I declared.

'It's the only way to get some food down the poor little mite. The child is skin and bone. If I don't secure her, she'll run away. You're a little monkey, aren't you, Miss Beth?'

'I'm sure Mama and Papa wouldn't like it if they knew,' I said.

'Your mama knows exactly how I feed her, and thoroughly approves. "The child has to learn, Nurse Budd," she said, her very words. And if she's not encouraged, she'll starve. Is that what you want, Miss Rose?'

'I want my sister to be happy,' I said.

'I think she's happy enough in her own way, dear,' said Nurse Budd. 'You wait, a few weeks' more training and she'll be a docile little sweetheart. I dare say she'll be feeding herself soon.'

'Why don't you let her feed herself now? She's been doing it for years. She's not a baby,' I insisted.

'Very well then, Miss Rose,' said Nurse Budd, shrugging.

She undid Beth's belt and offered her the dish and spoon. Beth put her hands behind her back and went to crouch in the corner.

'Oh dear,' said Nurse Budd triumphantly.

I ignored her and walked very slowly towards Beth.

'It's all right, Beth, darling. Don't be frightened.' I picked up the bowl and spoon and sat down beside her. 'There now, Beth. Are you going to try a spoonful of semolina? Why haven't you got any jam to make it tastier? Our brother Algie puts a whole pot of jam on his pudding!'

'A whole pot of jam on his pudding,' Beth murmured, looking astonished.

'Well, I don't mean *literally*.' I looked over at Nurse Budd. 'Why hasn't she got any jam?'

'Miss Beth's sweet enough, dear,' she replied.

'Don't you worry, Beth,' I said fiercely. 'I'll talk to Cook and make sure she puts a big spoonful of jam on all your milk puddings.'

I balanced the bowl of semolina on her lap and tried to get her to take the spoon. She took it, but smacked the surface of the semolina so it splattered all over the place.

'Mind, Miss Beth, you're getting it on your dress,' said Nurse Budd.

'Don't listen, Beth. You feed yourself any way you like,' I said.

Beth held the spoon in the air.

'She'll make a mess, Miss Rose,' Nurse Budd warned.

'Mess,' said Beth, and smashed the spoon down into the bowl with all her might. Semolina spurted

135

everywhere – over her hands, her dress, her stockings, even the carpet.

'You see,' said Nurse Budd, lips tight. 'Now I'll have to clean her up. Why don't you go to the nursery and supervise your other sisters and brothers, Miss Rose?'

I gave up and went to find Nurse settling Phoebe into her cot for her nap.

'Nurse, Nurse!'

'Ssh now, Miss Rose, Baby's just nodding off,' she hissed.

'Rose, come and play soldiers with us!' Algie called.

'Now then, Master Algie, it's not playtime now, not straight after lunch. You look at your nice storybook and have a little doze,' said Nurse. She shook her head at me. 'I should run along, dear, you're just unsettling them.'

'I'm worried about Beth, Nurse. Nurse Budd is being so horrible to her, tying her on her chair and forcing her to eat. Can't you stop her?' I implored.

'I wish I could, Miss Rose. But she's in charge of Miss Beth now, and there's nothing I can do about it. I had words with your mama because I don't hold with being so strict. She said I was too soft with her, and this was the only way to deal with a child like Miss Beth,' said Nurse.

'That's nonsense!'

'I think it's nonsense too, but who am I to say? *I* couldn't control poor Miss Beth. Maybe if I'd done better with her earlier, she wouldn't be like this now. She was a dear little baby too, like a little lamb. But when she turned two she started getting into all these passions and developing her funny ways until I was at my wits' end. I've tried and tried, but I can't cope with her, especially with Master Algie being such a handful into the bargain.' Nurse fidgeted with her apron, pleating it into folds. 'Some days I think it's time to retire. Your dear father has promised to look after me. Perhaps I should go now.'

'Don't be silly, Nurse. You can't go. You're part of the family,' I said, though I suddenly saw how old and tired she looked.

It's very strange. For years Nurse seemed so big and strong, able to pick me up and put me to bed in disgrace, even when I struggled and kicked. But now I'm as tall as her, and much stronger, and it's very unnerving.

'Don't you worry, Nurse,' I said, and fled the room.

I could hear Beth howling now. I couldn't bear it. I wished Papa were at home. Beth's cries were heart-breaking.

I went rushing into the dining room. Mama and Mr Walker were sitting on either side of the long table, eating chocolate pudding with whipped cream. Why did we get fobbed off with milky slop while they had such a treat? I was sure Beth would eat up every mouthful.

'For goodness' sake, Rose, must you burst in on us like this?' Mama said angrily.

'I'm sorry, Mama, but this is an emergency. I simply have to tell you. Nurse Budd is forcing Beth to eat in such a cruel way, and now she's crying. Can't you hear her? You have to stop Nurse Budd, she's making Beth so unhappy. I've told Nurse, but she says she can't do anything.'

'Please calm down, Rose. Really! This is hardly an emergency,' said Mama. 'Nurse Budd is an excellent professional and knows best how to care for Beth. Now, I think we've bored Mr Walker long enough with nursery matters. Run along, please!'

Run along! As if I were Clarrie's age! I hate Mama at times. And I hate, hate, hate it that Paris Walker was *smiling* at her.

11

WHEN PAPA CAME HOME, I told him about Nurse Budd. He winced when I described the belt restraining Beth, the hand clamping her shoulder, the spoon clanking against her teeth. He went to see Beth for himself, and then he had a long talk with Nurse Budd. I lurked nearby, but I couldn't hear what he was saying, just the tone of his voice, very calm but very serious. We all know we are in trouble when Papa talks to us like that. We'd sooner he shouted. It wouldn't make us feel so bad.

I hoped he'd actually dismissed Nurse Budd. When he emerged, I said *I* would devote myself to Beth's care from now on, and I was sure we'd muddle along somehow.

'You're a very sweet sister, Rose, but that won't be necessary,' said Papa. 'Nurse Budd and I have had a long talk. She's explained her regime very carefully, and I can see that she's only trying to help Beth behave. Her methods might look a little harsh, but apparently she gets excellent results. She's assured me that in this short space of time she's grown to love Beth like her own child.'

'Are you sure she means it, Papa?' I asked.

'I'm absolutely certain,' he said. 'Now, you mustn't worry about it any more. Your old pa has taken care of everything.'

Poor gullible Papa. Much later, when everyone was asleep, Nurse Budd crept into my room.

'Night night, Miss Rose. You mustn't worry your little head about my methods. You will find I only want the best for Miss Beth. Don't go troubling your poor papa any more. You don't want to worry him. You do understand me, don't you?'

I understood her all right. She was making a veiled threat. I'm going to make it my mission to spend as much time in Beth's room as I can so that I can protect her.

'Don't forget I'm here, Beth. I'm on your side against Nurse Budd. If she starts doing anything you don't like, just shout for me and I'll come running,' I whispered to her.

Beth doesn't seem grateful at all. She sometimes even seems to *like* Nurse Budd. She looks at her expectantly and tries to please her. But when I approach her, she cowers away, as if *I'm* the cruel one.

Next week Rupert will be back for his half term, but I don't suppose I can count on him to help me protect Beth. He will probably be at the Feynsham-Joneses, visiting Pamela. I wonder how many letters he has written to her. He still sends Mama and Papa a short, dutiful letter every Sunday, telling them about sport and lessons and meals, and his friends Hardy and Martin. Those are their surnames. These chaps don't seem to have Christian names, though one has a Latin appendage: Robinson Minor. There's also Mackinley, who treats Rupert like his personal servant. It's ridiculous and demeaning – I can't understand why Rupert goes along with it.

Each time he sends me a paltry postscript. It's usually *Say hello to Rose* or, slightly more affectionately, *Give my love to Rose*. In his last letter I got two sentences: *Send my love to Rose. Why hasn't she written to me recently?*

I'll tell you why, Rupert Rivers. You haven't written a single letter to me since you went to that wretched school, yet you're writing pages and pages to that simpering girl and signing each one *Your loving friend, Rupert*.

Well, you're not *my* friend any more, and you're not loving. You don't care a jot about me. I'm not sure Mr Walker does either.

I *wish* I could sketch him adequately. I've tried a dozen times, but I can never make it look right. I pulled the drawings out of my sketchbook and tore them into shreds. I kept just one, hidden inside the precious copy of *Robinson Crusoe* that sat in my bookcase.

The next morning I didn't go to the studio. I couldn't face it after Mama had excluded me like a little girl. I didn't go the following day, or the one after that. Mama didn't comment. She was very happy to have Mr Walker all to herself.

Papa had finished his sketches of street children, so he went to his studio again, working on the design for the book cover. At least *he* noticed my absence.

'Have you got tired of drawing, chickie?' he asked. 'Well, I dare say Miss Rayner is glad to have her star pupil back in the schoolroom.'

She wasn't at all. I'd become too much of a liability. She tried to set me challenging work – mostly arithmetic, not my favourite lesson. Sometimes it was so difficult, I couldn't work it out at all. Miss Rayner told me all the correct answers, but only because she had the little crib book to hand. When I asked her to show me the workings of each sum, she blustered for a bit, but she didn't have any idea and we were both embarrassed.

She also set me a project on riding because she thought I *wanted* to learn. She gave me a little book on how to sit side-saddle. It was very kind of her, so I had to pretend to be pleased, and drew several boring sketches of saddles and stirrups and Lord knows what else.

Papa didn't seem to care that I'd stopped sketching. He'd become interested in Sebastian's lurid paintings now. Sebastian had discovered a picture of a pretty male saint being shot full of arrows, and was delighted to discover that he was his namesake. He took the Winsor & Newton paints and used up a lot of Yellow Ochre for St Sebastian's long hair, and nearly all the Crimson Lake for the blood dripping from his arrow wounds. Miss Rayner didn't think the subject matter quite suitable, but Papa was amused and gave Sebastian high praise.

Algie borrowed the paintbox next, and painted little Crimson Lake spots all over Montmorency. He meant them to look like arrow wounds, but poor Montmorency just looked as if he had measles. He didn't like being cleaned with a damp cloth, and made a sudden dash for freedom.

It caused chaos because Edie is ludicrously scared of mice and refused to come out of her attic room all day in case she encountered him. Mama threatened to dismiss her without a reference, but Edie said she didn't care, she wasn't having no mouse running up her skirts, not for love nor money. Then Jack Boots bestirred himself and stamped around the house on a mouse hunt. He might have stamped on Montmorency himself if he'd actually spotted him.

Luckily Montmorency had the sense to take refuge in Beth's room and make himself a cosy little nest in Marianne's silk skirts. She was back from her stay in the doll's hospital and looked as good as new, her eyes properly in place, but Papa had wasted his time and money. Beth wouldn't go near her. She wouldn't even let me introduce Marianne to Marigold.

'But you love Marianne!' I said. 'Don't be frightened of her.'

'Frightened of her,' said Beth.

Perhaps it was because Marianne's eyes wouldn't shut any more. She stayed sitting in the corner, staring resolutely ahead, while Beth whispered to Marigold. Montmorency wasn't discovered until Nurse Budd decided to put Marianne away in the nursery toy cupboard that evening. Montmorency panicked and ran up Nurse Budd's starched skirts. She shrieked her head off.

We found this tremendous fun. Even Nurse chuckled happily. Sebastian retrieved Montmorency and took him back to his cage, stroking and scolding him alternately.

Algie and Clarrie took it in turns to be Nurse Budd. Algie was particularly clever at imitating her flapping hands.

'You're a card, Algie,' I said, laughing at him.

But I didn't feel like laughing the next day, when I discovered that he hadn't just painted Montmorency. He'd also coloured in the pictures in *Robinson Crusoe*, and now the first few pages were stuck together with blotches of paint. It had been Papa's book when he was a little boy, and he'd given it to Rupert and me when we were six. Nurse tried to read it to us, but she stumbled over the words. She said reading such a long book made her throat hurt, and why couldn't we be content with *Struwwelpeter*? We loved *Struwwelpeter* because the rhymes were so funny, though the red-legged Scissorman gave us both nightmares.

But we still wanted to read Papa's book, so we started doing it together, taking turns with each chapter. It became our special desert island world. While Nurse was busy with Beth and Sebastian and Algie and Clarrie, we acted out the stories. Rupert insisted on being Robinson Crusoe. I was Man Friday. Rupert occasionally commanded me to be Robinson's dog, or even his pet parrot. We constructed our own ship from upturned chairs, while the nursery rug was our island. It was green rather than yellow like sand, but Rupert decided that it was a tropical forest.

Rupert insisted, Rupert commanded, Rupert decided – and I did what he wanted. He refused to play with me if I didn't stick to his rules. That's the way it's always been. I simply got into the habit of doing what he wanted, right up until the beginning of September.

After he'd left for school I went up to my room and cradled the large red volume, remembering all our childhood games. When Nurse persuaded me to come and have bread and milk with the others in the nursery, I took *Robinson Crusoe* with me, and slept with it under my pillow that night, though it gave me a terrible crick in the neck.

Now it lives on my bookshelf, head and shoulders above the other stories. It was my most precious book, and now it was spoiled. I felt like throttling Algie. Nurse had taken all the young ones out for their afternoon walk, so I had to wait to get hold of him.

I was sitting on the window seat halfway up the stairs, shaking my head over the ruined pages, when Mr Walker and Mama came out of the dining room. Mama said goodbye in a very gushing manner, even holding Alphonse up to give Mr Walker a 'kiss'. Then she went off to the drawing room, the dog under her arm. Mr Walker took his old jacket off the hook in the hall – and then looked up and spotted me.

'*There* you are, Rose!' he said, coming up the stairs. 'Where have you been? I've missed you! I asked your mama and she said you'd become tired of drawing. Is that right?'

I didn't dare look up at him in case I blushed. He'd *missed* me!

'I'm not really any good at drawing,' I said, staring hard at the ruined page in *Robinson Crusoe*, too bashful to look him directly in the eye.

'Well, you're certainly not that great at painting,' he said, looking at the splodged page and sitting down beside me.

'My little brother Algie decided to do some colouring,' I said ruefully. 'You know what children are like.'

'Children! So what are you, an old lady?' said Mr Walker, smiling.

'Don't tease me,' I said.

'So how old *are* you, Rose? Twelve?'

'Thirteen!'

'Still a little girl, but only just.'

'I'm not little,' I said indignantly. 'Do I seem it?'

'Sometimes,' said Mr Walker. 'And sometimes you seem as old as the hills.'

All at once I heard cries coming from Beth's room. 'Oh dear. That's my sister Beth again.'

'Yes. She's an invalid, isn't she?' Mr Walker asked delicately.

'She can't manage to be like other people,' I said. 'Some hateful people call her an imbecile, but she's not – she's very clever.'

'I'm sure she is.'

'I'd better go to her,' I said.

'You're such a good sister,' said Mr Walker (though this isn't true). 'And I'm positive you're good at drawing too. Please come back for the morning sessions. We miss you.'

We miss you? He surely couldn't mean Mama! I knew she'd be enjoying having him all to herself. But it meant so much that he'd said it – *twice*.

I rushed upstairs to rescue Beth. I was sure I'd find her tied to a chair again, but she was sitting on the floor in the corner, scratching herself. She does this sometimes when she's very agitated, and it looks so sad and horrid.

'Please don't do that, Beth, you'll hurt yourself,' I said, kneeling beside her.

I looked at Nurse Budd. 'Why is she crying?' I asked suspiciously.

'Because she's having a little paddy, bless her,' said Nurse Budd. 'She's got to learn that she can't always have what she wants.'

'What do you want, Beth?'

'Want! Want! Want!' Beth said, but she wouldn't tell me.

'She'll calm down soon enough, won't you, Miss Beth?' said Nurse Budd. 'I wouldn't pay her any attention, Miss Rose. You're only making her worse.'

147

I took no notice and tried to hold Beth's hands to stop her scratching. Beth shouted and wrenched them free.

'You see?' said Nurse Budd.

I got as near Beth as I could. 'Is Nurse Budd mean to you, Beth?' I whispered. 'Does she smack you?'

But Nurse Budd had sharp ears. 'Oh, Miss Rose,' she said sorrowfully. 'I'd never smack any of my charges! Miss Beth, Nurse Budd never smacks, does she?'

'Never smacks, does she?' Beth mumbled between sobs. Her nose was running unattractively.

'Here, Beth darling, let's wipe your nose,' I said, pulling my handkerchief out from my sleeve. I tried to mop her face but she wouldn't let me. She started rocking backwards and forwards.

'Oh, Beth, you look so unhappy,' I said helplessly. I tried to put my arms right round her to rock with her. I used to do that when Clarrie had a tantrum, and it often made her stop crying and snuggle close.

But Beth went rigid and struggled away from me.

'There now! Please stop it, Miss Rose. You're not helping the little lamb,' said Nurse Budd.

I couldn't argue with her. I wasn't helping at all. I gave up on poor Beth and went to my own room. I felt so sad about my sister – and yet I was still so happy, happy, happy that Paris Walker really seemed to like me.

I started to draw yet another sketch of him. Perhaps it might work better from memory than observation.

Then I suddenly remembered!

I leafed through all the pages of *Robinson Crusoe*, easing apart the ones that were stuck together with paint, tearing several in my hurry. I'd hidden my best sketch of Mr Walker there – and now it was missing!

12

I RAN TO THE nursery and peered under Algie's pillow, inside his toy fort, in his own torn books, looking for my sketch without success. I thought of his desk in the schoolroom. I was surprised to discover Miss Rayner still there, though she was only employed till one o'clock.

'Hello, Rose dear! I'm trying to work out how to do those fiendish sums I set you,' she said. 'I'm afraid I'm not making much progress!'

'Could I just take a peep inside Algie's desk, Miss Rayner?'

'Oh dear. Has the little scamp been up to no good?' she asked sympathetically.

'He's coloured in some of the illustrations in my *Robinson Crusoe*. He's ruined it. The pages are all stuck together now.'

'I'm so sorry! I should have kept a better eye on him,' said Miss Rayner, looking horrified.

'And there was a little drawing tucked inside my book – homework set me by Mr Walker. I wonder if he's put it in here?' I said, opening Algie's desk.

It was in a terrible mess, books and pencils and broken toys and spilled ink and apple cores.

'Oh dear, oh dear, I should check it more often and try to help Algie be tidier,' said Miss Rayner.

'It's really not your fault, Miss Rayner. We both know how messy Algie can be,' I said as I scrabbled through all the clutter. There was no sign of my drawing. 'It's not here. Oh, Algie, you little beast, what have you done with it?'

'He's a naughty little chap, but he's got such winning ways. I can't help laughing at him,' said Miss Rayner, shaking her head.

'I don't know how you put up with us all, Miss Rayner,' I said. 'We're such an unruly bunch. Don't you ever feel tempted to go and find a more rewarding set of children to teach?'

'Oh, Rose, you and your brothers and sisters are like my family,' she said, beaming at me.

I felt ashamed. None of us thought of poor Miss Rayner as family. Was that why she hung around half the afternoon even though she was only employed for the morning? Did she wish she lived with us? I realized I had no idea where she actually lived. I decided to ask her.

She seemed startled by such a direct question. 'In Clerkenwell, dear,' she said.

'*Clerkenwell?* But isn't that miles and miles away?'

'I suppose it is. But if I'm tired I take the omnibus.'

'But why do you live so far away? Do you have a house in Clerkenwell?'

'Hardly, dear! But I have a very nice room,' Miss Rayner said. 'Really quite spacious.'

I think she meant to reassure me, but I was shocked. A *room*? What did she mean? She lived and slept in the same room? And what about her meals?

'Do you cook for yourself, Miss Rayner?' I asked.

'No, there are no private facilities for cooking. My landlady serves a bowl of porridge in the mornings and does a hot meal in the evening, quite simple, but I'm sure it's nutritious,' she said cheerfully.

I looked at her. She was very large, barely contained by her corsets.

Miss Rayner knew what I was thinking. 'I sometimes buy myself little treats on the way home,' she told me. 'Especially if I happen to pass a baker's. I can never resist a penny bun. Or an iced bun for that matter. Or a slice of cherry cake on a Saturday. And if it's a very cold day I *have* been known to buy a bag of fried potatoes from a stall – I'm finding they're much warmer than a pair of gloves!' She giggled.

'If you're partial to cake, you must ask Cook to give you some of ours. There's always some left over from teatime,' I said.

'That's so sweet of you, Rose, but I couldn't possibly. I'm sure the teatime leftovers are pounced upon by the servants for their own tea,' Miss Rayner said. 'I wouldn't want to deprive little Mary-Jane or Jack.'

I was surprised she knew their names.

'Oh, we sometimes have little chats on the back stairs. I like children,' said Miss Rayner.

'Miss Rayner, don't you think it strange that we Rivers children are nurtured and educated so carefully while Mary-Jane and Jack have to look after us and don't have any education at all?' I asked.

'My goodness, Rose, you and your questions! It's just the way of the world, dear. You were born into a rich family and Jack and Mary-Jane into poor ones.'

Looking at Miss Rayner's patched dress and old worn boots, I realized that she was poor too.

'I shall ask Papa if he can pay you a better wage so that you can have more treats – *and* a warm pair of gloves,' I said.

'That's a very kind thought, Rose, but please don't. I think I'm being paid ample already, especially as I no longer teach Rupert and Beth – and I'm clearly inadequate when it comes to giving you tuition.'

'I think you're doing a valiant job, Miss Rayner,' I said, and resolved to be much nicer to her in future.

I went to ask Cook if she could bake a cake specially for Miss Rayner. She said she didn't see why she should bake extra, her budget was tight enough already, and it wasn't as if Miss Rayner was undernourished. She smiled nastily as she said this, and Maggie and Mary-Jane tittered.

Then I waited impatiently for Algie to return from the afternoon walk. The children had been out for a long time. Nurse was all in a fluster when she brought them back at last. Phoebe was crying because she needed a fresh napkin. Sebastian was crying because some horrid boys had sniggered at his long hair, calling him a girly-boy. Clarrie was limping, complaining that her boots were too tight. And Algie was soaking wet because he'd waded right into the pond to rescue his boat.

'Dear Lordy, what a to-do! There there, baby, Nursie will change you in just a moment. Master Sebastian, don't take on so, dear – they were just naughty rough boys and I dare say they call everyone names. Miss Clarrie, wait just a few seconds and I'll take off your boots and rub those poor tootsies, but I must get Master Algie's wet clothes off him or he'll catch his death,' said Nurse. 'Look at him dripping all over the carpet!'

'He's a little drip himself,' I said. 'Don't worry about Algie, Nurse. *I'll* get his clothes off and find him some dry ones while you attend to the other children,' I suggested.

I scooped him under my arm like a rolled-up rug and hauled him along the corridor before he could protest.

When we were in the night nursery he started kicking, so I dropped him on his cot and then sat on top of him.

'Kick me once more and I'll slap you,' I hissed. 'I'm so cross with you! How dare you paint my precious *Robinson Crusoe*!'

'I was trying to make it look nice for you! The pictures were so grey and boring,' said Algie.

'Well, you've absolutely ruined it. And what did you do with *my* picture?'

'What do you mean, *your* picture? I haven't seen any picture.'

'Don't play the innocent with me, Algie Rivers. What have you done with it?'

'I haven't done anything,' he wailed. His teeth were starting to chatter.

I knew that he was fibbing – but I also knew that he was soaking wet and getting very cold.

'Keep still while I take your clothes off,' I commanded, unpeeling each of his garments until I was down to his drawers. Then I yanked those off too.

'Stop it! Get off me! Let Nurse do it!' Algie yelled, struggling to escape.

'*I'm* doing it.' I grabbed a towel. 'Here, I have to get you dry. You really need a bath after being in that stinky pond, but it will take ages to get enough hot water.' I started rubbing him vigorously.

'Leave off! You're too rough! You're hurting!' Algie protested.

'Stop being such a baby,' I said. I wasn't *really* hurting him, but I didn't feel like dabbing him gently.

I was all set for a serious interrogation, but I'm also a responsible sister. I had to get him dry first. It would be just like Algie to take a chill and die and then haunt me for the rest of my days. When at last he was warm and pink, I went to the children's wardrobe. Algie jumped up on the bed and started leaping around, stark naked.

'For goodness' sake, Algie, stop it!' I commanded.

'I'm not Algie. I'm a Whirling Dervish!' he said, spinning like a top.

'Stop whirling, Mr Dervish, and get dressed,' I said, bringing an armful of clothes with me and sitting him back on the bed. I'd thought of a devious plan.

I put a vest and some drawers on him so that he wouldn't suspect anything too soon, and then I pulled Clarrie's dress over his head and got all the buttons fastened down the back before he realized that anything was up.

'This shirt feels most peculiar!' he complained. 'It's all tight and itchy.'

'That's because it's a dress,' I said. 'I've decided that you're such a horrid little boy that I'm turning you into a girl.'

'No! No, stop it! I can't wear a *dress*!' Algie shrieked. 'I won't, I won't!'

Even as a baby Algie had hated wearing skirts. He couldn't wait to be dressed as a proper boy. So now he grew frantic, trying to tear off the frock, but his pudgy little fingers couldn't reach the buttons at the back. Thank goodness they were tightly sewn. 'Get it *off*!' he roared.

'What's the matter with Master Algie?' Nurse called from the day nursery, busy with Phoebe.

'Oh, he's just being silly, Nurse,' I said, my hand over Algie's mouth. He did his best to bite my fingers but I hung on determinedly. I put my head close to his and whispered, 'Now, you're going to stay a little girl until you give me back my drawing!'

'Haven't got your silly drawing,' Algie said indistinctly. 'Who wants a drawing of stupid old Mr Walker anyway?'

'So you *have* taken it. Where have you hidden it?'

'I've forgotten,' said Algie. He tried to get the frock off again.

'Algie! I'll tell Nurse,' I said.

'I'll tell Nurse you're being beastly. *And* I'll tell her, you've got a silly pash on Mr Walker,' said Algie. 'I'll tell her right now!'

'And I'll tell her you stole my precious drawing, and she'll get very angry and she'll tell Mama, and then she'll have you whipped,' I said.

This wasn't likely at all. Nurse rarely told tales on us, partly because our behaviour might reflect badly on her. Mama was strict, but we would have had to do something truly dreadful to be whipped. And who was to do the whipping? Papa would refuse outright. He'd never so much as smacked us. Mr Hodgson might be willing, but he was very old and frail now. And surely *I'd* be the one in trouble for drawing Mr Walker in the first place.

Luckily Algie didn't think of this. He just heard the word *whip*.

'I won't be whipped! I'll grab the whip, and then I'll whip *you* – *lash, lash, lash,*' he said, cracking his imaginary whip.

I tried to grab him. Unfortunately I caught hold of his borrowed frock, and the silk ripped with a terrible sound, paralysing us both.

'What was that?' Nurse called sharply.

'Nothing, Nurse!' I called, wondering how on earth I was going to mend Clarrie's dress when I was so terrible at needlework. But it was too late anyway.

Nurse came into the room with a wailing Phoebe on her hip. She saw Algie, red-faced in the torn frock, and smacked him hard across the backs of his legs.

Algie screamed his head off.

'Now stop that shrieking, Master Algie, I barely touched you,' said Nurse. 'How dare you rip Miss Clarrie's frock! It's her best silk too – I doubt I'll be able to mend it without a patch, and then it'll only be good enough for playing at home. What are you doing in Clarrie's frock anyway? I won't have such goings-on in my nursery. Master Sebastian's bad enough without *you* starting too,' Nurse scolded.

'I haven't started anything!' Algie sobbed furiously. 'It wasn't *my* fault! It was Rose – *she* did it!'

'Hush now! It's bad enough getting into such mischief, but downright wicked to blame your poor sister,' said Nurse.

It was glorious to get my own back on Algie, but when Nurse said that Algie had to go straight to bed without any tea, I decided I couldn't let him suffer any longer.

'Algie's actually telling the truth, Nurse,' I said. 'I dressed him up for a joke and then I accidentally tore the frock. I'm so sorry.'

'Miss Rose!' she said, shocked.

She didn't smack *me* about the legs – I'm too old for that sort of treatment now – but she gave me a severe telling-off and sent me to my room. *I* was the one to go without any tea, but I didn't really care. In a couple of hours I would be dining with Mama and Papa, and I'd started to find the plain nursery tea a very dull meal.

Even so, missing tea would have been torture for Algie. He seemed impressed that I'd taken the blame. Half an hour later he sidled into my room with his hands behind his back. He found me sitting up on my bed, head bent, arms clasped round my knees.

'You're not crying, are you, Rose?' he asked. 'You can cheer up now. Look!' From behind his back Algie produced my drawing of Mr Walker, flourishing it like a conjuror at a birthday party.

'So where did you hide it?' I asked, grabbing it.

'I *didn't* hide it! Absolutely not! You probably just left it somewhere or maybe Edie picked it up and tidied it away or perhaps Papa saw it and thought it was his,' Algie suggested. 'Or, I know, Alphonse could have mistaken it for the newspaper and run off with it in his mouth.'

'Or perhaps a little pig flew in through an open window and seized my drawing and made off with it,' I said.

'Perhaps it did,' said Algie happily. 'Anyway, I've been searching and searching for it for you because I knew how upset you were, and then at long last I came across it and here it is.'

'So where was it?' I persisted.

'I forget,' said Algie.

I didn't have the energy to persist. I smoothed out the crumples and put it back between the pages of *Robinson Crusoe*.

'Mr Walker will get squashed in there,' said Algie.

'I'll squash *you* if you're not careful.'

'You really do love him, don't you?'

'Of course I don't,' I said, feeling my cheeks grow hot.

'You've gone all red!'

'No I haven't,' I insisted.

'Yes, you are in love with him, I can tell! That's stupid, because you're just a little girl still and he's a man like Papa,' said Algie.

'If you go on like that I shall spread equally silly rumours about you, Algie. I'll go round telling everyone that you're in love with . . . Cook!'

'I *am* in love with Cook,' Algie declared. 'Every afternoon I tell her I love her, and she gives me a slice of pie and lets me scrape the cake mix out of the bowl. When I'm big I'm going to marry her and she'll make me jam roly-poly every day, even for breakfast, and we'll live happily ever after, so there!'

160

It's a waste of time trying to outwit Algie. And he's right, isn't he? I think I *am* in love with Mr Walker. I fizz all over at the thought of him, I daringly whisper his name, Paris, over and over again as if it were poetry, and I remember every word he says, every look he gives me, every gesture, every smile.

I've gone back to the daily portrait sessions. I knew that Mama would be annoyed – it's obvious she wants Paris all to herself, but I can be as artful as Algie.

I went to see Papa first. I sighed and moped until he said, 'What's the matter, chickie?'

I ducked my head and acted shy, and then at last I burst out, 'Oh, Papa, I wish I had *your* talent. My work is so stiff and clumsy compared with yours.'

He put his arms round me and told me that I was already a very promising little artist.

'Of course, you haven't quite got *all* the skills yet, darling. It will take years of practice before your pencil glides over the page. My goodness, it's still a struggle for me, and I've been sketching for the last twenty years! Have you seen the number of times I tear out a page and chuck it at the wastepaper basket? My drawings of street children have been so challenging. I want to keep them simple and true to life, showing them in their sad rags and sordid surroundings, yet I also want to show their liveliness, their joy when they run around and play their funny games.

'There's one child who haunts me. I first came across her in the doll-maker's shop, the one I mentioned. She looks like a little gypsy – she's grubby and bashed and bruised, poor mite, and yet she's the sparkiest of them all. She looks after all the children in her alley better than a mother, inventing so many fanciful games. She's always burdened with a baby on her hip, but she joins in with enthusiasm. She runs faster than any of the boys, and gives a clout here and a kick there, but she's so gentle with one little lad with withered legs, always letting him play too. It's a joy to see her.'

'I wish I could meet her, Papa,' I said.

'I've very nearly finished the drawings, but I tell you what, Rose, when they're done we'll start up our own special sketching sessions, you and me. We'll wander all over London and select our subjects and draw all morning, and then we'll come back to the studio and see if we can develop our rough sketches into something worthwhile. It will be good to have my studio back. I can't seem to work there while Paris is painting his portrait of your mama. But you should watch him. He has great talent and you could learn so much. One day I'm sure he'll paint a truly great portrait that will set the world on fire.'

'Like your painting of Louisa in her black dress?' I said.

Papa shook his head and didn't reply. I'm sure Louisa was more than his muse. I think she was his sweetheart too. I feel so sorry for him.

I am sad for Papa but I'm so happy for me, resuming my so-called sketching sessions.

Needless to say, Mama is not at all pleased.

'I thought you had got tired of drawing, Rose. You haven't been making much progress, as far as I can see. Maybe you should run along back to the schoolroom.'

'Papa wants me to persevere,' I said.

'And quite right too,' said Paris. 'I think we should encourage her, Mrs Rivers.'

'Oh, well, if you think so, Mr Walker,' said Mama, suddenly all smiles.

When she's with him she acts in an embarrassingly girlish way. I wouldn't have been surprised if she'd produced a fan and tapped him on the wrist with it.

We settled into the morning session, Mama posing in her blue dress, Paris painting her, and me sketching the pair of them, though my hand was shaky and I couldn't draw properly. I watched Paris most of the time. His portrait is astonishing. Mama comes to peep at it whenever she needs to stand up and stretch.

'I hope the portrait pleases you, Mrs Rivers,' said Paris. 'You make me feel anxious when you come and look at it.'

'You need have no qualms on that score, Mr Walker. I am extremely pleased. It's a remarkable likeness,' said Mama complacently.

I hung around when she went to change out of the blue gown for lunch.

'I'm glad you've come back,' said Paris.

'I'm glad too,' I said. I looked at Mama's portrait.

'A remarkable likeness?'

We exchanged glances.

'You've seen my work. Let me see yours.' Paris reached for my sketchbook.

I was so ashamed of my childish scribble that I tore the page out, crumpled it into a ball and tossed it in the wastepaper basket.

'Oh dear,' said Paris. He bent over the basket to retrieve it.

'Please don't!' I said. 'It's quite terrible, truly.'

'Then show me a sketch you're proud of.'

'I'm not proud of any of them. Mama's right, I'm not making any progress whatsoever,' I said.

'Show me!'

I stepped away so that he couldn't see as I flicked through the pages of my sketchbook. I was so relieved that I'd torn out all the portraits of him. I chose one of Papa, blushing as I held it out.

'You see? It's no good, is it?' I said.

I expected him to argue, and tell me I showed promise, like Papa. Instead he shook his head.

'Do you want me to be truthful?' he asked.

'Yes please. Absolutely truthful. I shan't mind a bit,' I said.

'All right,' he said. 'It's good enough, quite competent, but it's just a schoolgirl sketch.'

I knew this, but I found I minded after all.

'I'm sorry. I think I've been too harsh,' said Paris.

'No, not at all,' I said, my voice a bit wobbly.

'I'm comparing your sketches with students' work at the Academy, which is ridiculous of me. They're really . . .' He was obviously searching for the right word.

'Promising?' I said.

'Yes!'

'That's what Papa says. With that exact intonation,' I said, sighing. 'I think Mama is right: I *am* wasting my time.'

'Do you *enjoy* sketching, Rose?'

'Not really.'

Not at all, actually. It's so boring sticking to what I can see. I go tense and my hand gets tired and my neck aches from looking up and looking down. I don't know how Paris and Papa can paint all day, working on the same little patch of canvas.

'What do you like to do most then?'

'Reading. Writing. Daydreaming! I *do* like drawing, but only my own comic nonsense.'

'What sort of comic nonsense?' Paris asked. 'Show me.'

'I just scribble silly stuff. Papa laughs at it but says it's time for me to start doing serious work. Perhaps I'm simply not a serious person,' I said.

'Let's see. Please.'

I ran to fetch my old drawing book. He held out his hand.

'They're very childish. I did most of them ages ago,' I said breathlessly.

Paris flipped through the book. He chuckled at the goblin Algies and paused at the Wild Girls.

'Oh, Rose,' he said. He stared long and hard, turning his head this way and that, noting every detail. Then he looked up at me, his eyes shining.

'They're good. They're *really* good. Witty and wicked and wonderful! Your papa is quite wrong, bless him. This *is* serious work. Seriously original, seriously funny! You must carry on in this vein, Rose. I think they've got enormous potential.'

'Truly? You're not just being kind now?'

'I'm not kind. I'm honest,' said Paris. 'I don't believe in flattery.'

'That's not true! You're forever flattering Mama!' I protested.

'That's true, I grant you, because I'm hoping to be royally paid for the portrait,' said Paris. 'I flatter all potential patrons – but I'm brutally honest with my friends.'

He counts me as his friend!

13

I **DEFINITELY DIDN'T WANT** to sketch any more – but I didn't want to miss out on the morning studio sessions! Up till noon every day I *pretended* to sketch. Whenever Mama glanced over she saw me bent over my sketchbook, working hard. I was doing my own comic drawing.

I worked on a series of cartoons called *The Artist and His Model.* I drew Mama posing, simpering and self-conscious, while behind his easel Paris put his hand to his brow, despairing. He painted a life-like portrait of a foolish fat woman, and then crossed it out and started a flattering portrait. I ended up with a cartoon of Mama grinning like the Cheshire Cat at the finished painting, while a smiling Paris went off with a huge sack of money.

If Mama had seen this she would have been mortified! I would have to hide my sketchbook carefully now. Heaven help me if Algie got hold of it. He seems to have a sixth sense about my secret things. I know he often searches through my drawers for hidden trinkets. I can always tell, because he leaves my ribbons and sashes and stockings in a tangle. He is the worst brother in the world.

Sebastian is also in my bad books. He rescued a little brown mouse from a trap that Cook had set in the kitchen, christened her Miranda, and gave her to Montmorency as a bride. They seemed wary of each other initially, but soon settled into wedded bliss.

'I think she might be going to have babies soon!' Sebastian announced one day. 'She needs a separate cage now – I've read all about it in *Suitable Pet Animals for Boys.*'

He made her a little private residence in an old dented copper kettle, lining it with soft leaves and moss, liberally sprinkled with cheese crumbs.

He looked at it, frowning. 'I can't keep it in the night nursery because Nurse will see it and make me set Miranda free in the garden, and then Mistletoe might catch her when he goes for his nightly prowl,' he said.

So I let Sebastian hide Miranda's kettle in my room, because I rather liked the idea of baby mice, but later, when she was cleaning my room, Maggie knocked the kettle onto its side and Miranda and all her children escaped. Sebastian caught a couple, but couldn't find the rest, and now I'm kept awake by scuffles and squeaks from behind the wainscoting.

So both Algie and Sebastian were out of favour. I disliked *all* my brothers, especially Rupert, because he'd betrayed me and hadn't written to me even once. I didn't let myself get excited at the thought that he was coming home for half term, from Friday afternoon till Tuesday morning.

Mama told Cook to prepare all Master Rupert's favourite dishes, until the kitchen table and the larder shelves and even the windowsills were crowded with plates and bowls, and poor Mary-Jane was sobbing under the table because Cook had boxed her ears for letting the custard curdle.

Papa painted a huge banner saying: *Welcome Home, Rupert.* He hung it over the door, flapping above the stone lions. The children were in such a state that Miss Rayner abandoned lessons and let them play Battledore and Shuttlecock in the garden to let off steam. Beth became overly excited too, saying Rupert's name over and over again, tossing her head from side to side and wringing her hands until Nurse Budd gave her a dose of her medicine to calm her down.

'I don't know why you're all getting in such a state,' I said coolly. 'Who cares if Rupert is coming back?'

Mama and Papa went to the railway station to meet him. The whole household stood on the front steps, servants at the back, Nurse and the children at the front, while Nurse Budd and Beth peered out of the upstairs window.

I was too proud to join them. I went to the window seat and sat there with a book, although I have to admit that I read a very long poem by Tennyson without taking in a word of it. I heard a great cheer as the hansom cab drove up. Then the entire household burst in through the door, laughing and shouting and clamouring like the crowds at the Queen's Golden Jubilee.

I stared at my page, the lines flashing up and down like skipping ropes. Then the book was snatched from my lap and tossed aside.

'Hey, Miss Head-in-a-Book!' Rupert was laughing in my face – the old Rupert, my twin, his hair tousled and falling in his eyes, his cheeks flushed with merriment.

I burst into tears and threw my arms around his neck so violently I nearly tumbled both of us down the stairs.

'Oh, Rupert, I'm so glad to see you,' I sobbed.

'Stow it, you silly,' he said briskly. 'Let me get my frightful uniform off. This collar is murder on a chap's neck.'

His uniform was actually very grand, the tail coat making him look like a real gentleman, though the trousers were already too short.

'You've grown!' I said.

'It would be more surprising if I'd shrunk,' said Rupert.

'So what is school like? You're so lucky! Can you speak Latin and Greek yet?' I asked.

'What was it they said about Shakespeare? "Small Latin and less Greek." So far I can only chant about love and war and tables in Latin, and I can barely get through the Greek alphabet. Shame I can't crib off you, Rosy Posy, you'd learn it all in a flash,' said Rupert.

He might have been an inch taller, but he was still my dear funny brother. He hadn't turned into a ridiculous lovestruck ninny, even if he was pining after loathsome Pamela.

We didn't have time to talk properly for ages. Mama insisted we take tea in her drawing room, which was hard on the little ones because they were banished to the nursery. Rupert took them up a plate of cakes afterwards – cream buns and jam puffs and brandy snaps. They fell upon them with cries of joy. Algie and Clarrie seized a snap each, pretending they were cigars. Sebastian delicately licked the cream off his bun, and then, after two bites, put it in his pocket for Montmorency.

Nurse protested that the cakes were much too rich and would give the children stomach ache. Rupert told her she was an old fusspot and insisted she had a jam puff to celebrate his homecoming. Nurse would have been sharp with me if *I'd* called her a fusspot, but she just giggled and said, 'Really, Mr Rupert!'

Mr Rupert? So he'd stopped being Master since he went away to school? We were exactly the same age, but he was treated like a man now, whereas I was still a child.

Rupert didn't forget Beth. He selected a meringue with pink whipped cream, and asked Cook to serve it on a little gold-rimmed pink plate from the best Sèvres china.

'I hardly dare, Mr Rupert. Not for one of the children!' she said, shocked.

I was astonished too. 'For *Beth*?' I asked.

'I want her to have the very best,' said Rupert.

'I want that too, but you know how she throws things.'

'She won't throw the plate. If she feels like throwing things she'll chuck the meringue instead,' said Rupert.

'At Nurse Budd! Oh, I do hope she does.'

'What's she like, this Nurse Budd? Mama waxes lyrical about her in her letters.'

'I can't stand her. She pretends to be so fond and warm, but she's really as cold as a steel trap,' I said.

'I can't wait to meet her!'

We went to her room and knocked until Nurse Budd put her head round the door.

'How do you do, Nurse Budd. I'm Rupert, the eldest son,' he said.

'Eldest by fifteen minutes,' I insisted.

'I'm glad to make your acquaintance, Mr Rupert,' said Nurse Budd.

'We've brought Beth a treat, Nurse Budd,' he said, proffering the plate.

'That's very kind, Mr Rupert, but she's having a little nap just now. Too much excitement! I'll give her a little taste when she wakes up,' said Nurse Budd.

172

Rupert stood his ground. 'We'll wake her up now,' he said firmly. 'And I don't want her to have just a little taste. I'd like her to eat it all. I know she's got a sweet tooth and I want her to have a treat.'

I stared at him. He spoke with such calm authority. He really *did* seem older now. No wonder the servants called him Mr.

'I really don't think that's wise, Mr Rupert,' said Nurse Budd. 'I'm a trained nurse and—'

Rupert didn't listen. He walked straight past her into the room.

Beth was lying on her bed, fully dressed apart from her shoes, fast asleep with Marigold beside her. Her hand was gripping the doll's china fingers.

'Wake up, Beth,' said Rupert, sitting down on the edge of the bed. 'It's me, Rupert.'

'Rupert,' she murmured.

'Yes, that's right. Sit up a little. Prop her pillows up, Rose. Look, Beth, we've brought you a treat,' Rupert said, coaxing her.

Beth wriggled up and peered at the cake. 'A treat,' she said.

'Yes, you can eat it all.'

'Eat it all?'

'Yes, because you're my special sister,' said Rupert. 'I love baby Phoebe because she's so sweet, and I love Clarrie because she's so funny, and I love old Rosy-Posy here because she's my twin and my best friend, but you're my very special sister, Beth. I miss you very much when I'm away at school.'

'Eat it all?' Beth repeated, running her finger round the gold rim of the plate.

'All the cake. I wouldn't eat the plate too because it might cut your lips, but I dare say you can lick it,' said Rupert.

Beth doesn't seem to understand jokes. She seized hold of the cake and took a huge bite, getting cream all round her mouth and spraying the front of her dress with crumbs.

'Oh dear, you're making such a mess, Miss Beth. Let me mop you up,' said Nurse Budd, darting towards her with a handkerchief.

Beth ducked away, protesting.

'Leave her be, Nurse Budd. Let her enjoy her cake,' said Rupert.

We waited while Beth gobbled it all up. She ate with such abandon that she even had a smear of cream in her hair.

'There, special sister! Was it good?' asked Rupert.

'Good!' said Beth, licking her lips.

'Bless her,' said Nurse Budd. 'Still, someone's not going to want their nice nourishing bowl of bread and milk for supper!'

I hated her slightly menacing tone.

'Do you think Nurse Budd is horrid to Beth when we're not there?' I said when we were out on the landing.

'How do I know?' said Rupert. 'You always fuss about things, Rose. Just be happy that Beth enjoyed a topping cake. It was actually the one *I* wanted most. Didn't she just wolf it down!'

'You were lovely to give it to her. But I can't *help* worrying about her. Nurse Budd keeps her practically a prisoner.'

'After I've left school I'll set up home, and Beth can come and live with me. I'll make sure she has the sweetest, kindest nurse ever, and she'll be so happy she'll never, ever throw another tantrum,' said Rupert, swaggering down the stairs.

He had his future all mapped out. He didn't even have to make his own way in the world. Grandpapa would make sure that he had a huge allowance, and leave the Scottish jute mill to him. It was all so easy for Rupert.

'What?' he said, seeing me looking wistful. 'You can come and live with me too, Rose, you know that.'

'What about your future wife?' I asked him. 'Won't she mind Beth and me living with you?'

'I'm not sure I want to bother with a wife. I intend to have capital fun leading a bachelor life.'

'Does Pamela know this?' I asked before I could stop myself.

'Pamela?' said Rupert. He tried to sound astonished but he went very red. Rupert rarely blushes, but when he does it's always painfully obvious. Even his ears go red. He suddenly didn't look so grown up and dashing standing there on the stairs, the Sèvres plate held loosely in his hand. He seemed to have forgotten he was holding it.

'Watch the plate!' I warned.

Edie was scurrying out of the drawing room with the left-over tea things on a silver tray. Rupert carefully put the plate on it.

'Could you return this to Cook for me and tell her that Miss Beth was utterly delighted,' he said, composed again.

'Certainly, Mr Rupert,' said Edie, bobbing him a curtsy with difficulty because she was clutching the tray.

Mama was calling for Rupert, but he suddenly linked arms with me.

'Let's take a stroll in the garden,' he said. 'I'm not sure I can take any more of Mama just now. "Well, darling boy, are you captain of the rugby team yet? Are you top of the form? Have you made many friends and are any of them titled?"' His imitation was cruelly accurate.

We made for the servants' quarters so that we could slip out through the back door. This meant that Rupert had to compliment Cook on her cake, ask Mr Hodgson about his rheumatics, tease Maggie, and give Jack Boots and Mary-Jane a polished penny each.

'You're quite the little lord of the manor now,' I said.

'It's good to be home,' said Rupert, squeezing my arm.

'Why didn't you write to me, Rupert?'

'I was missing you so much,' he said smoothly. 'I might have blubbed in front of the other boys.'

We let ourselves out of the stout back door and wandered through the vegetable garden picking blackberries, circled the greenhouse and then walked the length of the lawn, asters and Michaelmas daisies on either side, until we reached the long grass beneath the apple trees. This was our favourite place. We had always eaten windfalls until we had stomach ache, and climbed the old oak right at the end of the garden.

'So which do you like best, home or school?' I asked.

'*East, West, Home's Best*,' said Rupert.

'So I gather you're *not* captain of the rugby team or top of the form or the most popular boy in the class?' I asked.

'Mama's hopeless. You don't get to be in the team at all till you're at least fifteen. Though I am third in the form actually, which is not bad considering Robinson Minor is top and Newburg is second, and they are both sad brainboxes who are definitely *not* the most popular boys,' said Rupert.

'Papa told me he hated school.'

'Yes, well, Papa would. He's not very good at fitting in.'

'But you are?'

'You have to be, or they pick on you and make your life a misery,' Rupert explained.

'The masters?'

'No, they're not too bad. Apart from old Beetlebrow – he beats anyone who so much as sneezes in his class.'

'He's beaten *you*?'

'Yes, because I deliberately played the fool to annoy him and amuse the other boys. *That's* the way to be popular.'

'But didn't the beating hurt terribly?'

'It's not too bad, especially if you pad your under-things with a nightshirt. And he's old so he hasn't the strength to make really deep weals with his cane,' Rupert said. 'The other boys can hurt you far more – kicking or flailing with wet towels. Don't look like that, Rose. No one lays a finger on me. I reckon I *am* the most popular boy in the class. The only boy who tells *me* what to do is Mackinley. He's quite decent actually. He's only punished me once so far.'

'He's *allowed* to punish you?'

'He's in the upper sixth. I have to be his servant,' said Rupert. He said it matter-of-factly, though I could tell that he was embarrassed.

'Why do you?'

'The boys at the top of the school get the new boys to do their chores,' he said.

'What sort of chores?' I asked.

'Oh, I have to make his breakfast every morning,' Rupert said cheerily. 'Of course, *we* all have to take our brekker in the House dining room, but the upper sixth take theirs in their study. Mackinley has a little stove. Most days I cook him sausages. He sometimes lets me have one. Then I have to make sure he's got hot water. And I clean his boots. He's very particular about those blessed boots.'

'So you have to act like Cook and Maggie and Jack Boots for this boy just because he's older than you?' I asked incredulously. 'You must be mad, Rupert. Tell him you're not his servant!'

'Now that *would* be mad. It's the tradition. All the new boys have to do it. Some of the sixth form make their lives hell. Newburg gets beaten practically every day. The other boys hear him snivelling at night, and then they jeer.'

'That's horrible! Can't you stick up for him?'

'Then they'd start on *me*,' said Rupert. 'If I start championing poor old Newburg, I'll be in trouble. You have to put yourself first at school. That's the way it is. You have to get people on your side.'

'You're so good at that. You can charm everyone. All these horrible boys, all the family, all the servants,' I said. Then, pulling a face, I added, 'And Pamela.'

'Don't let's mock Pamela,' said Rupert. 'My so-called charm's not enough to win over all the chaps at school. It's my knowledge that holds them in thrall.'

'But you're not the cleverest. You said Newburg and that other boy were brainier than you.'

'I know stuff that they don't. Things that boys talk about,' said Rupert.

'What stuff?'

'You wouldn't understand it,' Rupert said maddeningly.

'I *would*! I know just as much as you, apart from Latin and Greek!'

'This is filthy stuff,' said Rupert.

I was baffled. 'You mean the sort of silly nonsense Algie comes out with?'

'No! Well, a bit like that. But it's about . . . bodies.'

'*Bodies?*'

'Do stow it, Rose!' said Rupert hastily, looking at the fence behind us as if half of Kensington were crouched there, listening. 'It's what people do with their bodies,' he whispered.

My heart started thumping.

'They talk about it all the time at school. Even Mackinley and his friends. It's the main topic of conversation in our dorm, especially after lights out,' said Rupert. 'And anyone who knows just a little bit more than anyone else is Top Man.'

'But you don't know anything, do you?' I asked.

'I read a racy booklet. I actually bought it off a chap down a back street.'

'You didn't!'

'He said I was too young, but I gave him twice what he was asking. I wanted to find out all about it.'

'You *are* too young!' I said.

'Anyway, I know more than the other boys now. I made out I'd actually got a sweetheart and done some of the things in the booklet.'

'*Rupert!*'

'Hardy and Martin and all the boys in my dorm believed me. But Mackinley got wind of it and found it funny, though he punished me for telling lies. So then I thought I might try to manufacture some proof to show him. I wrote this letter to Pamela.'

'You wrote a filthy letter to *Pamela*?'

'Not a filthy one, idiot. She'd have thrown it away – or shown it to her mama!' said Rupert.

We both went into peals of laughter at the thought of Mrs Feynsham-Jones reading such a letter.

'It was all lovey-dovey, gush-gush stuff about how I'd grown fond of her and was missing her. Nothing too dreadful.'

'But it *is* dreadful to string her along when you don't mean a word of it,' I said priggishly, though inside I was rejoicing. So he didn't really care about her at all!

'It's not dreadful, not when she seems so happy. She wrote back and said ridiculously soppy things, declaring she kissed my letter every night and longed to be close to me again. I showed it all round the dorm and they were very impressed. Mackinley was still suspicious and thought it was a letter from my sister.'

'How dare he! As if I'd ever write such a letter!' I said furiously.

'Yes, but he doesn't know you, does he? So then I asked Pamela to send me her photograph and she did, and then he could see that we're not a bit alike, and anyway his people vaguely know the Feynsham-Joneses. He recognized Pamela. He laughed his head off and clapped me on the shoulder. Now Mackinley and half the upper sixth call me Casanova. He was a famous Italian chap who had lots of affairs,' said Rupert, swaggering.

'He was a man though, not a boy,' I said. 'Rupert, you're only thirteen!'

'People say I look more like sixteen. *Pamela* says,' he told me, laughing. Then he pulled a silly girly face and said in a high-pitched voice, 'Oh, Rooooopert, you're so grown up now!'

I couldn't help laughing too as we went indoors. Algie and Clarrie came running up, demanding to know what we were laughing at. Rupert made a fuss of them, giving them piggybacks and galloping so fast that they squealed in delight.

I saw that Sebastian was watching. Rupert offered him a piggyback too, but he shook his head shyly.

'I don't think Montmorency would like it,' he explained.

'Well, we mustn't upset Montmorency, because he's such a good-natured, handsome fellow, the lord of all little rodents,' said Rupert.

He was teasing, but Sebastian glowed.

The children complained bitterly when Nurse came to chivvy them upstairs for supper and bed. Rupert and I joined Mama and Papa for grown-up dinner. Mama monopolized the conversation, making plans for the weekend.

'I'd really like to keep you all to myself, my darling, but I also want to show you off to our friends. You've grown so in just half a term! I dare say when you come home at Christmas you'll be as tall as your papa,' she said. 'Though of course you're not so very tall yourself, are you, Edward? Rupert clearly takes after my side of the family. My papa is well over six foot, and still very spry and slender. He looks very manly in the kilt. We'll have to get you measured for a new kilt for Hogmanay, dear boy.'

'So which friends are you going to invite, Mama? How about the Feynsham-Joneses? I believe Rose has chummed up with the girls while I've been away at school.'

Mama thought this an *excellent* idea.

14

MAMA INVITED THE Feynsham-Joneses for afternoon tea the next day. I felt ill at the thought of seeing them again, especially Pamela. It's a great relief to discover that Rupert doesn't care for her in the slightest. Still, I do wish he wouldn't talk about her in such a sordid way at school.

Pamela's been so carefully brought up. She surely wouldn't even let Rupert hold her hand. They're only *children*, though they both look much older than me. Why is Rupert like this? He's the one who always jokes around. This morning he actually slid down the banisters and landed smack on the floor. It must have hurt him, but he just laughed.

Mama cried out in consternation, and Papa came running down from his studio.

'Really, Rupert, must you always act the fool?' he said, shaking his head. 'You're worrying your mama and your sister.'

Papa put his arm round my shoulders. 'Glad to have your brother back, poppet? Are you happy now?'

I nodded.

'How's the sketching going, eh? Is Paris helping you at all?'

'I really don't think I have much talent, Papa,' I said.

'I'm not sure *I* have sometimes,' he said. 'Not any more.' He said it lightly, and smiled, but he looked very tense.

'Papa, are *you* happy now?' I whispered.

He looked startled. 'Of course I am, my pet. And your mama is clearly in seventh heaven now that Rupert is back. She's plotting a splendid tea party this afternoon.'

Mama wanted to include the younger children, but planned to have them play prettily in the garden as soon as they'd had a bite to eat. She thought Beth too great a risk and told Nurse Budd to take her out for a walk shortly before the Feynsham-Joneses were due to arrive.

However, the sky suddenly darkened and there was a serious downpour. Nurse Budd had only just bundled Beth into her coat and hat and boots, and now she had to take them off again. Beth protested noisily.

'Oh my Lord,' said Mama, almost in tears. 'I was banking on Nurse Budd keeping Beth out of the way. And now she's started one of her turns. We shall have to cancel the party!'

'Rose,' Papa murmured. 'Go and comfort your mother.'

I refused. She wouldn't appreciate my comfort. Anyway, I *wanted* the party to be cancelled.

Papa looked at me, and then gave my shoulder a squeeze. 'All right. You run upstairs and see if you can calm Beth. *I'll* look after your mama.

'There now, Jeannie.' He put his arms round her and held her close, there in the dining room in front of everyone.

I thought Mama would push him away, but she gave a little sob and rested her head on his chest. We all stared, Algie and Clarrie nudging each other and giggling.

I hurried upstairs. Beth's screams were deafening now. She was lying on the floor, half in and half out of her coat, drumming her boots on the carpet.

'Beth, for heaven's sake! You must stop making such a row! Mama is going frantic and we're expecting visitors,' I said, seizing hold of her.

Beth only cried harder.

'There now, Miss Rose, leave her to me. I'll soon quieten her,' said Nurse Budd. 'It's pointless trying to reason with her when she's in such a paddy.'

'Perhaps we might give her some cake,' I suggested.

'Cake! She was sick three times in the night after that great creamy cake she had. Three changes of sheets!

I don't want that performance again tonight, thank you very much.'

I tried sitting down beside Beth and talking to her, but she was screaming so hard the veins on her forehead stood out.

'I'm scared she's going to have a fit,' I said.

'This will calm her,' said Nurse Budd, going to her case by the washstand. 'A little dose of Godfrey's Cordial and she'll be as right as rain. It'll soothe her.'

'But it seems to make her so sleepy,' I said.

'Well, a nice little nap never did anyone any harm, Miss Rose. Here, Miss Beth, hold still a minute for your spoonful of magic medicine. You don't want to spill it over your coat, now do you?'

Beth was suddenly still as still, though she was still gasping and sobbing, tears streaming down her face. She swallowed the cordial and then let Nurse Budd ease her out of her crumpled coat.

'There now, dear. Time for bye-byes,' said Nurse Budd. 'Off you go, Miss Rose. There'll be scarcely a peep out of her now.'

I went downstairs again, feeling a little anxious. Rupert was lounging in front of the fireplace. Nurse had taken the little ones upstairs to be suitably prepared for the party.

'Where are Papa and Mama?' I asked Rupert.

'Upstairs,' he said. 'He's calming her down.'

'They're so strange, aren't they? They snap at each other all the time, and then they act like two lovebirds,

187

just the way they used to. Remember when we were little and Papa used to toss us up in the air – and then once he tossed Mama up in the air too.'

Rupert raised his eyebrows. 'I don't remember them romping around like that!'

'They did, they did,' I insisted.

Papa would sometimes take Mama on his lap, dandling her like a little child. He'd kiss her cheek and pet her and pull out her hairpins so that her dark curls came tumbling down past her shoulders. She always protested and tried to slap his hands away, but you could tell she didn't really mind.

When did they stop being fond of each other? Was it after Beth was born, or after Sebastian and Algie and Clarrie? There was a gap after Clarrie. Mama had had another baby then, before Phoebe, but it was very small and puny, and died after only a few days. I remember being taken in to see it, a tiny boy lying in a much-too-big christening gown. His face was yellow like an old wax doll. I dreamed about him for weeks. Perhaps Mama did too, because for a long time she was very sad. That was about the time Papa started painting Louisa.

I wished Mama and Papa could be happy together again. They came back downstairs hand in hand, Papa as gentle with Mama as if she were an invalid. She had changed into the blue dress she'd worn for her portrait. She'd smoothed her hair and put on some powder. Her eyes were a little red, but otherwise she looked perfectly composed. Papa had changed too, discarding his paint-spattered corduroys for a formal suit and tie – very dull and ordinary, though I suppose he looked handsome.

Nurse managed to get all the children washed and brushed and in their best clothes before the Feynsham-Joneses arrived. Baby Phoebe was looking exceptionally sweet, her fluffy hair sticking up in ducks' tails. Rupert looked lankily elegant in his colourful waistcoat, the gold chain of Grandpapa's watch gleaming brightly. He seemed very grown up and dashing. I could see why Pamela was so taken with him.

At first she sat right at the other end of the room, pretending to take an interest in Clarrie, asking her endless questions about her dolls and her dresses. Clarrie was pleased to have the attention of a much older girl, especially a pretty one with blonde curls. Clarrie now longed for long, wavy fair hair like the princesses in her storybooks. She sometimes walked around with Papa's yellow silk scarf draped over her head as a makeshift wig.

She stared at Pamela's beautiful hair for several minutes, and then put out a hand and fingered one of the curls as if checking it was real. Clarrie's hands are usually sticky, so I didn't blame Pamela for pushing her away. Clarrie pouted and went to sit with Algie at the end of the table. Sebastian slid onto her vacated seat and started talking to Pamela. He *is* interested in dresses and dolls, though he's not allowed either.

But Pamela edged away from him and Lucinda-May stood up in terror, remembering her last visit, when

Montmorency made a bolt for freedom. Sebastian promised them that Montmorency was safely locked in his cage, but they didn't seem convinced.

'Perhaps you'd like to run and check on him, Sebastian,' said Papa.

Then Rupert took the chair beside Pamela and spoke in a low voice, his head very close to hers. I couldn't hear properly, but Pamela soon calmed down and started smiling.

Suddenly I caught a glimpse of my face in the looking glass above the mantelpiece. I was scowling. Was Rupert playing a game or was he really fond of Pamela?

Letting the little ones have tea with us was a bad idea. They spilled their milk on the tablecloth and ate with their mouths open, and Algie had a coughing fit and sprayed everyone with crumbs. Mortified by their behaviour, Nurse took them up to the nursery as soon as she could.

I was stuck between Lucinda-May and Cecily. That morning they had gone riding in Rotten Row and talked about it endlessly, while I yawned.

'It's such a shame you don't care for riding, Rose,' they said, and smirked at each other.

I wished I'd been sent back upstairs with the little ones. At least I could eat with gusto there. Mama kept frowning at me and dabbing at her lips with her napkin, so I gathered that I had smears of jam or cream on my cheeks. Cook had made an enormous batch of choux buns, but when I reached for a second one, Mama shook her head vigorously.

The Feynsham-Jones girls all ate daintily, nibbling like Montmorency, choosing the smallest, plainest cakes. Pamela scarcely ate anything, her eyes on Rupert.

He glanced out of the window. 'It's stopped raining, thank goodness,' he said. 'Pamela, you look a little flushed. Would you care to take a stroll around the garden if you've finished your tea?'

'I *am* rather hot. Yes, that would be a good idea,' she said.

Lucinda-May and Cecily clamoured to go out as well.

'Of course. Come along, girls, we'll all take a turn,' Rupert said smoothly.

'What a little gentleman,' Mrs Feynsham-Jones murmured. 'My girls think the world of him. You're so lucky to have a son, Mrs Rivers.'

She clearly wasn't thinking of Sebastian or Algie! I was pleased Lucinda-May and Cecily were joining the party. *Serve Rupert right*, I thought. *Now he's stuck with all three and he will find it very tedious.*

But when I went to the window five minutes later, I saw Lucinda-May and Cecily galloping up and down the path together, their hands out in front as if they were holding reins. They were whinnying at each other, playing their own private game. Rupert and Pamela were at the very end of the garden under the oak tree, scarcely visible.

Why did he have to take her down to *our* part of the garden? I saw that their heads were very close together. What was he whispering to her?

I rested my forehead on the cool glass. I was feeling hot too. I wondered about going out and joining them, but I was too proud. I just watched, my heart beating fast as they started wandering back again. They paused by the greenhouse, and then Rupert opened the door and they went inside.

He seemed to be showing Pamela the plants. Then he picked up some pruning shears. Was he going to cut a flower and make her a little nosegay? She was giggling and shaking her head. Then she ran her fingers through her long curls, holding them out in front of her, examining them carefully. She chose one that was perhaps a little longer than the others. Rupert leaned forward, holding the shears. Then I saw the steel flash as he gave a quick snip.

They came out of the greenhouse and walked up the garden. Pamela was looking at Rupert, hanging on his every word. But Rupert was looking towards the house, straight at me, as if he knew I'd be watching from behind the curtain. He patted the pocket where he'd put the lock of hair, and smiled.

'Did you see?' he said later, when the Feynsham-Joneses were gone at last. 'She actually let me cut off a curl!'

'I saw. You've cast such a spell on her she'd let you shave her head if you begged her,' I said. 'You should be ashamed of yourself, Rupert.'

'The boys in my dorm will go wild when they see it. I'll spin them all kinds of stories.'

192

'You're horrible. I feel sorry for Pamela,' I said.

'You can't stand the girl,' said Rupert.

'I can't stand you either,' I told him.

'You're just jealous,' he said, looking smug.

'Jealous of *you*?'

'Jealous that you're not part of a romantic intrigue yourself.'

'How can you call your horrid scheming romantic?'

'You hate the idea of any kind of romance, Rosy-Posy. You'll end up a sad old spinster, scowling at other folks' fun. You'll never know what it's like to love.'

'Well, actually you're quite wrong,' I said heatedly. 'I *do* know!'

'Yes, you love Papa and Mama and me and Beth and Sebastian and Clarrie and the baby, and I dare say deep down you even love Algie, but that's not what I mean. You're still too young to understand.' Rupert shook his head at me in mock sorrow.

'I understand perfectly. And I do love in just the way you're implying. I love someone who's nothing to do with the family,' I said rashly.

'You can't fool me,' said Rupert. Then he looked at me properly and saw that I was blushing. 'What? Hey! You're serious! You've got a pash!' He started laughing.

'Don't use that horrid word,' I said. 'And stop laughing!'

'It's such a joke. You're in love! Who *is* it?'

'I'm not telling you.'

'I can always wheedle stuff out of you,' said Rupert. 'So who can it be? You don't *know* anyone, that's the trouble. I can't think of any boys your age. Oh, hang on! It's Jack Boots!' He started making up a ridiculous story about Jack writing love letters in boot polish.

I stayed disdainfully silent, so Rupert switched tack.

'Of course, you're such a serious bluestocking that you'd tire of an uncouth young lad in five minutes. No, you'd go for a mature gentleman . . . one with a certain standing and excellent manners. It's obvious! You've got a pash on Mr Hodgson!'

I rolled my eyes and yawned, but perhaps Rupert had seen me tense when he said the words 'mature gentleman'.

'Or maybe . . . maybe it's one of Papa's friends,' he said.

I tried hard to keep my expression blank, my breathing even.

'It's dear old Mr Rossetti! You'll have to grow a lot taller and sprout a massive head of hair if you want him to paint you, but I'm sure he's not too fussy in his fuddled old age,' said Rupert.

'You're the one who's fuddled, because he's been dead for years! And don't talk about him like that! He was a genius. Really, Rupert, you can be so crass sometimes.'

'So are you, fancying yourself in love when you're still a little stay-at-home ignoramus. I expect the mystery man in your life is having a good laugh at you,' he said.

Rupert has always had a streak of cruelty running through him. When I was little he tormented me, making me play Hide-and-Seek at night and then running off into the pitch-black attics, even though he knew I was scared of the dark. He hid the little pink velvet pig I used to take to bed with me, and only 'find' him when I was frantic. He pushed me over and pretended I'd tripped, he stole my lucky sixpence and scribbled all over my best drawings. He could be every bit as maddening as Algie – and yet he could also be so sweet and gentle that I was willing to forgive him anything.

I'm not going to forgive him now.

15

IF PARIS HAD COME to the house as usual, Rupert would have guessed that I loved him. Luckily the portrait painting had been abandoned for a few days as Mama wanted to spend as much time as possible with Rupert.

All Sunday he behaved like a dutiful son, attending church so that Mama could show him off to the entire congregation.

'What shall we do for your last day at home, darling?' she asked him at breakfast on Monday morning.

'I rather thought I'd take myself off for a trip to the Kensington museums,' said Rupert.

Mama's face fell.

'Why don't we all take a little trip?' Papa suggested. 'Yes, let's go on a family outing.'

'All of us?' said Mama.

'Why not?'

'But where would we go?'

'We could *all* go to the Kensington museums – or perhaps go to see the Egyptian mummies in the British Museum,' said Papa.

'Algie and Clarrie would run amok!' said Rupert quickly. 'And I dare say the mummies would frighten Sebastian and give him nightmares. No, I think it's better if I simply slope off for the morning. I've taken a fancy to seeing the stuffed animals in the Natural History Museum.'

Rupert had told me that those stuffed animals with their sad eyes made him shudder. I looked at him sharply.

'I wonder if the Feynsham-Jones girls are going there with their governess this morning,' I said.

'Why on earth would you think that?' Rupert said, glaring at me.

But he'd given Papa an idea. 'Bother the stuffed animals! Why don't we go and see some real ones? Let's all go to the Zoological Gardens! We haven't been there since you were a little boy, Rupert, but remember how you loved it, especially the elephant ride!'

'I'm a bit old for elephant riding now, Pa,' said Rupert.

'Nonsense! *I* intend to ride the great beast,' said Papa. 'Think how the little ones would enjoy the zoo, especially Sebastian. And if Algie misbehaves, we can always put him in a cage with the monkeys.' He put his arm round me. 'We'll sketch, Rose, and make sure we get all the creatures' legs the right way round.'

Papa was so persuasive that we all decided it was a good idea. If Rupert really *had* suggested meeting Pamela in the Natural History Museum, he seemed happy now to change his plans. I thought of her wandering mournfully round and round the glass cases looking for him. Poor Pamela!

Sebastian, Algie and Clarrie were wild with excitement. Nurse was less keen, especially when she was told she must come too, with little Phoebe. This meant carrying her, as there was no way she could get a perambulator into a cab.

'It'll scare her senseless anyway, seeing all them wild creatures marauding around and biting each other,' Nurse protested.

But Phoebe adored the animals, especially the bears. She peered down into the bear pit and stretched out her arms, whimpering urgently, wanting to be lowered down to play with them.

Algie and Clarrie liked the lions best, because they roared in a thrilling fashion when their meat was thrust into their cages.

'Thank the Lord Beth isn't here,' Papa murmured to me. 'She'd likely start roaring too.'

He sounded heartless, but earlier that morning he had wanted Beth to join us.

'Beth's behaviour has improved a good deal since I employed Nurse Budd, but I don't think she's reliable enough to trust on a family outing,' said Mama.

'Then Nurse Budd can accompany us too, and ensure that Beth behaves. Beth is family too, my dear. Rose, go and tell Nurse Budd to get Beth ready.'

I ran upstairs eagerly, but Nurse Budd stopped me at the door.

'Ssh now! You can't just burst in here, Miss Rose. I'll thank you to remember to knock,' she whispered. 'Now, I'm afraid I'm going to have to send you away. Your sister isn't ready for visitors right at this moment.'

'Why can't I see her?' I asked. Had she done something cruel to Beth? I imagined her tied to the chair, a gag about her mouth. I took a deep breath. 'You might be trained as a nurse but you are still our servant. So just jolly well let me see my sister.'

I pushed past her into the room. Beth was lying in bed, quite still.

'Beth! Beth!' I cried, rushing over to her. 'What's the matter? Are you ill? What has she done to you?'

'Oh dear, Miss Rose, there's no need to get yourself into such a silly state. My little Beth's simply staying in bed this morning because she had a disturbed night,' said Nurse Budd, shaking her head at me. 'Don't raise

199

your voice, dear, she needs to catch up on her sleep. She had a nightmare, and then when she woke she was too scared to get out of bed onto her pot so she had a little accident, naughty girl. But I wouldn't dream of punishing her. I know the poor soul can't help it.'

'But Papa wants Beth to come with us to the Zoological Gardens.' I shook Beth gently. 'Come on, Beth, wake up. You must come and see the lions and the bears and the elephant with us.'

Beth murmured something crossly, and pulled the sheet over her head.

'I don't think she wants to, Miss Rose, do you?' said Nurse Budd.

'Papa will be upset,' I said.

'I'm sorry about that, but I do know what's best for your sister.'

'But you never want her to have any treats!'

'Oh, it's easy enough to spoil the poor child and get her over-stimulated. You're all very good at doing that. But you're not the ones who have to soothe her during the day and stay up with her half the night. You seem to upset Miss Beth every time you come near her, Miss Rose. I know you're full of good intentions, but it is a little trying at times. Do you really think that you could care for her better than me?'

I didn't have an answer for Nurse Budd, and she knew it. I had to give up. Beth stayed at home.

Afterwards I felt unsettled, and couldn't stop thinking about Beth as I wandered around the zoo. Nurse Budd is right: Papa loves Beth and makes a fuss of her sometimes, but he's certainly not prepared to look after her.

Mama rarely goes near Beth, even when she's quiet and docile. She doesn't seem to have time for any of her children, apart from Rupert, though when we're out on show she acts as if she adores us. She was especially animated at the Zoological Gardens, hanging onto Rupert's arm, forever fussing over the little ones.

'See the funny monkeys, Clarrie!'

'Algie, say hello to Mr Hippopotamus. See, he gets even muddier than you!'

'Is Montmorency peeping at all these big animals, Sebastian?'

'Yes, Phoebe precious, look at the pretty birdies!'

Nurse encouraged the children to reply politely, though she muttered under her breath, and put her handkerchief over her nose when we went into the lion enclosure because it smelled so rank.

Papa was making a big effort too, carrying Clarrie when her small legs got tired, and chanting all the Edward Lear rhymes he could think of as we trekked from cage to cage.

I mooched around by myself most of the time, but I heard a couple commenting on us.

'What a jolly family!'

'So happy, bless them!'

When we got home, Beth was awake and dressed, but she looked pale and listless. She crooned quietly to Marigold, and didn't seem interested when I told her about the animals.

The next morning she still didn't seem herself, and had dark circles under her eyes. I reported this to Mama, but she barely listened – she was too busy supervising the packing of Rupert's tuck box for the second half of term.

I tried telling Papa, but he was in an unusually bad mood as he pored over his post.

'Can you credit this, Rose? The wretched art editor at the Religious Tract Society doesn't care for my illustrations! He says the street children look too low and vulgar. He wants me to clean them up and turn them into little Kate Greenaway moppets! How dare he!'

'I'm sorry, Papa. I wonder, could you come and see Beth for a moment? I don't think she looks very well,' I said.

'Oh, for goodness' sake, Rose, do stop fussing over your sister,' he said irritably.

I felt cross with everyone. When Rupert left for school I didn't even say goodbye to him properly. Well, I *said* goodbye, but I was very cool. He didn't seem to care.

The minute the cab had disappeared round the corner I wanted to give him a proper hug. I nearly ran after it. I could probably have caught up with him in the jam of cabs and carriages and omnibuses in Kensington High Street. But I didn't go, and now I wouldn't see him until Christmas.

I started to write him a letter, but suddenly wondered if he might show it to his loathsome friends, pretending that I was yet another sweetheart, so I tore it up. I tried drawing instead. I was in such a bad mood that my sketches were very dark. I drew Beth lying in bed, her hair fanned out across the pillow, with Nurse Budd hovering over her like a ghoul. I drew Rupert in his dormitory, with evil-looking boys sniggering over his stories. I drew Mama and Papa having terrible arguments, screaming at each other, while the children cowered on the stairs. I even drew Mistletoe running off with little Montmorency in his mouth. And I drew myself sitting on the window seat, moping.

I had real cause to mope the next day: Paris didn't come. Mama and I went up to Papa's studio early, Mama squeezed into her blue silk, me wearing my best green dress. My hair was up too. At first I'd stuck pins here and there until I resembled a pin cushion, but as soon as I shook my head my hair had tumbled down.

I'd asked Nurse to help me – she used to do my hair in schoolgirl plaits and her fingers are still nimble – but she shook her head at me. 'You're too young to put your hair up, Miss Rose,' she said firmly.

I didn't waste time begging her. She doesn't know the latest styles anyway. I tried Edie instead, trapping her in Mama's dressing room.

'I have enough trouble doing your mother's hair, Miss Rose, especially now that it's thinning and she has to have false locks woven in to puff it out,' she whispered.

This came as a surprise. I hadn't dreamed that Mama's abundant hair was anything but her own.

'Is Mama going bald?' I asked bluntly.

'Hush, Miss Rose! No, no, of course not. What will you come out with next! I should have held my tongue. It's just natural thinning as she gets older – and having all you children hasn't helped,' she said. She patted her own thick hair complacently. 'Catch me having any. Well, I might consent to one when I marry my Harold, but no more. It's like a bear garden in this house with all you children. Though Mr Rupert seems to have turned into a young man in a matter of weeks.'

'Yes, he has. And I'm growing up too, Edie. So please would you help me with my hair?' I asked humbly.

'I've a hundred and one things to do this morning, and your mama had me pin her sapphire brooch this way and that, wanting it at exactly the right angle for her wretched portrait,' said Edie, sighing. 'She's taken a real fancy to that young artist fellow, hasn't she? I don't trust him an inch, even though he's done a pretty enough picture of her. He's simply stringing her along to make some money, the ne'er-do-well,' she said, shaking her head.

'You're utterly mistaken, Edie,' I said hotly. 'Mr Walker is entirely honourable. He's a protégé of my father. He's extremely talented.'

'I'll say. He's clearly stringing you along too, Miss Rose,' said Edie.

I didn't want to get into a dispute with Edie because I badly wanted her to do my hair.

'Do you have any jewellery yourself, Edie?' I asked, changing tack.

She peered at me. 'Oh yes, I've got diamond rings galore, and ruby necklaces and emerald earrings,' she said sarcastically.

'Perhaps you would like to borrow some of *my* jewellery for when you go out with your Harold,' I suggested. 'I haven't anything truly precious like Mama, but I've got a gold link bracelet, a pearl necklace, and several Scottish agate brooches sent to me by Grandmama.'

Edie looked interested. I ran and showed her the contents of my jewellery box. I didn't care for any of them, but she picked out an agate brooch with a lucky rabbit's paw attached. The thought of a rabbit hobbling around on three legs made me feel sick, but Edie said it would look pretty on the collar of her coat.

We struck a bargain. Edie sat me down, and in five minutes she had transformed me. When I peered into the looking glass I looked quite different. My hair was wound up in a great shining coil, with several strands left drifting to soften the look.

'Oh my!' I said in awe. 'I look at least fifteen! Sixteen, even.'

'You're a funny little thing, Miss Rose. I didn't think you gave a fig about your appearance,' said Edie. 'Oh well, it suits you, I'll give you that.'

It was all wasted effort. When I went into the studio Mama took one look at me and exploded.

'For heaven's sake, child, what do you look like? Take your hair down at once!'

'But, Mama, don't you think it suits me?' I was genuinely surprised. Mama was forever nagging at me to tidy my hair, and now it looked exceptionally neat.

'Of course I don't! You're just a little girl. You look ridiculous with a grown-up lady's hairstyle – and such a vulgar one too!'

This was perplexing. Mama repeatedly begged me to grow up and stop looking like a hoyden. And how could she possibly call the styling vulgar when her own maid had fashioned it for me, arranging it in much the same way as Mama's?

I peered at myself in the hand glass Mama keeps beside her to check that she isn't too flushed or shiny. Did I really look ridiculous? I still liked the gleaming coils and the soft little wisps. I saw how the new hairstyle emphasized my cheekbones and the line of my neck. I hadn't even noticed that I had prominent cheekbones and a long white neck before!

'Stop preening in that ludicrous way!' Mama snapped, and she reached out, removing handfuls of pins and scrabbling at my hair until it had tumbled past my shoulders in its usual tangles.

I struggled not to burst into tears.

'Don't make that sulky face now! Pull yourself together. I'm not having you showing me up in front of Mr Walker,' said Mama. She looked at the carriage clock on the mantelpiece. 'He'll be here any minute.'

But he wasn't. We waited and waited, but he didn't come.

Later, Papa came up to the studio. 'My goodness, where's our golden boy?' he asked.

'He's not here yet, as is obvious,' said Mama, her voice strained. 'I think something must have happened to him. Do you know where he lives, Edward? Perhaps we should send a message.'

'I don't think that's really necessary, Jeannie. I'm sure he's fine. He's a lovely chap, but he can be a little unreliable at times. I dare say he'll come tomorrow.'

He didn't come. Not the next day, or the next, or the next.

Maybe he's never coming again.

16

IT'S SO WRETCHED without Paris. I haven't been able to hide my misery. Luckily everyone thinks I'm simply missing Rupert.

The whole household is out of sorts. Beth is no longer suffering from that terrible languor, but she's so restless, and scratches her arms incessantly, making them bleed. Nurse Budd painted the scratches with gentian violet to stop infection and cut her nails really short – though Beth still managed to scratch. Now her hands are confined in big padded mittens, tied tightly at the top so that she can't pull them off.

The little children are fretful, and even baby Phoebe cries because she is teething, her cheeks scarlet. Papa is out a great deal, and Mama stays in the drawing room, issuing peevish orders to the servants. She wangled Paris's address from Papa after all, and sent an urgent message to his lodgings. His landlady replied that he had taken himself off on a little holiday and she had no idea when he might return.

'A *holiday*?' Mama said, outraged. 'But he's still got to put the finishing touches to my portrait. He didn't ask me!'

'For heaven's sake, Jeannie, he's not your servant,' said Papa. 'Artists like to feel free to come and go.'

'And they also like to eat and drink,' said Mama. 'How can he go gallivanting off without so much as a by-you-leave when I haven't paid him a penny yet?'

'Perhaps he's found another benefactress,' Papa said.

He didn't mean this seriously, but it upset Mama. Me too. I miss him so. I can't seem to draw without him. I can't even read properly. Every day I sit on my window seat with a book on my lap, but I'm generally daydreaming. Anyway, I know a lot of Tennyson by heart. I can recite the whole of *The Lady of Shalott*. I took a melancholy delight in chanting loudly, chanting lowly, just like her, though Algie and Clarrie hung over the banisters listening, and then mimicked me cruelly.

I felt as if I were under a spell too, though I didn't have a web to spin. Whenever there was a knock at the door I ran down to see if Paris had come back from his holiday. I told myself not to be ridiculous, and next time the doorbell rang and Edie's boots tapped across the hall tiles to the front door I stayed where I was. I heard Papa's deep voice.

Algie heard him too. He came flying down the banisters and landed with a thud. Clarrie thumped down the stairs after him, with Sebastian scurrying behind. Papa often comes home with a bag of sweets in his pocket so they always greet him eagerly.

I leaned forward to peer down into the hall, nearly falling off the window seat, and realized that Papa had brought a little girl home with him. I couldn't see her properly, but she looked like a street child, though she was wearing clean, neat clothes. Did he want to sketch her for Miss Smith's book?

I could hear Algie showing off, Clarrie giggling, Sebastian murmuring shyly. Alphonse was yapping in the drawing room, sensing a stranger, but Mama failed to put in an appearance. Upstairs, Beth was silent, while Phoebe babbled at Nurse. I stayed on the window seat, feeling too wretched to greet Papa and his small guest.

A few minutes later he came up the stairs, looking rather flushed. 'Hello, Rose darling,' he said, coat swinging, scarf dangling. 'Are you drawing?'

'Reading Tennyson,' I said.

'Good for you! But I hope you've not abandoned your drawing just because Paris isn't around at the moment.'

'You really don't know where he is?'

'I haven't a clue, my dear. Your mama is most put out. But I dare say he'll be back soon.'

'Do you really think so, Papa?'

'Of course. He wouldn't leave the portrait unfinished. And he hasn't been paid!'

'Do you think that's the only reason he comes here – just to make some money?' I asked.

'Well, a chap's got to eat, darling. I've sometimes spent weeks painting the most terrible bores simply for a pocketful of chink.'

'So he thinks we're terrible bores?' I asked, my voice wobbling.

'No, of course not! He says he loves coming here. I'm sure he enjoys painting your mama. She's still a very beautiful woman. I don't think my portraits have ever done her justice. And he finds you children fun.'

'So he thinks I'm "fun",' I murmured, wondering how one small word could be so humiliating.

'Yes! And talented and lively and gifted,' said Papa, tweaking my nose.

Did Paris really call me talented and lively and gifted? Maybe Papa was just saying that to make me feel better. But perhaps he really *did* say it.

'Oh dear, I didn't hurt your nose, did I? It's gone very pink. In fact, your whole face is pink, my love. Are you blushing?'

'Of course not! You're actually rather flushed yourself, Papa.'

'That's because I've been having an adventure!'

'An adventure?'

'A real one, involving hiding behind doors and a sudden dash for freedom, pursued by a wicked witch of a stepmother! I've rescued a child from Miss Smith's Home for Destitute Girls!' said Papa.

'You've *rescued* her? But I thought that was what *Miss Smith* did. Aren't you going to take the child back?' I asked.

'I can't, because the mad woman is pursuing her. The child had to make a run for it. I couldn't let her roam the streets by herself – she's only a scrap of a thing. She's that dear little child I met at the doll-maker's. Such a fetching girl, with a mass of black hair and a tiny pinched face that's already seen too much sorrow in her short life. I *had* to bring her back here, didn't I?' Papa's voice wavered.

'Yes, of course, Papa,' I said. I thought he'd behaved admirably, and felt a sudden rush of love for him. It was wonderful to have such a gallant, impulsive father – but I couldn't help wondering what on earth Mama was going to say.

I glanced up in the direction of the drawing room.

'I think your mama is resting, Rose. I didn't want to disturb her. I thought I'd introduce her to my little waif later, when she is feeling refreshed,' said Papa.

'Oh, Papa!' He was bold enough to rescue a child from the streets and yet too cowardly to tell his wife what he'd done.

'What will you do if Mama says this child has to go back where she came from?' I asked.

'She won't do any such thing. I'm sure she'll be delighted,' said Papa, clearly trying to convince himself. 'The child will be a delightful addition to the household. I'm going to employ her as a little nurserymaid.'

'Oh, Papa, you're going to get rid of Nurse Budd!' I said excitedly.

'No, no, I couldn't possibly expect one small girl to handle Beth all by herself.'

'Surely you're not going to send Nurse away?' I asked, shocked. 'I know she's getting old and struggles a bit, but what would she do without us?'

'I wouldn't dream of sending Nurse away! Nurse is part of our family, and always will be,' said Papa firmly. 'No, I've employed the child to *help* Nurse, as she gets so tired nowadays. She will be very grateful.'

I stared at him. He didn't seem to understand the womenfolk in his household at all.

'I'm sure it will all work out splendidly,' he went on. 'Anyway, I must go and apply myself to my drawing. Fighting dragon stepmothers and rescuing tiny damsels in distress has been very time-consuming. I need to get on with some work!' He blew me a kiss and then scuttled on up the stairs.

I was keen to meet this poor little destitute child. She was still down in the hall with Algie and Clarrie and Sebastian. They were dancing around her, fascinated, and she was telling them that she had magic powers.

I looked at her curiously. She really *was* little, the same size as Sebastian, but you could tell by her pale, careworn face that she was older. She had an incredible tangle of dark hair, and she was wearing an institutional blue frock that was much too big for her, and strange soft felt boots, but she looked very pleasing all the same.

'Are you saying you're a witch?' I asked.

'I could be,' she said, chin up. 'And *you* could be Beth and have a doll called Marigold.'

I laughed. 'You're not a very clever witch then. I'm not Beth. She's in the nursery, tucked up on the chaise longue because she's not very well. I'm Rose and I'm too old for dolls. Who on earth are you?' I asked her.

'I'm Clover,' she said. She was looking at my book, trying to read the words upside down. I saw her lips moving, spelling out *The Lady of Shalott*.

'Do you like poetry?' I asked.

'Maids don't read poetry!' said Algie rudely. He grabbed my book and wrinkled his nose at all the verses. He doesn't read poetry either. 'Papa says she's our new nurserymaid. We don't want one, do we?'

'Algie!' said Sebastian. 'You'll hurt her feelings.'

'I *do* like poetry,' said Clover indignantly. She took my Tennyson from Algie and held it carefully, fingering the fine leather binding. It was clear that she liked books and knew how to handle them. She had spirit, and argued fiercely, just like one of us.

'Can you do magic tricks if you're a witch?' Clarrie asked. 'Can you magic more sweets?'

'Nurse isn't going to want her either,' Algie said.

'Oh, bother Nurse,' I said.

Clover swallowed hard. 'I'd better go and introduce myself to her,' she said.

She was going to get a frosty reception, I thought. I felt sorry for her. It must be so bewildering to fetch up in this house, dealing with difficult children and hostile staff. She still had Mama to contend with. Papa had abandoned her. I decided *I* was going to take care of her now.

'In a minute,' I said. 'Come to my room first. I'll show you my books. Come on, Clover. Not the rest of you though. You've all got sticky hands. Go and wash!'

As I took Clover's hand, I felt her trembling. She was obviously frightened, though she was doing her best to hold her own. I took her to my room, shutting the door firmly behind us so that we could have some peace from the little ones.

'Oh!' she said, peering around at everything. She swallowed again and walked on tiptoe over the rug, touching the books on the shelves with one finger. She ran the back of her hand across the silk of my bedspread, touched the toes of my old dolls and stuffed animals on the windowsill, and then stopped when she caught sight of herself in the looking glass. She put her hands to her mouth, startled.

'I – I'm sorry . . . Rose. *Miss* Rose. I shouldn't be here,' she said.

'Of course you should. I invited you in! Don't look so worried. Do you like my room?'

'Of course I do,' she said. 'It's so clean and pretty and full of so many beautiful things. So it's all yours? The others don't sleep in the bed with you?'

'I should think not!' I said, imagining the awfulness of sharing a bed with Algie.

She flushed. 'Sorry, miss,' she said.

'Please, please, please don't call me Miss. Well, not when we're by ourselves. So was your room very different at your home?'

'The rooms at Miss Smith's home are all neat and clean, but nowhere near as nice as this,' said Clover. 'And back in Cripps Alley, where I come from, they're *very* different.'

'Tell me,' I said, sitting down on the edge of my bed. I patted the space beside me. 'Come and sit down beside me, Clover.'

She sat down, but she pressed her lips together and wrapped her arms tight around herself. They were painfully thin, her wrists as fragile as birds' legs, but her hands looked strong, rough and red with hard work.

'You've obviously had a very hard life,' I said softly.

I meant to sound sympathetic but she gave me a sharp glance. I realized I sounded patronizing. 'I'm sorry. That sounded awful. I just wish I knew what it's like to be you,' I said earnestly.

Clover shrugged her skinny shoulders.

'It seems so unfair that I have such an easy life, and yet you and Jack Boots and little Mary-Jane have to slave for me and my family when you're children just like me,' I told her.

'Little Mary-Jane?' asked Clover.

'She's really young, but she's already been sent into service by her horrible mother. I believe you've got a horrible mother too,' I said.

Clover clenched her fists. 'I had a wonderful, dear, sweet, kind mother,' she said.

'I'm sorry! I didn't realize. I thought she was the reason Papa rescued you.'

'I was running away from my *stepmother*, Mildred. My real mother died when I was very small but I remember all about her. I loved her more than anyone, apart from Megs,' said Clover.

'Megs?'

'Megs was my sister. She died too,' said Clover, and a tear suddenly rolled down her cheek.

'I'm sorry,' I said wretchedly. 'I didn't mean to make you cry.'

'I'm not crying,' she said, wiping her eyes with the back of her hand. 'You want to know what it was like at my home? We were all crammed into two bedrooms. All us children squashed up together in one of them. My father and Mildred had the other. Mildred hated me and I hated her. Then Megs got the fever and – and she died, so Mildred kept me shut in a cupboard and didn't even want me to go to the funeral, but when I got out, my friend Mr Dolly – he makes the most beautiful dolls—'

'I know. Beth's Marigold,' I whispered, reluctant to interrupt her now she was in full flow.

'He made me my funeral outfit, and then I ran away and some rough lads stole my money, but a lovely lady who dances at the Gaiety Theatre looked after me,' said Clover. She said it proudly. I was impressed to find that she knew a dancing girl, but knew that Mama would have been horrified.

'And then you went to the Home for Destitute Girls? Was it very severe? Did they beat you?' I asked.

'No! Miss Smith is very kind. I was happy there. I liked looking after the little ones. But then Mildred came to get me and *she'd* beat me soon as look at me, but your pa rescued me. I begged him to let me be your nurserymaid,' said Clover.

'Well. Not mine exactly. I'm rather too old to be confined to the nursery,' I said. 'But I expect you'll be looking after Algie and Clarrie, poor you. Sebastian is easy enough, so long as you're not afraid of mice. And baby Phoebe's a dear little thing,' I said reassuringly.

'A baby! I'm good with babies,' said Clover.

There was a sudden high-pitched cry from along the corridor.

'That's not a baby!'

'No, that's my sister Beth. She often cries – she's poorly, you see,' I started, but Clover was already running out of the door and along the corridor.

She followed the sounds of Beth's cries until she got to the right door and then hurtled in without knocking. I rushed after her.

'For pity's sake, how many times do I have to tell you not to come barging in here, Miss Rose!' Nurse Budd started – and then she broke off, startled to see that the intruder wasn't me at all. She was out of breath from wrestling with Beth. 'Who in God's name are you?' she asked.

'I'm Clover Moon, and I think you should let go of that poor child immediately!' said Clover.

'I *beg* your pardon?' said Nurse Budd. She saw me standing in the doorway. 'Miss Rose, run for Mr Hodgson. There's a lunatic child broken into the house and she's very likely dangerous!'

'No, no, Nurse Budd, this is Clover, our new nurserymaid,' I said.

'A child like that! Don't be ridiculous!' she scoffed.

'I'm here to help,' said Clover. 'I can see you need help too. You're frightening that poor girl into a fit. Can't you see that she hates being held like that? You're practically throttling her! It's downright cruel.'

'How dare you address me in such a way! As if I'd ever be cruel to my dear little patient. But Miss Beth can be very fierce, bless her. She's just bitten me – look!' Nurse Budd held out her arm to show us the tooth marks on her wrist.

'I'm sure she didn't mean to, Nurse Budd,' I said.

'That's right, poor pet. But I have to tell you that, in the hospital where I was trained, if any sick child bit persistently, we had the surgeon come along to extract their teeth.'

'Teeth!' Beth cried, terrified.

'Sometimes it's the only way,' said Nurse Budd. '*Will* you stop struggling, Miss Beth!'

'Just let her go!' I cried.

'Well, if you say so, Miss Rose, as you always know best, don't you?' said Nurse Budd.

She let go of Beth so suddenly that she tumbled to the floor, crying even louder.

'Oh, Beth! Poor Beth!' I said, kneeling down beside her, trying to put my arms around her.

Beth carried on screaming, her whole face contorted. Her eyes were wild, her nose was running, her hair was tangled, her hands were flapping – I couldn't help feeling a little scared of her.

'Beth! Please don't cry so,' I said imploringly.

'Don't try to hold her, Miss Rose, it will just upset her,' said Clover.

'Don't start giving orders here, missy!' said Nurse Budd. '*I* am in charge of Miss Beth. When Mrs Rivers employed me, she made it clear that I'm the only person able to look after Miss Beth because I'm a professionally trained nurse and I won't let any child get the better of me.'

'When *Mr* Rivers employed me, he made it quite clear that I am the new nurserymaid and I am to help you because you're getting old and can't cope with the children,' said Clover. 'Trained nurse! That's a likely story.'

'Don't you talk to me like that!' said Nurse Budd, and slapped her across the face.

I gasped, but Clover didn't flinch.

'You don't frighten me. I dare say you slap this poor girl too. But I'm going to keep my eye on you. I know your sort. You're just like my stepmother. No, you're *worse*,' said Clover.

'Oh, bravo!' I said, astonished by her courage.

But it didn't get her anywhere. Nurse Budd was much bigger and stronger. She took hold of Clover by her skinny arm and literally dragged her out of the room.

'Stop it! You're hurting her!' I cried.

I tried to prise Nurse Budd's hands away, but she was too strong for me too.

'You'd better mind your own business, Miss Rose! What are you doing, consorting with this little guttersnipe? What will your mama say, I wonder? Well, let's find out!' she said.

She pulled Clover along, with me following. Beth was so shocked she stopped screaming and huddled in a corner. Edie was nipping up the stairs, adjusting her cap as she went. She stared up at the three of us, her hands still raised comically in the air.

'My Lord, what's going on, Miss Rose?' she asked.

'Miss Rose and this grubby little child have invented some cock-and-bull story that she's been sent to help me with Miss Beth,' said Nurse Budd. 'Tell Mr Hodgson to send for a constable. She needs to be locked up! Doubtless she's come from a den of thieves and will rob us all!'

'Don't, Edie! Papa really *did* bring Clover here!' I said, panicking.

'Now now, Miss Rose, you'll be in trouble for telling such a silly fib,' said Nurse Budd.

Edie straightened her cap, arranging two little curls to peep out at the front. She smiled. She has no time for Nurse Budd either.

'I think *you're* the one who's going to be in trouble, Nurse Budd,' she said. 'Miss Rose is telling God's honest truth. The master *did* take it into his head to bring the child into the house. *I* should know, because I let them in. I don't know whether she's to help you or old Nurse, but the master says she's to be a nurserymaid.'

'That's nonsense!' said Nurse Budd, flushing crimson.

'I agree with you on that one. She's had no training for service and it's clear she's come from the streets, even though they've scrubbed her up a bit,' said Edie, wrinkling her nose at Clover.

'How dare you talk about her like that!' I said. 'Shame on you both, when Papa has welcomed her into our house.'

'I'm not so sure she's welcome, Miss Rose. Lord knows what your mama's going to say about it,' said Edie, frowning at Clover.

Mama had plenty to say when we all trooped into the drawing room.

Nurse Budd was threatening to leave at once if she wasn't able to take sole care of Beth, as arranged.

'Please believe me, Nurse Budd, I know nothing of this! I promise that we will stick to our arrangement. You *must* stay. We couldn't do without you now! I will talk to my husband. This has to be a dreadful mistake,' said Mama.

Nurse Budd gave me a dark look and went back upstairs.

Papa was still skulking in his studio, but Mama sent Mr Hodgson himself to fetch him.

'I can't believe you could behave so irresponsibly, Edward!' she said when he came in. She gave Clover a withering look. 'This girl's far too young and inexperienced to be a nurserymaid. She's not at all the right sort of girl in any case. We don't know anything about her background. I'm sure she hasn't got any references.'

'Now, Jeannie, let's calm down,' said Papa. 'I'm sorry to spring Clover on you at such short notice – well, no notice at all – but I really had no alternative. I'm sure she'll work hard for us, and she has a marvellous knack with children. She'll be a boon to dear old Nurse. Let's see what *she* thinks.'

Nurse was summoned, and arrived with the baby on her hip. Phoebe was wailing irritably, her cheeks bright red.

'Oh dear, hark at little Phoebe,' said Papa quickly. 'Poor Nurse, it looks as if she's getting to be quite a handful.'

'I can manage her, sir,' she said quickly.

'Yes, but it must be a struggle with Sebastian and Clarrie – not to mention that young demon Algie!' Papa continued.

Nurse's cheeks were almost as red as Phoebe's. 'I can still do my job, sir,' she said.

'Yes, I know, and splendidly too, but I think it's time you had a little help. So here's your very own nurserymaid to give you a hand,' said Papa, putting his hand on Clover's shoulder. 'Miss Clover Moon.'

Nurse was so shocked she very nearly dropped Phoebe.

'I don't need help, sir – and certainly not from a child straight off the streets. It's madness! I've known you since the day you were born. You've been so soft-hearted you've lumbered yourself with this girl, and now you're trying to palm her off on me. Shame on you, sir!' she said, trying to hush the baby. Phoebe only cried harder.

Papa squirmed as if Nurse were sending him to bed without any supper, but he went on, 'Clover will prove a veritable asset in the nursery, you mark my words.' He patted Clover on the shoulder. She was standing tensely, her green eyes darting from one to the other. I ached for her.

'I know Clover will be very capable,' I said.

'Don't be so ridiculous, Rose,' Mama snapped. 'As if your opinion counts! Nurse, why is the baby crying so? She's very red in the face. She hasn't got a fever, has she?'

'Beg pardon, madam, but she's just teething. It's hurting her. I've tried rubbing jelly on her gums but it only soothes her for so long,' said Nurse, jiggling Phoebe up and down.

'Teething jelly's useless,' said Clover. 'She just needs distracting. Give her here.'

She reached out and took poor wailing Phoebe in her arms before Nurse realized what was happening.

'Oh dear, is it those toothy-pegs?' said Clover, shaking her head at Phoebe. 'Those cheeks look very red and hot. Let's cool them down, shall we?' She blew very gently into the baby's face. Phoebe stopped mid-cry, looking surprised. 'Yes, it's nice, isn't it. Again? And in those hot little ears too?' She blew, and Phoebe wriggled and smiled.

'There now!' said Papa. 'Didn't I say she had a way with children? Bravo, Clover! Look, little Phoebe's chuckling now!'

'Give the baby back to Nurse this instant, Clover Moon, or whatever your name is,' Mama commanded. 'I don't trust you for one moment.'

'Clover's in our employ now, Jeannie, whether you like it or not,' said Papa, quietly but firmly. 'I'd like you all to remember that I am the head of this household.'

I was sure Mama was going to argue, but she pressed her lips together and nodded. She was holding Alphonse very tightly, and he started yapping furiously, as if he were expressing Mama's feelings for her.

'Follow me, then, girl,' Nurse mumbled to Clover, sniffing her disapproval.

Clover did as she was told, still holding Phoebe. She looked demure, but when she passed me she gave me a tiny wink.

She kept Phoebe quiet and amused, had a long conversation about the breeding habits of mice with Sebastian, complimented Clarrie's dolls, and played a new card game, Snap, with Algie, letting him win every time.

When I came back from a very frosty dinner, with Mama and Papa saying scarcely a word to each other, Clover had given the children their supper and got them all into bed. Nurse sat sulking by the fire, warming her sore bunions and muttering to herself.

Clover kissed each child goodnight. She tried to see Beth too, but Nurse Budd was guarding her fiercely.

'Goodnight, Beth! Sleep tight. And make sure the bugs don't bite!' Clover called through the door.

'Don't bite, don't bite,' Beth called back, calmer now.

Nurse kept Clover up doing the darning till late. I heard her pattering along the corridor in her soft felt shoes.

I lay awake, wondering how she was feeling, having to cope with this strange new life and all these people who were set against her. Would she fall asleep as soon as she put her head on her pillow, or was she lying awake too, feeling lost and lonely?

I wondered where she was sleeping. There was no room in the night nursery, unless she shared Nurse's bed, and I was sure they'd both hate that. Nurse Budd certainly wouldn't let her in with her. Perhaps she had to share a room in the attic with Edie and Maggie. I didn't think they would be very kind to her.

The house was silent. When I heard midnight strike, I decided to go looking for Clover. The house seemed intensely dark, even with my candle. I climbed the stairs to the attics, shivering, though I kept reminding myself that there was nothing to be frightened of. I wasn't a governess like Jane Eyre, confronting a mad woman. I was the daughter of the house, concerned about the welfare of one of our servants.

I peeped into Edie and Maggie's room. They were both fast asleep, Edie with her hair in curling papers, Maggie flat on her back and snoring. I peered under the bed, but there was no sign of Clover.

Then, back on the narrow landing, I heard a muffled sound, soft and regular. Someone was crying. I crept along until I found the right door, and then knocked timidly. The crying stopped abruptly.

'Clover?' I whispered. 'Clover, it's me, Rose. Can I come in?'

She murmured something, so I opened the door and slipped into her bedroom. But it wasn't a bedroom at all. It wasn't even a proper room, but a cupboard – a junk room stuffed with a three-legged armchair, a lopsided table, a battered nursery screen, and any number of trunks and suitcases. I couldn't see them properly in the dark, but they made large, oppressive shapes in the tiny space. I stumbled over a bucket on the floor to catch drips from the roof.

Clover hadn't even been given a proper bed. She was curled up under a blanket on a mattress on the floor.

'Oh, Clover, are you crying?' I asked foolishly.

'No,' she said, but her voice was thick and snuffly, and when I bent down and touched her face I felt the tears on her cheeks.

'You poor thing,' I said, and I squatted on the mattress beside her and pulled her into my arms.

She clung to me and I rocked her gently. I'd rarely held any of my brothers or sisters. Rupert and I had been very close, but if I tried to cuddle up to him he always laughed and called me a softie. Even when she was little Beth hated being touched. Sebastian would sit on my lap when he was tiny, but declared he was a big boy now. Clarrie was far too fidgety, and I'd never wanted to go anywhere near Algie. I'd have loved to hold Phoebe, but Nurse was sure I'd drop her.

It felt so good to hold Clover, especially when she relaxed against me and stopped trying to smother her sobs.

'That's it, you have a good cry,' I said. 'No wonder you're sad. Everyone's been so horrid to you and you've been so brave.'

'No, it isn't that. I'm crying because I miss my brothers and sisters, especially little Bert, though he doesn't really need me any more. And most of all I miss my sister Megs, but she's dead now, and I try to imagine her as an angel, but I want her *here* so that I can look after her,' Clover sobbed.

'Of course you do,' I said. 'I feel so ashamed that they've stuck you in this horrible poky room. Listen, why don't you come down to my room? My bed's very soft, with heaps of room for the two of us.'

Clover sat up and sniffed. 'I can't sleep in your bed, Miss Rose! What would they say if they found out?'

'I don't care what anyone says. And don't call me *Miss* Rose, it's horrible. When we're alone together, promise you'll always call me Rose, like a proper friend.'

'All right. But I still can't come to your room. You know the other servants would tell on me, and your mama would be horrified,' said Clover, wiping her face with her sleeve. 'They'd send me away.'

'Then I'll creep up here every night and we'll curl up together. They can't send *me* away, though I often wish they would!'

I wriggled down onto the mattress and pulled Clover close beside me. The mattress was very lumpy and didn't smell quite clean, and the blanket was very thin. Clover's hair was long and wild and got in my face. I can't say it was comfortable – and yet within minutes we were both fast asleep.

17

I HAVE A TRUE friend at last – but we have to lead a double life. When we're with other people in the house, family or servants, we stick to the rules. I might nod at Clover, but mostly I pretend to ignore her. Clover isn't allowed to ignore me back. Nurse insists she bobs a little curtsy and murmurs, 'Good morning, Miss Rose,' or 'Good afternoon' or 'Good evening'. I'm not a nursery child any more, but if Nurse notices that my hair needs brushing or my dress is crumpled or I've kicked off my boots and exposed a hole in my stocking, she gives Clover a little nudge.

'Find Miss Rose's hairbrush for her, Clover! You need to get that dress ironed for Miss Rose, it's all over creases! Ask Miss Rose to change her stockings and get that hole darned right away!' she commands crossly, shaking her head at Clover as if it's somehow *her* fault.

Nurse is forever criticizing her, though any fool can see that Clover's made a huge difference in the nursery. She gets the children up, and washes and dresses and feeds them in double-quick time, and then she *plays* with them. She makes up the sort of games that Rupert and I used to play. Sebastian and Algie and Clarrie stop being small children in a stuffy nursery: they're pirates sailing out to sea, or princes and princesses in a palace, or polar bears and penguins in Arctic realms.

'Such nonsense!' Nurse sniffs, rocking Phoebe.

She won't let Clover near the baby, but when she dozes after lunch Clover sits Phoebe on her lap, takes off her woolly booties and plays This Little Piggy with her toes. Phoebe chuckles and claps her fat little hands in delight. She adores Clover. All the children do, even Algie. He follows her around and does whatever she asks.

She never sighs or shakes her head at him the way we do. She says, 'Perhaps *you* can help Miss Clarrie button her shoes, Master Algie, as you've got such nimble fingers. I think *you* might read the story today, Master Algie, because you read with such expression. Can you help Master Sebastian hunt for Montmorency, Master Algie, as your eyes are much sharper than mine?'

It works! Algie does as Clover suggests, and she always lavishes praise on him. It should have made him unbearably conceited, but he simply nods and says, 'Happy to oblige,' as if he's her little servant.

Clover has to be careful not to get on the wrong side of Nurse Budd, who complained to Mama, saying that she was insolent and impertinent and not to be trusted. Mama daren't go directly against Papa's wishes: she cannot actually dismiss Clover, but she says she must mind her manners or she will be sent to the kitchen as a second scullery maid.

'I have to bite my tongue whenever I'm near Nurse Budd,' Clover told me one night, when we were curled up together.

'I'd sooner you bit Nurse Budd instead,' I said, and we both giggled. 'I can't bear her, Clover!'

'I hate her too,' she said. 'I hate her second only to Mildred, my stepmother. She pretends to be so fond of Beth, but I don't think she likes her at all.'

'I've said as much to Mama and Papa, but they won't listen to me,' I said. 'They don't *want* to listen. They're embarrassed by Beth. Mama wants to hide her away and pretend she doesn't exist. Papa makes a fuss of her, but then forgets all about her.'

'He took the greatest care when buying her doll,' said Clover. 'Oh, I do miss Mr Dolly. He was so kind and gentle to me, and he taught me so much. He was more of a father to me than my pa ever was.'

Clover told me stories about her pa and her hateful stepmother and all the children she looked after. I tried to imagine what it would be like to care for half the children in my street as well as all my siblings. I find it tiresome enough playing with Sebastian and Algie and Clarrie for more than a few minutes. Perhaps I take after Papa.

I wished I took after him artistically. I don't think I have any true talent. It meant so much to me when Paris praised my comic drawings, but I'm sure he was simply trying to be kind.

I still didn't know why he'd stopped coming to paint Mama's portrait. I missed him dreadfully, but he wasn't quite real any more. It was as if I'd made him up. I wasn't sure now that I actually *loved* him. Perhaps it was all a fancy in my head because I was so lonely without Rupert. I'm not lonely any more because I have Clover for a friend.

I crept upstairs nearly every night, though I couldn't risk it if I heard Beth crying. If Nurse Budd caught me she'd tell Mama, and then there would be terrible trouble. I'd be confined to my room for a week on a bread-and-milk diet. That's how they punished Algie last year when he experimented with matches and set fire to the Persian hearthrug.

I could put up with any silly punishment – but Clover would be sent away. She couldn't go home because her stepmother would hurt her – I'd seen the long red scar on her forehead. She couldn't go to her doll-maker friend or return to the Home for Destitute Girls because Mildred would find her there. She couldn't get another position as a nurserymaid because she didn't have any references. She would have to beg on the streets.

I worried that I was being selfish, but she was always so pleased to see me.

'I've been so used to cuddling up with Megs and baby Bert and all the other children. It feels lonely up here all by myself,' she said. 'I can't get to sleep when I'm alone, no matter how tired I am. Don't laugh, but I'm afraid someone is waiting to get me behind all this furniture.'

'I'll never laugh at you, Clover,' I said, my heart turning over. She has to be so grown up during the day, and yet she's still only little herself. 'I don't know how you cope with the children the way you do, especially Algie!'

'I love Algie – he's got such spirit, and he makes me laugh. I love *all* the children. Clarrie's a dear, with all her funny notions, and Sebastian's such a kind boy. Phoebe's a darling. I'd bounce her on my knee all day if I had my way. I haven't got to know Beth properly because Nurse Budd is always guarding her, but she seems a very interesting girl. She reminds me of one of the little ones at Miss Smith's home. I wish I could talk to her more.'

'You make us all sound like such model children,' I said.

'Well, you are.'

'Even me? I'm untidy and unladylike and I get in such a strop at times.'

'And I like you the most.'

'You'll prefer my twin brother, Rupert, when he comes home at Christmas. Everyone likes him best. He can be

234

very charming when he wants. I used to worship him,' I said, sighing.

'But not any more?'

'He's changed so.' I hesitated. It seemed disloyal to say anything bad about Rupert. 'I don't always approve of him,' I added, and then blushed in the darkness because I sounded so prim.

'That's boys for you,' said Clover. 'My brothers can be real pickles – like a lot of the lads down our alley. But not my friend Jimmy Wheels. He's the best.'

'Jimmy *Wheels*? That's a strange name.'

'Well, it's not really his name. Folk all call him that because his legs don't work so he lies on a little wagon and wheels himself along.'

'Oh my goodness, the poor boy.'

'He's very speedy. He's got a lovely mother who was very kind to me.' Clover paused. 'My own mother was lovely too. She died when I was little but I still remember her.'

'*My* mother isn't lovely, is she?' I said, not caring if I sounded disloyal now.

Clover fidgeted. 'Well . . .' she said.

'You don't have to be tactful. She's horrible to you. And to me, even though I'm her daughter.'

'She doesn't hit you,' said Clover. 'And perhaps she fusses because she cares about you. She wants you to grow up to be a fine lady.'

'You can't seriously think that,' I said. 'And who wants to be a fine lady anyway?'

'I wouldn't mind,' said Clover. She didn't say it sharply, but I blushed again.

'I'm sorry – that was such a stupid thing to say,' I apologized.

'It was stupid of me too, because obviously *I* can never be a fine lady,' said Clover. 'I can't see a girl from Cripps Alley going to a ball like Cinderella and meeting a handsome prince.'

'What sort of man would you like to meet, Clover?' I asked.

'I've met him. Mr Dolly is the sweetest man in all the world. When I'm older I'd like to set up a new shop with him – miles and miles away from Mildred. It'll be just Mr Dolly and me, and all our dolls. They'll stay still and silent, never needing to be fed or washed or changed,' said Clover, chuckling.

'But isn't he an old man?'

'Yes, he's been just like a father to me.'

'Wouldn't you like to meet someone more romantic?' I asked.

'I don't much care for romance,' said Clover. I felt her wiping her mouth with the back of her hand. 'Big boys used to grab me and kiss me, and I hated it.'

'But you're only a child!'

'It's different where I come from.'

'So kisses don't feel good?' I asked shyly.

'I suppose it depends. No one's kissed you then, Rose?'

'No! And I don't want anyone to either,' I declared, not quite truthfully. 'Let's go to sleep now. It must be very late and we have to be up before six.'

236

Phoebe still woke at dawn for her early-morning feed, and Clover had to be up to prepare it. I scurried silently down to my room before the rest of the household stirred.

I didn't mind waking early. I stretched out in my comfortable bed, enjoying the soft pillows. The next night I decided to take one with me – and my thick pink quilt because it was so cold in the attic. I sorted out little gifts for Clover too: a spare bar of lavender soap, half a bottle of my rainbow shampoo, a tortoiseshell comb, two handkerchiefs and a little box of sugar plums.

The sugar plums were actually Algie's, a present from a sentimental old lady in the park, but he'd only have eaten them all at once and made himself sick. When he discovered they were missing he kicked up a terrible fuss, but everyone was sure he'd eaten them himself. I know it's despicable to rob your little brother, even if he's Algie, but I felt that Clover was more deserving.

I gave her books too, though she's got no time to read them. I've chosen *A Little Princess* and *Jane Eyre*, because they're about girls with troubles and I felt that Clover might identify with them. I told her to read only the first ten chapters of *Jane Eyre* as she doesn't care for romance. I don't either.

I'm never going to let a boy make an idiot of me like poor silly Pamela. I think falling in love is foolish. It doesn't make you happy. It doesn't last. Look at Mama and Papa. Mama has a daguerreotype that was taken on their honeymoon. She keeps it in an ornate frame on her dressing table. The couple standing together are barely recognizable as my parents. Mama is gazing up at Papa, a radiant smile on her face, and he is clasping her hand and looking down on her ardently. Now they cannot be in the same room together without snapping.

I think Papa still longs for Louisa, while Mama languishes on her chaise longue thinking of Paris. They are so foolish. Especially Mama. Paris is half her age, and he is obviously never, ever coming back.

I'm the foolish one! Paris *has* come back!

He arrived at half past nine this morning, carrying his battered bag of paints and brushes in one hand, his palette in the other, whistling as he walked across the hall and up the stairs. I was sitting on the window seat, scarcely able to believe it was really him. He gave me a cheery smile.

'Hello there, Rose,' he said casually, as if he hadn't been missing for four whole weeks.

I gaped at him foolishly.

'Whenever I pulled a face like that, my old nurse used to say the wind might change and then I'd be stuck with a mouth like a goldfish for ever,' he said.

'You had a nurse?' I said.

I'd imagined him being brought up in a romantic garret with glamorous artistic parents who didn't give a fig for society and its rules. I was genuinely astonished.

'Was your mother an artist too?' I asked, thinking she probably scraped together a nurse's wages so that she was free to paint.

'My mother?' said Paris. 'Well, I think she did a little genteel watercolouring when she was a girl.'

'What about your father?'

He laughed. 'He's a stockbroker. I don't think that's a very artistic profession, do you?'

'Well, maybe not.' I took a deep breath. 'Mr Walker, where have you *been*?'

'I've had a little holiday abroad,' he said. 'But now I'm all set to get your mother's portrait finished.'

'Abroad?' I repeated. 'But you didn't say you were going.'

'I didn't know I was until the opportunity arose. That's what being an artist is all about, Rose – acting spontaneously!' he said. Then he looked more serious. 'Is your mother very cross with me?'

'I don't think she's a very spontaneous person herself. I'm not sure she'd understand your going away on a whim,' I said.

'Mmm,' said Paris thoughtfully. He moved closer. 'Budge up a bit.'

He sat down beside me on the window seat. I breathed in his distinctive smell of oil paint and tobacco and cologne.

'Can you help me concoct a convincing story to appease Mama?' he said. 'I'd really like to continue with her portrait.'

'And get paid,' I added.

'Absolutely,' said Paris. 'You're very sharp, Miss Rivers.'

'It would probably help if you told me where you really were,' I said.

'I told you. Abroad. In my namesake city, as a matter of fact. Have you ever been to Paris, Rose?'

'Hmm,' I said vaguely.

'It's such a beautiful city,' he said, shaking his head.

'Yes, isn't it,' I agreed, though apart from learning that Paris was the capital of France I knew nothing whatsoever about it.

'What do you like most about Paris?' he asked.

I was stuck. 'Just . . . the atmosphere,' I said.

He laughed. 'You've never been there, have you?'

'No, of course I haven't.'

'I loved it there – for the light, the pale creamy grey of all the beautiful buildings, the green of the Seine, the vibrant colours of the pretty girls in their fashionable clothes – and the art galleries most of all. I spent entire days in the Louvre, wandering around in awe. But the new painters are the most exciting – Monet, Renoir, Degas. How I would love to paint like them! I don't suppose your mother would let me start her portrait all over again and paint in the new way? No tedious detail, no delicate little brush strokes, just big bold impressions that get right to the truth of the subject.'

'I don't think Mama would care for that approach,' I said. 'But *I* think it sounds very exciting.'

'Perhaps I'll paint *your* portrait then, Rose. Sitting on the window seat in your green dress, with the sun streaming in and highlighting your hair. Would you like that?'

Would I? I wasn't sure if Paris was joking or not. I knew that Mama would never pay for a portrait of me.

I wasn't sure she would even pay for her own portrait now. She'd feel that Paris had let her down badly by gadding off to France.

'What made you suddenly decide to go to Paris?' I asked.

'French friends of mine,' he said. 'They were very persuasive.'

'Are they artists too?'

He nodded. 'Mostly.'

I thought of Paris with those other young men, wandering around the city, gazing at paintings, drinking wine in bars, singing under the stars.

'You're so lucky,' I said enviously. 'I'd give anything to be an artist.'

'I think you'll become a brilliant graphic artist, known for your sharp wit,' said Paris.

'I wish you wouldn't tease me,' I said.

'I'm not teasing. Run and fetch your sketchbook. I want to see your latest drawings.'

'There aren't any,' I said. I hadn't put pen to paper since Paris abandoned us. 'I just haven't felt like it,' I went on. I didn't want to tell him why, but he must have guessed.

He cupped my face with his hands, looking into my eyes. 'Listen, Rose, if you're going to be an artist, then you have to put your work before everything else. There'll be many times when you don't feel like it, but you mustn't let it stop you. No matter what else is going on in your life, work is always there. It's worth persevering, even in

241

the depths of despair. Promise me you'll carry on with your art, no matter what.'

It was difficult concentrating on what he was saying when we were so close and his hands were on my face, but I nodded and said yes.

'That's a good girl,' he said. 'So, what shall we tell Mama?'

'Perhaps you could say you were suddenly called abroad because your mama had been taken ill, maybe at a holiday resort?' I remembered that Mama had been terribly impressed when Lady Robson told her about her stay at a spa town in Germany. 'Baden-Baden! Yes, she became dangerously ill, and you received a telegram and had to rush off immediately, unable to warn anyone. You've been at her bedside constantly, and for several weeks it seemed as if you were going to lose her and you were distraught – but now, miraculously, she's recovered, and you accompanied her home at the weekend and she's still a little fragile but the doctors are very pleased with her.' I stopped, out of breath.

It was Paris's turn to gape. 'My Lord, you're a genius! Perhaps you're destined to be a writer as well as an artist! And an actress into the bargain because you sound so convincing!'

'I am a girl of many talents,' I said, though I wasn't sure that even Mama would believe such a story.

18

MAMA BELIEVED EVERY word of it! I think Paris could have spun her a tale about being captured by cannibals and she'd still have nodded sympathetically. She was just so pleased to see him. When I took him into the drawing room she blushed a deep, painful crimson. Even her throat was mottled red.

'Mr Walker!' she said, and for a terrible moment I thought she was going to burst into tears.

I was mortally embarrassed for her as she hung on his every word, gazing at him as if she couldn't quite believe he was here. She even patted his arm as if to reassure herself. Then she rushed off to change into her blue dress while Paris went up to the studio to prepare his paint.

But Mama couldn't find the sapphire brooch she'd been wearing to set off the neckline of her frock. She had Edie search in every drawer and cupboard and feel down the back of every sofa and chaise longue. She made Maggie run her feather duster across every mantelpiece and sweep all the corners.

Nurse Budd objected bitterly. 'I'm not having you coming in here with that broom! You'll disturb my little Beth,' she said. 'Surely it's not necessary, madam. You never come into our room so you couldn't have dropped it here. And I hope you don't think that *I've* got your brooch!'

'Of course not, Nurse Budd – but perhaps Beth took a fancy to it? I know she likes sparkly things,' said Mama.

'I supervise my little charge every minute of the day,' she replied. She paused. 'I'm not one to tell tales, but the other day I saw the younger children with your big jewellery box.'

She followed Mama down to the drawing room, and Nurse and Sebastian and Algie and Clarrie were sent for.

'Have you touched my jewellery box, children?' Mama demanded.

All three quivered guiltily. Nurse looked at them, shocked.

'You have!' Mama looked at Sebastian. She looked at Clarrie. Then she looked at Algie. He was biting his nails anxiously.

'What have you done with my sapphire brooch, Algernon Rivers?' she demanded.

'I haven't got your old brooch!' he protested. He ran to Mama and thrust his arms round her waist, while Alphonse snapped at his ankles irritably. 'Mama, I promise, promise, promise I haven't taken it.'

'Are you sure, Algie?' she asked. 'I don't think I believe you. You're such a bad boy. If you've stolen my very precious sapphire, then you will have to be soundly whipped.'

'He's a naughty little monkey, but I'm sure he'd never steal, madam,' said Nurse indignantly.

'Don't whip Algie, Mama!' said Clarrie. 'We played Pirate Treasure with your jewellery box but none of us took any brooches.'

'I tried on a pearl necklace and a gold bracelet, but I was very careful and I put them right back,' said Sebastian, who was always painfully honest.

'Really, Nurse, whatever's got into you! How dare you let the children ransack my jewellery box!' said Mama.

'It's nothing to do with me, madam,' said Nurse. 'I didn't know anything about it. They've been running wild, getting thoroughly over-excited. Pirate Treasure! It's one of the games that Clover Moon invented, I'll be bound.'

'Clover Moon!' said Mama, her lips tightening. 'I might have known it.'

'Please, Mama, I'm sure Clover had nothing to do with it,' I said hastily.

Mama took no notice, and sent for Clover. She was in the middle of bathing Phoebe, and had to bring her to the drawing room wrapped in a towel.

'How dare you bring the baby into the drawing room like that!' said Mama, momentarily distracted.

'I'm sorry, missus – Mrs Rivers – madam,' Clover stammered. She still forgets how to address her so-called betters. I don't think it matters a hoot, but it doesn't impress Mama.

She drew a deep breath now, her nostrils pinched, and glared at Clover. 'I cannot believe my husband employed you,' she said. 'You're the most useless servant girl I've ever known.'

'Mama, that's nonsense, Clover is absolutely wonderful with the children. She can even make Algie behave – and I'm sure if she were allowed to look after Beth she'd manage her far better than Nurse Budd,' I declared.

'I'll thank you not to contradict me in front of the servants,' said Mama.

She turned back to Clover. 'Did you let the children play with my jewellery box?'

'Yes, madam,' said Clover.

'My goodness, the brazen hussy!' said Nurse Budd.

'I can scarcely believe my ears! You let the children play with sapphires and rubies and diamonds!' said Mama.

'I didn't know they were precious stones, madam. I thought they were just coloured glass,' said Clover.

'As if a lady in my position would wear coloured glass!' said Mama. 'How can you suggest such a thing! And how dare you let the children play with my possessions in any case!'

'I'm sorry, madam. I knew the children shouldn't be playing with your jewellery, but they were having such a lovely game of pirates that I wanted them to find treasure. I won't let it happen again.'

'There won't be an opportunity, miss. You're not staying in this house a moment longer! I shall have you locked up in prison, where you belong. Now give me back my sapphire brooch!' Mama demanded.

'I haven't touched your brooch!' said Clover, shaking.

Nurse Budd pointed at her triumphantly. 'There, look, she's trembling. A picture of guilt!'

'Mama, you can't accuse Clover when you have no proof whatsoever that she's stolen your brooch!' I cried.

'Poor Clover!' Algie agreed.

'We love Clover,' said Clarrie.

'She would never steal your brooch,' said Sebastian.

'You've managed to turn my own children against me, Clover Moon!' Mama said. 'We shall settle this once and for all. Nurse, take Phoebe. Edie! Maggie! Where have you got to? Take this wicked girl away and search her thoroughly. And call for Mr Hodgson and Jack Boots to scour her room from top to bottom.'

'No!' I cried. I thought of the little comforts I'd taken there – the soap and shampoo and handkerchiefs, the pillow and the coverlet. They would all think that Clover had stolen them too!

I ran out of the room and, while poor Clover was being led away and Mr Hodgson sent for, I ran up the stairs, along the corridor, up the narrow servants' stairs, and straight to the tiny junk room. I seized the coverlet, threw the little trinkets onto it, and bundled it up – and there, lying on the threadbare sheet, was the sapphire brooch.

I stood still, the blood drumming in my ears. Oh, Clover, Clover, Clover! How *could* she? But perhaps I couldn't blame her. We had so much and she had so little. Was it really such a dreadful thing to do?

Thou shalt not steal.

I didn't care what the Bible said! I wasn't going to let them send for a policeman and drag poor Clover off to prison. I had to protect her.

I snatched up the brooch, then ran down the back stairs clutching the blanket, thrust it into my wardrobe, and then opened my hand.

I knew that Mama wouldn't rest until she had her brooch back. It was no use hiding it.

I ran down the stairs so quickly that I slipped and landed in a heap at the bottom, jarring my spine. It hurt horribly, but I picked myself up and hurried into the drawing room.

'Look!' I said breathlessly, holding the brooch out in the palm of my hand.

There were general exclamations from everyone.

'My brooch!' Mama exclaimed. 'Where did you get it, Rose?'

'From your room!' I said. 'I went to have another look because I couldn't bear you thinking that Clover had stolen it. And she didn't! It was there all the time.'

'I checked your jewellery box three times, madam – you saw me yourself,' Edie declared.

'And I swept that floor thoroughly, I swear I did,' said Maggie, coming back into the room, hauling Clover with her.

'The brooch was right in the corner, behind the long curtains,' I said, lying fluently. 'It must have rolled there while the children were playing. You see, Clover *didn't* steal the wretched brooch. We should all apologize to her!'

We all stared at Clover. She was deathly pale and shaking, her eyes bright with tears.

'I'll do no such thing,' said Mama. 'She should be punished for allowing the children to play with my jewellery. See to it, Nurse! And one more transgression and I will dismiss you, girl, do you understand?'

There was a long pause.

'Yes, madam,' Clover muttered.

Nurse shook her head at her, and told her sharply to get back to the nursery. She wouldn't let Clover carry baby Phoebe, but she couldn't stop Sebastian and Algie and Clarrie hanging miserably onto her skirts.

I followed too, and while Nurse was busy giving Phoebe another bath to warm her up, and the three young ones went to the schoolroom, I seized hold of Clover and pulled her out into the corridor where we wouldn't be heard.

She winced as I held her arm, and I wondered if Edie and Maggie had been unnecessarily forceful when they searched her.

'It's all right,' I hissed. 'I won't tell, I swear I won't. I don't blame you in the slightest.'

I expected her expression to soften, but she stared at me as if I were her enemy instead of her friend.

'I don't know what you mean,' she said, her chin jutting.

'Oh, Clover, I saw the wretched brooch there, in the middle of your bed! Why didn't you hide it? They'd have found it straight away!' I said.

'I didn't put it there. I never stole the brooch,' she said through gritted teeth.

'But – but surely—' I stammered, flustered by her attitude. I thought she'd be so relieved, so grateful that I'd saved her from dismissal, maybe even from prison.

'I'm not a thief,' she said, her green eyes glittering. 'I stole a torn picture book off a barrow once, but that was long ago. I'd never steal so much as a penny from your family!'

'But I saw the brooch in your bed!'

'I didn't put it there,' she said, tears starting to spill.

'All right. I believe you,' I said, to comfort her.

'No, you don't,' said Clover, and she went back into the nursery and slammed the door on me.

I heard Nurse telling her off, and warning her never to go near the mistress's room ever again. Clover didn't say a word. What was the matter with her? Why was she acting so strangely?

I stared at the closed door, suddenly doubting. I *knew* that the brooch had been in Clover's bed – but it had been left in such an obvious place, almost as if she *wanted* someone to find it. Why would she do that? Or could someone *else* have put it there?

I opened the nursery door.

'What is it now, Miss Rose?' said Nurse.

'I need to talk to Clover.'

'Stop interfering, Miss Rose. Clover hasn't got time to talk to you now. We're all behind like the lamb's tail after all the to-do. Run along,' she said firmly.

So I went up to the studio. Mama had the brooch pinned on her dress and was sitting talking to Paris, her eyes as blue and sparkling as the brooch. It seemed incredible to think that she'd been in such a fury ten minutes ago.

She kept tossing her head and simpering, posing with one finger pressed into her plump cheek to make a dimple. Paris gazed at her intently, making little strokes on his canvas with his paintbrush. It seemed uncomfortably like stroking Mama herself.

I hovered, not sure what to do. I was keen to be with Paris, but revolted by Mama's pantomime. I feared that I might have acted in the same way when we were in such close proximity on the window seat. Dear heavens, had I sparkled and simpered too?

I didn't think Paris had even noticed me creep in, but as I backed towards the door he looked up.

'Where's your sketchbook, Rose? Half the morning's gone already. Here, use my drawing pad,' he said, offering it to me. 'You'll find pencils in my jacket pocket on the door hook.'

'I think Rose is tired of drawing,' said Mama. 'And I'm not sure it's a good thing for her to keep missing her lessons.'

'Of course you know best, Mrs Rivers, but I wonder if she can learn much more from the dear old biddy I've seen with the other children,' said Paris.

'Oh, you're so right!' I said. 'Miss Rayner tries hard, but she teaches us from those little Peter Parley books – lists of facts that we have to learn parrot fashion. I wish Mama would let me attend a proper school like my brother.'

'Young girls don't need serious schooling,' said Mama. 'If you're going to be argumentative and distract us, then you'd better go away. Mr Walker is an artist and needs to concentrate.'

I found a pencil and sat down at the side of the room, where they couldn't see what I was doing. I flicked through the pages of Paris's drawing pad as silently as I could, unable to help myself.

I looked at his recent sketches – studies of Mama's hands, her rings very tight on her fingers, and of her eyebrows, her nose and her little pursed mouth. It was strange seeing her dissected like that.

There was also a sketch of me sitting on the window seat! I stared at it. Had Paris drawn me from life, looking up from the hall or down from the landing, while I was too absorbed in my book to notice? I couldn't work it out from the angle of the drawing. Maybe he'd done it from memory. I was thrilled to think that he'd wanted to draw me – though it wasn't a flattering portrait.

In every sketch he had softened Mama considerably, but he seemed to have hardened me. I was frowning in a very intense way as I looked down at my book. There were two little pinched lines above my nose, and my eyes were narrowed. My hair was looped back untidily behind my ears and I'd kicked off my shoes and socks. The shading on my bare feet made them look grubby.

I knew what I looked like, of course. I saw myself in the looking glass every day. But I hadn't realized I was so fierce, so harsh, so untidy. I could understand why Mama was so impatient with me.

Was it a good thing or a bad thing that Paris had drawn me with such accuracy? Had he not bothered to flatter me because I wasn't his patron and wouldn't be paying him? Or could he possibly like me the way I was?

I couldn't decide. Then I flicked back another page and saw a sketch of a stranger. She was a beautiful dark-haired woman wearing a long embroidered silky gown that was slipping off her shoulders. She stared straight out of the page, smiling.

There were more sketches of her, page after page. I saw her in an evening dress with her hair up; in a demure white blouse and neat tie; in her corset and lace-edged drawers. There was even a drawing of her in her tin bath wearing nothing at all. It was a back view, but she was looking round at the artist, smiling again.

I turned the pages gingerly, as if the paper were scorching hot. I saw a city scene with a wide, tree-lined river and a graceful bridge and little stalls selling old books. I didn't need to see the medieval buildings in the background and the CAFÉ DE PARIS sign outside a restaurant to realize that this was France. Sitting at one of the little tables outside the restaurant was the dark-haired woman with a glass of wine in her hand.

So *she* was the friend Paris had mentioned. I flipped through several more sketches, scowling at them all. Then I turned back to the first clean page and started my own drawing. It was a set of pictures that told a story, like a little child's reading primer. At the top of the page I printed *The Artist Tells a Story*, and drew a little caricature of Paris. *Here is the Artist. He is a nice man.*

Then I drew him painting Mama, making her look very fat and very silly. *He paints pictures.*

I did another picture of Paris smiling at Mama while she simpered coquettishly. *He tells the lady she is very pretty.*

I made Paris yawn behind his easel, his mouth wide. *He finds this very tiring.*

The next little sketch showed Paris packing a bag, a long scarf wound round his neck. *He needs a holiday.*

I'd filled up my page, so I started another. I drew him on a big boat looking out to sea. The dark woman was at his side. *He takes a trip with his friend.* I drew them strolling by the Seine. *They have a lovely time*; dancing in a bar. *They have lots of lovely times*; then in a restaurant with the waiter presenting a bill. Paris was patting his pockets, the woman peering into her purse. *Oh dear, they ran out of money!* I did another drawing of the pair on the boat going the other way. *The Artist has to go home.*

I was on the third page now. I drew Paris looking sorrowful, talking to Mama. *The Artist has to tell the rich lady a story.* In the next picture Mama was smiling as Paris resumed the portrait. *The Artist is very good at telling stories.*

I filled up the rest of the page with a drawing of Paris looking quizzical, and printed at the bottom: *Do you still think the Artist is a nice man?*

I was so absorbed that I forgot all about the real Mama and Paris. I jumped when Mama raised her voice.

'Really, Rose, I think you need an ear trumpet! For the third time, put down your pencil and run along. It's long past nursery lunchtime.'

I stretched and wiggled my shoulders.

'You've been working really hard all morning,' said Paris. 'Let's see what you've done.'

'Oh no, it's just nonsense,' I said, starting to tear my three pages out of his drawing book – but he quickly snatched it away.

'Don't be bashful, Rose. Let me see,' he said, and peered at my drawings. I felt sick. How could I have let myself get so carried away! What would he think of me?

'Oh my goodness!' he said, laughing.

'Are her sketches very comical, Mr Walker?' asked Mama.

'They're certainly that.'

'Let me see.' Mama held out her hand.

'No!' I gasped.

But Paris was master of the situation. 'I don't want to embarrass Rose. I think it best you don't see these sketches, Mrs Rivers. I don't think you'd be impressed. Let's give her a few weeks' practice first,' he said smoothly.

'I'm sure you know best, dear boy,' said Mama. 'I hope you'll join me for lunch . . . I'll just go and change.' She wandered off in a rustle of silk and a waft of lavender cologne, Alphonse pattering along at her heels.

'Thank you,' I said weakly.

'You're a girl to be reckoned with, aren't you!' said Paris, peering at my work again.

'I'm so sorry. I didn't mean to be so rude. I just couldn't seem to help it,' I said.

'Rose, they're excellent. Astonishing, in fact. I tried to do some satirical drawings for that humorous journal

Punch, and sent them to the art editor – he's an old friend of mine. He turned them all down, saying they didn't have the right tone. They were too childish. Yours are anything but! They're brilliant!'

'You're just saying that to be kind,' I said.

'Come now! You know full well I'm not necessarily a kind person. My, you're sharp! So, you've found me out, Miss Rose Rivers. Do you disapprove terribly of my French entanglement?'

'I don't care a jot,' I said, my cheeks burning.

'I find it hard remembering that you're still a child.'

'About to go and have my nursery lunch.'

'I wish I could join you. I think it would be much more fun,' said Paris.

'If you saw Sebastian letting his pet mouse eat from his plate and Algie slurping his food and Clarrie spitting out her cabbage, I think you'd soon change your mind,' I said.

'And what about your other sister, Beth?'

'She has to eat with Nurse Budd now – she acts like her jailer. Beth is the real beauty of the family. You should be painting *her* portrait, not Mama's.'

'I'd sooner paint yours, Rose. Shall I suggest it to your mother?' Paris asked.

'So you can make some more money?'

'No! Oh dear, you *have* got a poor opinion of me! Rose, could I keep your sketches for the moment and show them to my friend at *Punch*?'

'No!'

'You really won't let me?' Paris said, looking disappointed.

'They're not good enough. And they're too personal,' I said.

'They *work*, Rose. Let me show him.' He reached out and took my hand. 'Please.'

How could I resist?

19

CLOVER WASN'T IN THE nursery at lunchtime.

'I've sent that young madam off to Bethnal Green,' said Nurse.

'You've done *what*, Nurse?'

'Don't you speak to me like that, Miss Rose. You're not mistress of this house yet!'

'But *why* have you? What's at Bethnal Green? Is it – is it a workhouse? Or a *prison*? She didn't take Mama's brooch!'

I was beginning to think that Clover really *couldn't* have taken it. I'd been sleeping in her room night after night, and there certainly hadn't been any sign of the brooch then. It had been lying in such an obvious place. Someone had put it there deliberately so that Clover would get the blame. I wondered if that someone could possibly be Nurse. She'd hated having Clover foisted upon her, hated seeing how much the children loved her. She'd blamed Clover for allowing them to play with Mama's jewellery box.

'Don't get in such a state, you silly girl,' said Nurse. 'Of course she's not going to any workhouse or prison! My, my, what an overactive imagination! She's gone to that nursery equipment shop over in Bethnal Green because there's something wrong with the steering on little Phoebe's perambulator. I dare say Master Algie bouncing it about didn't help. So, as a punishment, I've made Clover trundle the wretched thing there. By the time it's fixed and she's wheeled it all the way back to Kensington she'll have learned not to encourage the children in their wild games.'

'But it must be miles and miles, there and back,' I protested.

'Then it will teach her a lesson, won't it? When I was a lass I'd think nothing of walking ten miles,' said Nurse.

'Yes, but I'm sure you had proper boots. Clover only has those soft felt things. They'll be worn right through!'

Nurse looked a little guilty. 'I hadn't thought of that. Well, perhaps I'll send her on a trip down Monmouth Street tomorrow, and she can kit herself out with a good pair of second-hand boots. I'll lend her a shilling. She's not a bad girl, for all her wildness. And *I* know full well that she's not a thief, Miss Rose, so you've no call to act high and mighty with me.'

I felt ashamed. I decided that Nurse couldn't have planted the brooch in Clover's bed. She sounded almost fond of her now.

I kept thinking of Clover trudging all that way across London. It had started to rain too, not a downpour, but enough to make felt boots sodden. She must have been feeling so miserable. And she still thought I suspected she'd stolen the brooch.

I felt so badly about it. I tried to be nice to everyone so that I could feel like a better person. I read *The Arabian Nights* to the children when they lay down after lunch. I accompanied them on a cold, dreary walk to the rose garden, the flowers all finished and the bushes cut back to prickly stumps. I even joined Mama when Mrs Feynsham-Jones came calling at four o'clock.

I sat and sewed my tedious cross-stitch sampler while they batted conversation back and forth as if they were playing Battledore and Shuttlecock. Mama scored points boasting about Paris and the pains he was taking with her portrait.

'Will he show it at the Academy?' asked Mrs Feynsham-Jones.

'I dare say,' said Mama complacently. 'He's very talented, you know.' She glanced at the other blue dress portrait over the mantelpiece. 'Edward's portrait of me was considered very fine, but I think Mr Walker's is superior. Oh, I've just had the most novel idea! Perhaps one of the galleries might care to display both portraits side by side so that people can make up their own minds!'

I can't believe how silly and deluded she is. Even when she was young and slender Mama was never a society beauty like the Honourable Louisa Mayhorne. Now she's too old and plump to be any kind of beauty. Besides, she's shunned by real society because her money comes from Grandpapa's jute mills. Even ugly old Lady Robson has stopped calling. I think Mrs Feynsham-Jones only comes so that she can feel superior.

She was clearly disconcerted by Mama's non-stop chatter about her portrait, and tried to score her own point.

'I think you ought to know, Jeannie dear, that my girls told me they'd seen Sebastian and Algie and Clarrie behaving very strangely in Kensington Gardens the other day. Apparently they had feathers in their hair and were making whooping noises as they danced around the bushes,' she said. 'That little nurserymaid was joining in too, leaping about and waving a stick like a tomahawk!'

Mama winced. 'Oh dear Lord, that wretched Clover Moon again! I'd be delighted to send her packing, but Edward has made it his mission to keep her under this roof. You know how obsessed he is with all these little waifs and strays. He's influenced by that Sarah Smith who writes those dubious stories about slum children.'

'I never let my girls read them when they were little. I don't think they're at all suitable,' said Mrs Feynsham-Jones. 'And another thing, Jeannie – when are you going to have Sebastian's hair cut? He really could be mistaken for a girl. If I were blessed with a son I'd make sure he looked like a little man.'

'Sebastian seems gentle, but he's got the strongest will of all my children. Nurse says he screamed blue murder and tried to bite her when she approached him with the scissors,' Mama said weakly.

'He needs a good whipping! One cannot pander to children's whims. And as for Beth! Well, truly, my dear, if your nursery staff had only been a little firmer with her, I'm sure she'd behave like a little lady now, even if she is backward,' said Mrs Feynsham-Jones.

I wanted to stab her with my embroidery needle. 'Beth isn't backward. She's very intelligent. She just gets upset easily,' I said.

'That's enough, Rose. Nurse Budd is trying a firmer approach. She came on Lady Robson's recommendation. I've noticed a big improvement already,' said Mama.

'Really? I heard that Lady Robson's daughter-in-law had to dismiss her. Seems there was something seriously wrong with her son,' said Mrs Feynsham-Jones.

Then she turned to me. 'And how are you, Rose?' she asked, her voice syrupy sweet. 'I see you're stitching a sampler. How quaint at your age! My girls all completed theirs before they were ten. Still, it's good to see you with your head out of a book for once, attempting to join in the conversation. All that reading can't be good for you. I'm sure it's eyestrain that has given you that unfortunate scowl.'

Mama didn't even try to defend me. She simply shook her head and sighed, then steered the conversation to Rupert's last letter and his progress at school. At last she was in her element, because her golden boy was doing so splendidly. Mrs Feynsham-Jones had scored several points, but Mama held the trump card.

'Dear Rupert,' said Mrs Feynsham-Jones. 'My girls miss him dreadfully, especially Pamela. She struck up a firm friendship with Rupert in the summer – did you know?'

'Dear Pamela,' said Mama, but she sounded uncertain. She wanted *me* to be firm friends with the Feynsham-Jones sisters, but she wasn't so sure they were good enough for Rupert.

When Mrs Feynsham-Jones had left, Mama asked me if I'd known that Rupert and Pamela were 'firm friends'.

'I'm not sure you could call it that,' I said.

'Mmm, I thought as much,' said Mama. 'Still, I suppose Rupert could do worse. For the moment. Of course, Rupert and Pamela are still children. It's not as if they're seriously courting!'

'Rupert certainly isn't serious,' I told her.

'For all he's grown into a little gentleman, he has a head full of sport and tuck and japes. He's years away from thinking about sweethearts. The very idea!' said Mama fondly. She glanced at me. 'Dear goodness, they'll be telling me *you're* firm friends with some boy next!' She laughed as if this were a great joke.

I don't want to be romantically involved with any boy, but I couldn't help feeling hurt that Mama found the idea so funny. I kept thinking about Paris's sketch. I looked so fierce and plain. Positively ugly in fact. No matter how much I brush my hair or how often I change my dress or how scrupulous I am about keeping my hands ink free and my stockings unwrinkled, I am never going to be pretty.

I didn't want to be an insipid pink-and-white girl like Pamela. I wished I could be an exotic, dark-haired beauty like Paris's friend in France. I wondered what it would be like to go abroad with him. In a few years' time, when I was old enough, perhaps it might be possible.

I thought about it at dinner as I looked at my unappealing fatty chop and mashed potato.

'Do eat up, Rose. You've been toying with that chop for the last ten minutes. Edie is waiting to serve us our dessert,' said Mama.

'Sorry, Mama. I'm just not very hungry,' I said, pushing my food to the side of my plate.

'Less of that nonsense! Eat it up at once. You're thin as a rake. You'll make yourself ill if you don't eat properly,' said Mama. 'Edward, make the child eat up.'

'A few more mouthfuls please, Rose,' said Papa. 'Though I must admit, you look the picture of health, even though your mama feels you're wasting away. Look at those lovely pink cheeks!'

I was blushing because, inside my head, Paris and I were dining in a little French restaurant. I wasn't sure what French people ate. I could only conjure up frogs' legs, which didn't sound very palatable – but I wouldn't care. I'd have eaten sautéed frogs, toads, newts, indeed, any kind of reptile, just so long as I could share the meal with him. We were washing it down with red wine. Rupert and I had once shared a half-full bottle of wine to see what it was like to be drunk. It had been such an unpleasant experiment that just the smell of wine made me feel ill now – but in my daydream I sipped away happily, raising my glass to Paris as he sketched me.

I managed the mouthfuls Papa demanded, ate half my strawberry tart and custard, and then escaped. I went to see how Clover had fared on her trip to Bethnal Green, but she was busy bathing the children and Nurse told me I was in the way. Clover didn't even look at me.

I decided to wait till later, when everyone else was asleep. At last the children had settled down, and I could hear Nurse snoring. There was silence from Beth's room. I hoped Nurse Budd was asleep too. I was unnerved by the thought that she might be sitting behind the door listening, but I summoned my courage and tiptoed along the corridor.

I opened the door to the servants' stairs cautiously to stop it creaking, and then hurried up the narrow steps. The wood was cold on my bare feet, and so worn and splintered. The family stairs were all thickly carpeted, with polished brass stair rods.

I crept past Edie and Maggie's room. I could hear them whispering. 'Honestly, it makes me so flaming cross,' Edie was muttering. I wondered what it was that made her angry. Was it us? Did they even like us? I knew so little about them, and yet they knew everything about us. Maggie emptied our night-time chamber pots and dealt with our dirty clothes, washing and ironing them and sewing on all the missing buttons. She must think us a trial.

Edie wasn't so involved with us children, but she knew Mama intimately. She held out her towel when she bathed, and squeezed her into her corsets, and powdered her bosom. She padded out her thinning hair and applied rouge to give her cheeks a girlish blush. She was snippy with us, but always flattered Mama:

'Oh, madam, that blue suits you beautifully!'

'No one would believe you'd had seven children!'

'What tiny feet you have! Those pearl kid boots set them off a treat!'

Edie can't really think that. She is as adept at wheedling as Paris. She even makes a fuss of Alphonse, giving him little titbits – yet once, when he snapped at her, I saw her bend down and bare her own teeth, imitating his growls. She was larking around for Maggie's benefit, but she looked truly menacing, and Alphonse ran away in fright.

Perhaps Edie wants to bare her teeth at us too. Maybe all the servants disliked us. Cook might secretly spit into our food as she stirred our stews and puddings. Mr Hodgson might be quietly selling off the silver and vintage wine and pocketing the profits. Jack Boots and Mary-Jane might pull faces and do cruel impersonations behind our backs. Our own nurse had dandled and rocked us to sleep, but perhaps she was sick and tired of us now. And I was sure that Nurse Budd hated us, for all she sounded so sugary sweet.

Nurse Budd! She hated Clover too. She wanted to get rid of her. It seemed so obvious now. *She'd* taken the sapphire brooch and put it in Clover's bed!

I burst into Clover's room. I thought she'd be crying in the dark, but her candle was lit and she was sitting up in the tattered petticoat she wore as a nightgown. I saw that the pillow and all the little presents I'd given her were neatly parcelled up beside her.

'Clover?' I said, forgetting to whisper.

'I should lower your voice, Miss Rose. Here are your things. Please take them away.'

'Oh, Clover, don't be like this,' I begged. 'I didn't *really* think you'd stolen the wretched brooch. And I didn't tell on you, did I? I lied because I wanted to protect you.'

'Thank you, Miss Rose,' she said coldly.

'Please don't call me *Miss* Rose. I'm your friend! And listen to me, I'm sure I know how the brooch came to be in your bed. Nurse Budd put it there! She hates the way you try to protect Beth. She was trying to get you dismissed.'

'Have you only just realized that? And you're supposed to be so clever! *I* worked that out the moment you told me you'd found the brooch in my bed,' said Clover. 'You thought I'd stolen it, just like everyone else, because I'm just a slum child from Cripps Alley.'

'All right, it was dreadful of me, and I feel deeply ashamed now. Please say you'll forgive me,' I implored her.

'As if you care whether I forgive you or not! You're the daughter of the house. I'm just the servant,' she said.

'Will you stop this! I care *dreadfully*!' I sat down beside her and tried to put my arm round her, but she flinched.

'Please be friends with me, Clover. I made a mistake, and now I'm sorry. For goodness' sake, friends can sometimes behave badly to each other, can't they? Rupert used to say terrible things to me, and I had to put up with it. I still *liked* him.'

'Well, *I* don't like you any more,' said Clover. 'That's one thing you can't make me do, even though I'm your servant. Now please take your things and go back to your room.'

'I won't! Not till we make up. I'm not budging from this room until you say you truly forgive me,' I said.

'Then we're neither of us going to get much sleep,' said Clover. 'You can make me say anything you want, but you can't make me feel it in my heart.'

'But you're breaking *my* heart,' I declared. 'You're my one true friend in all the world.'

Clover sniffed. 'Is that right, Miss Rose? How long have you known me? I might have told you little things about my life, but you don't really know anything about me.'

'I *want* to know! I *want* to be your friend.'

'You can't force people to be friends. You thought you were being so kind and splendid making friends with a girl like me, but when you saw that brooch so obviously planted in my bed, you thought I was a common thief like all the others. You felt so clever and noble pretending that you'd found it in your mother's room. You were probably thrilled to get a chance to protect me. You wanted me to be humble and grateful and in your debt for ever.'

'How can you *say* that!' I said, but my heart started thumping. I knew it was partly true. I burst into tears.

'Ssh!' she said. 'Edie and Maggie will hear!'

I cried harder, unable to stop. Then I heard a door opening and the scuffle of bare feet. Clover put her hand over my mouth.

'Clover?' It was Maggie. 'Is that you howling?'

I held my breath, shaking.

'Yes, Maggie!' Clover said, pretending to sob.

'Don't take on so. I reckon Miss Rose saved your bacon today,' she said.

'I didn't steal that brooch!'

'All right, keep your hair on,' said Maggie. 'What you crying for then?'

'My feet hurt. They're blistered from all that walking,' said Clover.

'It was quite a hike for a little kid like you. Want me to come and rub your feet for you?' Maggie asked.

'No, they're too sore. But thank you. I'll be all right now.'

'Go to sleep then. You'll feel better in the morning, you'll see,' said Maggie. 'Night night.'

We heard her shuffle back to her room. Clover kept her hand over my mouth until I was quiet, though I still shook. She sat still for a minute, and then sighed and leaned against me.

'There now, Rose,' she whispered. 'Don't take on so. I'm sorry I was cold with you. I didn't mean to upset you so. I know you were trying to act for the best.'

'Do you really hate me now?' I whispered.

'Don't be daft. You mean the world to me. That's why I was so hurt that you thought I'd steal from your family.'

'Can we still be friends?'

'Yes, if you still want to be friends with me.'

'And you'll keep all the things I gave you?'

'Yes!'

'And can I stay the night with you?'

'Yes, of course, only keep quiet!'

We cuddled up together. It was such a relief that we were friends again. I had hiccups from crying, but did my best to smother them. It made us get the giggles.

'Do you still miss your sister dreadfully?' I whispered.

'Yes,' said Clover. 'We were so close, Rose.'

'I know just how much I'd miss Rupert if something happened to him.'

'Is he like you?'

'Not at all, even though we're twins. He has such charm. He can make anyone like him. Like Mr Walker,' I added, without thinking.

'The artist who's painting your mother's portrait?' Clover whispered. 'Do you like him then?'

'Very much! He likes my comical drawings. He's going to show them to an art editor friend of his. He thinks I have real talent!' I said, unable to help boasting.

I remembered that Papa had said Clover liked drawing too.

'Can I see something *you've* drawn, Clover?' I asked.

But Clover was already asleep, her head lolling against my back, her wild hair tickling me.

When we woke early the next morning, I asked her if she'd draw something for me.

She screwed up her face at the thought. 'You don't want to see my scribbles. I just draw little pictures to amuse the children, that's all. Hush! Isn't that Phoebe wailing? You'd better run back to your room quick before Nurse starts stirring.'

I took her at her word, thinking she probably copied illustrations out of nursery books. When Papa was working on his sketches that afternoon, I told him that she liked drawing.

'I know she does, Rose. Thank goodness the unfortunate business of the missing brooch has been resolved. I'm so glad you've taken her under your wing. She's a dear girl, isn't she?' he said.

'I think she's splendid, Papa. And it's interesting that she likes drawing, isn't it?' I said. 'Have you seen any of her pictures?'

'I have indeed. She's very talented,' said Papa.

'Really talented?' I asked him, surprised.

'I have one of her sketches here,' he said, leafing through his portfolio. 'Yes, here it is.'

He showed me a drawing of a child sitting on a step. Perhaps it was her sister Megs, because it was drawn with such care and tenderness. Papa had taught me enough to realize that some of the shading wasn't quite right, the figure not quite centred on the page – but there was no mistaking its quality.

'It's remarkable, isn't it?' he said.

'Yes, it is. Far better than anything I could do.'

'Your sketches are more technically accomplished,' Papa said. 'But certainly this child has a raw talent that is very rare.'

'So why are you wasting your time teaching *me* to sketch? You should be teaching Clover!'

'I would like to, but the child is kept so busy with all your siblings. And I'm sure your mama would not think it proper.'

'Mama fusses so about propriety, but she doesn't actually come from a long line of gentlefolk herself. It's ridiculous!' I said.

Papa looked shocked. 'I don't think it's seemly to talk about your mother like that, Rose. You're too sharp at times. If you can't show Mama the respect she deserves, at least feel a little compassion,' he said. 'Her life hasn't always been easy. And I don't suppose *I* have helped. Now run along, I have work to do.'

I felt well and truly snubbed, but I suppose I deserved it. I felt humbled too by the quality of Clover's artwork. Still, I'd never set out to sketch seriously. I only ever wanted to do my comical drawings. It was wonderful that Paris thought so much of them. He is younger and more in touch with current fashion than Papa. I hoped his art editor friend would like my drawings too.

I imagined casually strolling into Papa's studio and saying, 'Have you read *Punch* this week? There's an amusing little piece towards the end . . .' I'd flap the journal at Papa and he'd glance at it quickly – and then stop, astonished. He'd surely be impressed if my art appeared in *Punch*. Then he'd *have* to be proud of me.

But the opportunity will never arise. A few days later Paris told me that his friend rejected my sketches.

'Don't look so cast down, Rose. He's very impressed by your work, especially when I told him that you were still a child. He'd love to see more of your drawings in the future. He feels they're a little too sharp for *Punch* just now,' he said. 'But don't worry, I'll show them to some other people. I still think they work wonderfully.'

I couldn't listen to him any more.

Too sharp, too sharp . . .

Nurse used to say that to me. 'Really, Miss Rose! You're so sharp you'll cut yourself one day.'

I feel as if I am cut now. And bleeding.

20

I'VE STOPPED GOING UP to the studio. Paris hasn't commented on it. I think he feels embarrassed about leading me to believe that my work was any good. Mama is pleased to have him to herself.

I've spent my time reading in my room. I found a translation of *Madame Bovary* hidden behind the five volumes of Vasari's *Lives of the Artists*. It is an astonishing book. Mama would faint if she read certain passages.

I've spent time with Beth too. I persuaded Papa to tell Nurse Budd that I must visit Beth daily. I hated the way she was always shut away from us now. I needed to keep an eye on her.

'Of course, sir, whatever you say – though I think all these visits will interfere with my regime. Miss Beth's behaviour is much improved. I believe dear Mrs Rivers is exceptionally pleased. It would be a shame if Beth became over-excited,' she said.

'I am not suggesting that Beth should be visited by a troupe of circus clowns, Nurse Budd. Rose is Beth's *sister*. And I am her father, and intend to visit her whenever I wish too,' said Papa firmly.

'Very well, sir,' Nurse Budd said, meekly enough, though her eyes gleamed with malice when she looked at me.

I'd confronted her outright about the sapphire brooch.

'Did *you* find Mama's sapphire brooch after the children had been playing with her jewellery, Nurse Budd?' I asked.

'You're very forgetful, Miss Rose. *You* were the one who found the brooch,' said Nurse Budd.

'Are you sure you didn't put it in a certain place to make it look as if Clover had stolen it?' I persisted. 'I think you did!'

'What a strange fancy, Miss Rose,' she said. 'Why should I want to do that?'

'Because you dislike Clover. You don't want her spying on you.'

'Oh my, Miss Rose, your imagination really runs away with you sometimes. I think you should write storybooks when you grow up,' said Nurse Budd.

I was *sure* she'd taken the brooch, hoping that Clover would be blamed. But I had no proof – and Nurse Budd knew it.

All I could do was visit Beth as often as I could and make sure that Nurse Budd wasn't tormenting her. Beth didn't seem particularly glad to see me. She was very quiet now, often sitting on the floor in a corner, clutching Marigold.

'Why don't you sit on a chair, Beth? You'd be much more comfortable,' I said. 'Does Nurse Budd *make* you sit on the floor? Is it a punishment?'

Beth didn't reply, and Nurse Budd gave a false tinkly laugh.

'The very idea, Miss Rose! I'd prefer Miss Beth to sit up nicely in her chair too, but she likes that corner. It's her own little place.'

'Own little place,' Beth murmured to Marigold.

'You're like little Jack Horner in the nursery rhyme, Beth,' I said, sitting down beside her.

I chanted my way through it, and all the other nursery rhymes I could think of. She used to like to join in. I knew she was word perfect, but she didn't even repeat the last word of each line. She simply held onto Marigold and rocked to and fro.

I tried rocking too. It was surprisingly difficult to keep up, and it hurt my behind. I started to feel giddy, the room seeming to whirl around me. I wondered if that was why Beth rocked. She wanted to be in her own world, not ours.

'Don't mock the poor child, Miss Rose,' said Nurse Budd.

'I'm not mocking her! I'm trying to understand her,' I retorted.

'Understand!' she said, sniffing. 'She simply needs the right handling and a regular routine.'

'I suppose she *is* quieter than she used to be,' I said to Clover.

'I don't think children should be quiet,' she replied. 'I wish *I* was allowed to look after Beth. Still, Nurse lets me care for Phoebe now. She's such a sweet baby. I do hope your mama has another baby soon.'

'I don't think Mama would care for that! And surely you don't want to spend the rest of your life looking after babies!' I said. 'Papa showed me your drawing, Clover. It's so good! Papa thinks you've got real talent. Perhaps you could be an artist one day. Don't look like that, *some* women are. You'd be free to paint all day and keep company with other artists. You could even go to Paris if you wanted. Mr Walker says it's a wonderful city.'

'I don't care what Mr Walker says. I don't like him very much.'

'You don't really know him.'

'I know the type,' said Clover, sniffing.

I felt irritated, but I kept my temper. 'Anyway, in Paris you could stroll along the River Seine and drink wine at bars and stay up all night,' I said.

'I can stroll along the River Thames, but I would never drink wine because I've seen too many drunks in my life.

I certainly wouldn't want to stay up all night – I like my sleep,' said Clover, being deliberately contrary.

'Oh, for heaven's sake, you don't have to be so *literal*,' I protested. 'Don't you have any ambition?'

'I could have all the ambition in the world, but where would it get a girl like me, Miss Rose?' she said.

We were dangerously close to quarrelling again so I kept quiet. Of course she's right. It's much harder for a girl from a poor background to achieve anything in life. It's much harder for *any* girl. Perhaps that's why Mama won't let me go to school. She wants to keep me in my place.

I must be way behind Rupert now. Perhaps I could get him to tell me what he's learned when he comes home for the Christmas holidays. We could pore over his textbooks together. I loved this idea!

But when Rupert came home at last, he was appalled.

'Give a chap a break, Rose!' he said as we sat together on the window seat. 'It's rotten enough having to concentrate on all that stuff when I'm at school. I'm so sick of Latin and Greek and mathematics! That's the last thing I want to think about now it's the holidays.'

'Well, what *do* you want to think about?' I said. 'Your dear friend Pamela, I suppose!'

He went red.

'You're blushing!'

'No I'm not. It's just so hot and stuffy here at home. It's freezing at school. We don't have any heating in the classrooms, and the dorms are so cold you have to crack the ice in your water jug in the mornings. Look, I have chilblains!' He waved his fingers at me.

'Poor little rich boy,' I said, mocking him. 'That's not a chilblain, that's just a wart, and you've always had it. You're blushing because of Pamela – and no wonder! You tell such lies about her. Imagine how she'd feel if she found out.'

'I don't talk about her any more.'

'Don't lie, Rupe. I can always tell when you're lying.'

'No you can't, because I'm telling you God's honest truth,' he said. 'Let's change the subject because it's becoming boring. Who's the new little servant girl, the one with the amazing hair exploding out of her cap?'

'She's called Clover Moon,' I said.

'Where on earth did she spring from?'

'Papa found her.'

'What, she's one of his little street children? I bet Mama had something to say about that!' said Rupert.

'She wasn't pleased at first, you know what she's like, but Clover's wonderful with the children. Even Algie does as he's told.'

'Good Lord!' said Rupert. 'Maybe she's bewitched him. She's got the most astonishing green eyes, have you noticed?'

'Of course I've noticed. She's my friend,' I said.

'Your *friend*?' said Rupert, raising his eyebrows.

'Yes. She's the dearest, kindest, most talented girl, even though she comes from some awful slum and has led a terrible life. Don't you dare mock, Rupe,' I said fiercely.

'I'm not mocking. As a matter of fact I've got a friend who's a servant too, this chap Jack.'

'Jack *Boots*?'

'No, not *our* Jack! This is someone at school, one of the gardener's boys. Kilbourne has massive grounds, and I like to wander around them. I came across this chap cutting back the brambles and we got chatting. He's good fun. His father's a boxer, one of those fairground chaps. Jack's teaching me to box too.' Rupert clenched his fist and punched me lightly. 'Apparently women box at the fairs too. There's an interesting job for you, Rose! And a way of letting out all your aggression.'

'Oh, very funny,' I said. I was intrigued by this new friendship, though I knew that Rupert had never been a snob. 'Are your friends learning to box too?'

'I don't hang around with those chaps any more, actually. They've started to get on my nerves.'

'That's a shame. Mama's desperate for you to invite some of your school chums to tea over Christmas.'

'Is she? Well, I'll invite Jack, that'll show her,' said Rupert. 'He's actually a capital chap, Rose. I wish I *could* invite him.'

'I wish you could too. But, seriously, Mama's really keen to meet your school friends, the ones you write about in your letters.'

'I write any old tosh in those letters. As a matter of fact I don't *have* any particular friends at the moment.'

Rupert yawned and stretched as if the whole subject bored him, and then started talking about his eccentric mathematics teacher. I was interested, and longed to ask Rupert more about the subject, because I only knew the most basic arithmetic, but I was worried by his hasty change of subject.

'What do you mean, you haven't got any particular friends?' I asked.

Rupert always had friends. Everyone vied to befriend him. He was the most popular boy wherever he went.

He shrugged.

'You mean you're friends with everyone?'

'No, the exact opposite. I'm friends with no one. Or, to be precise, no one is friends with me.'

'What about Hardy and Martin?'

Rupert shrugged. 'They can't stand me. They all despise me now. Don't look so devastated! I have my new pal Jack if I want company.' He was trying to pretend he didn't care, but I saw that he was near tears.

I reached out and took his hand. He gripped mine back tightly. I tried to think of the right thing to say – but then Algie and Clarrie came clattering down the stairs to spend their token time with Mama in the drawing room.

'You come too, Rupert, please!' Clarrie begged, and Algie tried pulling Rupert's legs to tip him off the window seat.

'Play with us!' he commanded.

'Leave Rupert alone, you little horrors,' I said quickly. 'He's feeling tired after his journey. He's not up to any rough stuff just now. Tomorrow!'

They trailed off, complaining. A minute later Sebastian followed – with one of Clarrie's pink satin ribbons in his long hair.

'Sebastian!' I exclaimed, momentarily distracted. 'I don't think it's a good idea to wear that ribbon. Mama won't approve and Papa will laugh at you.'

'Nurse put it on me because I won't let her cut my hair. She said if I wanted to look like a girl, then I might as well dress like one too,' said Sebastian. 'It's to shame me.'

'She's so mean sometimes. She was always nagging me for being such a tomboy,' I said. 'Just take the ribbon off, Seb.'

'But I like it,' he told me. 'I think it looks pretty. And it feels nice.' He fingered the satin complacently and sauntered off.

'I hope that poor little tyke doesn't get sent to Kilbourne,' said Rupert. 'They'll make his life hell.'

'Why are they making *your* life hell, Rupe?' I asked softly.

He sighed. 'It was the Pamela thing,' he said. 'It started to get a bit out of hand. It became a game, and they started making up things about her themselves. Really filthy things. It got a bit too much. I remembered what you said and started to feel guilty. So I told them that she was a decent girl and would never do the things they were suggesting.

'They thought it was because I was in love with her, so they teased me and called me the Lovelorn Swain and made kissing noises at me. I could cope with that, but then Hardy got a letter saying that his family have been invited to Lady Robson's party, and the Feynsham-Joneses are all going too.'

'Oh no!' I said.

'Oh yes! He said he was going to make a point of cosying up to Pamela. He seemed to think she'd fool around with *him*. I couldn't bear the stuff he was saying, so I hit him,' said Rupert.

'Good for you!'

'But he's better at fighting than me. He bloodied my nose. I was sure he'd broken it! I doubled up, and Hardy pushed me over, and then my watch fell out of my pocket – and I didn't see it and stepped on it and it broke.'

'Grandpapa's gold watch!'

'I was so horrified I started blubbing right in front of them all. And they jeered, and now they call me Blubber Baby.'

'Oh, Rupert. Do you think you can get the watch mended?'

'It's completely smashed. God knows what the parents will say when they find out.'

'And are they still calling you that stupid name?'

'Boys I don't even know poke me or try to trip me up so I'll blub for them,' said Rupert.

'Can't you tell one of the masters?'

Rupert looked at me pityingly. 'You never tell tales. The whole school would hate me if I ratted on them. Well, they do already. And it's your fault in a way. If you hadn't given me that little lecture, I wouldn't have started to worry about Pamela's feelings. It's all very well for you, Rose. You tell me how to behave and yet you don't have the slightest inkling what school is like. You're so lucky. You can just loll about at home and do nothing.'

'I don't *loll*,' I said. 'As a matter of fact I've been sketching. Not just with Papa – with Mr Paris Walker.'

'Paris! Dear goodness, what a name!'

'I think it's a beautiful name,' I said stiffly.

'Oh well, it probably suits him. These artist chappies are all weirdos.'

'Papa isn't! And neither is Mr Walker!'

I felt immensely sorry for Rupert, but he was starting to annoy me. How could he twist things and say it was *my* fault that those idiotic boys called him names? He should never have boasted about Pamela in the first place. And why did he have to be so horrid about Paris when he didn't even know him?

He wasn't particularly nice to Clover either – even though he knew that she was my special friend. He kept pretending he'd forgotten her name, and called her Daisy or Buttercup or Dandelion. The children roared with laughter, and Nurse smirked too.

I was furious with him. 'How can you call her silly names when you know how *horrible* it is?' I hissed.

'*She* doesn't mind. She laughs too,' said Rupert.

I had to admit that this was true. When I crept up to her room that night, I apologized to her and said that Rupert didn't mean any harm.

'I know that. He's just teasing. He's a boy. They all do it,' said Clover.

'I know it's no excuse, but he's not having a very good time at school,' I said. That sounded rather ridiculous. 'I don't suppose the boys from your alley still go to school at thirteen?'

'No, they start at the factory at twelve and work a ten-hour shift,' said Clover.

I felt terrible. What must she think of us all?

Thank goodness Papa is so sweet with Clover. The next morning he announced that he had to go on an important seasonal mission and needed to find the right person to accompany him.

Sebastian and Algie and Clarrie clamoured to be chosen, sensing that Papa might be buying Christmas presents.

'No, chickies, I need someone who is an expert in this particular field. Someone who is especially interested in dolls,' said Papa.

'Sebastian!' said Algie, screaming with laughter.

'I quite like dolls, Papa,' said Clarrie. 'I like the little ones who live in their own houses. I *wish* I had a doll's house and a family of little dolls,' she added, putting her head on one side and doing her best to look cute.

Papa laughed and tousled her hair, so that her ribbon came undone.

'Really, Edward, Nurse has just fixed the child's hair,' Mama said irritably.

'Sorry, Clarrie. Naughty Papa. If I see Father Christmas on my travels, I'll have a word with him about that doll's house. But I need advice about *big* dolls.'

'Beth has Marigold. I think she's a splendid doll, but Beth will never let me play with her,' said Sebastian wistfully.

'Don't be so silly, child, boys don't play with dolls,' said Mama. 'Edward, you can't possibly be suggesting that *Beth* goes shopping with you! I don't feel she's quite ready for that sort of outing.'

'I tend to agree with you, my dear,' said Papa. 'I have someone else in mind.'

I thought he was looking in my direction, and smiled – but he was looking past me, to where Clover was deftly retying Clarrie's ribbon.

'Little Miss Moon, would you be kind enough to accompany me to the doll-maker's?' he asked.

Clover gave a gasp, and clasped her hands. Her green eyes shone. 'Oh, yes please!' she breathed.

Mama gave a very different kind of gasp. 'Really, Edward, have you lost your senses? If you need a servant to help you carry parcels, I suggest you take Maggie, who's a good strong girl – or Jack Boots, who is growing quite sturdy too. Clover Moon is so small she could barely carry a matchbox!' she exclaimed. 'She would be bound to drop something.'

'I've seen the child carry our baby daughter on her hip half the day and she hasn't dropped her yet. In fact, I've seen her haul young Algie around when he's playing up, and that's a task fit for a strongman in the circus. Show off the muscles in your skinny little arms, Clover!' said Papa.

Clover hesitated, not sure whether he was being serious or not. She dropped a curtsy instead and said, 'I am quite strong, missus, and I'll be very careful.'

Mama winced at the 'missus'. 'You should address me as Madam, Clover – and only speak to me when I ask you a direct question,' she said imperiously.

Clover's eyes flashed, but she curtsied again meekly and said nothing.

'Off we go, Clover. No time to waste,' said Papa, and he whisked her off before Mama could object further.

'Well, really!' she said. 'Your papa has no sense of propriety whatsoever.'

She was soon distracted, because Paris was coming for his last portrait-painting session before Christmas.

I thought Mama might cancel it so that she could make the most of Rupert, but it seemed she'd sooner spend the morning with Paris than with her beloved eldest son.

'I have other plans anyway,' said Rupert.

'Aha!' said Mama, wagging her finger at him. 'Might that possibly involve a visit to the Feynsham-Joneses?'

Rupert went red, which made her squeal. 'Oh, Rupert, you're blushing, bless you! It must be love! How sweet!'

Algie made disgusting kissing noises, while Clarrie and Sebastian giggled.

Poor Rupert walked out of the room without responding, trying to look dignified, but Algie had left his spinning top on the floor. Rupert tripped over it, nearly falling flat on his face.

This made everyone laugh out loud. I burned all over and rushed after him.

'Don't mind them, Rupert, they're all such fools,' I said, catching hold of his arm. 'You're not really going to see Pamela, are you? If I were you I'd keep away.'

He brushed my hand aside. 'When I want your advice I'll ask for it,' he snapped, and when he got to his room he slammed the door on me.

I was left feeling tearful and aggrieved. Sitting with Rupert on the window seat, I'd felt so close to him, but now he wanted to shut me out. I didn't know what to do with myself. I didn't fancy making paper chains with Miss Rayner and the little ones. Nor did I want to sing 'Bye Baby Bunting' to Phoebe ten times in a row. I didn't want to brave Nurse Budd and sit with Beth, though I knew I should.

So I went up to the studio though Mama made it plain that she didn't want me there.

'Really, dear, you don't need to come if you've lost interest in drawing,' she said.

'I'd like to set you a new task, Rose,' said Paris. 'Why not attempt a Christmas scene? Depict a typical family Christmas – in your own style.'

'I don't think I could,' I told him.

'Nonsense!'

'I don't see the point.'

'You could give the finished picture as a little Christmas gift.'

'No one would want my stupid stuff,' I said, determined to feel sorry for myself.

'*I* would,' said Paris. 'In fact, you can give *me* the picture as *my* Christmas present.'

'Dear Mr Walker! You're so kind to humour the child,' Mama murmured.

I started drawing and Paris started painting. Mama talked the whole time. She'd heard that Lady Robson was giving a party on Christmas Eve and was upset because we hadn't been invited. Mama insisted that Christmas Eve was a ridiculous day to hold a party, and said it should be family time. We should gather round the piano together and sing carols. She ignored the fact that, even though we have a piano, none of us can play it adequately. I have failed again as the eldest daughter of the house. I have no musical ability whatsoever.

We're not very good at singing together either. Mama says she is a natural soprano, but she has such a high, affected voice you can barely hear her. Papa sings very loudly and in a jolly manner, but he is so off-key it makes painful listening. Rupert had a reasonably pure voice, but it's started to crack. Sebastian won't sing at all because he says it disturbs Montmorency. Algie can sing a little, but he generally substitutes rude words for the proper ones and then snorts at his daring. Clarrie forgets the words completely and makes do with la-la-la-ing.

Beth is the only one who sings really beautifully. She used to have piano lessons and did well, though she played with her head down, crooning to herself. The teacher insisted that she should sit up properly, and tried to lift her chin. This frightened Beth and she threw such a tantrum that her piano lessons ended there and then.

Mama convinced herself that our family Christmas Eves were the Eighth Wonder of the World, and suddenly invited Paris to join us.

'Why didn't I think of it before? You will have such fun, dear boy. And why not stay the night and spend Christmas Day with us? Cook makes the most marvellous Christmas dinner, and we have a slap-up tea too! I dare say I shall scarcely fit into this dress afterwards.' Mama scarcely fits into it now, and every seam strained as she described our Christmas revels. 'It will be such fun playing Charades, Mr Walker! You'll enjoy the chance to dress up and act.'

'My dear Mrs Rivers, you are quite right, I do enjoy acting,' he said. 'But I'm afraid I can't join you and your family for Christmas, much as I'd like to. I have to be with my mother. She is still rather an invalid.'

I admired his quick thinking – but Mama was swift with her own response.

'Why not bring the dear lady too? If she is still frail, she can recline on my chaise longue. We have a trained nurse on the premises, should she need medical attention.'

'That's so kind of you, Mrs Rivers, but I think the travelling would be too much for her, and any company tires her, no matter how congenial. She leads a very quiet life now,' said Paris.

Mama was silenced for only a few seconds. 'Then I have a better idea. Join our family for New Year's Eve instead. I'm sure your mother will understand, as she will wish to spend it quietly. We always have a splendid ball up in Scotland, you know – a true Hogmanay. My parents have a country estate in Angus, and we have such a jolly time. Our parties are legendary. Oh, you must come, Mr Walker! And, as an artist, you will be inspired by our grand Scottish scenery. My husband finds it immensely stimulating. Please say you will come!'

'You're too kind, Mrs Rivers,' said Paris. He didn't say yes, but he clearly couldn't think of any more excuses.

Mama sat back triumphantly, sure she had won. I wondered if Paris *would* come! I doubted it, but it would be such fun if he did! Mama wasn't exaggerating about the ball. Grandmama organizes it, with a piper, and a band for dancing the Eightsome Reel and the Dashing White Sergeant, much more exciting than prim ballroom dancing. Papa used to say he fell in love with Mama as he twirled her around in the Gay Gordons. I pictured them: Mama a slender girl of eighteen in a white dress with a tartan sash, Papa older but still trim and gallant, leaping about in a borrowed kilt.

There's an age gap of twelve years between them. As I worked on my Christmas picture I realized that there was a similar age gap between Paris and me. I couldn't help feeling that this was significant.

When it was time for lunch I snapped my sketchbook shut.

'Aren't you going to show me?' asked Paris.

'It's not finished yet,' I protested.

'Oh, Rose, stop being so childish!' said Mama. 'Let us both see. You've certainly been very absorbed all morning, hunched up over that drawing. Did you know that your tongue sticks out when you're concentrating? It looks quite comical.'

Mama certainly wouldn't find my picture comical. I'd drawn our family sitting around the dining-room table eating Christmas dinner. I'm afraid I'd pictured Mama bursting right out of her dress, but still gobbling away. Papa was sliding slowly under the table, a large glass of wine in his hand.

Rupert had some wine too, and was nibbling a chicken drumstick in a supercilious way. I sat beside him, scowling. I drew Beth sitting with her back to everyone. Sebastian was feeding Montmorency from his plate. Algie was on all fours under the table, snipping hems and boot buttons with a pair of scissors. Clarrie was being sick into a plant pot. Nurse was in the background holding Phoebe, who was howling. Nurse Budd and Clover were having a fist fight in a corner – and Clover was winning. The rest of the servants were slyly helping themselves to the desserts on the sideboard.

I spent the afternoon in my room colouring my picture in festive reds and greens with my Winsor & Newton paints. At first glance it looked like a gay and happy scene, the kind you find on a tuppenny Christmas card. I was pleased with the effect.

When the paint was dry, I turned the page over and wrote lightly in pencil: *Happy Christmas, Paris. See what a treat you have missed!*

I spent a good ten minutes wondering how to sign myself. On cards for my family I put: *With love from Rose.* I wrote the same on Paris's picture, but then wondered if this was too forward. I rubbed it out, and simply signed my name with a tiny drawing of a rose.

Then I wrapped it in decorative paper and secured it with my best hair ribbon. As soon as the picture was hidden I started to worry about it, wondering if it was too sharply satirical. But I'd taken such pains with the ribbon I couldn't bear to open it up and check.

I decided that I was getting in a state about nothing. Paris had clearly been joking when he asked for my drawing as a Christmas present. He would forget all about it. How could I give it to him anyway? He wasn't coming back till after Christmas.

But on Christmas Eve he appeared with a basket of gifts!

'I should have grown a large belly and a white beard overnight, and then I could be Father Christmas,' he said.

He'd brought a huge tin of sugar plums for the children, a bottle of claret for Papa, and two slender boxes – one for Mama and one for me!

Mama opened her present immediately. It was a little silver pencil studded with blue beads, with a silky blue tassel at the top.

'Oh my Lord, Mr Walker, what a *dear* little pencil!' she cried. She gushed about it for a full five minutes, but I think she was disappointed. Perhaps she'd hoped the box might contain jewellery.

'I saw it in the shop and thought of you. The blue is the exact shade of your dress,' said Paris. 'I thought you could use it to keep the score when you play Bridge with your friends.'

'What a charming thought,' said Mama, though she never plays Bridge and has few friends. 'You must open *your* box now, Rose.'

'I'd sooner wait till Christmas Day,' I said. I was sure it was another pencil.

I ran to fetch my present for Paris and shyly gave it to him.

'Thank you, Rose,' he said, smiling.

'Open it now, Mr Walker. I'd love to see what Rose has drawn for you,' said Mama. Then she whispered, 'It was so sweet of you to get the child a present so she wouldn't feel left out.'

'Bless you, Mrs Rivers. However, I'd sooner save my present for Christmas Day too,' said Paris, tucking my sketch into his portfolio.

I haven't been able to wait for Christmas Day. I opened my present in my room and discovered that it wasn't a pencil at all. It was a small dipping pen with a rose-red stem and its own tiny bottle of black ink. There was a message too, tucked inside the box.

For your artwork!

21

CHRISTMAS EVE WAS SURPRISINGLY jolly. Mama made a big effort for once. She organized an early supper and then summoned everyone to the drawing room – all the servants, and the children in their nightgowns, even Beth. She seemed half asleep, so that Nurse Budd had to steer her into the room, but when she saw the Christmas tree with all its candles lit she became entranced and stood in front of it, head raised in awe. Her eyes shone, reflecting the candles. My heart turned over and I longed to go and give her a hug, but I knew she was better left alone.

Clover was almost as much in awe of the Christmas tree as Beth. She helped roast chestnuts in the fire, and both family and servants had their fill, though the children kept burning their fingers on the red-hot shells. Then Mama clapped her hands and called for us to sing Christmas carols, just as she'd boasted we'd do to Paris. We gave a very uncertain rendering of 'Once in Royal David's City', not sure of the tune, but then Mr Hodgson hurried off and returned with a mouth organ!

He saved the day. We'd had no idea that he owned such an instrument, let alone that he could play it with such enthusiasm. The servants were more musical than us. Clover has a fine, pure voice, though she didn't know all the words, and Jack Boots sang like a little choirboy.

Beth ignored everybody at first, still staring at the Christmas tree, but when we started 'Silent Night' she joined in, her voice soaring above all the others.

> 'Silent night, holy night,
> All is calm, all is bright
> Round yon virgin mother and child.
> Holy infant,
> So tender and mild,
> Sleep in heavenly peace
> Sleep in heavenly peace.'

Beth was word perfect. She sang it effortlessly, like a nightingale. We were all near tears, and I could scarcely breathe.

Rupert reached out and squeezed my hand. 'Happy families, eh?' he murmured.

He seemed surprisingly relaxed when, at that very moment, the hateful Hardy might be approaching Pamela Feynsham-Jones at Lady Robson's party. On the way up to bed I stopped him on the landing and gave him a quick hug.

'Hey!' he said, wriggling away, but he was smiling.

'Oh, Rupe, do you think Hardy really is going to Lady Robson's party? He isn't just pretending?'

'He's going all right,' said Rupert. 'His grandmother is her first cousin once removed or some such nonsense.'

'Then he really might say dreadful things to Pamela!'

'Let him,' said Rupert airily. 'Don't worry so, Rose.'

'You were in a cold funk when you told me!'

'Well, I've calmed down now. All is calm, all is bright, like the carol.'

'It won't stay calm and bright if Mrs Feynsham-Jones comes knocking at the door! And *Mr* Feynsham-Jones will be ready to horsewhip the young blade who's been spreading such disgusting rumours about his precious daughter!'

'Have you ever met Mr F-J? He's a timid little man with a droopy moustache and a nervous cough. I'm hardly shaking in my shoes,' said Rupert.

'You're not taking this seriously enough!'

'I've sorted everything out, Rose. Where do you think I went yesterday? I went to see Pamela and confessed.'

'You didn't!'

'Of course I did. Mrs Feynsham-Jones thought it so sweet of me to come calling by myself. Seeing as we're old family friends she allowed Pamela to walk in the gardens with me unaccompanied,' said Rupert.

'And you actually told her that you've been saying all those things about her to your nasty little chums?'

'They're not my chums any more. And of course I didn't put it like that. I simply said that the boys had started ragging me because they'd got hold of one of her letters. I said truthfully enough that Hardy had insulted her, and so I had defended her honour and hit him. I said that he'd blubbed like a baby—'

'But that was *you*!'

'Well, why would I want to admit such a thing to my sweetheart?' said Rupert. 'I warned her that Hardy hates me now, and might well say beastly things about me. Pamela was touchingly concerned. I think she'll send Hardy off with a flea in his ear.'

I stared at Rupert. 'But you haven't told her the truth!'

'I've told her *my* version of the truth. Now go to bed and stop worrying so, Rose,' he said.

Of course I was worried. If Rupert's ploy were successful, Hardy would hate him even more. I hoped Boxer Jack was a good teacher. Rupert would need to stand up for himself when he went back to school. And what was he going to do about Pamela now? He called her his sweetheart. Did he really think of her in that way?

Perhaps one day I might have a sweetheart myself. Paris! Why not? When I am older, the age gap between us will seem insignificant. I knew he had a sweetheart – that dark girl – but I hoped she might be temporary. Artists led wild lives and had many sweethearts before they settled down.

I imagined Paris and me together. Whatever would Mama say! I decided not to confide in Rupert. I knew he would mock me. I sometimes think the only person he really cares about is himself.

I didn't tell Clover any of this. For a girl from a slum she's got a firm moral sense, though she doesn't think much of church-going. Our family attend the morning service, while the servants go in the afternoon.

'I don't generally listen to the vicar though. I don't like him very much,' said Clover. 'He is forever judging us and finding us wanting. We sing that hymn about the rich man in his castle, the poor man at his gate. He definitely looks down on the poor.'

'He judges *us* too. And his sermons are interminable,' I said. 'The children get so bored they fall asleep and tumble off the pew. I yawn and wriggle and stretch until Mama pokes me in the ribs.'

'I stare at the beautiful coloured-glass windows. I like it when the sun shines through and makes a pattern. I fancy it's Megs up in Heaven saying hello to me,' said Clover.

'You won't go all pious on me, will you?' I asked anxiously.

'I don't think so. Mr Dolly doesn't approve of religion – he says it makes people bigoted,' she said. 'Oh, Rose, it was so lovely, lovely, lovely to see dear Mr Dolly again!'

Papa had reunited Clover with her dear friend and protector when he went to choose another doll for Beth. Clover was terrified that her stepmother, Mildred, might spot her, but Papa dressed her in my green coat with the furry collar. She tucked her hair up inside the big matching hat and pulled it down past her eyebrows so that hardly any of her face showed, but she was still anxious.

'But I didn't see Mildred or anyone else who knows me – just dear Mr Dolly,' she went on. 'When he saw me, he gave a little cry and swept me up into his arms. I hugged and hugged him. He's a very small man and rather crooked, so I very nearly toppled him over! It was wonderful to see him. We've missed each other so much. He let me paint a doll's face while your papa was choosing a Christmas present for Beth! If only Mr Dolly didn't live so near Cripps Alley. Then I could work for him and be a doll-maker too!'

I was happy for Clover but couldn't help feeling a little jealous. I'd hoped that she would feel so happy here that she wouldn't dream of going back to her old life. I couldn't understand why this funny old man meant so much to her. She seemed far fonder of him than she was of me.

Papa has a more generous spirit. He must have been touched by Clover's relationship with the old doll-maker because he invited him to our house for Christmas tea.

'Wasn't that wonderful of him!' Clover exclaimed.

'Yes, it was,' I said, proud that Papa had acted so kindly, though I was sure Mama would object. 'So he's coming?'

'I'm afraid not. He's already been invited to spend Christmas Day with Jimmy Wheels and his mother,' said Clover.

I wondered if that poor lame boy minded being called Jimmy Wheels. We call our servant boy Jack Boots. What would my nickname be . . . ? Rose Sharp-tongue?

'Your papa says Mr Dolly must come to tea another day instead, perhaps in January. And meanwhile he's invited another guest for Christmas tea – his friend Miss Sarah Smith. He illustrates her children's books. She's *my* Miss Smith who runs her Home for Destitute Girls. I don't love her the way I do Mr Dolly, but she's been very kind to me,' said Clover.

I looked forward to meeting Miss Smith. I read her book, which Papa is illustrating, and I liked it, though Mama doesn't think it suitable reading material because Miss Smith writes about street children. She also does good works, running this home for girls, and is a governor of the Foundling Hospital. Perhaps this is the sort of work I could do if I don't marry.

But perhaps one day I'll marry Paris! We'd probably be very poor, but I wouldn't mind living in a garret with him. He would paint and I would draw, and whenever we sold some work we'd holiday in France . . .

'Are you asleep already, Rose?' Clover whispered.

'No, of course not! Though it must be after midnight now. Happy Christmas, Clover!'

'Happy Christmas, Rose!'

'What's Beth's new doll like? Is she as grand as Marigold?'

'Well, she's very beautiful. Mr Dolly is experimenting with wax dolls now. Your father chose a life-size baby doll. It has little wisps of real hair and eyelashes. It's a work of art. You really could mistake it for a real baby. I think it looks a bit too real for Beth.'

'I don't think Beth really cares for babies,' I said. 'She doesn't seem to like Phoebe very much. She always covers her ears when she starts crying.'

'Still, Mr Dolly was delighted, because the baby doll was very expensive. Your papa proved to be an excellent customer. He bought a doll's-house family for Clarrie and even insisted on a doll for little Phoebe. I helped him choose this time,' said Clover. 'It's small enough for her to grasp, but not so small that she could swallow it. It's wooden – very stoutly jointed and unpainted, because Phoebe will suck things so . . .' Clover paused.

'What's the matter?'

'I'm just wondering if my own baby brother, Bert, remembers me at all. I carried him around everywhere. He used to suck my fingers,' she said softly.

I wondered what it must feel like to lose contact with your family. I don't think I'd mind as much as Clover. I shall try to make a bit of a fuss of her tomorrow. I have a special present for her.

When I was little, Miss Rayner encouraged me to make presents for Mama and Papa. I spent hours and hours knitting comforters and constructing cross-stitch purses, and they always received them with delight, even Mama – but as I grew older I realized that Mama never once used her purse or her blotter or her glove holder, and Papa wore his knitted items for only a day or two, and then managed to 'lose' them.

I can't say I blamed them. My handicraft skills are frightful, in spite of Miss Rayner's encouragement. I once gave the worst of my purses to her because I'd managed to misspell the greeting on the front. I knew Mama would scoff if I presented her with a purse saying *Merry Chistmas*. I'd run out of red thread too, so half the message was in green. It was probably the worst home-made Christmas present in the world, and yet Miss Rayner seemed thrilled with it. She still keeps it in her bag.

I wondered about getting up and making Miss Rayner a proper purse with a sentimental message sewn on the front – maybe *Best Governess in the World*, even though she isn't. But I won't be seeing her until after we come back from our trip to Dundee. I decided it could wait. Maybe I will make it on the long train journey. Or maybe I won't. I'm often full of good intentions, but rarely act on them.

At least I've got Clover's present ready. I'm going to give her my coloured pencils. They aren't new, but I've sharpened them all and tied a ribbon round the box.

22

WE HAD THE USUAL early-morning Christmas Parade. Papa gets up first and comes to the nursery in his nightshirt and dressing gown. He is always respectably covered, but the very idea alarms Nurse. She gets up even earlier and puts on her corset underneath her nightgown and pins up her hair, and then climbs back into bed and pretends to be asleep. She rubs her eyes and acts surprised when Papa comes bouncing in, but she doesn't fool anyone. She's always changed and fed the current baby of the family too, so that it isn't damp and screaming when Papa plucks it out of its cot.

This was Phoebe's first time as the star of the ceremony. She behaved perfectly, chuckling happily as Papa lifted her up to give her a Christmas kiss. Then he took her to the next youngest, Clarrie, who was also feigning sleep, quivering with excitement under her eiderdown. He bent down and helped Phoebe to give her elder sister a Christmas kiss. I was watching slyly from the doorway, feeling surprisingly fond of them all, even when Algie baulked at kissing poor Sebastian and made a silly rude noise instead.

It was Sebastian's task to wake Beth – but none of us knew how that would turn out. No one had warned Nurse Budd about our family tradition. She leaped out of bed, outraged, her nightcap lopsided, looking so comical that we couldn't help sniggering.

'Mr Rivers! What is the meaning of this!' she demanded.

'Merry Christmas, Nurse Budd. This is our special Christmas Parade. We have come to wake Beth with a kiss. I'm sorry we startled you,' said Papa.

'Oh my goodness, Mr Rivers! What a pity no one warned me. Still, Merry Christmas to you all. Could you wait a couple of minutes while I prepare Miss Beth? She finds it hard to manage surprises. I'm sure you understand,' she said, and she shut the door in our faces.

Papa frowned but stood there meekly.

'Take no notice, Papa! Let's go straight in,' I said.

'I can't, Rose! Perhaps Nurse Budd is performing some private ablution,' he replied. 'We'll be patient for five minutes.'

When Nurse Budd opened the door, she was still in her nightgown, but she'd changed her nightcap for a nurse's cap. Beth was awake, but still lying in bed, licking her lips. Perhaps she'd already been given her dose of Godfrey's Cordial. Sebastian went up to her and blew her a kiss. Beth looked worried, but was distracted by Montmorency, who was peeping out of his nightshirt pocket. She started twitching her own nose in imitation.

At that point I flew back to my room so that she would find me in bed. Papa led her along the corridor, and she sidled through the door, looking down at the carpet. She wouldn't come over and kiss me, but when all the other children made encouraging kissing noises, she copied them, smacking her lips together.

'Happy Christmas, Rose,' they chorused on Beth's behalf.

Then I had to lead the way to Rupert's room. He seemed genuinely asleep, and lay sprawled on his back, hair tousled, mouth open.

'Oh, let's drop a penny in his mouth as if he's a slot machine!' Algie chortled.

Rupert woke up and seized hold of him. He turned him upside down – not a pretty sight as he wore nothing beneath his nightgown. Then Rupert led the parade to our parents' bedroom.

They don't usually share this room any more. Papa uses the bed in his dressing room instead. He moved there when Mama had Phoebe, and he's stayed there ever since. But now he climbed into the big bed beside Mama and we all piled in as well.

Mama must have got up earlier too, because she smelled of cologne, her hair was carefully brushed, falling past her shoulders like a young girl's, and her nightgown was fresh and uncrumpled. She looked surprisingly pretty. She played along with the kissing game, sighing happily when Rupert kissed her cheek.

'Happy Christmas, my dear boy,' she said. 'It's so lovely to have you home again. My own family, all together!' She kissed Papa and then each of us in turn. I clung to her for a few seconds, wishing she could always be like this, so soft and warm and playful.

'The stockings, the stockings, the stockings!' Algie clamoured, rushing over to the fireplace. Six woollen stockings hung there side by side, with one little sock for Phoebe. Previously they'd hung from our own bedposts, but last year Algie had run riot at two in the morning, opening not only his stocking but everyone else's too.

Algie snatched them down now and distributed them. My stocking contained a little purse, a handkerchief, a plaster rabbit, a tin of toffees, an orange and a handful of nuts. The others had similar small trinkets. Phoebe's sock contained a tiny blue stuffed monkey, a rusk, a soft hairbrush and a little silver bell.

Beth took a fancy to the bell. She snatched it and rang it again and again.

'No, Beth, no!' said Mama. 'Perhaps we should send her back to Nurse Budd.'

'Let her play with it if she wants,' Papa said quickly. 'I'm sure Phoebe doesn't mind.'

Phoebe seemed content to suck the end of her hairbrush instead. Mama said the constant ringing was giving her a headache, but at least it kept Beth quiet until breakfast time.

After we'd eaten our bacon and eggs we had our main presents in the drawing room. The servants joined us too. Papa dressed up as Father Christmas, with a false beard – Algie kept trying to pull it off. He'd stored the big presents in the boot room, and led us all down there blindfold before revealing the exciting packages. There was a great to-do as they were all brought upstairs by Mr Hodgson and Jack Boots. I took advantage of the general fuss to wish Clover a happy Christmas and thrust the box of crayons at her.

'Oh, Rose! Sorry, *Miss* Rose!' she said, her green eyes filling with tears as she peeped inside the wrapping.

'Run and hide them, quickly,' I said.

Clover was back in time for the start of the family present-giving. As she passed by, she very quickly squeezed my hand.

Nurse Budd was watching, and sniffed contemptuously.

'Present time, present time, present time!' Algie and Clarrie shouted.

'Very well, my chickies. So what has Father Christmas brought for this fine family of children?' said Papa. 'Aha! A very *small* present for the eldest son!'

Rupert's little package from Father Christmas was a gold signet ring set with a bloodstone. It was very fine and fitted him perfectly.

'And *Mother* Christmas has a present for you, darling,' said Mama, giving him another small box.

It was a gold pocket watch, almost identical to Grandpapa's.

'But he already has the watch your father gave him, Jeannie,' said Papa, surprised.

'Yes indeed, but I think it's better if he saves that one for special occasions. This can be his everyday watch,' said Mama smoothly.

Had Rupert confided in her too? Had she simply noticed he wasn't wearing Grandpapa's watch any more? Rupert gave Mama a special hug, and she smiled at him indulgently.

My own present was an exquisite Japanese water-colour of a persimmon tree.

'What a strange little painting,' said Mama. 'Are you sure it's finished, Edward? The tree is right on one side and most of the paper is blank.'

'Father Christmas thought Rose would appreciate the painting as she admires Japanese art,' said Papa.

'Indeed I do, Papa,' I said. 'I shall hang it above my bed. Please thank Father Christmas for me.'

I had a present from Mother Christmas too, a set of three silver bangles. I thanked Mama graciously, but I didn't like the way they jingled on my arm. I'd have preferred a pocket watch too.

Beth didn't care for her big baby doll either. She seemed frightened of it, not sure whether it was real or not. She kept giving it little sidelong glances to see if she could catch it moving.

'What a lucky girl you are, Miss Beth,' said Nurse Budd. 'Why don't you give baby a cuddle?'

She held out the doll, but Beth kept her arms by her side, fists clenched.

'Don't be silly now, Miss Beth. Hold the lovely baby dolly your kind papa has bought you.'

'It was Father Christmas's present – but maybe he got it wrong,' said Papa.

'Wrong, wrong, wrong!' Beth said, and started to cry.

'Perhaps she'd like Marigold just for now. I'm sure she'll love the baby doll when she gets used to it,' said Clover. 'Best not press it on her now, Mr Rivers.'

Mama gasped at Clover speaking her mind.

'Hold your tongue, girl!' Nurse Budd hissed.

'No, no, Clover's being very sensible,' Papa insisted firmly. 'Can you go and fetch it for her, dear?'

Mama winced at the word 'dear'.

Nurse Budd winced too. '*I'll* fetch it, sir,' she said. 'Of course we all want to make dear Miss Beth happy, but might I point out that it's not always sensible to indulge her every whim. The precious child has to learn to behave. We don't want her to grow up with the manners of a street urchin, do we?' she added, with a horrible dig at Clover.

Beth cried even harder.

'I think you'd better take Beth away for a while, Nurse Budd. See if you can distract her,' said Mama.

'Certainly, madam. Come with me, Miss Beth,' said Nurse Budd. She held Beth by one hand, the wax baby dangling in the other. Its legs swung as she walked, as if it were kicking in protest. Beth struggled to get away too, but Nurse Budd held her fast.

'Papa!' I cried. 'Please don't let Beth be taken away, not on Christmas Day!'

Papa looked at Mama helplessly.

'Nurse Budd knows best,' she said firmly.

So Beth was dragged away screaming. For a couple of minutes the other children were subdued and anxious, but they were soon distracted by their presents from Father Christmas.

Beth was returned to the drawing room half an hour later, red-eyed and subdued. She kept her hand over her mouth. Perhaps she was trying to stop herself crying. She'd missed the rest of the present giving, but didn't seem to care. She stood with her back to everyone, fascinated by the fairy at the top of the big Christmas tree, and wouldn't be distracted even when Clarrie kindly offered to share her own present – a splendid doll's house.

Sebastian played with the doll's house instead, rearranging the furniture and making the little doll family wander about the rooms trying out the beds and sofas and chairs. His own present was a big set of the Reverend Wood's nature books. I leafed through one and found it fascinating. I wondered if I could become a naturalist and discover a new breed of animal or an exotic plant. Unfortunately there's not much chance of stumbling across anything out of the ordinary in Kensington.

Algie's present was the most splendid of all, a dapple-grey rocking horse with a flowing white mane and tail and a scarlet saddle. It's so huge it has to be stabled in the nursery, where it occupies half the room. It took Papa, Mr Hodgson and Jack Boots to haul it up there, and Nurse wasn't pleased.

The servants got presents too. Mama took care of the women: Cook and the two nurses were given lengths of white linen to make into starched aprons and caps, and Edie and Maggie and Mary-Jane got black material for their dresses. They didn't seem like proper Christmas presents at all, especially as they had to make them up themselves. I heard Edie whispering to Maggie, saying that she was going to take her material back to the draper's to exchange it for some green silk she'd been eyeing for months. Mama ignored Clover, and gave her no present at all.

Papa was more generous with Mr Hodgson, giving him a gold sovereign. He gave Jack Boots a half-crown, and a knife with a special device for taking the stones out of horses' hoofs, which delighted him.

'You're the tops, sir!' he said hoarsely.

Papa had a present for the little servant girls too. Mary-Jane got a blue bead necklace – and Clover her own sketchbook and a large set of pastels. I was so happy for her, though it made my own present of half-used coloured pencils look insignificant.

'Really, Edward, you seem to have more money than sense,' said Mama, frowning at him.

But her own gift from Papa was the most lavish: a pair of sapphire drop earrings to match her brooch. Mama held them up to see how they would look.

'They suit you, Jeannie,' said Papa.

'They're magnificent! But they must have cost a fortune!' she gasped.

'We *have* a fortune, my dear,' he replied.

It was actually *Mama's* fortune, but she seemed delighted that Papa was spending it on her. She'd bought Papa a wallet – a fine one, made of silky soft leather, though it wasn't in the sapphire earrings league.

'I simply *had* to buy them when I saw them in the Bond Street jeweller's window,' Papa said.

'They match my brooch beautifully,' said Mama.

'I bought them because they match your blue eyes.'

'Oh, Edward.'

Mama was in such a jolly mood that she made a real effort to play with the children. She knelt in front of the doll's house, making the little dolls talk in high, squeaky voices. She flicked through Sebastian's nature books, though she squealed when she turned to the section on spiders and beetles. She even went up to the nursery and climbed onto Algie's rocking horse. She rocked to and fro energetically, her skirts flying out.

'See, Rose, *this* is the way to ride a horse!' she cried, tossing her head, her new earrings shining.

'Oh, Mama, get down from my new rocking horse! You'll break him! You're too old and fat!' Algie cried.

Mama struggled off immediately, adjusting her skirts, her face very red.

'That's extremely rude, Master Algie,' Nurse scolded. 'How dare you say such a nasty thing to your mama.'

'I didn't say anything *rude*,' Algie protested. 'I only said she's old and fat, and she *is*.'

'You'll go to bed with a smacked bottom if you persist, Christmas or not,' Nurse hissed. 'Trust you to show me up! I'm ever so sorry, madam. I'll wash his mouth out with soap.'

'No, it's of no consequence,' Mama murmured. 'The child meant no harm.' She tried to smile bravely.

I felt so surprisingly sorry for her that I went and put my arm round her. 'Algie thinks any grown woman is old and fat, even someone young and slim like Edie,' I said.

This only made it worse. Mama pulled away and strode out of the room with a swish of her skirts.

Nurse gave Algie a shaking, and this made him feel so aggrieved that he played up and started showing off dreadfully. It was a relief when Mr Hodgson banged the gong in the hall to announce that Christmas lunch was about to be served.

It was a splendid lunch, with a turkey so huge that Maggie had to help Cook carry it in on its immense silver platter. Papa set about dividing it into portions, waving the carving knife in the air theatrically and stabbing at the carcass as if it were still alive. We had a side of ham too, and little sausages, and stuffing, and golden roast potatoes, and cabbage and carrots and parsnips, and then we had Christmas pudding flaming in brandy, and then we had mince pies and oranges, and *then* we had chocolate peppermints and Turkish Delight. The little ones drank lemonade. I had lemonade too, but most unfairly Rupert was allowed a glass of wine like Mama and Papa, and a cup of strong coffee at the end of the meal.

'Why can't *I* have wine and coffee?' I complained. 'I'm exactly the same age as Rupert.'

'Rupert is more mature and grown up,' said Mama. 'Besides, it's not seemly for such a young girl to drink wine.'

She drank several glasses herself, though I noticed she ate very little, just a slice of turkey and one potato, which seemed a terrible waste. Perhaps Algie's remark was preying on her mind.

Beth barely ate anything either. Mama had risked allowing her to join us at the family table. Nurse Budd insisted she wear a great bib like a baby in case she spilled food on her best red velvet frock. Beth kept plucking at it, trying to undo the strings, but Nurse Budd had tied them in a tight knot. She whimpered when she was served her vegetables because the cabbage had touched her potatoes and the carrots and parsnips were heaped on any old how. She likes each item of food to be entirely separate on her plate, and then she eats them in turn.

'Really, Beth, you mustn't be so pernickety,' said Mama, frowning.

Beth bent her head and slid so far down her chair that she was nearly under the table. Alphonse was lurking there, hoping for scraps. He snapped at her irritably and Beth cried out.

'Oh, for pity's sake,' said Mama. It looked as if Beth might be taken away again, but mercifully she subsided, nibbling listlessly, nearly asleep.

By the time we'd finished the vast meal we were all drowsy. We lolled around in the drawing room, utterly stuffed with food. Mama had a doze on her chaise longue, with Alphonse stretched out beside her, snoring. Papa had forty winks too. Phoebe fell asleep in her cradle. Beth nursed Marigold, her head nodding. She looked like a painting by Sir John Everett Millais, posing so sweetly in her red velvet dress, with her hair shining.

Clarrie and Sebastian played with the doll's house, Clarrie making the little family climb up the walls one by one to camp on the roof. She let the smallest doll fall, and announced in a matter-of-fact voice that it was dead. She wanted Sebastian to help her organize a funeral, but he was busy setting all the rooms to rights. He took all the furniture out of the biggest room and made a cosy nest of straw at one end, with a water bowl at the other. It was obvious he was preparing it for a new resident.

Algie was very bored with all this and plagued Rupert to play with him. Rupert gave him several games of Snap, and then showed him some card tricks he'd learned, perhaps from his new friend, Jack. He kept making cards disappear and then reappear in his pocket, as if by magic. Algie demanded to see the trick again and again.

I wished Rupert could make *Algie* disappear. I grew bored and wandered off by myself. I went up to my room and set out a piece of scrap paper, the little bottle of black ink and the new pen Paris had given me. I needed to practise. I'm not very skilled with pen and ink and usually make blots. This pen was finer though, and after a shaky start I got used to the nib and learned to control the thin, steady flow of ink.

I drew Beth asleep in her chair, with ivy and brambles growing all around her like Sleeping Beauty. I was trying to think of a handsome prince who could release her from the enchantment when I heard a knock at the front door.

I wondered for a mad moment if it could be Paris visiting after all. I ran out onto the landing and heard Edie talking, and then a lady's voice, deep and resonant, answering her. I'd forgotten that Papa had asked his writer friend, Miss Sarah Smith, to share our Christmas tea.

I ran down to the drawing room. Mama was sitting up, patting her hair, her cheeks flushed. Perhaps she thought it was Paris at the door too. Papa was still dozing.

'Mama, Papa's friend has come calling. Papa, I think Miss Smith is at the door,' I warned them.

'Oh my Lord, what a silly day to choose for a visit! Edward, how could you invite this lady on Christmas afternoon!' Mama grumbled.

Papa woke with a start and ran his fingers through his tousled hair. 'Dear goodness, I'm still so full I feel I need to undo my trousers!' he said.

'Don't be so vulgar!' Mama hissed. 'Children, I want you to behave yourselves for our guest. Let us hope she will leave immediately after tea. Nurse Budd, take Beth away – she can't cope with strangers.'

'For pity's sake, Jeannie, let the child stay and be part of the family,' Papa protested. 'If she's wary of strangers it's because she never meets any. I'll not have poor Beth locked up in her own house!'

'She's never locked up, sir,' said Nurse Budd indignantly. 'I do my best to take care of her. But I feel that Mrs Rivers is right. It would be kinder to take her away for a little rest. Come along, Beth, my sweet.'

I hated the way she used those false endearments. It clearly irritated Papa too. Perhaps he decided it was time to stand up to Nurse Budd.

'I take your point, Nurse Budd, but I think she should stay all the same,' he said. 'Beth has no need to fear my friend Miss Smith. She is used to little girls.'

Edie led Miss Smith into the drawing room. She was a tall, dignified lady, very plain, but elegantly dressed in black silk. She wasn't alone. She had a child with her, a thin, red-haired girl in the quaintest of uniforms: a tall cap and starched apron and a brown stuff dress with short sleeves, in spite of the wintry weather. She had sharp little elbows and her fingers were red with chilblains, but her blue eyes were bright with wonder and curiosity.

'Merry Christmas, Mrs Rivers!' said Miss Smith. 'It's very kind of you to invite me to join you for Christmas. I hope you don't mind my bringing an extra little guest with me.'

'Merry Christmas!' replied Mama stiffly. 'Is this quaint child a *foundling*? Good heavens, whatever next!'

I'd read all about the abandoned children in the Foundling Hospital. I stared at the girl, wondering what it must be like to live in such an extraordinary place.

Mama was looking appalled. Foundlings are the children of fallen women, and so she thinks they are tainted. She threw Papa an indignant glance and suggested that Nurse take the foundling girl to the nursery.

'I'm not a baby!' said the girl, with spirit.

Nurse shuffled forward, still sleepy herself after her Christmas lunch in the servants' quarters. Nurse Budd marched forward too, still bristling from Papa's rebuke.

The foundling didn't flinch. She wasn't even looking at them. She was staring at Clover.

'Clover Moon!' she declared.

'Hetty Feather!' said Clover. 'Oh, my!'

They were acting as if they were old friends. Miss Smith laughed, and explained that she'd once taken them out to tea together. Then she quietly reminded little Hetty Feather of her manners. She promptly dropped a curtsy to Mama, and said she had a beautiful room.

I wondered what the rooms in the Foundling Hospital were like. I was sure they must be very bleak, like Lowood School in *Jane Eyre*.

Papa seemed enchanted with Hetty Feather and asked if Miss Smith had brought her out because she was the best behaved of all the foundlings.

Hetty smiled ruefully. 'I rather think it's because I am the *worst* behaved,' she said, which made me like her enormously. I wanted to befriend her at once, and yet I hung back, feeling strangely shy and uncertain. *She* might not like *me*. Clarrie had no such qualms, and showed off her doll's house. Hetty seemed fascinated. I suppose she'd had no experience of grand toys. Perhaps she didn't have any toys at all in the Foundling Hospital.

Clarrie started giggling, telling Hetty how Algie had insisted on taking every member of the doll family to visit the miniature lavatory – and then there was a to-do because we all suddenly realized that Algie had mysteriously gone missing.

We all played Hunt Algie until Clover discovered him hiding inside the biggest ginger jar. There was an even greater fuss trying to get him *out*, but then Rupert seized him by the shoulders and pulled hard. Mama was very vexed, especially as her precious ginger jar nearly got broken in the process, and threatened Algie with a whipping. She didn't mean it of course. None of us have ever been whipped in our lives.

I saw Hetty Feather shudder. She had clearly taken Mama seriously.

'Do they ever whip the children at the Foundling Hospital?' I asked her.

She told me a little about her life there. I'd thought a servant's lot was dreadful enough, but a foundling child suffers terribly, frequently cold and hungry, and forced to do the dreariest chores. Miss Smith was upset because she is a governor of the hospital, and resolved to try to make changes. Papa suggested she write a book about a foundling's life – but Miss Smith said that Hetty herself might write that book one day.

It turns out that she has been writing her memoirs! I was amazed. I didn't think she'd even be able to read and write. Apparently she's already written hundreds of pages, sitting up night after night and scribbling by candlelight.

Algie pestered Mama to know what a foundling was. She was very blunt and told him that it was the child of a degenerate woman who had abandoned her baby. I'm sure they can't help being degenerate, and wouldn't abandon their babies if they could help it. I felt it was very cruel of Mama to say this in front of Hetty Feather.

She clearly thought so too, and flushed with fury. 'That's not true!' she said, her eyes flashing.

Miss Smith hastily whisked her out of the room to wash her hands, with Clover showing them the way. They were gone for a very long time, and when they came back at last Hetty Feather seemed in quite a different mood, pink and smiling and whispering to Clover.

I wondered if they were whispering about *us*. I wanted to talk to them, but felt too awkward. It was a relief when tea was served, though we were all still uncomfortably full of lunch.

Hetty ate enormously though, helping herself from every single plate. She must have been wretchedly starved in that institution. She munched her way through the savouries, the jellies, the iced creams, and chose every kind of cake. I wondered how such a small thin girl could possibly devour so much food so rapidly. Clarrie was fascinated too. She is a very greedy little girl, but even she can't manage more than three cakes at a time.

Then Papa gave out the crackers. They delighted Hetty. At first she didn't want to pull hers because she thought it looked so pretty – and then, when she discovered a whistle inside, she blew it for all she was worth, nearly deafening us all. When Cook brought in the flaming fruit so we could play Snapdragon, Hetty thought the bowl was on fire and offered to run for a bucket of water. I asked her to hold my new silver bangles while I thrust my hand into the flames. Nurse Budd said I was a fool to trust a foundling child. I thought I'd trust this funny, lively red-haired girl implicitly, whereas I didn't trust Nurse Budd an inch.

When we played Blind Man's Buff, Hetty was very gentle with Beth, pretending she was the fairy on the Christmas tree. Nurse Budd said she must be simple, but Hetty Feather is actually very clever. We played Charades together, Miss Smith and Hetty and Beth and I – and Clover, to make up the numbers, though Mama objected. We won too – an old lady, a foundling, a troubled child, an ignorant girl who's never been to school, and a servant!

It was delightful plotting our play up in my bedroom, though I felt embarrassed when Hetty admired my furniture, my old toys, my much-thumbed books. Hetty came up with our Charade phrase – *Foundling Hospital* – and we acted it out, playing foundlings ourselves in the last scene. It was such fun. If only I could play with girls like Hetty and Clover every day.

We won, and I gave Hetty a hug. She was still wearing my silver bangles when she said goodbye, and I wanted her to keep them, though Miss Smith gently protested. Clover said they were beautiful – she didn't think I should give them away either. In the end I decided to give one bangle to Hetty, one to Clover, and to keep the last for myself. We were three girls with matching silver bangles. Three friends.

23

OF COURSE, MAMA MADE a great fuss when
she discovered what I'd done. She insisted that
Clover give her bangle back immediately, behaving as if
she'd stolen it, but there was nothing she could do about
Hetty's. Every night I take Clover her bangle, and she
dances around in her petticoat pretending she's a grand
lady at a ball with the bangle gleaming on her arm in the
moonlight.

One morning we overslept. I rushed down to my room,
praying I wouldn't bump into Maggie or Edie on the
servants' stairs, while Clover scrambled into her clothes

and dashed to the nursery to supervise the little ones. But she'd forgotten to take off the bangle! When she rolled up her sleeves, Nurse Budd saw it.

'Aha! You wicked little thief!' she cried. She met Papa on his way into Mama's room with the early morning post.

I heard the hullabaloo and hurried down to defend Clover.

'My goodness me, ladies! Could I suggest we all calm down and conduct this conversation a little later, when we are all dressed?' said Papa, peering at us from over his reading glasses.

'I beg your pardon, sir. I'd never intrude on you normally, but this is a matter of urgency. Clover Moon has stolen Miss Rose's silver bangle! She's wearing it now, as bold as brass. She deserves to be sent packing immediately, madam!' said Nurse Budd, turning to Mama.

'No, Mama! Please, it's not Clover's fault. *I* gave her the bangle back. Oh, I can't bear it if she gets into trouble because of me,' I said, starting to sob.

'Don't cry, Rose dear,' said Papa.

'Yes, Rose, there's no need to get in such a state,' said Mama. 'You really must learn not to be so familiar with the servants. You certainly should never lend them your jewellery! You should be ashamed of yourself for accepting it, Clover, but I suppose you don't know any better.'

We all gaped at her. Was that *it*?

'Oh, Mama, thank you for being so understanding!' I said, wiping my eyes with the back of my hand. Clover bobbed her a little curtsy while Nurse Budd stood there stiffly, clearly astonished.

'Calm down now, Rose. We all have a lot to do today, packing for our journey to Scotland. You run off to the nursery, Clover, and help Nurse pack for the children,' said Mama.

I couldn't understand why she was so serene. She enjoyed spending New Year's Eve in Dundee, but normally the effort of organizing all our trunks drove her into a frenzy, and she snapped and scolded all day long.

'You'd better go and attend to Beth, Nurse Budd,' said Papa. He paused. 'This is the second time poor little Clover has been falsely accused of stealing. I hope you now realize that she's a good honest girl who's never stolen so much as a sixpence in her life. Perhaps you owe her an apology.'

'If you say so, sir,' said Nurse Budd, tight-lipped. 'I beg your pardon, Clover.' She turned on her heel and marched out of the room, her boots squeaking on the polished floor as if they were protesting.

'Good for you, Papa,' I said, smiling at Clover.

She bent her head gratefully.

'So you are not to be sent packing after all, little Miss Moon,' said Papa. 'You are required to *do* the packing for our jaunt to Bonnie Scotland. It should be a very jolly trip this time because we'll have company. Paris is joining our party.'

'Really, Papa?' I said, my heart thudding.

'I met up with him at the Arts Club on Boxing Day and waxed lyrical about the Scottish moors and mountains. Apparently your mama has already invited him to make the trip to Dundee with us. It seems an excellent idea. I did my best to persuade him to come and do some landscape painting with me, and he's just written to say he'd be delighted to accept the invitation.'

So *that* was why Mama was in such a good mood! She sang as she selected suitable clothes and had Edie fold them into her big leather travelling trunk. Edie was cheerful too, because she could stay at home with Maggie and Cook and Mr Hodgson and Jack Boots and Mary-Jane. Perhaps they all feast on steak pies and suet puddings and Papa's wine while we're away. Edie and Maggie are free to see their young men too.

Nurse always comes with the family to look after us. This year Nurse Budd would be joining us – and Clover too! Nurse Budd didn't look too pleased and had a word with Mama, suggesting it might be better if she and Beth stayed at home. Mama was tempted by the idea. Last year Beth had cried for the whole journey and had nearly driven us all insane. But Papa wouldn't hear of it.

'Beth is part of our family. I will not have her left behind,' he said firmly. 'If you find looking after Beth on a long train ride too much of a challenge, Nurse Budd, I'm sure Clover will help amuse her.'

'I don't think that will be necessary, sir,' said Nurse Budd stiffly.

Clover was wildly excited at the thought of going to Scotland.

'I've never seen a real mountain. I want to climb to the very top! And I want to see Highland cattle because they look such strange beasts in picture books. And I also want to see if all the men really do wear skirts and boldly show off their legs,' she said, giggling.

'Wait till you see Papa in the kilt,' I said. 'He thinks he cuts a dashing figure, but his legs look so funny in their woolly stockings.'

'I'm sure Mr Rivers looks splendid in a skirt,' said Clover, who admires Papa and will never hear a word said against him.

Papa wore his kilt for travelling, though I dare say he found it uncomfortable, because he likes to lounge with his legs well spread, which means careful attention to his skirts if he is to maintain his dignity. Mama insisted that Sebastian and Algie wore their kilts for the train journey as well. Sebastian was only too delighted, and wore the kilt with pride, careful of his pleats whenever he sat down because he didn't want to crease them. Algie protested bitterly. He liked wearing his Scottish woollen socks and tucked his knife down them eagerly (it was only a pretend knife, of course – Algie certainly couldn't be trusted with a real one), but he absolutely hated the kilt.

'It's a skirt and they're for girls and I'm not a stupid girl,' he yelled, and he lay down and refused to put it on, even when Nurse smacked him. At last Clover managed to talk him into it, but he glowered and sulked all the way to the railway station. Clarrie wore a kilt too, and she wasn't happy either. It was last year's, and rather too small for her now, emphasizing her round stomach and chubby knees, and she kept clawing at the neck of her Aran jumper, saying it was itchy. Phoebe fretted too, wrapped so tightly in her large tartan shawl that she could scarcely draw breath.

Beth wore her kilt without too much fuss. I think Nurse Budd had given her a large dose of Godfrey's Cordial to keep her calm for the long journey. She slept nearly all the way, her head lolling, mouth open, snoring softly.

'Bless her,' said Nurse Budd, and read her copy of the *Nursing Times* until she fell asleep herself.

I wore my kilt too. Mine was last year's as well, and still roomy enough, but it was very short and showed too much of my skinny legs.

'I can't wear it, Mama. It doesn't look decent,' I said, going into her dressing room and tugging at the hem.

Mama was looking at her own reflection with complacency. She was wearing a new deep blue velvet travelling dress with a high white lace collar that hid her double chin. Edie was pinning her dashing new hat in place. It had tartan trimming and several grouse feathers secured at a jaunty angle.

'Don't be so silly, child,' she said, not even turning round.

'But I'm *not* a child. I don't look right in the kilt any more,' I said. 'Look!'

Mama gave me a quick glance.

'Hold still, madam, I've just got to the tricky bit,' said Edie.

'You look perfectly respectable, Rose. I think girls wearing the kilt look very fetching,' said Mama.

'*You* don't wear one,' I said.

'Don't be ridiculous. I'm a grown woman.' Mama peered at her reflection.

Yes, grown *out*wards, I thought, looking at her bulging bosom and behind. I had to wear the wretched kilt with my cream Aran jumper, looking like a lanky eight-year-old. I walked hunched up to try to make my kilt look longer.

'Why are you walking like that? Have you got stomach ache?' asked Rupert.

He looked incredibly handsome in his new kilt. He had grown too, but was far too slim to wear Papa's old one, so Mama had ordered him a kilt in the correct tartan. It was the perfect length. His legs looked very shapely, not matchsticks like mine.

'You cut a fine figure in the tartan, Rupert darling,' said Mama. 'My, what a shame Pamela can't see you in your outfit!'

Rupert laughed carelessly. He had got away with it. Apparently Hardy was very forward with Pamela at Lady Robson's Christmas Eve party, and she objected furiously. He became cross too, and asked why she was so high-and-mighty with him when she was so free with Rupert Rivers. Pamela was horrified, and went straight to her mother. Mrs Feynsham-Jones descended on

Hardy like the wrath of God and insisted he leave the party immediately, before her husband had him horsewhipped.

'But Hardy will be furious with you when you go back to school, Rupe,' I said anxiously.

'I'm not sure he'll even *be* at school,' said Rupert. 'Mrs Feynsham-Jones seems determined to write to the Head complaining about his behaviour. I do hope he gets expelled! Then I won't have to try out my new boxing skills after all.' He clenched his fists and made a few playful jabs in the air.

'What about the other boys? You said they all joined forces against you.'

'Hardy egged them on. Martin wasn't quite so bad. I dare say he'll want to be friends again, and the others will come round too. But what do I care if they don't?' said Rupert, swaggering. 'They're only silly schoolboys. They don't mean anything to me.'

'And Pamela?'

'She's got a pash on me, you know she has.'

'But doesn't that mean you're stuck with her for ever? Imagine how furious Mrs Feynsham-Jones will be if you stop pursuing her daughter.'

'I could do a lot worse than Pamela,' said Rupert. 'She's got a sweet nature, she's well connected, she thinks the world of me and, even if she's not quite a beauty, she's already got a startling figure.'

'How can you talk about her in that cold-blooded manner?' I said. 'You clearly don't love her at all.'

'Love!' said Rupert mockingly. 'You don't know what you're talking about. You're still a little girl.'

He was so wrong. I knew all about love. I was struck dumb when Paris met us at King's Cross station. It was a very chilly day but I went hot all over, and knew I was blushing.

'My dear Paris, how lovely to see you!' said Mama. 'But you're not entering into the spirit of our festive enterprise! Where is your kilt?'

He was wearing his usual crumpled trousers and scuffed boots, and the ancient greatcoat that had apparently cost sixpence from a market stall.

'I'm afraid I don't happen to have a kilt in my wardrobe, Mrs Rivers,' he said.

'You should have said! You'd cut such a fine figure in proper Scottish dress. Still, I dare say there will be kilts going spare at Pennycuik. That is the name of my family home. I think you will find it very pleasant. It is up on a hill, with sea views, and the air is bracing. We are miles away from those murky jute mills,' Mama declared.

It was the profits from those murky jute mills that had purchased every grey stone and piece of slate that made up Pennycuik. The mills had paid for the Chinese wallpaper and the Venetian glass chandeliers and the Persian carpets and the William McTaggart paintings hanging on the walls and the new gas lighting illuminating every corner. They also paid the wages of all the indoor servants who looked after Grandmama and Grandpapa, attending to their every whim, and the outdoor staff who

334

kept up the stable of horses and the well-sprung carriages and the rolling green lawns.

It seemed bizarre that so much wealth should come from a humble product used to back carpets, but when I thought of all the carpets in houses all over Britain it made more sense. *Rich* people's houses. Poor people made their own rag rugs or made do with bare floorboards. If Paris lived in a garret, perhaps he didn't have a carpet either.

He was embarrassed when Papa took care of his ticket to Dundee.

'Nonsense, Paris. I always take a whole train carriage and there would have been a seat going spare anyway. My wife and I, the two nurses – three counting little Miss Moon, though she's too tiny to take up a whole seat. Young Phoebe travels on Nurse's lap. Then there's Rupert, Rose, Beth, Sebastian, Algie and Clarrie. That makes eleven of the Rivers household. Still one seat left for you, Paris, old chap.'

'For goodness' sake, Edward, we can't expect Mr Walker to be squashed up with all these noisy children,' said Mama. 'The three of us will travel in peace and comfort in first class.'

Papa seemed taken aback. 'But that's rather a waste of money, Jeannie, and I doubt there will be spare seats left now.'

'Leave it to me,' said Mama, swapping Alphonse from one arm to the other so that she could reach her purse.

'Really, Mrs Rivers, I would love to travel with the children. I find them great fun,' said Paris.

'I think you'd regret that decision before we were even out of London,' said Mama. 'Now, no more arguing!'

Papa looked angry, but he could see that it was embarrassing to haggle over the matter in public. Mama marched off, taking Paris's arm, while Papa followed behind.

'There, now we can spread out properly,' said Nurse happily, but we were all upset that Paris and Papa had been taken from us. I don't think any of us minded doing without Mama.

At first the children enjoyed peering out of the windows and nibbling crystallized ginger to ward off travel sickness. When they got fidgety we tried playing I-Spy, and then I read aloud, but Algie kept kicking his heels and complaining that the story was boring.

In desperation Nurse unpacked the lunch hamper, though it had only just turned midday. Cook had made us a big veal-and-ham pie and a potato salad, with a fruit tart and the remains of the Christmas cake for dessert. The children got crumbs all over their clothes. Algie insisted on eating two huge slices of cake, and then lay back pale and damp and yawning, saying he thought he was going to be sick. Luckily he wasn't, but it was a near thing.

Instead he had a nap. In fact nearly everyone had a nap. Nurse nodded over Phoebe, cradling her reverently like an ancient Madonna. Clarrie lolled against Algie, and Sebastian rested his head on Montmorency's cage. He'd been severely warned about letting his mouse out on the journey, and had to make do with posting titbits through the bars.

Rupert swung his new gold watch to and fro until he fell asleep. Beth slept too, hunched up into a little ball. Nurse Budd had her eyes closed but was sitting bolt upright, and I couldn't tell whether she was really asleep or not. Clover was awake and I longed to chat to her, but I couldn't talk naturally just in case Nurse Budd was listening. We tried mouthing messages until Clover's eyes drooped and she fell asleep as well.

I wondered if Mama and Papa and Paris were dozing. I was sure Mama would have contrived to sit between the men. We saw the three of them whenever there was a stop at a station and we got out to stretch our legs or use the conveniences.

In the afternoon there was a fifteen-minute stop, so Papa bought us all an iced bun and a bottle of ginger beer at a stall, which was very jolly. Paris started a game of Follow My Leader along the platform to stretch the children's legs. I dithered about joining in, not sure whether I was a child or not. Mama walked Alphonse up and down on a lead, encouraging him to relieve himself, while Nurse fussed over Phoebe, who was crying plaintively. Beth had woken up at last, but was flapping her arms like a wounded bird. Nurse Budd nagged at her. I'd hoped to snatch a few moments with Clover, but she had to dash after Algie, who had bolted along the train to chat to the engine driver.

It was pitch dark well before we neared Dundee. Everyone held hands when the train crossed the brand-new bridge.

'Why is everyone holding hands?' Clover asked, bewildered.

'The old bridge collapsed into the river Tay with a train on it, and everyone drowned,' I explained.

Her eyes opened wide, and she reached across and clutched my hand hard. There was a great whoop of relief when we made it safely across. Then we scurried to find hats and coats and possessions, and waited a long time on the freezing cold platform while Papa organized porters to take care of our luggage. Paris and Rupert found enough cabs to transport us all the couple of miles to Pennycuik.

'Come in this one, Rose,' Rupert called, but I wanted to be with Clover, so I squeezed in with her and the two nurses, and Phoebe and Beth. They were both wailing miserably because of the deathly cold wind and the unfamiliar, harsh accents of the porters and cabbies. Clover was shivering in her thin shawl and the wind was whipping her hair about her head, but I could see her green eyes shining in the eerie glow of the gas streetlights.

'I'm in a foreign country!' she said.

'Don't be silly, girl. Scotland's part of Great Britain,' said Nurse, wrapping yet another shawl around Phoebe.

'It feels foreign and it smells foreign and they even talk foreign,' said Clover.

She gasped when the cab jolted to the top of the bray and she could see the turrets of Pennycuik, the moonlight giving the grey stone a softened pearliness. 'It's a castle!' she declared.

'It's just a freezing great house,' said Nurse. 'I'm always chilled to the bone, no matter how many blankets I have on my bed.'

'It has turrets so it's certainly *like* a castle! Can we go up into the turrets? Are the servants' bedrooms actually *in* the turrets?' Clover chattered excitedly.

'You're not to go anywhere near those turrets! You'll encourage the children, and if Master Algie goes up there he'll fall to his death, I just know he will,' said Nurse.

'There aren't any proper rooms in the turrets. Just stone steps that go up and up until you get to the roof. Rupert and I explored last year,' I said.

'Hush, child! If I'd known that I'd have had the pair of you whipped! How dare you be so reckless,' Nurse grumbled. 'You know those turrets are strictly out of bounds.'

One black night Rupert had dared me to explore them and we'd crept up together. We had a candle, but I was shivering so much I managed to drop it and the flame went out. Rupert still insisted on climbing right to the top, feeling our way in the dark. The stone walls were cold and damp, and the steps beneath my bare feet were slippery. I clung to Rupert's nightshirt and gabbled prayers inside my head.

It felt as if we were inching up and up for ever, but at last it grew a little lighter, and we reached the top at last. Our heads poked out like sweep's brushes, and the wind made such a noise we had to shout to make ourselves heard.

Rupert had pulled himself up until he was leaning right out.

'Come back, you fool! You'll slip!' I said.

'No, you pull yourself up too. There's a fantastic view!' Rupert cried.

'How can there be? It's dark. Come back, Rupe,' I begged.

He took no notice, and leaned out even further, resting on his hips. And then his hands slipped and he very nearly toppled right over. I screamed and caught hold of his legs, pulling with all my might. He managed to scramble back down to the step, landing in a heap.

'For pity's sake, Rose, you nearly had me over!' he said, as if it were my fault.

'Oh, Rupert, you almost fell!' I gasped.

'Nonsense,' he said, but he was shaking, and I knew he'd been just as scared as me. 'Perhaps we'll leave it for tonight. I don't want you getting upset, old girl. We'll come back when it's not so breezy, all right?'

It was *always* breezy at Pennycuik, the wind coming straight off the North Sea, fierce and wild and salty. We both knew we'd never dare go up there again.

'Don't worry, I'm not going anywhere near those turrets,' I said.

'Turrets, turrets, turrets,' Beth mumbled.

'There now! You've set her off with your silly talk, Miss Rose,' said Nurse Budd. 'Stop that now, Miss Beth, dear. Turrets are bad, bad things.'

'Bad, bad things,' Beth repeated anxiously.

'Don't worry, Beth. You're not going near any turrets,' said Clover. 'They're just the top bits of the castle. See the castle down there? It's like a castle in a book of fairy tales. Remember how much you liked the Christmas tree fairy?'

'Fairy,' said Beth. Her brow cleared. 'Fairy!'

'Such nonsense,' Nurse Budd murmured. 'Why encourage her with all this fancy? She's fanciful enough as it is. Firm but fair discipline, that's what she needs.'

'How can you talk about disciplining a girl like Beth when she's in her own little world and doesn't understand when she's being naughty?' I said angrily.

'Now now, Miss Rose,' said Nurse, but she patted my knee to show that she understood.

'Some people might think you'd have benefited from a little more discipline in your own upbringing, Miss Rose,' said Nurse Budd. 'Of course, *I'd* never suggest such a thing.'

'No, it's not your place to do so, Nurse Budd,' I said.

She leaned towards me and murmured, 'You wait, Miss Rose, you'll get your comeuppance one day.'

I did my best to ignore her. Then we arrived at Pennycuik, and all the servants had lined up with lanterns in the freezing cold to meet us. Grandmama and

341

Grandpapa were standing in the doorway. Grandmama wore her furs, a long coat down to her tiny boots, a fur hat on her head, and an extra fur stole wrapped round her shoulders. With her beady little eyes and long thin nose she looked like a furry creature herself, a small bear opening her arms to give us each a hug. Grandpapa didn't even wear a greatcoat. He was holding a lantern aloft, wearing only his tweed jacket and kilt, legs planted wide apart as if daring the weather to have any effect on him. He hugged us all and gently burrowed his hand into Phoebe's shawls to tickle her under her chin.

'She's a rare bairn,' he said, making little clucking noises at her as she was carried into the house.

Nurse Budd was new to him, and he shook her hand stiffly and then ignored her, but he seemed very taken with Clover, who was marshalling the sleepy little ones into some semblance of order, and removing their coats and hats and mittens in the hall.

'Who's this little elf?' he asked, shaking his head at her wild hair and tiny figure. 'Haven't you enough children of your own, Jeannie, to go adopting a mischievous little fairy?'

'Fairy,' Beth murmured, and Grandpapa gave her a little wink and tried to pat her on the shoulder, but she shied away.

'Don't be ridiculous, Papa,' Mama replied. 'The girl is a little nurserymaid wished upon me by Edward – one of his whims. Papa, let me introduce Edward's dear friend

342

Mr Walker. He is painting my portrait and, though I shouldn't say so myself, it's a masterpiece. It will attract attention at the Academy, you mark my words.'

Paris protested, and Papa laughed and thumped him on the back.

'You mustn't believe a word of it, sir,' said Paris.

'No, no, Jeannie's right. You will be the English Leonardo and Jeannie your Mona Lisa,' said Papa.

They were clearly joking, but Mama giggled delightedly. Grandmama tutted, and when one of the maids helped Mama off with her coat she shook her head at her.

'My, Jeannie, you've certainly been putting on the beef since the last baby. Look at you, lassie! You make two of me now,' she pointed out.

Mama laughed awkwardly, but she'd gone scarlet, and her hands went helplessly to her thickened waist. I had forgotten how sharp Grandmama was with her. It is strange how cruel mothers can be to their daughters. If *I* have a daughter I shall cherish her and make her feel loved.

We were all swept into the dining room, and given game soup and bread and cheese and oatcakes, adults and children alike. Nurse and Nurse Budd were for once united, protesting that this was far too rich for the little ones.

'Nonsense,' said Grandpapa briskly, cutting himself at least a quarter of a pound of Scottish Cheddar and eating it straight off the knife. 'The kiddies need feeding up. Look at the girls – skinny wee creatures.'

If Grandpapa thought Clarrie skinny, he needed spectacles! He seemed specially fond of her, pulling her onto his lap.

'How's my wee bairn?' he said, gently pinching her cheek.

She pretended to be a baby, cooing in a tiresome manner, but Grandpapa played along, and even mimed giving her a bottle. Perhaps she misses Nurse's attention now that she's no longer the baby of the family.

Phoebe was given an oatcake to chew on after she'd finished her bottle of milk.

'She'll choke on it!' Nurse warned, but Phoebe gnawed on it happily for five minutes and then fell asleep, dribbling.

'Bless the wee lamb,' said Grandmama.

'Would you like to hold her for a minute, madam?' Nurse asked politely.

'Good heavens, no! She'll dribble all over my velvet,' she exclaimed, as if Nurse were quite mad. 'You'd best take her up to the nursery. It's all prepared. Take the little ones too. And poor Beth.'

Beth was already asleep, her head on the table, and protested irritably when Nurse Budd shook her awake.

'I'll carry her upstairs,' said Papa, but Beth struggled when he tried to lift her.

'I think she wants a piggyback,' said Paris. 'Here, Beth, up we go. I'll be your horsy.'

'Horsy!' said Beth. 'Horsy, horsy, horsy!' she cried as Paris galloped out of the room with her on his back. Nurse Budd went marching sternly in their wake, sniffing at such nonsense.

'She likes horses, does she?' Grandpapa asked. 'We'll see if we can find a good steady plodder for her to ride tomorrow. And how about you, Rose? Do you fancy a canter?'

'I'm afraid not, Grandpapa. I don't care for riding,' I said quickly.

I don't think Beth likes horses. She likes Paris. We are all in his thrall.

'So you've taken a shine to this young artist, Jeannie?' Grandmama asked when the children had been swept upstairs. Rupert and I were treated as token grown-ups and allowed another hour in their company. Rupert was even offered a tot of whisky and water, though I had to make do with raspberry cordial.

'He's Edward's friend. He invited him,' said Mama, her chin in the air. 'Is that not right, Edward?'

Papa nodded. He doesn't say much when we're at Pennycuik. He isn't quite himself. Grandpapa and Grandmama are still cool with him. When Mama and Papa first eloped, the family refused to have anything to do with them. They treat Rupert like the real man of the house now, and of course he loves it.

'Mr Walker is practically part of the family,' said Mama. 'Such a dear fellow, and so talented.'

'And so poor,' said Grandmama. 'His shirt cuffs are frayed and he has a rip in his trousers!'

'Yet he acts the dandy with his drooping purple scarf and his down-at-heel pointed boots,' said Grandpapa.

'Mr Walker is an artist,' Mama declared indignantly. 'Of course he dresses unconventionally.'

'He is also my friend, and I'll thank you not to talk about him when he's barely left the room,' said Papa.

There was an awkward silence. Rupert and I exchanged glances. Was there going to be a family row already, when we'd only just got here?

Grandmama quickly changed the subject. She turned to Rupert and started asking him about school. He replied fluently, lying so convincingly I almost believed he really *was* the golden boy who was everyone's favourite.

'*Was* that all lies in there?' I whispered when we were sent upstairs to bed.

'I was being polite,' said Rupert. 'It's the eleventh commandment. *Thou shalt not disturb your relatives unduly, for it will trouble them and have dire consequences for yourself,*' he said. 'Night, Rose.'

He sauntered off to the blue room. I followed him and peeped inside. It was one of the best guest rooms, and I'd always longed to sleep there because there was an elaborate blue and white Dutch tulip vase on its own ebonized table. Grandmama always had it filled with flowers. Obviously tulips were in short supply in December, but she had used red poinsettias and they looked wonderful. The bed was splendid too, a four-poster, with midnight-blue velvet curtains.

By rights Paris should have been given this bedroom, but Grandmama had sent his things up to one of the attic rooms where the servants slept. Mama had protested, but she shrugged her shoulders.

'There's no option, Jeannie. We've got a full house – well, we will tomorrow, when the Lord Provost and his wife and daughter come, plus old Lord and Lady Allingham – and the Jessops if they over-imbibe,' she explained.

'But Mr Walker could at least have a decent room tonight!'

'Please don't worry on my behalf, Mrs Rivers. I shall be very happy to sleep in the attics. I'm sure it will be much more comfortable than my garret bed,' he insisted.

'You poor boy. But don't fret, once my portrait is shown I'm sure you'll be the toast of London and all society will come flocking. You will soon find yourself able to afford a beautiful house with a studio,' said Mama, patting his arm. I wished she wouldn't clutch him like that, as if they were a couple.

I feared that Grandmama had put me in the nursery, where Rupert and I had always slept before, but I was in the big amber room – with Nurse Budd and Beth! It's another beautiful room, with a large display cabinet of amber beads from the Baltic. It has a four-poster bed too, with deep yellow damask curtains. I'd have loved to sleep there by myself – I wouldn't even have minded sharing it with Beth – but I was appalled at the thought of Nurse

Budd sleeping with us. Were we all going to have to squash up together?

Thank goodness a servant appeared with a truckle bed, indicating that Nurse Budd was to sleep there.

'Nonsense, girl,' said Nurse Budd. 'I am not one of the servants. I am a trained nurse. I need a proper bed. I shall sleep in the four-poster, Miss Beth may have the truckle, and Miss Rose will sleep in the nursery with her siblings.'

The servant looked at her. The Scottish staff are far more inclined to say what they think.

'Oh my, what's that bleating? You'd think there was a nanny goat in the room! But no, it's not a goat, it's a nanny – and, dear goodness, what a fuss she's making,' she said to Beth and me. She turned to Nurse Budd. 'Know your place, and don't go calling me "girl", lassie,' she said, and flounced off.

Nurse Budd had gone a deep red. 'I shall report her in the morning. She shall be sacked for insolence! I am not sleeping in a truckle bed,' she said, and she gave it a kick with her boot.

'Truckle bed,' Beth said, backing away from it as if it might bite her.

I ended up sleeping in it. Beth had to sleep in the four-poster with Nurse Budd. That was the worst option. It was horribly embarrassing getting ready for bed together. Nurse Budd undressed herself in bed behind the yellow curtains, but she had no qualms about whipping all Beth's clothes off and leaving her shivering stark naked before putting her nightdress on over her head. Then she went to her little leather case and gave her a large spoonful of Godfrey's Cordial.

'Why are you giving her that when she's already yawning her head off?' I asked.

'She won't sleep through the night without it,' said Nurse Budd. 'Please leave me to do my job, Miss Rose.'

Perhaps she took some cordial herself, because five minutes after she'd put the light out she started snoring. Beth snored too, slightly out of time with Nurse Budd. I curled up in my truckle bed and pulled the blankets over my head. Nurse Budd insisted on having the window open for fresh air and the room was freezing.

I couldn't get to sleep. I imagined Clover lying awake too, missing our chats. I wondered if I dared go and find her. I waited another half hour or so, and then eased myself out of bed, wrapping one of the blankets around me like a shawl. I tiptoed across the room. Nurse Budd and Beth kept snoring steadily.

I opened the door, turning the handle very slowly, and then slipped out into the corridor. It was so dark I had to feel my way along until I got to the servants' stairs.

I crept up the steep steps to the attics and then paused, wondering where to go next. I didn't know which room they'd put her in. There were so many. I didn't dare call Clover's name in case I woke someone else.

I listened at each door. I heard loud snoring, someone coughing repeatedly, and someone else muttering – but

Clover didn't snore like that, she didn't have a constant cough, and the mutterer had a thick Dundee accent.

I had gone halfway down the long corridor when I suddenly stopped dead. I heard the soft, steady patter of bare feet following me.

24

I **DIDN'T KNOW WHAT TO** do. Should I run? Dart into someone's room? I prickled all over with fear. I was scared it might be Nurse Budd.

She was bigger and stronger than me. She detested me. She'd threatened me. What might she do to me now, in the pitch dark?

The footsteps were getting nearer. I turned and, in the darkness, made out a shape. The footsteps stopped. There we were, facing each other.

I breathed in and smelled cologne.

'*Mama?*' I whispered.

'*Rose?*'

She came towards me and caught hold of my shoulders. 'What are you *doing* here, child?' she whispered, her breath hot on my face.

I swallowed. I couldn't think of a single feasible excuse. 'What are *you* doing here, Mama?' I asked in turn.

'I – I thought I heard someone crying,' she said.

'Ah, yes, so did I,' I returned.

We both stood there silently. I knew *she* was lying. She knew *I* was lying.

'Well, evidently they have stopped,' Mama said at last. 'Go back to bed at once, Rose.'

'Yes, Mama.'

'I am going back to bed too, of course. Come on.'

We shuffled along the dark passageway together, blindly feeling our way. Mama was breathing heavily. When at last we were down the stairs and back on the carpet of the first floor, she gave me a push in the small of my back.

'Return to your room this instant, Rose. I won't have you wandering about the house in the dark. It's disgraceful behaviour. What might people think?'

What might people think if they discovered you *were out wandering too?* I thought it, but I didn't dare say it.

I went back to the amber room, scared now that I'd wake Nurse Budd after all, but I heard two sets of snores behind the yellow curtains. I climbed into bed and tucked my feet up into my nightgown. I was shivering so much I made the bed creak.

I kept thinking about Mama. Had she realized that I was looking for Clover? Why was *she* up in the attics?

I wondered about it all night long, turning over and over in my truckle bed, still very cold and uncomfortable. I kept thinking about the warm four-poster, but I'd sooner have slept on a glacier with prowling polar bears than shared it with Nurse Budd.

I started composing in my head a series of scenes called *Rather Than Sleep with Nurse Budd*, with a centrepiece of Nurse Budd lying in bed, her eyes gleaming slits, her teeth bared, her hands crossed piously over her nightgown, but her fingers clawed. In each corner I'd put a comic vignette of myself: I'd drown under a waterfall; bake in a desert with a pride of lions circling; writhe on a bed of a thousand knives; lie upon an operating table while a surgeon sawed off my arm.

I thought of getting up very early and drawing it with my new ink pen. Then I could show my picture to Paris. I'd have to be very careful not to let Mama see.

What was I going to say to Mama in the morning? I didn't know how she would react. I felt ill at the thought of seeing her. Perhaps I'd go to the nursery for bread and milk with the little ones, or share the breakfast tray ordered for Nurse Budd and Beth.

It was painful watching Nurse Budd get Beth washed and dressed for the day. She was quick to attend to her own needs, dressing herself behind the yellow curtains and emerging fully clothed. She had surprisingly long hair, brushing it vigorously until it crackled. She looked softer with it hanging down her back, but as soon as she'd wound it fiercely round and round and pinned it into its daytime bun she lost all hint of girlishness.

She didn't grant Beth any such privacy. She didn't even wake her properly. She just announced, 'Time to get up, Miss Beth,' and pulled her out of bed, ignoring her sleepy protests. She yanked off her nightgown, and Beth closed her eyes tight. Perhaps she thought we couldn't see her if she couldn't see us. Nurse Budd washed her and forced her into her underwear and a navy woollen dress, with a crossover tartan wrap wound about her narrow chest. Beth scratched at her arms and fidgeted, reaching out towards the washstand.

'In a minute, Miss Beth. Just let me get your hair done,' said Nurse Budd.

She started brushing her hair with such force that she jerked Beth's head.

'Can't you do it more gently? You're hurting her!' I protested.

'I have to get all the tangles out. You could do with brushing your hair properly yourself, Miss Rose. I always get a lovely shine on Miss Beth's,' said Nurse Budd.

She brushed and brushed, while Beth started whimpering, her gaze still fixed on the washstand.

'What is it then? You've had your wash,' said Nurse Budd. Her eyes were gleaming, and I realized that she was playing a nasty game with Beth.

Beth grunted and pointed. There was nothing there, apart from the soap and flannel – and the medical case containing the black bottle of Godfrey's Cordial.

'Oh! Is *that* what you want?'

'Want!' said Beth urgently. She started trembling as Nurse Budd made a performance of unlocking the medical case, taking out the bottle of cordial, uncorking it and pouring a large spoonful.

'Careful now, Miss Beth. No spilling on your pretty frock,' said Nurse Budd, holding it above Beth's head, out of reach.

Beth did her best to control herself, whimpering.

'Easy now. Swallow it down in one go,' said Nurse Budd, holding the spoon to her lips.

Beth sucked it clean and then grunted pleadingly.

'Very well, my dear. Just one more spoonful.'

I hated seeing Beth beg like this.

'Isn't that too much?' I said. 'It says just a teaspoon.'

Nurse Budd rolled her eyes at me. 'It's completely harmless.'

Soon the maid appeared at the door with the breakfast tray and, while Nurse Budd was lifting each silver cover, I held the bottle of Godfrey's Cordial up to the light. It was still almost full, and I felt reassured.

'Perhaps I shall take breakfast here too,' I said as Nurse Budd started setting out the plates and cutlery on a side table.

'There's not enough for three,' she said, which was ridiculous, because Grandmama's provisions were always lavish and there seemed enough porridge and scrambled eggs and bacon to feed five families.

'Enough for three,' Beth repeated, dragging Marigold to the table with her, and sitting her on a little stool.

I could have gone without breakfast, but the food smelled so delicious. Resolutely I set off down to the dining room. It was a great relief to be joined by Rupert on the stairs.

'You look as pale as a ghost, Rose,' he said. 'Didn't you sleep well? I always sleep like a top at Grandmama's.'

'I'm sure *I'd* sleep wonderfully if I had the blue room all to myself,' I said sourly. 'It's so unfair. Why should *I* have to share with Nurse Budd and Beth?'

'Well, you can hardly expect me to take your place, old girl,' said Rupert. 'Come on, cheer up. Grandpapa is taking me riding this morning. I dare say he'll get a pony saddled up for you too. One with spirit, as you're such a natural horsewoman. Pamela has told me how much you love riding.'

'Stop being so mean.'

'I'm only teasing. No need to take it to heart. What is it, Rosie? What's the matter?' Rupert stood there looking at me.

'I don't know. Well, last night I crept upstairs, trying to find Clover—'

'Clover?'

'When we're at home I often go to her room. We talk long into the night,' I said.

'There'd have been a real to-do if you'd been caught. Mama would be outraged if she knew,' said Rupert.

'Perhaps she suspects.'

'Strewth! She caught you on the stairs?'

'No, right up in the attics. She was creeping around in the dark too. We gave each other a terrible fright.'

'Good Lord!' said Rupert. '*Mama* was creeping about up there after we'd all gone to bed? Was she in her *nightgown*?'

'Yes, I think so. I couldn't really see, but it was about two in the morning.'

'What did she say she was doing there?'

'She said she thought she'd heard someone crying. I suppose she might have. Clover sometimes cries. Only I didn't hear her last night.'

'As if Mama would care whether little Clover was crying or not,' said Rupert. He opened his eyes wide. 'So who else was she looking for up in the attics? Think, Rose!'

'Shut *up*, Rupert!'

'Well, grow up!'

We heard footsteps coming down the stairs. We looked round and saw Paris, jaunty and smiling, a blue spotted scarf tied round his neck, as if to match the splashes of blue paint on his black corduroy trousers. We both started guiltily.

'Are you two quarrelling?' he asked.

'No, of course not,' I said quickly. 'Did you hear what we were saying?'

'I heard Rupert telling you to grow up,' said Paris. 'Don't you dare! You're perfect just the way you are, Miss Rose Rivers,' he said, and carried on down the stairs.

357

'You've gone crimson!' said Rupert.

'No I haven't,' I insisted, though I could feel my cheeks burning.

'Dear goodness, what's that chap's secret? He looks such a scruffy oaf to me, and yet both you and Mama seem to have lost your heads over him.'

'That's nonsense.'

'Is it? Rose, what were *you* really doing up in the attics? Were you looking for Clover? Or were you running after Mr Walker too?'

'Don't be disgusting,' I said, and I slapped his face hard.

Then Papa came down the stairs, and put his arm round both of us. 'Good morning, my twins. My, you're both very red in the face. Have you been running up and down to work up an appetite? Let's go and have some breakfast. It's actually sunny this morning, though freezing cold of course. Paris and I have decided to avoid all the household preparations for the party. We're going sketching. I thought I'd show him Monifieth – it's wilder than the Ferry. You should come too, Rose. You might get inspired.'

'Oh, Papa, I'd love to!' I said, not daring to look at Rupert.

'That's marvellous, Rose. I was worried you'd become disheartened with your sketching. It's good to see you so enthusiastic.' Papa clapped me on the back and ushered us both into the dining room.

Grandmama had already finished her breakfast. Grandpapa was still leisurely sprinkling salt on his porridge, a strange Scottish habit that always astonished me. Mama wasn't down yet, much to my relief.

'Where's Jeannie then, Edward?' Grandmama demanded, dabbing her lips with her napkin.

'Oh, she's getting ready. I think she's already changed her dress twice and torturing your little maid because she doesn't care for the way she's done her hair,' said Papa jovially.

'Wee Morag is my own maid and she's extremely competent,' said Grandmama. 'It's not her fault if Jeannie demands all those fussy ringlets.'

Grandmama's hair is iron grey and straight as a ruler. She wears it scraped back so tightly it must make her scalp tingle. She sat bolt upright, drumming her fingers on the tablecloth.

'Where *is* the girl?' she demanded. 'I need to discuss one hundred and one things about the party tonight.'

'Now, dear, Jeannie is a guest in our house. You shouldn't rope her in to help organize everything,' said Grandpapa, munching. Pennycuik porridge is peculiarly thick. Rupert says the ingredients are oats, water, and a pound and a half of glue.

'She's my *daughter*,' said Grandmama. 'It's her duty to help her mother!'

It seemed you were never excused daughterly duties, even when you had seven children yourself.

Mama came into the room when everyone else had breakfasted and the servants were shuffling their feet, waiting to clear the dishes. She was wearing her best blue silk, the dress she wore for her portrait. It seemed a strange choice, especially as Pennycuik was so cold. She was wearing her new sapphire earrings as well as the brooch, and she'd applied her cologne so liberally she overpowered the smell of bacon and eggs.

'My Lord, Jeannie, you're not dressed for the party already!' said Grandmama.

'Of course not, Mama,' she said.

Paris stood up for her as she joined the table. 'Your dress looks stunning as always – and, my goodness, your earrings are beautiful,' he said. 'I think I shall have to add them to your portrait, Mrs Rivers.'

'By all means,' said Mama, smiling at him. She let him settle her in the chair next to his.

'Well, eat up, my dear, though there's scarcely any porridge left,' said Grandpapa.

'Don't dally, Jeannie. There's so much we have to do,' said Grandmama. 'The Christmas greenery is looking very tired. I'll ask the gardener and his boys to fetch some more, and I thought you might arrange it for me. You've always had the knack of making flowers look pretty. And then you can be in charge of wrapping the party favours. I need your help on the dietary front too. I only discovered yesterday that the wretched Lady Provost has such a delicate constitution she can't consume animal products, so what on earth am I going to give her? Can *you* think of an equivalent to Arbroath smokies and good Angus beef? Apparently she can't even eat Clootie Dumpling because of the suet! Did you ever!'

Grandmama droned on and on like a Scottish Mrs Beeton.

Mama was barely listening. 'Perhaps a medley of vegetables, Mama? But I'm not sure I'll have time to do any chores. Paris has brought his painting equipment, so I thought this would be an ideal opportunity for him to work on my portrait,' she said. 'Wait till you see it, Mama. It's a work of art.'

'Don't be ridiculous, Jeannie, it's a work of art by very definition,' said Grandmama.

'I would have loved to continue, Mrs Rivers, but I've failed to bring the portrait itself. I didn't want to risk damaging it on the journey,' Paris said quickly.

Mama didn't seem perturbed. 'Of course! But never mind – perhaps you'd care to start some preliminary sketches for the *next* portrait, in profile this time? I thought that would be a novel idea,' she said, turning her head and demonstrating, her hand at her throat to hide her double chin.

'It would be a great honour, but I'm not sure I can manage to make a start today,' Paris said.

'You're not quick enough off the mark, Jeannie,' said Papa, draining his cup of tea. 'I've bagged Paris for myself. We're going sketching. I thought I'd take him up the coast to Monifieth. Rose is coming too, aren't you, my dear. She seems very keen.'

'I dare say she is,' said Mama icily. She looked at me for the first time that morning. 'But you must stay and help Grandmama.'

'Oh, Mama!'

'Don't spoil the lassie's fun, Jeannie. Let her go off gallivanting if she wishes,' said Grandpapa. 'I'm taking Rupert riding, and I've ordered the carriage to take Nurse and the little ones to Balgay Park. Come on then – let's be off and leave the womenfolk to their planning.'

I was off before Mama could think of another ploy to keep me there. I rushed up to the amber room to fetch my coat and hat and sketchbook and pencils. I found Beth back in her underwear, shivering and crying, while Nurse Budd wagged her finger at her.

'What on earth are you doing?' I asked. 'You're frightening her! What have you done with her dress?'

'Miss Beth took it upon herself to spit her porridge all down her bodice,' said Nurse Budd. 'I've scrubbed hard, but it's stained.'

'Well, it isn't very smooth porridge, and you know she hates to eat anything lumpy. You shouldn't have forced her to eat it,' I said fiercely.

'What am I supposed to do, let the child starve to death? She's skin and bone as it is,' said Nurse Budd, taking hold of one of Beth's thin arms and giving it a little shake.

Beth screamed and hit out at her.

'Now now, that's very naughty, isn't it, Miss Beth. You don't want to make Nurse Budd cross, do you?'

'Don't, Beth! Do calm down,' I said. I tried to distract her the way Clover did. 'Shall we see if we can find you another dress to put on? Then you can go on an outing with Nurse and the others to Balgay Park. It's lovely there – do you remember? There's that little bridge you like to run across, and the wooden summer house. When I was young I liked to pretend that it was my own little house. You and Clarrie could play house together,' I said.

'Play house together,' said Beth, looking at me.

'I'm afraid *I* can't come to the park, Beth. I've got to go sketching with Papa and Mr Walker,' I said, sighing as if it were a tiresome duty, and then bolted out of the room.

I bobbed into the nursery to find Clover. She was trying to get Algie and Clarrie into their warm Scottish outfits while Nurse fed Phoebe, grumbling that Cook had given her the wrong kind of milk.

'I know this is far too creamy and rich and it'll upset her,' she kept muttering, though Phoebe was guzzling down her breakfast with evident relish.

'I'm *not* wearing that stupid skirt again,' Algie shrieked, running around in his drawers.

'I'm not either,' said Clarrie, copying him.

'Don't be silly, Miss Clarrie, you wear skirts every day,' said Clover, catching her and swinging her up in the air to stop her pouting.

'Yes, but the kilt is so stiff and it makes me itchy,' said Clarrie. 'And so does my jumper. And my under-things. '

'Mine too,' said Algie, pulling down his drawers and kicking them off. 'We're not wearing anything at all!

We'll be monkeys!' He started making monkey noises and pulling faces.

Sebastian laughed. He was already dressed in his own kilt and sitting carefully in a nursery chair, his woollen socks pulled up neatly and his black shoes tied just so.

'I'll take you straight to the Zoological Gardens and put you in a cage,' said Clover. 'Though you haven't a clue how to make real monkey noises. Listen, it's like this.' She demonstrated loudly, scratching under her arms for extra authenticity.

Algie and Clarrie were so impressed they let Clover pull their underwear back on and buckle up the dreaded kilts.

'What a terrible row! Call yourself a nurserymaid. You're worse than the whole pack of children rolled together,' Nurse grumbled.

'Don't be silly, Nurse, Clover's magical,' I said. 'She can get the children to do anything she wants. Clover, I came to tell you. Papa's organized a sketching party this morning, just for the three of us.'

Her green eyes shone. She thought I meant that Papa had invited her too! I felt terrible.

'Papa and Mr Walker and me,' I amended.

'Oh,' said Clover. 'Yes. Of course.'

I couldn't bear to see the way she drooped. 'But perhaps – perhaps I could ask if you could come too,' I said.

'Have you taken leave of your senses, Miss Rose?' said Nurse. 'As if the master would take a little maid out sketching! And anyway, even if he were so soft, she couldn't possibly go. She has to help me look after these four.'

'You're always protesting that you don't need any help, Nurse,' I said.

'I'll thank you not to be impertinent, Miss Rose. You might think yourself a little lady, but you're not too old to go over my knee and be smacked with the hairbrush,' said Nurse.

'I'd like to see you try, Nurse!' I replied.

She shook her head. 'It doesn't do to stir young Clover up and pretend there's no difference between her and you. She has to know her place,' she said quietly.

'*Why* does she? Why do we have this ridiculous idea of class anyway? Why am I a lady and Clover a servant just because we happened to be born into different homes?' I asked.

'It's only right and Christian,' said Nurse.

'Christ was a carpenter, which is a decent profession, but it doesn't make him a gentleman,' I declared.

'Button your mouth, Miss Rose, and get out of my nursery. I'll not listen to such wicked blaspheming,' Nurse declared, shaking her head.

I felt guilty going off sketching with Papa and Paris, but I reasoned that it wouldn't help Clover if I stayed behind. And it turned out to be the most tremendous fun. Papa and Paris joshed each other like schoolboys, striding out across the tufty grass and boggy glens while I bobbed along behind. Whenever we came to a big ditch they seized me by the hands and swung me across, and as soon as I started lagging they sang to cheer me along. Papa warbled Scottish laments while Paris sang ridiculous comic songs from the music hall. Papa joined in, word perfect, and said they took him back to his youth.

At last we reached Papa's perfect spot, and he got the provisions out of his bulging knapsack – strips of home-cured ham and shortbread triangles. We devoured them eagerly, though we'd had breakfast less than two hours ago. Papa and Paris took sips of whisky from a flask, saying it kept out the cold. Papa only had ginger beer for me. I could have done with some of their whisky – it was even colder crouching above the beach, with the wind blowing straight off the sea.

I hoped that Papa and Paris would carry on singing and joking merrily, but after a few minutes each became absorbed in his work, and when I attempted conversation Paris gave short, abstracted answers and Papa simply grunted. I tried to concentrate on my own sketch, but I found it frustrating. I didn't know how to draw the heaving sea or the heavy clouds or the vast expanse of sky.

'Draw what you see, Rose,' Papa said when I flicked my page over yet again. 'Get the outline right – the line of the sea, the sand, the rocks. Look where the light is, the shade. Then start filling in the details.'

But I couldn't get the outline right, and there weren't any interesting details. I made them up, peopling the deserted beach with my siblings. I drew Rupert posing on a rock playing with his pocket watch in a languid manner, Beth staring at the waves, Sebastian sitting primly on a tartan rug so he wouldn't get his kilt sandy, Algie tearing off his own kilt to go swimming, Clarrie building a sandcastle, with Phoebe crowing and kicking beside her.

When we were all completely frozen, we took a break and jumped up and down to get the blood circulating.

Paris looked at my sketch and laughed. 'Well done, Rose! You've drawn each child splendidly! Look, Edward. See how talented your daughter is!' he said enthusiastically.

I glowed, in spite of the cold, but Papa looked disappointed.

'Oh, Rose! You're back to your nonsense again. It's wittily done, but you could have drawn it just as well at the house. I want you to learn to sketch from nature,' he said.

'Nature is just a little bit *dull*, Papa,' I said, which made Paris laugh.

'I have *seven* children, and yet none of them seems to have an artistic soul,' said Papa, sighing.

'You can hardly expect Phoebe to sit up in her cradle and start painting,' said Paris. 'I grant you that young Algie and merry little Clarrie don't seem artistic – but Sebastian is a sensitive soul.'

'I dare say he is, but he doesn't care for painting any more,' said Papa. 'He says he doesn't like the smell, yet he cleans out that mouse cage happily enough.'

'I think he'll end up being a zoologist, Papa,' I said.

'What career do you predict for Algie?' he asked.

'Oh, that's easy – he'll be a clown in the circus.'

'And Rupert? He's clearly not interested in being an artist. He's far too worldly,' said Papa. 'I suppose he'll inherit his grandfather's fortune one day. Do you see him as a Jute King, Rose?'

'No, I think he'll hire a man to manage the mills while he *spends* the fortune,' I said.

'What about you, Rose?' Paris asked. 'What do you want to do when you grow up?'

'So you see my girl as a New Woman, with a career?' Papa asked with interest.

'I don't see how I can pursue any worthwhile career when I have no education to speak of,' I said bitterly.

'Don't start, my dear. You know your mother doesn't approve of schooling for girls.'

'But you approve, don't you, Papa?'

'Possibly. But I don't control the purse strings. I'm allowed to buy my wife expensive jewellery, but I can't send my bright daughter to school,' said Papa. I think he meant to say this lightly, but it sounded harsh.

There was a little silence. Both men sat down again and went back to sketching. I had lost heart. I tried to sketch properly, but my hands were now so cold that I had even less command of my pencil. I stared at the sea, the sand, the sky until they all blurred into each other. I tried sketching Papa and Paris crouched on their separate rocks, but I couldn't get the shapes right. Papa ended up with a head much too big for his body, and Paris's right arm was twice the length of his left. I wished I had an India rubber, but Papa didn't approve of rubbings out.

'Look hard until you see exactly how the line should go, and then you won't need to rub out,' he said.

I was looking so hard my eyes watered in the wind, yet my lines were all over the place. I gave up altogether and sat there daydreaming, wondering what my New Year's resolution was going to be.

25

I **WAS CHILLED TO** the bone when I got back to Pennycuik.

'Did you have a good time sketching?' Clover asked me when she'd settled the children for their afternoon nap.

'It was so cold! I'm still freezing now, feel,' I said, touching her with my icy hand.

She took hold of it and rubbed it briskly back to life. 'Was it wonderful?'

I hesitated. 'It was fun to be with Mr Walker and Papa,' I said truthfully. 'We sang all the way there and back.'

'What's the sea like? Is it very vast and wild?' Clover asked eagerly.

I felt terrible when I realized she'd never seen the sea herself. She begged to see my sketches. I felt ashamed when I showed her. She seemed a little puzzled, but was very polite, and laughed at my caricature of the children on the beach.

'You don't have to be kind, Clover. I know I'm useless at art,' I said.

'Well, so am I. Your papa says I must try to find time to practise,' she said, waving her right hand in the air to demonstrate drawing.

I saw she had coloured smudges on her fingers. 'Have *you* been sketching with your new pastels?' I asked.

She flushed. 'Just for a little while when the children were quiet and Nurse was feeding Phoebe. I kept an eye on them to make sure they weren't getting into mischief,' she said anxiously.

'Oh, for goodness' sake, you don't have to justify yourself to me. You're a wonderful nurserymaid. You must sketch at every opportunity!' I assured her. 'Let me see what you've done!'

'You'll laugh at me. I don't know anything about drawing. In the past I just chalked silly pictures on the pavement. No, please, I *can't* show you,' she said, but I made her fetch the sketchbook from under the cushion where she'd hidden it.

I stared at her picture. She had sketched the view from the window – the garden with its dark trees, their branches bare and clipped, solitary shrubs in the flower beds, and orderly gravel paths crossing the grass in severely straight lines, a garden so formal and dull it made the heart ache. But behind the deep green rhododendron bushes that circled the grounds she'd added the tangle of forest and the distant purple hills and the great grey sky.

I was utterly silent.

'Please give it back. I know it's dreadful,' said Clover.

'It's wonderful,' I whispered.

I'd been brought up in an artistic home, given special tuition by my famous father, been taken to sketch for hours in a picturesque spot – and produced nothing worth keeping. Clover had snatched a half hour and had created a landscape so powerful it made me shiver.

'I must show it to Papa,' I said.

'No! Please don't! It's not good enough. And if Nurse finds out, I'll get a telling-off for wasting time when I should have been mending,' Clover protested.

'I *have* to show him,' I said firmly, and marched off with her sketchbook.

Papa and Paris were in the billiard room, tucking into a plate of mutton pies, a cheeseboard, a fruit cake and two tankards of beer.

'We filched these from Cook. Here, Rose, have some cake. You must have worked up a healthy appetite after that long walk,' Papa said.

'In a minute, Papa. You must look at this drawing. You too, Mr Walker!'

Papa took the sketchbook from me and stared at Clover's drawing. Then he looked up at me, his face a picture in itself. 'Did *you* sketch this, Rose?' he asked.

'Of course not, Papa,' I said impatiently. 'You know full well I'm no good at drawing. *Clover* did it, just now, when the children were resting.'

'I knew the child had ability. That was partly what drew me to her in the first place. It seemed so valiant, somehow, a little girl from the gutters chalking pictures and painting faces on dolls. But this is something else – look, Paris!'

Paris stared too. He liked my comical drawings, he found them amusing – but my work didn't make his eyes light up like this.

'Which one's Clover? The little moppet with all the dark hair? And she hasn't had any training?'

'None – but I'll make sure she does now,' said Papa. 'I shall instruct her myself.'

'That's marvellous, Papa – but what about Mama? She surely won't allow it,' I said anxiously.

'She won't know. I'll make sure of that. I'll think of some ploy,' said Papa. 'I'll go and find Clover right this minute.'

'You won't get her into trouble, you promise?' I begged.

'Don't worry.' He gave me an absent-minded pat on the shoulder and then hurried off.

I was left alone with Paris. He was watching me intently.

'Do you mind your father being so bowled over by the little maid's work?' he asked.

'No, I'm truly pleased for Clover. She's my friend. I just wish Papa could be as proud of me,' I said, trying to be completely honest.

'*I'm* proud of you and your work, Rose,' said Paris.

'But we both know I'm nowhere near as talented as Clover.'

'You have a different talent, that's all.'

'Not good enough for *Punch* though.'

'I think it's simply the wrong journal to appreciate your work. It's run by a brotherhood of self-satisfied men. They don't want a slip of a girl showing them up,' said Paris. 'It was stupid of me to get your hopes up, Rose. I'm so sorry. Here, have a slice of cake.'

'For goodness' sake, you and Papa keep offering me cake! I'm not Clarrie,' I said indignantly, but I took a slice all the same, and a chunk of cheese.

'What do you think of Pennycuik?' I asked.

'Well, it's very interesting,' Paris said. 'I've always wanted to go to Scotland – but perhaps I was thinking more of the Highlands.'

'I don't suppose it compares to France,' I said.

'It was very kind of your father to invite me. Well, your mother too.' He paused. 'I'm afraid I've offended her.'

'In what way?' I asked huskily.

'She was clearly thinking I'd continue with her portrait while we were here. And then she wasn't pleased when your papa whisked me off. How can I make it up to her?' Paris asked.

Did he really care about hurting her feelings? I wondered. Or was he simply worried she might not pay for the portrait?

'I think if you dance with her tonight she will find it easy to forgive you,' I said.

'Oh dear Lord, do I have to dance? I have two left feet when it comes to the waltz,' said Paris.

'It's not that sort of dancing, it's Scottish reels,' I said.

'That's worse!'

'It can be quite good fun actually. It's very fast, and you whirl round and round.'

'Then you'll have to take pity and show me what to do,' said Paris.

'Very well,' I said, sighing as if it would be a chore. Secretly I was thrilled that he was actually asking me to dance with him.

I took another slice of cake and munched it happily.

Papa came back beaming, still clutching Clover's drawing pad. 'There, I've talked to your mama, Rose, and it's all fixed! I shall be giving young Clover a drawing lesson every weekday morning,' he said triumphantly.

I stared at him in astonishment. 'Mama's never agreed to that, surely?' I said.

'Well, not exactly,' he admitted. 'I found Clover in the nursery reading a story to Sebastian and Clarrie, and showered her with praise. She nearly burst into tears, bless her. She's clearly not used to praise. But then we heard a terrible roaring downstairs. Young Algie had sneaked off to slide down the banisters, and had fallen and bumped his head. It was only a little bump, but he wouldn't stop crying until Clover caught him up in her arms and said she needed to mend his head with vinegar and brown paper, just like Jack's crown in the nursery rhyme, and that cheered him up immensely.

'Your mama was very put out and inclined to blame Clover for Algie's naughtiness, but I did my best to defend her. I said that the Queen of England herself could not quell our number three son. Algie took offence at that and started roaring again, declaring it wasn't fair, he wanted to be my number *one* son, bless him. He's not a bad little chap, you know. I think he just needs more attention,' said Papa indulgently.

'I think he gets too much attention already,' I said. 'But I don't see how Algie sliding down the banisters led to Mama letting you give Clover lessons.'

'I said I'd rather like to do a portrait of him. Your mama said he would never be able to sit still, which was reasonable, but I said the sessions would only last a half hour, and Clover could sing him nursery rhymes or make up little stories to amuse him. Mama said Nurse wouldn't be able to manage without Clover, but Nurse loved the idea of Algie being spirited away, even for half an hour. So it's all settled. When we get home I shall start a portrait of Algie and, while I'm painting, Clover can be my little apprentice, learning how to mix paint and work out perspective and achieve special effects.'

'While gabbling nursery rhymes?' I said.

'Oh, come along, Rose, I'm sure it will work splendidly,' said Papa. He looked at me carefully. 'You don't mind, do you, darling? I thought you'd taken Clover under your wing.'

'I have, I have. Of course I don't mind, Papa, I'm happy for her,' I said.

'That's all I want – for everyone to be happy,' he said. He clapped Paris on the shoulder. 'You're happy too, aren't you, my friend? You've certainly made me happy this New Year's Eve. I don't usually care for these trips to the frozen north. My in-laws can be a little forbidding, especially my father-in-law. I don't think he's ever forgiven me for enticing his precious daughter down south.'

Grandpapa might ignore Papa, but he's fond of us children, especially Rupert. Grandmama had several sons, but they all died in infancy, so their firstborn grandson has a special place in their hearts.

Grandpapa and Rupert came back glowing from their ride, Grandpapa full of praise for Rupert's natural horsemanship.

'You'll have to come and stay longer. You've got the makings of a fine horseman. I'll take you out hunting,' he said as they went upstairs to get changed for the party.

'I'd love that, sir,' said Rupert.

'That's the spirit,' said Grandpapa. He saw me trailing after them. 'I'd take you too, Rose, but I hear you don't care for horses.'

'That's putting it mildly, Grandpapa,' I said.

He seemed tickled by my response. 'So you're determined to be an artist like your father, eh?'

'No. I haven't got the talent,' I said, sighing.

'So what *do* you like to do, lassie?' he asked.

I thought carefully. 'I like to read, especially poetry and novels. I like to learn. I like to study.'

Grandpapa peered down at my legs.

'Grandpapa?'

'Just checking the colour of your stockings. Seems to me you're turning into a bluestocking,' he said, chuckling.

Rupert joined in the laughter. I was furious. Why was it so funny? I couldn't stop Grandpapa, but I thumped Rupert hard on the back.

I spent a long time in my bath, moodily mulling things over, not wanting to go back to the amber room because of Nurse Budd. I let the bath get lukewarm, and when I tried to top it up the water ran cold because so many other people had taken baths too.

By the time I trailed back to the bedroom in my dressing gown I was shivering. Beth was shivering too, standing in her underwear, refusing to put on her party frock. She was peering at the ropes of amber in the glass display case, intent on counting each round yellow bead. Every time Nurse Budd pulled at her she lost count and cried with frustration.

'Now come along, Miss Beth dear, stop that silly counting and put on your lovely dress or Nurse Budd will start to get cross,' said Nurse Budd.

'Cross, cross, cross!' said Beth, stamping her stockinged foot.

'Hurry up, dear, do!'

'Do, do, do!' Beth parroted, and started counting all over again.

'Look, Beth, I'm putting on my party frock,' I said, fetching my white organdie. 'We like wearing these dresses. Papa says we look like snowdrops.'

Beth ignored me altogether, muttering, '*Twenty-two, twenty-three, twenty-four . . .*'

'Just let her get to a hundred and then I'm sure she'll stop,' I suggested.

'She'll stop,' Beth agreed. '*Twenty-five, twenty-six . . .*'

The grandfather clock in the hall chimed the half hour.

'We're meant to be downstairs to meet everyone . . . *Ninety-nine, a hundred* – there, you're finished now. Into your dress,' said Nurse Budd, lowering the flimsy white material over Beth's head.

She screamed and struggled frantically, unable to see. Her fingers caught in the sleeve, and there was an ominous ripping sound.

'You little devil,' said Nurse Budd, and she smacked Beth hard.

'Don't hit her! It's cruel and wicked!' I cried, though I'd had more than my fair share of smacks from Nurse in the past.

'I'm simply trying to calm her down,' said Nurse Budd, panting. 'That's it, Miss Beth, stop struggling or you'll

379

tear your dress more. Keep still while I sort you out. Then you can have some medicine.'

Beth was suddenly docile, letting Nurse Budd pull her head and arms free.

'She already had some this morning,' I protested.

'Well, she needs some more now,' said Nurse Budd, fetching the bottle and pouring out a big spoonful.

'Surely that's too much?'

'Who's the trained nurse, you or me?' said Nurse Budd, ramming the spoon into Beth's mouth.

'Careful, she'll choke!' I warned.

But Beth opened her mouth wide like a baby bird and then whined for more.

'Just one more then, so long as you're a good girl now,' said Nurse Budd.

'Good girl now,' Beth said, sucking on the spoon.

She had little crusts of black medicine at the corners of her mouth. Nurse Budd licked a handkerchief and wiped them away.

'Now, let's see the damage,' she said, peering at Beth's dress.

There was a little tear along the seam that joined the sleeve to the bodice.

'There's no time for sewing now. You'll just have to keep your arms down by your side, do you hear me?' said Nurse Budd.

Beth nodded, calm now, and co-operated as the tartan sash was wound about her chest.

'There, just your shoes now. One foot first, then the other – that's the way.'

'That's the way,' said Beth dreamily.

'Don't just stand there gawping, Miss Rose. Get dressed,' said Nurse Budd, putting on a clean apron.

I struggled into my frock. I liked the light, silky feel, the skirts floating around my calves. I even liked the tight crossover, because it hid my flat chest and gave me more of a waist. I wanted to see myself in the looking glass, but I didn't want Nurse Budd to mock me for being vain. She was busy brushing Beth's hair and fixing a large white satin ribbon on one side. I hastily tied a matching ribbon in my own hair, hoping it didn't make me look too childish. If Edie had come with us I'd have begged her to pin my hair up again, even if it made Mama angry.

When I went downstairs Mama was worrying about her own hair. It had been styled differently, with loops on either side of her parting and little curls to set off her new sapphire earrings. There was a thin blue ribbon wound in and out of her bun at the back, with a bow right in the middle.

'Does my hair look all right?' she whispered to me. 'The maid insisted it's the new French style. What do you think, Rose?'

I was surprised that she had asked my opinion. I thought she looked like an elaborately decorated parcel, but I knew she didn't want me to be truthful. I murmured something about it looking very decorative. She kept fiddling with the curls, winding them round her fingers, and patting the bun to make sure that the ribbon was still in place. She fidgeted with her dress too. She was wearing an elaborate version of her daughters' white organdie frocks, with a tartan sash, but the girlish outfit only made her look matronly.

When Papa saw her he seemed surprised, but told her gallantly that she looked very charming. Paris was flatteringly inventive, saying she looked like a Botticelli maiden as he kissed her hand. She took him seriously and blushed.

Grandmama was blunt.

'Good Lord, Jeannie, you're dressed up like the Queen of the May!' she said, raising her thin eyebrows.

Grandmama's hair was in its usual severe knot. She was wearing a grey silk dress with a very high lace collar, a rabbit's-foot brooch set with topaz pinned to her meagre bosom. Clarrie kept begging to stroke Grandmama's little bunny, which made Algie snigger dreadfully.

We all lined up in the hall to greet the guests as soon as they'd shed their coats and the ladies had visited the downstairs cloakroom. We stood in strict order of seniority: Grandpapa, Grandmama, Papa, Mama, Rupert, me, Beth, Sebastian, Algie and Clarrie. Nurse stood back several paces, holding Phoebe, who was dressed in her best lace christening gown. It was rather too tight for her now and she wriggled irritably, her face very red. Nurse Budd stood to attention in case Beth had one of her turns.

Poor Clover had been told she wasn't needed and sent up to the attic.

I think Grandmama would have liked to send Paris there too, but he was placed beside the nurses and introduced to everyone in clipped tones as 'Edward's artist friend'. Only the most important people had been invited to dine with us before the ball began. Even Grandmama seemed a little overawed by the Lord and Lady Provost and their daughter, though the parents looked brown and plain and rather whiskery, like otters. The daughter had a smooth complexion but unfortunate teeth.

'Welcome to Pennycuik,' said Grandmama, as if it were Balmoral itself.

There was a huge fire, and steaming hot punch served from a great silver cauldron. There were platters of tiny sausages, bite-sized game pies and smoked-fish patties.

Grandmama encouraged us children to pass these around. Rupert was charming and self-assured and offered his dish to all the ladies with a flourish. I was shy and awkward, and mumbled whenever anyone spoke to me. Beth wasn't trusted with a plate, though she was quiet because there was a vast Christmas tree in the corner. She stared up at the fairy and muttered, *'Fairy, fairy, fairy,'* to herself. Sebastian handed his plate round carefully, looking earnest. Algie and Clarrie didn't offer their plates to many guests. They hid behind the sofa and stuffed their faces.

I wished I could hide too. The guests were eyeing us children up and down, commenting on how much we'd grown in the past year as if it were an extraordinary phenomenon. Rupert was especially admired for his height, his general bearing, his polished manners.

'That laddie's going to break so many hearts!' was the general verdict.

I was a disappointment by comparison. I heard one woman say, 'Poor Rose. She's getting plainer and plainer. It's hard to believe she's Rupert's twin.'

Last year Beth had thrown a tantrum and had to be removed, but now her demeanour and beautiful hair drew praise.

'That lassie's come on by leaps and bounds. You'd never think she's not right in the head. Look at her – quite the little lady,' they pronounced.

Nurse Budd glowed smugly in the corner while Mama burbled on about Lady Robson's personal recommendation.

Sebastian divided opinion. The Lady Provost and all the other women thought him charming, admiring his long fair hair and quaint manners. The men were less impressed. The Lord Provost said he needed to be fed more beef. Sebastian looked anxiously at Nurse, hoping she couldn't hear. Sebastian dislikes meat because of the fat, and spits most of it out into his handkerchief.

No one could say that Algie needed more meat. His pink cheeks and stocky build were admired, but his exuberance was overwhelming. Clarrie was considered a nice enough wee girl, although also inclined to be boisterous.

Little Phoebe was thoroughly inspected too, all the ladies clucking at her like hens. Phoebe liked this sort of attention and smiled chirpily, so was pronounced a fine infant.

'I dread to think how you're going to portray this occasion,' Paris whispered in my ear. 'What will the title be? *Does the Family Pass Muster?*'

I giggled. Mama frowned and beckoned me to her side.

'Pass the plate round to all the guests, Rose. You mustn't monopolize Mr Walker,' she hissed.

She seemed determined to monopolize him herself, making sure he sat next to her at dinner, though Grandmama had originally placed him down at the far end. Rupert and I were invited to dinner, but the children were led back to the nursery for their supper.

'When the music starts you may come down and join in the fun for half an hour, my dears, but you must be in bed by nine,' Grandmama said firmly.

Algie and Clarrie complained bitterly, wanting to stay up till midnight, but after dancing the Gay Gordons they were both exhausted and Clover had to be summoned to help Nurse carry them off to bed.

'Here, Clover, let me give you a hand with these little dumplings,' said Papa.

Clover looked dazed by the ballroom, with its great chandelier and pink Chinese wallpaper and potted palms and little gilt seats. She tried a little slide on the highly polished floor and stared into one great looking glass after another, glimpsing multiple ballrooms at every turn.

The guests looked like figures from a fairy tale, the ladies in their white dresses, the men sporting their tartan. Clover was startled by the wheeze and wail of the bagpipes and put her hands over her ears. I hate the noise they make too, though I can't admit it to my fervently Scottish grandparents.

Clover gave a timid smile when she saw me watching her. I wondered what she was thinking. Was she wishing she could swap places with me? Was she contrasting this ostentatious display of twinkling glass and over-bright gilt with her hovel in Cripps Alley? Was she planning the picture she'd draw tomorrow? Would Papa contrive to send her to art school when she was older? Might she be a serious painter, with her work exhibited at the Academy?

'You're looking very earnest, Rose,' said Paris, sitting down beside me. 'What are you thinking?'

'I'm just daydreaming about Clover. She's really talented, isn't she?' I said.

'Yes, she is. Much better than I was at her age,' he agreed. 'My, this is an amazing room, isn't it?'

'I used to be dazzled by it, but now I find it too ornate and bright. I wish Grandmama would commission you to redecorate it. I know you'd make it much more simple and elegant,' I said, remembering the rooms he'd designed at the Palace Hotel.

'I don't think my decorative style would please your grandmama at all. She certainly doesn't care for my *personal* style,' said Paris, smiling ruefully.

He was the only man in the room not wearing the kilt.
He wore his smartest suit, which wasn't very smart at
all. It was well cut, the cloth good, but it was terribly
worn at the cuffs. His white shirt was clean but crumpled,
and he wore a crimson knotted scarf instead of a tie.

'I rather think she'd prefer it if I didn't appear on the
dance floor – but would you be my partner if we lurked in
a distant corner?' Paris asked.

'I would love to dance with you,' I said.

'You will have to teach me the steps.'

'I'm not sure of them myself. I'm pretty hopeless at
dancing,' I admitted.

'That's very comforting. We'll encourage each other.
Come on, let's have a go,' said Paris, offering me his arm.

I hoped he wouldn't feel me trembling. I'd never danced
with anyone who wasn't a relation. I generally danced
with Rupert, though Papa occasionally took me up for a
reel. I'd danced with Sebastian, who was a surprisingly
good dancer. But I'd never danced with a strange man –
though of course Paris wasn't strange at all.

I didn't dare look in Mama's direction.

The floor was very crowded and we had to struggle
round the edge. The Lord Provost and his wife lacked
one couple for their set. Perhaps people were too overawed
to join them. The wife beckoned to Paris, clearly not
minding his bohemian dress.

'You're very kind, madam, but I'm afraid neither Rose
nor I are accomplished dancers. We are going to caper by
ourselves in a corner,' he said, bowing to her.

She gave a squeaky giggle of regret, her nose very pink.

'Who was that eager lady with the hairy husband?' Paris murmured when we were out of earshot.

'They're the Lord and Lady Provost. They're very grand. Grandmama is thrilled that they're attending,' I explained.

'Goodness,' he said, pretending to be impressed. He looked around the crowded room. 'Do you know all these people, Rose?'

'Hardly any of them. They're not just from Dundee – there's a whole contingent from Perth, and Lord Mackay from Forfar has a large party from London staying with him. Grandmama's so excited to have real lords and ladies at her ball!'

'And one dissolute impoverished artist,' Paris said.

'I think you're a very distinguished guest,' I said. 'Wait till you've had a painting hung in the Academy. Mama is right, people will flock to your side. I remember what it was like when Papa did his famous portrait of the Honourable Louisa Mayhorne.'

'So you think people will be agog to see my portrait of the very worthy Jeannie Rivers?' Paris asked, eyebrows raised.

I felt a delicious thrill when he mocked Mama – yet I was also uncomfortable, because she was still my mother. *I* was free to mock her, but somehow it didn't feel right when Paris did.

'Perhaps,' I said. 'Right, we've reached the corner. Let's dance!'

I showed him the steps, pointing my feet alternately, and then we whirled around, doing our own independent reel. The floor was so crowded that no one could see us. Paris proved to be a good dancer – better than Papa, who often started with the wrong foot or set off in the wrong direction. It wasn't quite like dancing with Rupert either.

I craned my neck to see if *he* was dancing. Yes, with a real beauty, an older girl with flaming red hair and a green tartan sash, the most striking young woman in the whole room. Trust Rupert! She looked a little like Hetty the foundling girl, though much better fed.

Paris saw me staring at her. 'My word, Rupert's very bold! She seems charmed by him too. Is he *really* only thirteen?'

'Well, he's my twin, so of course he is,' I said. 'Though I know I look much younger.'

'You seem older than your age in many ways, Rose,' said Paris.

'But I don't look it, do I? It's so unfair. I agree, Rupert looks years older than me.'

'I think you look perfect just the way you are. I really do want to paint your portrait. Perhaps it will be *your* portrait that will set those crowds flocking!'

'They will flock to mock!' I said. It was difficult to talk and dance at the same time, so I stopped and leaned against the wall, and Paris did too. We were continuing our companionable chat when Mama suddenly came bursting through the dancers.

'*There* you are! Rose, what are you thinking of, skulking in a corner with Mr Walker,' she demanded.

'She's been teaching me to dance, Mrs Rivers. We've had to find a discreet corner so that I don't feel a laughing stock,' he said.

'Rose shouldn't keep demanding your attention! It's very naughty of her. You must come and mingle, dear boy. This is your opportunity to make the right contacts. I will introduce you to lots of wealthy, influential people. Apparently there are titled folk from London here too. My father hunts with Lord Mackay, so it shouldn't be too hard to gain an introduction,' Mama burbled.

She took Paris's arm and started steering him away. He looked over his shoulder at me, pulling a comical face. I followed in their wake, realizing that my sash had twisted and my hair ribbon had come undone.

Grandmama seized hold of me this time.

'Really, Rose, do tidy yourself up! Your mama is insisting on meeting Lord Mackay and his party, and you will have to be introduced too. Rupert is already a big hit with one of the London lassies, bless him.' She nodded at the flame-haired girl, who was dancing in a very lively manner. Her sash had stayed in place and her flying curls still looked decorative.

'Don't scowl like that, Rose!' Grandmama said sharply.

Grandpapa was talking to Lord Mackay, who started introducing Mama and Paris to his house party.

'May I introduce Lord and Lady Marchpane,' he said, presenting the most senior couple. Lord Marchpane was pale yellow, and damp from energetic dancing. I had to wipe my hand on my dress after I'd shaken his hand. Lady Marchpane was thin and white and brittle as chalk, looking as if she might snap at any moment. Then there was another older couple, Sir Edmund and Lady Fanshawe. Sir Edmund made a great to-do of repeating his name, with the emphasis on the *Sir*. Perhaps he was newly knighted. They were clearly very rich because red-cheeked Lady Fanshawe was glittering with diamonds: earrings, bracelets on both wrists, a necklace and a huge diamond ring. They made Mama's sapphires look very insignificant.

The last gentleman from London was Scottish, but he was presently living in Lord Mackay's townhouse near Regent's Park. He was a lord too – Lord Hirst, Lord Mackay's nephew by marriage. He was fair and square-chinned and broad-shouldered, very bluff, very bland.

'And you must meet my new wife – where has she got to? Ah yes, talking to those gentlemen over there! Louisa, my love, come and be introduced,' he called.

She was beautiful, tall and fair, with a pale porcelain complexion and very white shoulders that contrasted wonderfully with her black velvet dress. She was one of the few women not wearing white. Perhaps she was deliberately drawing attention to herself. She held her head high, though she seemed a little perturbed when she saw us.

She seemed so familiar. I knew that complexion, that pearly skin, that bold stance. She was the Honourable Louisa Mayhorne, Papa's muse!

Of course Mama knew her too. She gasped and took a step backwards.

'Jeannie! What on earth is the matter? Aren't you well?' Grandmama hissed. 'This is Lady Hirst.'

'I know who she is. I know who she was. I know *what* she was,' said Mama.

She looked round and saw Papa standing behind her, his face ashen, obviously taken completely by surprise. He swallowed, clenched his fists and swayed. I couldn't bear to see his expression of helpless longing.

Lady Hirst stared back, faintly flushing, her head high, smiling.

Mama's eyes brimmed with tears. She wrenched herself away from Grandmama. 'How *could* you invite her?' she said, and then she ran out of the room, pushing her way blindly through the crowd.

I don't know if Grandmama understood what was wrong or not, but she stayed in steely control.

'Please excuse my daughter. She hasn't been very well since her last confinement. Now, I do believe the band is tuning up for the Dashing White Sergeant. My husband refuses to join in the dancing, so I hope *you* will be my dashing white partner, Lord Mackay,' she said smoothly, offering her hand.

He bowed and led her onto the dance floor, to be joined by the Marchpanes, the Fanshawes and Lord and Lady Hirst. They started dancing, Lady Hirst mesmerizing in her dark velvet. Papa stood in the shadows, watching her.

'Good Lord,' Paris murmured. 'She's the woman in his portrait. *That* Louisa.'

'I don't suppose Grandmama realized. She would only have been given her married name. Oh, heavens, do you think everyone knows?' I whispered.

'They will if Edward keeps gawping at her like a moonstruck calf,' said Paris. 'Excuse me, Rose.'

He went over to Papa, murmured something in his ear, and then led him firmly away. I was left standing by myself. I looked around for Rupert, but he was dancing with the Lord Provost's daughter. She had clearly been wished upon him by her mother. He didn't look too pleased.

I didn't know what to do – whether to stay there or join one of the groups of ladies at the edge of the ballroom.

'Would you care to dance, Rose?' It was Grandpapa, bowing stiffly to me!

'But you don't dance, Grandpapa,' I said.

'That didn't deter your mother's young artist friend. You seemed to give him adequate instruction. I shall try too,' he said gallantly.

Poor Grandpapa truly couldn't dance. He shuffled around hopelessly, going left instead of right, and twirling me round at the wrong moment. We were both very relieved when the dance came to an end. He offered me a sherbet cup and we sat together at a gilt table, trying to make conversation. We were both surreptitiously watching the doorway.

Mama didn't come back. Papa didn't either. Eventually Paris returned, and I stood up and waved to show him where I was.

'Sit down, Rose,' Grandpapa said quietly. 'I think perhaps your brother might be a more suitable partner this time.'

He shook his head as Paris made his way towards us. Paris saw – and veered off in the other direction. At the end of the next dance Grandpapa beckoned to Rupert. He came over eagerly enough, and we stood up together for the Gay Gordons.

'Did you see me dancing with that poor girl with the teeth? But what about my *first* partner! What a beauty—' Rupert started.

'Do shut up, Rupert. Didn't you see what happened? The Honourable Louisa Mayhorne is here, you know, Papa's so-called muse – only she's Lady Hirst now. See the woman over there in the black gown?'

'Oh my Lord, she's still a stunner! No wonder Papa was besotted with her,' Rupert breathed.

'What is she *doing*, coming here so brazenly?' I said.

'Maybe she didn't know about the family connection? Or maybe she did, and wanted to come and flaunt her rich young husband in front of Papa,' said Rupert. 'Shall I take her up on the dance floor and ask her? Do you dare me?'

'No!'

'I will anyway,' he went on. 'Just wait till the Gay Gordons is finished!'

Rupert didn't really have the nerve to approach Lady Hirst. We sat with Grandpapa, and when Grandmama joined us, breathless after two dances with Lord Mackay, she was very firm.

'I think you had better retire now, my dears,' she said.

'But, Grandmama, you promised we could stay up until twelve!' Rupert protested.

'I did indeed, but perhaps you are both a little too young. I can't keep an eye on you all evening because I am the hostess and have to make sure all my guests are entertained. As both your parents have disappeared, you have no one to chaperone you. Off you go. Please don't make a fuss. I do not want our family to draw any more attention to themselves,' she said stiffly.

I looked at Grandpapa pleadingly, but he was nodding in agreement. Rupert and I were sent to bed like naughty children. When I got to the door I looked round – and saw Paris leading the girl with the flaming hair out onto the floor.

26

I DID MY BEST NOT to cry as we went up the stairs.

'Oh dear, poor Rose,' said Rupert.

'I don't know what you mean,' I said shakily.

'You were hoping to dance with Mr Walker again,' said Rupert. 'And now he's dancing with Miss Imogen Wentworth.'

'Who?'

'Miss Wentworth, the gorgeous redhead. *I* danced with her first.'

'Yes, and you looked ridiculous, a boy partnering a grown-up lady,' I snapped.

'She's not grown up, she's still studying,' said Rupert.

'She's never still a schoolgirl!'

'She's actually at a women's college at university,' said Rupert. 'You'd never credit it, would you? She doesn't look the swotty type, but she must be a brainbox.'

'I didn't think women could go to university,' I said.

'Well, *she* does. She's one of these new independent women. I think she's marvellous. She was jolly nice to me too.'

'She was simply being kind. She's probably laughing at you with all her friends.'

'Stop being so spiteful, Rose, just because you're upset that Mr Walker can't resist her either,' said Rupert.

'I don't give a fig about Mr Walker,' I said haughtily, praying I wouldn't burst into tears.

Rupert started mocking me, but broke off when we got to the top of the stairs. We could hear shouting and crying – two people in the midst of an almighty row.

Our parents.

'Oh Lord,' said Rupert, and he took my hand.

We stood there listening. They were in their room and their voices were muffled, but we could still make out what they were saying. It was dreadful.

'They'll wake the children if they carry on like this,' I whispered.

'I dare say the servants are all earwigging too,' said Rupert.

'I hate it. Why does it all have to be so horrible? Do you think all marriages are like this?' I asked, crying. 'I'm never going to marry. *You'll* probably get married several times!'

'When you're a lonely old spinster, and I've left my third wife and am too fat and bald to find another, then we'll set up home together, you and I,' said Rupert, and he gave me a hug as we said goodnight.

I was a little comforted, but even from the amber room I could still hear Mama's hysterical crying. Mercifully Beth was deeply asleep and snoring, though Nurse Budd was ominously silent behind the yellow damask curtains.

I took off my things and climbed into the trundle bed.

'Is your mama unwell, Miss Rose?' Nurse Budd whispered into the darkness. 'Do you think I should go and see if I can help?'

'She's perfectly well,' I said ridiculously, and then buried my head under the covers.

I couldn't cry properly because I didn't want Nurse Budd to hear me. I lay there burning, thinking of Mama and Papa and Louisa and Paris and Miss Wentworth. They whirled around me in a grotesque Scottish reel. Suddenly I heard bangs like gunshots and sat up, terrified – but then, through the chink in the curtains, I saw flashes of light and realized that it was fireworks to celebrate the start of the new year.

When I woke in the morning, it was hard to believe it had all happened. Perhaps it had been a bizarre nightmare. Had the Honourable Louisa Mayhorne really been at the ball? Surely Mama couldn't have rushed out of the room in tears, with everyone staring! I knew I'd danced with Paris – but had he then asked that red-haired Miss Wentworth up onto the floor?

I heard Nurse Budd and Beth stirring, then getting up. I lay there, pretending to be asleep. I didn't want Nurse Budd asking any more questions about Mama. Beth started whimpering and I peeped out at her. She was clinging to Nurse Budd, who was getting dressed underneath her nightgown.

'For pity's sake, wait a minute,' Nurse Budd told her.

Beth became more insistent, grabbing handfuls of nightgown.

'You'll have me over! Stop it! If you're not a good girl, you won't get it!'

Beth carried on making desperate little noises until Nurse Budd emerged from her calico tent.

'All right, all right, give me a minute,' she said. 'Let's get you dressed first.'

At this, Beth started howling.

'Stop that! You'll wake everyone up and they'll all have thick heads after last night's shenanigans. Here now.' Nurse Budd went over to the washstand, opened her leather case and brought out the bottle of Godfrey's Cordial. She gave Beth several spoonfuls. Beth went on licking the spoon even when it was clean.

'I don't think she should have all that!' I exclaimed.

'Oh, we've woken up, have we, Miss Rose? And *still* questioning my medical competence? Anyone would think *you* were the trained nurse, not me!'

'You gave her an awful lot, even if it's harmless,' I said.

'It's just to top her up. It makes her feel better, doesn't it, dear? She likes it,' said Nurse Budd, stroking Beth's tear-stained cheek in a way that turned my stomach.

'Likes it,' Beth mumbled. She looked dazed.

'You *have* given her too much,' I said.

'Nonsense. It was just a tiddly spoonful,' said Nurse Budd.

While she was struggling to get Beth dressed, I peered at the bottle. It was difficult to gauge through the dark glass, but it seemed there was only an inch or so left. Nurse Budd had opened the new bottle only yesterday.

I *had* to tell Mama and Papa – but would they even come down to breakfast together after last night? As I went into the dining room I felt sick with nerves. Grandmama was sitting at the end of the table, wearing a black woollen frock with a large cameo brooch pinned at the neck, making calm conversation with the Lord and Lady Provost. The Lord Provost had a little lump of porridge stuck to his moustache. It wobbled unattractively every time he spoke.

The daughter sat beside her mother, her brown hair tied in an elaborate topknot which didn't become her. She kept looking at Rupert, but he was giving his plate of bacon and eggs his full attention. They were the only guests to have put in an appearance.

'Good morning, Rose,' Grandmama said. 'What would you like to eat? There's porridge of course, and kedgeree, and bacon and eggs, and Scotch pancakes, and I dare say Cook will do you a kipper if you'd like one.'

'I'm very partial to kippers, but the taste does linger,' said the Lady Provost, and began to list her culinary likes and dislikes. The Lord Provost yawned, clearly knowing it by heart. Grandmama nodded politely like a perfect hostess, though I saw her stifle a yawn.

I took one rasher of bacon and a spoonful of scrambled eggs, though I really didn't want anything.

'Come and sit beside me,' Rupert said eagerly, still ignoring the poor daughter.

'Where's everyone else?' I said.

'The ball didn't finish until gone two. Some of them are still asleep or feeling poorly.' Rupert lowered his voice. 'I drank several glasses of wine myself but my head doesn't hurt a bit.'

'Where are Mama and Papa?' I whispered.

Rupert shrugged. 'They haven't put in an appearance yet.'

'And Mr Walker?'

'Grandmama said he breakfasted early with Grandpapa and they've gone for a ride together.'

'They've gone for a *ride*?'

'Yes, I just said. They could have waited for me!'

'*Mr Walker* has gone for a ride?'

'Do stop repeating things, Rose. You're sounding like Beth.'

'But *does* Mr Walker ride? I can't imagine him on a horse, he isn't that sort of a person,' I persisted.

'Perhaps he wants to canter over to Lord Mackay's castle to see the beguiling Miss Wentworth,' said Rupert.

'Do you think so?' I said miserably.

'Who knows?' Rupert leaned over and whispered, 'Do you think Papa's gone with them to see Lady Hirst?'

'Don't joke about it, it's horrible,' I said, laying down my knife and fork, unable to eat.

'Don't you want that bacon?' asked Rupert, spearing it with his fork and adding it to his pile.

'Rupert, dear, I don't really think we want nursery behaviour in here,' said Grandmama. 'There's plenty more bacon in the serving dish if you're still hungry.'

'Perhaps you'd like a little more, Portia?' Grandmama asked the Lord and Lady Provost's daughter.

'Oh, our Portia eats like a little bird,' said the Lady Provost. 'That's why she's so slender.'

'Skin and bone,' said the Lord Provost. 'But she's fit and healthy, aren't you, lassie?'

Poor Portia was now a painful crimson. They were discussing her like a brood mare.

'She loves her Scottish dancing, don't you, Portia?' said her mother. 'She's very light on her feet, isn't she, Rupert?'

'Yes, you're a very fine dancer, Portia,' Rupert was obliged to say, giving her a cursory nod. He gave me a little kick under the table to indicate his horror.

Papa came into the dining room looking pale and weary. We waited for Mama, but she didn't appear.

'Good morning, Edward,' said Grandmama.

'Good morning,' Papa said tersely. He bent down and murmured something in her ear.

She frowned. 'Is that really necessary?' she said in an undertone.

Papa whispered something else, and Grandmama sighed irritably and rang a little bell. A maid appeared almost instantaneously.

'Would you send for a doctor, please, Mary? Perhaps it had better be Dr Grimes, though he's further away. Dr Macdonald seemed a little the worse for wear last night. I believe Dr Grimes is a Rechabite, and therefore teetotal,' Grandmama said.

The maid bobbed off importantly.

'Oh dear, I do hope one of your grandchildren hasn't been taken ill,' said the Lady Provost.

Papa came and sat down heavily beside me. He looked so ill that I reached out and took his hand.

'Are you all right, Papa?' I asked anxiously.

'Yes, my dear. Just a little tired, that's all,' he said. 'It's your mama who's rather unwell.'

'My daughter's been in fragile health since her last confinement,' Grandmama said quickly, 'but I'm sure she's not seriously ill. She just needs a little tonic.'

'Oh, I do understand,' said the Lady Provost. 'I was bothered with my nerves for a full year after Portia was born. Perhaps I could go and give her a little womanly advice after breakfast?'

'I'm sure she'll be up soon,' Grandmama said firmly. 'Rose, go to your mother and wait with her until the doctor comes.'

I hesitated. I knew that Mama wouldn't want me there under any circumstances. I hoped Papa would make some excuse for me, but he was nodding.

'Yes, go to Mama, dear,' he said.

I looked at Rupert imploringly, but it wouldn't have been considered proper for him to come with me. I was the eldest daughter. It was my duty.

I trudged up the stairs, wondering what on earth I should do or say. I hated the thought of being alone with Mama, especially if she was in bed. I knocked timidly at her door. There was no response. I knocked again, and heard a low moan from within. I pushed the door open, alarmed.

The curtains were closed but I could see well enough in the half-light. The bedroom was in turmoil, Mama's white dress thrown on the carpet, a pillow flung into a corner, the water jug in pieces. Mama was lying face down on the bed, fists clenched on either side of her head, her nightgown rucked up and showing her plump legs.

'Oh, Mama,' I said, trying to cover her up.

'Leave me alone!' she mumbled.

'Let me help you tidy up. They've sent for a doctor,' I said, opening the curtains.

Mama moaned and put her hands over her face. Her fingers raked her long tangled hair.

'Can I brush your hair, Mama, and help you wash your face?' I asked.

'Get out of my room, do you hear me!'

'I'm just trying to help, Mama,' I said, grappling with her white dress.

'I don't want your help.' She reared up and I saw that her eyelids were swollen, her eyes bloodshot. Her nose was red too, her cheeks stained with tears. Her nightgown was torn at the neck, the skin beneath it red. She smelled strongly of perspiration – Mama, who was always so fragrant!

'Oh, Mama, I'm sure you have a fever,' I said. 'Thank goodness the doctor is coming.'

'A doctor can't help a broken heart,' said Mama, clutching her chest. 'Oh the pain, the unbearable pain!' She sounded so melodramatic that I was embarrassed as well as anxious. I felt my mouth twitch.

'You're laughing at me!'

'No, I'm not, I'm feeling sorry for you.'

'I don't want your pity.' Mama sat up properly and gave me a push. 'Go away!'

So I stood helplessly outside the door. Grandmama sent Morag to see if she could prepare Madam for the doctor's visit, but Mama shrieked at her too.

'She's off her head, miss,' Morag murmured to me, and scurried away. I walked up and down the corridor wondering what on earth to do.

Suddenly I heard a light pattering of feet on the servants' staircase and hurried towards the dividing door. It was Clover, running down to the kitchen for milk for Phoebe's bottle.

'Oh, Clover,' I said, rushing over. 'Everything's so awful! Mama and Papa had a terrible argument last night, and now Mama's ill and acting so strange and I don't know what to do.'

'I heard the crying and shouting. I got up to comfort the children. Nurse sleeps so soundly she never wakes for anything. They were all crying, even Algie. I had to climb into his bed and hold him close before he'd stop. What on earth was it about?'

'The Honourable Louisa Mayhorne was invited to the ball by mistake – well, she's Lady Hirst now, one of Lord Mackay's guests from London. She's the woman Papa used to paint. He was very fond of her.' I lowered my voice. 'Actually I think he was in love with her. And he still is – it was obvious from the way he was looking at her last night. Mama ran out of the room in tears, right in front of everyone.'

'But I thought your mama was besotted with Mr Walker?' Clover said.

'Yes, but he doesn't care for her.'

'Does he care for you?' she whispered.

I shook my head. 'No, I'm just an amusing child to him,' I said. 'He danced with me, but then he went off with a beautiful red-haired girl called Miss Wentworth.'

'She's considered beautiful and yet she's got red hair?' said Clover. 'I'll have to tell Hetty Feather that!'

'We had such a good time playing Charades at Christmas, you, me and Hetty, didn't we?' I said.

'Yes, we did,' said Clover. 'It was like we were three friends.'

'We *are* friends, aren't we, Clover?'

'Yes, we are.'

'And we'll stay friends, no matter what?'

'Of course.'

'I'm so worried about what will happen now. What if Mama and Papa never make up? What if Papa goes off with this Louisa? We will all have to stay with Mama and I'd much sooner be with Papa. And what about *you*? Papa said he was going to give you art lessons. How will he do that if he doesn't live with us?'

'I'm sure they will make up. All couples have their differences. My pa and Mildred often had arguments but they stayed together, though Megs and me wished she would clear off!' said Clover.

'You're such a comfort, Clover. No wonder the children all love you so, even Beth. I'm worried about her too. Nurse Budd is giving her much too much of that Godfrey's Cordial, but she keeps telling me she's a trained nurse and knows what she's doing.'

We heard firm footsteps coming along the main corridor.

'That might be the doctor! I'd better go,' said Clover. She ran down several steps, and then turned. 'Ask him about Beth's medicine. He's a doctor, so he'll know.'

It seemed like a good idea, but Dr Grimes was a thin, dour man who barely acknowledged me when I went back down the corridor. A maid led him into Mama's room and then seemed all set to hurry away again.

'You must stay with your mistress,' Dr Grimes said sternly.

'Yes, sir, but the lady's not actually *my* mistress, and I'm needed downstairs, if you please,' she gabbled.

He tutted and looked at me. 'Are you the afflicted lady's daughter?'

'Yes, I am.'

'Then you come in with me. I need a chaperone.'

'But Mama doesn't want me with her,' I said.

'Nonsense, girl,' said Dr Grimes briskly, and I had to follow him into the room.

I hoped that Mama's sense of propriety might have made her sit up and look respectable to receive the doctor, but she was still lying groaning on the bed. I cowered in a corner, frightened and embarrassed, but Dr Grimes seemed quite at ease.

'Good morning. Mrs Rivers, I believe? I am Dr Grimes, here to examine you. Sit up properly please,' he said briskly. 'Now, tell me, are you in any pain?'

'Here!' said Mama, clutching her chest dramatically. 'My heart is broken.'

'Is it indeed? Well, let's find out.' He approached Mama with his stethoscope.

She finally sat up, but fidgeted this way and that, still moaning.

'Keep still, madam,' Dr Grimes commanded.

He listened to her front and back while I watched, repelled but fascinated. Then he straightened up, shaking his head at Mama.

'Your heart seems to be beating very steadily so I hardly think it's broken,' he said. He grasped her plump wrist and took her pulse.

I tried copying him, feeling for my own pulse. Dr Grimes looked down Mama's throat, peered into her ears, even prodded her tummy. He made her look from side to side and asked her how many fingers he was holding up.

'For pity's sake, why are you asking such silly questions?' Mama said, suddenly sounding herself again. 'There's nothing wrong with my sight!'

'Exactly, madam. There's nothing wrong with you at all. I have been meticulous in my examination.'

'But I have such pain, in my heart and in my head.'

'I dare say. You are clearly very distressed and have been crying a great deal. But no matter what the cause, you will not recover lying here. I suggest you get a maid to bring you a restoring cup of tea and prepare you a hot bath. You will feel much better.'

'You don't understand! My husband, the father of my seven children, is in love with another woman,' Mama declared tearfully. 'He vowed that it was over, and I was fool enough to believe him, but then he brought her to my parental home, making a fool of me in front of everyone.'

I burned all over. How could Mama of all people, so conscious of decorum, blurt this out in front of a complete stranger.

'That's not true, Mama,' I said desperately.

'Why do you always have to contradict me, Rose?' she wept. 'I saw that woman flaunting herself. I saw the expression on your father's face.'

'But it was all a mistake. Grandmama didn't know that she was Louisa Mayhorne. It was nothing to do with Papa. Oh, please, don't let it distress you so,' I begged her.

'There! I think your daughter is talking sense,' said the doctor. 'I cannot help you any further, madam. I cannot counsel you on personal matters. I suggest you call a minister if you need spiritual help. Good day.'

He bowed stiffly and walked out of the room. I followed him, too cowardly to stay with Mama.

Papa was hovering on the stairs, looking very anxious. 'How did you find my wife, Dr Grimes? She seems beside herself. She has been in this state all night long. Have you given her something to calm her and help her sleep?' he asked.

'I can find nothing physically wrong with her. I don't believe in prescribing medicine for unhappiness. I'm sorry I cannot help you any further, sir,' he added, seeing Papa's despair.

'Dr Grimes, please may I consult you about something?' I asked timidly.

He sighed. 'I was called here on your mother's behalf, child. I came as a special favour, even though this is a holiday and I'd sooner be at home with my family. Do you have a physical ailment?' He hesitated. 'Perhaps you should consult your nurse.'

'It's about my sister's nurse,' I said. 'She gives her this medicine, Godfrey's Cordial.'

Dr Grimes raised his eyebrows. 'Nurses often use these wretched patent medicines when babies have colic. I certainly don't recommend it.'

'She's not an infant, she's ten.'

'Well, she certainly shouldn't be taking it at her age, but the occasional teaspoon shouldn't harm her,' said Dr Grimes.

'It's not an occasional teaspoon. It's a very large dose, morning and night – a whole bottle since we've been here,' I said.

'Good Lord! Are you sure, Rose?' Papa asked. 'Nurse Budd is a trained professional.'

'Then she must know what she's doing, and that makes the matter worse,' said Dr Grimes. 'Do you have any idea what the main ingredient in Godfrey's Cordial is? Opium! If what your elder daughter is saying is true, then your nurse is giving your younger child the kind of dose an addict would take in an opium den. I'd better examine the little girl immediately.'

'Oh dear Lord,' said Papa, shaking his head in horror. 'Yes, yes, of course.'

We trooped off to the amber room and Papa opened the door. Nurse Budd was dozing in her chair. Beth was gazing at the display of amber, muttering, '*One, two, three, four, five, six, seven, eight, nine, ten,*' and stabbing at the glass with her finger.

'Please knock before you enter!' Nurse Budd said, rubbing her eyes and adjusting her cap. 'Who is this strange man?'

'I am Dr Grimes. I have come to examine the child in your care,' the doctor said coldly. He approached Beth, who cowered away, covering her face the way she always did with strangers. 'There's nothing to be worried about, little girl. This isn't going to hurt,' he said.

'Hurt!' Beth repeated, whimpering.

'My daughter's troubled,' said Papa. 'She's very set in her ways and cannot manage to behave in social situations. That's why we employed a trained nurse.'

'Yes indeed. I do happen to know what I am doing, sir,' said Nurse Budd icily. 'I'm sure Mr Rivers will vouch for the fact that Miss Beth's behaviour has improved considerably since I've been with her.'

'I dare say,' said Dr Grimes drily. He took hold of Beth's head, gently but firmly, taking no notice when she protested. He tilted it back so that he could look into her eyes. 'Look at her enlarged pupils! See the tremor in her hands! This child is in a lamentable state of opium addiction.' He let go of her and marched over to the medical case by the washstand, then removed each bottle of Godfrey's Cordial and poured the contents into the bowl of soapy water, while Beth howled.

'You're a disgrace to your profession, madam,' said Dr Grimes. 'It's a wonder this child is still standing.'

'But what do we do with Beth now? Will she recover?' Papa asked anxiously.

'She will be very fretful and poorly for quite some time as she recovers from her addiction. She will need proper nursing and diligent care. I should get in touch with your own doctor as soon as you return home.'

'I shall indeed, Dr Grimes. I am very grateful to you. Rose, please see the doctor out. I wish to have a word with Nurse Budd,' said Papa sternly.

27

'**WELL DONE, YOUNG LADY,**' Dr Grimes said as we went downstairs. 'By speaking up, you have very likely saved your sister's life. Your papa should be very proud of you.'

'What about Mama?' I said tremulously. 'Do you think she will ever get better?'

'Oh, I dare say. I have often dealt with female patients suffering from heartbreak, palpitations and sick headaches. Most of them recover soon enough,' he said.

'What about the ones that *don't*, Dr Grimes?'

'Some patients try a water cure, but I'm not sure it's effective,' he said. 'I can't see why a cold bath in a spa hospital should do more good than a hot bath at home.'

'So what happens to the ones who are never cured?' I persisted.

'They are cared for in their own homes – or, if they become a danger to themselves or others, they may have to be taken away to an asylum,' said Dr Grimes. 'But don't fret, child, I'm sure your mama will recover.'

I hoped so fervently. I battled with Mama, but I hated the idea of her being dragged off to an institution. Would they keep her in her nightgown and lock her in a cell? And what about poor Beth? Was she really a drug addict? I had seen an engraving of men in an opium den in one of Papa's books at home. They looked evil as they lolled around in a dissolute fashion smoking oriental pipes.

I was in such a state that when I'd shut the door on Dr Grimes I sank down onto the floor and started crying. One of the maids came darting up immediately and shook my shoulder.

'I beg your pardon, Miss Rose, but you can't cry here. The Lord Provost and his lady have called for their carriage and will be leaving any minute. The mistress will be mortified if they see you in such a state,' she said urgently.

So I trailed upstairs, sniffling. Alphonse was trotting up and down the corridor whining, banished from Mama's bedroom. He usually snapped at me, but this time he came and licked my ankles, and when I sat down cross-legged on the floor he climbed onto my lap, quivering. I stroked his strange little head with its huge ears and he nestled close.

I thought about Mama, about Beth, about Paris. I had a pain in my heart too.

'Oh, my poor Rose,' said Papa, who was trudging towards me.

He sat down beside me and reached out absent-mindedly to stroke Alphonse, who snarled at him. Papa sighed heavily. 'He's never liked me, strange little mutt, though he doesn't seem to mind you petting him, Rose. Oh dear, oh dear. What a start to the new year!' he said wearily.

'Oh, Papa.' I wriggled closer and he put his arm round me.

'My dear little girl. I'd give anything to protect you from this upsetting business – but I suspect you've worked out why your mama is so upset,' he murmured.

'I think so,' I said, blushing.

'I didn't know – I didn't dream – it was all over long ago,' Papa said brokenly.

'I understand, Papa,' I said.

He sighed. 'I wish you did, Rose. But you're far too young and innocent to understand about love.'

'No I'm not,' I said. 'I know how much it hurts when you can't have the person you love.'

Papa put his arm round me. 'You're a funny little thing, sweetheart. I suppose you've been reading your mother's romantic novels.'

'I *never* read romances,' I said indignantly.

'If only there were happily-ever-after endings in real life,' said Papa, rubbing his forehead.

'Do you have a headache, Papa?'

'Yes, my head's aching. I'm in despair. I've caused your mama such torment, and I've employed an evil nurse who's endangered poor Beth's life. I've dismissed Nurse Budd. She's packing her things. I've given her the train fare back to London. I'm not having her near any of you children. I've taken Beth to the nursery for the time being. Nurse isn't happy about it and says she's too old to cope. I'm at my wits' end as to what to do now.'

'Oh, Papa, it's obvious! Clover will look after Beth.'

'Clover's just a little nurserymaid, far too young for such a responsibility.'

'I'm sure she would look after Beth splendidly, Papa. You say yourself that she has a wonderful way with children,' I insisted.

'She's certainly been a little treasure since she joined our household,' he said. 'And she's such a promising artist. Paris agrees with me that she has real talent. Thank the Lord he's had the tact to clear off riding this morning. He's a good chap, a true friend. Your mama thinks the world of him. Do you think there's any way *he* could calm her down?'

I looked at Papa, wondering if he could *really* be that blinkered. Couldn't he see how Mama felt about Paris? Perhaps he'd become so important to her because she'd lost Papa's love. Should I try to tell Papa? I worried that it might make him even more unhappy.

417

After Grandmama had said farewell to the Lord Provost and his family she came upstairs. She sniffed when she saw Papa and me squatting on the carpet.

'For goodness' sake, we have perfectly decent chairs to sit on!' she said. 'Pull yourselves together, both of you. I gather Dr Grimes's visit was a waste of time and money. I could have told you that would be the case, Edward. Is Jeannie not up yet?'

'She's still distraught,' Papa said miserably.

'Dear Lord, what's the matter with that girl? She's no grit whatsoever. I'll soon put her right,' said Grandmama, and she marched back towards Mama's room.

'Had you better go with her?' Papa asked me.

'No, I just seem to make Mama worse,' I said.

But I followed Grandmama all the same, and listened outside the door.

'Good heavens, Jeannie, look at the state of you!' I heard her say. 'How *could* you let the doctor see you like this! Have you no shame?'

'I'm not the one who's shameless!' Mama wept. She muttered incoherently about Papa and that woman and their scheming.

Grandmama told her to be quiet, explaining that it had been a genuine mistake, but Mama wouldn't listen. She went on saying dreadful things, speaking so fast her words ran into each other.

'Haud your whisht!' Grandmama shouted, her Dundee accent suddenly strong, and there was the sound of a sharp slap.

Mama was shocked into silence.

'There, that's stopped your rambling! Making a fuss because your husband's had another woman! I told you he'd never be constant, but you wouldn't listen. You were such a stupid wee lassie, running off with a penniless artist because you were charmed by a bit of flattery. And you're still gullible. Look at you now, bringing this young ne'er-do-well into my home, flaunting him in front of everyone, making a fool of yourself!'

Mama started sobbing again.

'Aye, you should be ashamed! And then you have a public fit of hysterics because your husband looks a little lovesick when he sees his old flame! When are you going to grow up? You're not unique. There's scarcely a woman in Scotland who hasn't had to put up with her husband's affairs. I've lost count of the number of times the lassies at the mill came to blows because one of them eyed up another's man. But you don't fight and scream and shout in decent society, Jeannie. You hold your head high and pretend you don't care – and after a while you might find you really *don't* care.'

Mama murmured something about heartache.

'Aye, you've got heartache, but at least you haven't got bellyache with hunger. That husband of yours isn't likely to run off because he knows which side his bread is buttered – but even if he does, you're a rich woman. Most lassies have to stick by their man even if he beats them, because they'd be penniless without his wages, and their bairns would starve. Your grandmother had it tough when your grandfather left home, Jeannie. I went to work at the mill to bring some money in, and I was proud to do it – but I'm far prouder that I've risen above my roots and can hold my own in the highest society. You've had it easy, my lass, and it's made you soft. It's time to toughen up, do you hear me? Now, up you get up and give yourself a good wash. Soothe those sore eyes, brush that tangled hair. You might be Mrs Rivers but you're still a Nairn at heart, whether it's broken or not. You're my girl, my one and only, and I want to be proud of you.'

I heard the bed creaking, the patter of footsteps and the sound of water splashing into a washbasin. It looked as if Grandmama's plain speaking had worked.

I scurried off to search for Rupert. I couldn't see him anywhere, and eventually found him mooching about in the wintry garden, punching the air with short, sharp jabs.

'Are you practising for when you go back to school?' I asked. 'Perhaps you can boast to all those horrid boys about your new Scottish girlfriend!'

'I'll punch *you* if you tease me about her. Grandmama insisted I say goodbye, and that awful girl made such a meal of it.' Rupert grimaced. 'Anyway, what's happening with Mama? Did the doctor come?'

'Yes, but it's Grandmama who seems to have brought her to her senses. I do hope so anyway. And, Rupert, you'll never guess what! I asked the doctor about Beth's medicine, that black treacly stuff Nurse Budd keeps giving her, and it's got *opium* in it. She's been drugging Beth! I *knew* there was something sinister about her. But now Papa's dismissed her and she's got to leave immediately.'

I wondered what the etiquette was for a dismissed member of staff. I hoped I wouldn't have to say goodbye. I hated the thought of interrupting her while she was packing, so I stayed in the garden with Rupert, even though I was freezing. He saw that I was shivering and wound his scarf around my neck.

'Let's run before you turn into a block of ice,' he said. 'We'll go all the way round Pennycuik. I'll race you.'

I knew I didn't have a hope of beating him because he went cross-country running at school and was much fitter than me – but I still chased after him. I kept within a few paces all the way round to the front, though I had a terrible stitch in my side. A carriage had drawn up at the front steps, with more of Grandmama's overnight guests on their way home, looking pale and weary now.

We had to slow down and bid them farewell, even though we couldn't even remember their names. One lady beckoned to me.

'How is your mother, dear? She seemed very unwell last night.'

'She's recovered now, thank you,' I said stiffly.

'What exactly was troubling her?' she asked, eyes beady with curiosity.

'Oh, Nurse sent for her because our baby sister had had a choking fit and poor Mama was very alarmed. But thank goodness she coughed up the offending item and all is well now,' Rupert said smoothly.

'You're such a liar!' I said as the carriage rolled on its way. 'I wish I could lie like that!'

Rupert set off again. 'Come on, we haven't finished our race,' he called.

It felt good to run and feel like a little girl again. I was level with Rupert as we hurtled round the side of the house and past the kitchen garden. A groom had brought a pony and trap round to the back steps, and Nurse Budd was climbing in, clutching her carpet bag!

'Oh my goodness. Quick, let's go back,' I said, but she'd heard our thundering footsteps.

She turned to me, her face contorted with fury. 'You interfering little madam!' she hissed.

'Don't you dare talk to my sister like that!' said Rupert.

'I was worried about Beth. I knew it was too much medicine. I *had* to consult the doctor,' I insisted.

'I wasn't doing her any harm. I was trying to keep her calm. I'm glad to be shot of you and your wretched family, wasting my training on the likes of you. You're not even proper society, you're just trade. You'll all come to a bad end, you mark my words. Especially you, Rose Rivers!' She said it with such venom that I backed away from her, clutching Rupert.

'Take the wretched woman to the station immediately!' he commanded the groom.

'Yes, Mr Rupert,' the man replied, and flicked the reins.

'Good riddance, you evil old harpy!' Rupert called after Nurse Budd.

'It was as if she were really cursing me!' I said, shivering.

'Don't worry, she's gone now,' said Rupert.

'Oh, Rupert, you don't think she's done anything to Beth, do you?'

'Beth's in the nursery with Nurse,' said Rupert, but he looked anxious too.

'Quick!' I said, and we ran up the steps and in through the back door, because it was nearest. We rushed along the stone corridors past all the sculleries and pantries and kitchens until we reached the narrow servants' stairs, and then we thundered up, nearly knocking a maid flying as she came down with a basket of sheets.

As soon as we burst through the dividing door we could hear cries and shouts. There was pandemonium in the nursery. Phoebe was wailing in her cot, Sebastian was cringing, and Algie and Clarrie were half laughing, half crying at Beth, who was yelling her head off, and flailing and kicking. Nurse was trying to hang onto her.

'Where's Clover?' I had to shout to make myself heard.

'Your father's sent for her, and I've been left to cope with all these children, and they're too much for me now, especially Miss Beth when she's in one of her states,' Nurse panted.

'You shouldn't hold onto her, Nurse, you know she hates it,' I said.

'Well, how else am I to stop her? Your father said she shouldn't go near Nurse Budd, she was to stay in the nursery, but she won't listen. She's set on going back to the amber room.'

'Why don't we let her go there, if that's what she wants? Nurse Budd has gone now. We just saw her leave, didn't we, Rupert. Come on, Beth, come with me,' I said, gesturing.

She didn't take my hand, but she paused to draw breath.

'Good girl. No more screaming now!' said Rupert.

Beth put her hand over her mouth and tried to stop.

'That's it. We can hear ourselves think now,' he told her. 'My, you need a handkerchief, Beth. Can you sort her out, Rose?'

I gave her my handkerchief and she scrubbed at her face.

'Not so hard, you'll hurt yourself. Come on, we'll go to the amber room, you and me and Rupert,' I said.

Beth scurried along beside us and ran into the room, heading straight for the washstand. She started whimpering, moving towels, peering into corners, looking underneath her doll, terribly agitated.

'What is it? What's she looking for?' Rupert asked.

'Her medicine. She's got so used to taking it,' I said. 'Poor, poor Beth. It's all gone now. Nurse Budd's gone too. She was bad. She gave you bad medicine,' I said.

'Medicine!' said Beth, weeping.

'Yes, I know you want it, but it wasn't good for you.' I tried to think of something to distract her. 'Let's count, shall we? Let's count all the amber beads. *One, two, three, four, five . . .*'

'*Six, seven, eight, nine, ten,*' Beth said automatically as she went over to the cabinet.

'Good old amber beads,' I said to Rupert.

'Amber beads! Amber beads!' Beth cried.

'Yes, count them, Beth.'

She shook her head and started stabbing at the glass. I looked properly and saw that the lock on the display case had been prised open. Every single strand of amber was gone.

'Nurse Budd must have stolen them! Good Lord! I wonder if we can catch her at the station?' Rupert said excitedly, all fired up for a drama.

But Grandmama said she didn't want to pursue Nurse Budd.

'She's a truly evil woman. I gave her a piece of my mind when I heard how she'd been poisoning my little granddaughter – and she had the nerve to come out with a mouthful of abuse in return. How Jeannie could ever have employed such a dreadful woman beggars belief. You should have heard what the Budd woman said about her! She even said terrible things about you, Rose!' said Grandmama, shuddering.

'What things?' I said, my heart thudding.

'Far too disgusting to repeat. That's why I don't want to go to the police and have the creature detained and charged. Lord knows what she'd start saying then. I haven't battled my way into society all these years only to be dragged down by scandalous rumours.'

'But what about your amber, Grandmama?' Rupert asked.

'Och, I've never cared for it particularly. All that foreign garish yellow! I like Scottish jewellery.' She sighed. 'I'm exhausted after all the shenanigans! What a start to the new year!' She squinted at the ornate ormolu clock on her mantelpiece. 'It's so fancy I can never make out where the hands are pointing. What time is it, Rupert, dear? Consult your pocket watch!'

I looked at Rupert anxiously, but he calmly took his new Christmas present out of his pocket and peered at it, shielding it casually with his hand.

'It's half past eleven, Grandmama,' he said.

'Good Lord, is that all? Still, your Grandpapa's watch has always been a marvellous time-keeper. Are you enjoying it, Rupert?' said Grandmama.

'Oh, very much. It is a real privilege to have such a beautiful watch,' said Rupert, slipping the replacement back into his waistcoat pocket.

'I'd better have a word with Cook about lunch. I wonder how many we will be? All the guests are gone now, thank heavens. By the way, little Portia seems to have taken a shine to you, Rupert, my boy!'

'She's a very sweet girl, Grandmama,' said Rupert, smirking.

'All the girls seem to be dazzled by Rupert, though heaven knows why,' I said tartly.

'I think I observe a flash of green in your eyes, Rose!' said Grandmama. 'Don't fret, dear. I'm sure you'll come into your own one day. Indeed, your mama was very childish-looking and plain until she was well into her teens, but then, thank goodness, she blossomed. I'm sure you will too.'

I swallowed, taking the insult on the chin.

'Now run along, dear, and see if you can help quieten your sister. I can still hear caterwauling again,' said Grandmama.

'You come too, Rupert. You're good at charming Beth,' I said.

'I dare say he is, but the nursery is hardly the place for young menfolk,' said Grandmama. 'Rupert's task is to sit and charm *me*. I don't see enough of you, dear boy.'

I walked out of the room seething, wondering for the hundredth time why boys had such an easy time – but then I realized that the crying upstairs had stopped abruptly. I ran up to the amber room, terrified in case Beth had hurt herself. But Papa was standing in the doorway, smiling. He put his arm round me, and I saw that Clover and Beth were sitting side by side on the bed, the yellow curtains drawn back. Clover had spread her new drawing book across their knees. She had a pencil in her hand. Beth had a yellow crayon.

'Now we're going to draw ten ladies,' said Clover. 'I'll draw lady number one.'

'One,' Beth repeated, sniffing. She needed my handkerchief again, but Clover wisely didn't try to wipe her nose. Beth started fidgeting, jogging Clover so that she drew a long straight line.

'I think lady number one wants long hair,' said Clover, adding more long lines. 'There we are. It's right down to her waist. She looks like you, Miss Beth. She's very pretty.'

'Very pretty,' said Beth, but now she was looking around the room, wanting that horrible addictive medicine.

'Try to keep still, Miss Beth. It's your turn now. Lady number one wants an amber necklace. You've got the magic yellow crayon. Give her necklace number one!'

'Necklace number one,' said Beth, and she crayoned enthusiastically. Each amber bead looked as big as an apple, and the necklace reached right down to the lady's knees, but Clover praised her extravagantly.

I saw that Papa's eyes were damp. 'Clover's such a clever little witch with Beth,' he whispered to me. 'She's going to have her hands full, but I truly think she'll manage her.'

Clover looked up, her green eyes bright. 'Now we'll draw lady number two. Here's her head. I think she'll have wild hair like mine. See – scribble, scribble, scribble. Now she looks like Clover.'

'Like Clover. Like Clover. Like Clover,' said Beth.

'There!' said Papa. 'Let's leave them to it. Perhaps I should see if your mama is feeling any better so that I can try and make my peace with her.' He took a deep breath and then walked off resolutely.

I WENT TO THE NURSERY, wondering if I might copy Clover and amuse the children by drawing with them. However, for once they were all playing peacefully. Nurse had found a huge box of bricks to keep them busy.

Sebastian was making a mouse castle for Montmorency, with ramps for him to run up and down and battlements for him to peer over. Algie was making a very wobbly fort with hairpin soldiers battling each other. Clarrie was making a Noah's Ark, wanting to float it on the pond in the garden.

I squatted down and tried to give a helping hand, but my suggestions only irritated them, even Sebastian.

'Thank you, Rose, I'll ask Montmorency if he'd like a four-poster bed with handkerchief curtains, but I rather think he'd nibble them and give himself a stomach ache,' he said politely.

'I don't want you to help me make a bigger, better fort. This one was the biggest, bestest fort ever, but the soldiers have blown most of it up, see. Watch out, there's going to be another explosion any minute!' said Algie, suddenly punching one of the flimsy walls and making it tumble down.

'You're stupid, Rose. Of course my Ark will float, and all the animals will be saved, and Mr and Mrs Noah and all the little children. It says so in the Bible!' Clarrie insisted piously.

I gave up and went to see if I could amuse my littlest sister, picking her up out of her cradle.

'For pity's sake, Miss Rose, I've only just this minute rocked the child to sleep. She was fretful all night because of the disturbance. Put her back before she starts crying,' Nurse grumbled.

I tucked her in again, but as soon as her head touched her pillow she started wailing.

'What did I tell you!' said Nurse. 'Really, what a waste of space you are!'

A waste of space. It was one of Nurse's favourite sayings. She said it about Sebastian when Montmorency got loose. She said it about Algie when he got up to some tomfoolery. She said it about Clarrie when she fell and dirtied her dress. She'd said it about Beth until Nurse Budd came along.

But I still couldn't help taking it personally. She was right. I *felt* like a waste of space. I had no charm like Rupert, no artistic talent like Clover, no knack with the children. I would never blossom, no matter what Grandmama said. No one would ever fall in love with me. I'd never stand a chance with Paris. He wanted girls like the red-haired beauty last night.

I stomped out of the nursery. I didn't know where to go. I didn't want to distract Beth if Clover was managing to amuse her. I didn't want to go near Mama or Papa. I didn't want to trail back to Grandmama and Rupert.

I wandered the house mournfully, peeping into the ballroom. It looked so different by daylight, empty except for two maids down on their knees at either end polishing the floor. They were red in the face, their sleeves rolled up, in spite of the cold. They still had a vast expanse to shine. They both looked up and nodded at me.

'Happy New Year, miss!' they chorused in unison.

I wished them Happy New Year back, though it didn't seem a very happy start to the new year for them. It certainly wasn't for me. There seemed to be an army of servants everywhere, sweeping, sorting, tidying, dusting. I couldn't find anywhere peaceful. I longed to curl up and read a book on the window seat at home. I had brought several with me, but they were up in the amber room.

I stopped a maid who was sweeping up pine needles from under the Christmas tree.

'I'm sorry, I can't quite remember – does Pennycuik have a library?' I asked. 'You know, a room full of books,' I added when she looked blank.

'A whole room?' she said. 'I don't think so, miss. I'm sure there's books in your grandpapa's study, but he doesn't like us to go in and dust too often because he says we muddle all his papers.'

'Do you think he'd mind me looking for something to read?' I asked.

'Hard to say, miss,' she said.

'I shall look all the same,' I said grandly, though I felt very anxious about going into Grandpapa's study. I knocked on the door several times, though I was pretty sure he was still out riding.

He had a very large Regency desk, its green leather top almost entirely covered with papers and receipts and account books. I kept well away, and went over to the bookcase. I opened the glass doors and peered at the large tomes, examining them one by one. There were histories of the jute industry, several books on Dundee, a general guide to Scotland, and various titles about hunting, shooting and fishing, all equally uninteresting. Then I saw a book tucked behind these big masculine volumes. *The Human Body – a Medical Guide.*

I eased it out and opened it up. At least there were illustrations – but what extraordinary pictures! I stared at a representation of a man in his prime, neatly drawn and carefully painted, his hair corn coloured, his eyes blue, his face pink – *all* of him pink! I'd never seen a naked man before. I'd seen my brothers in the bath, but this man looked very different and rather alarming – even more so when I opened a little tab on his torso and saw his insides, his heart and lungs and liver and kidneys and coiled intestines coloured in pink and yellow and red and brown.

I turned the page with a trembling hand, and found a woman this time, also naked, with another tab in the middle of her big tummy. I opened the flap and saw a baby inside, upside down, its legs curled up. I recoiled squeamishly.

Then I read the text, squinting at the strange words but gradually getting the gist. So *that* was what men and women did to have babies. The whole process seemed bizarre in the extreme. I never wanted to do any such thing!

When I heard the gong for lunch, I thrust the book back behind the other volumes and ran out of the study. It was a shock to see Grandpapa himself emerging from the gentlemen's water closet. I gave such a start he looked concerned.

'Good heavens, child, I'm not that hideous, am I?' he said gruffly.

'No, of course not! I was just surprised to see you. I – I thought you were out riding,' I stammered.

'I'm just back. That artist fellow came with me. I had no idea he was one of the Oxfordshire Walkers – his father's famous for his stables. Decent chap, though why they've given their son such a damn silly name I can't think. No wonder he's turned out arty. So what's this portrait of your mother like, missy?' Grandpapa asked.

'It's very fine,' I said.

'I dare say it's very flattering then.' Grandpapa sighed. 'Your mama got herself in a bit of a state last night. I hope she's better now?'

'I hope so too,' I said.

At lunch, to my astonishment, Mama truly did seem better. She sat next to Papa, her hair brushed and neatly twisted into a knot at the nape of her neck, showing off her sapphire earrings. Her dress was new, dark blue with a thin red stripe and a demure edging of crisp lace at the neck and cuffs. It had been cut cleverly to flatter her fuller figure. I thought of the picture of the woman in Grandpapa's book and wondered if Mama might be going to have another baby.

Papa still looked ill, with dark smudges under his eyes – but he was smiling resolutely at Mama. Paris was sitting on his other side. He looked very fresh and fit, his eyes bright and clear and his cheeks red from riding. He smiled at me, and gestured to the place next to him, but I went to sit beside Rupert.

'Are you all right, old thing?' Rupert murmured as we were served chicken and barley soup. 'Where were you? I went looking for you after I escaped from Grandmama, but you'd disappeared.'

'I was reading,' I said.

'Oh, you've always got your head in a book! Real life's much more interesting,' said Rupert.

'I think I've had enough of real life,' I muttered. 'It's too ugly and depressing.'

'But all the fuss is over now. Look at Mama and Papa. You'd never dream they were at each other's throats half the night,' said Rupert as Papa picked up Mama's dropped napkin and she thanked him.

'Rupert and Rose, don't murmur amongst yourselves, dears. Let us make proper conversation,' said Grandmama.

There was an inevitable silence while we ate our soup. I suppose we would normally be discussing the ball, but it was clearly not a sensible topic.

'Tell me your New Year's resolutions, everybody,' Grandmama said brightly as the soup plates were cleared and we were served cod in white sauce. She looked at Grandpapa. 'What are your resolutions, Angus?'

'You know very well that I never make resolutions,' he said, refusing to join in the game.

'What about yours, Rupert dear?' Grandmama continued smoothly.

'I resolve to become a little fitter,' said Rupert. 'I enjoyed my ride yesterday. Perhaps I might have riding lessons when I'm at Kilbourne, Papa?'

'You're already busy with boxing lessons,' I murmured.

'What's that? Boxing? Surely not!' said Grandmama.

'Rose was teasing me, Grandmama,' said Rupert.

'Really, Rose, you have such a strange sense of humour,' said Mama, frowning at me reprovingly. It was hard to believe that only a few hours ago she had been weeping despairingly. When she looked at Rupert her expression softened. 'I know why you want to improve your riding skills, you bold boy. You want to show off your horsemanship to little Pamela!'

'You always find me out, Mama,' said Rupert, smiling at her.

'I suggest that you also make a resolution not to be careless,' Grandpapa remarked out of the blue.

I stared at him. His eyes were still sharp. Had he noticed that Rupert was no longer wearing his precious gold watch? Rupert looked at Grandpapa a little anxiously.

'In what way is Rupert careless, Angus?' asked Grandmama. 'I would say he is the most care*ful* of all our grandsons. Unlike his little brother. I hear he ran amok this morning, slid down the banisters and collided with the umbrella stand.'

'Oh my goodness, was he hurt?' Mama asked.

'I don't think so, but the umbrella stand collapsed, and one of the walking canes snapped in half,' said Grandmama.

'He's such a naughty boy,' said Mama. 'Heaven knows what Nurse was doing letting him run wild like that. I shall have words with her after luncheon.'

'Poor Nurse was run off her tired old feet trying to look after Beth as well as the little ones,' said Papa.

'What is the matter with Nurse Budd? *She* should be in charge of Beth,' said Mama.

We all stared at her. No one had told her that Nurse Budd had been dismissed!

'That creature!' said Grandmama. 'Really, Jeannie, how could you have employed such a dreadful woman to look after that poor wee girl of yours?'

Mama flushed. 'How can you say that, Mama? She's a professional nurse, personally recommended by Lady Robson.'

'I don't care if she was recommended by the Queen herself, she's not fit to be looking after children,' Grandmama retorted. 'And now she's been sent packing, as she deserves.'

'What? How *dare* you dismiss her!'

'*I* dismissed her – because I discovered she'd been dosing Beth with Godfrey's Cordial,' Papa explained.

'Yes, I know, that's Beth's special medicine,' said Mama.

'Its main ingredient is opium, Jeannie,' said Papa. 'She has been giving our daughter copious draughts of it. We are lucky she has a strong constitution. Dr Grimes said it was a wonder that she survived.'

Mama flushed when he mentioned Dr Grimes. 'That sham of a physician?' she said heatedly. 'And why on earth was he taking it upon himself to query Beth's medication?'

'Rose had the common sense to consult him, Jeannie. She's been worried about Nurse Budd all along, and we haven't been listening to her,' said Papa.

'Rose! I might have known it,' said Mama, glaring at me. 'This is ridiculous. I won't hear a word against Nurse Budd. Lady Robson said she worked wonders with her grandson.'

'You were always so gullible, Jeannie, believing everything people say,' Grandmama said crisply. 'That Budd baggage has stolen all my Baltic amber into the bargain and I think those dull yellow beads were probably worth a fortune.'

'I rather think they were,' said Grandpapa, 'but I dare say I shall slave away until I can buy you some more.'

'Really, Angus! Anyone would think that you spin the wretched jute personally,' said Grandmama.

'Has Nurse Budd actually gone? I can't believe this stupidity! How on earth am I going to find a substitute? No one else seems able to cope with Beth,' Mama protested.

'Don't fret, my dear. I have appointed Clover as Beth's new little nurse – and judging from the happy silence upstairs she's doing her job splendidly,' said Papa.

'*Clover?* She's just a guttersnipe off the streets! If I had my way I'd send *her* packing. Are you sure *she* hasn't stolen the amber? Let us send the servants to search her room!'

'Enough, Jeannie! You've accused Clover of theft twice already – when she's honest as the day is long,' said Papa.

'Really, Edward, I despair of you and your little protégés,' said Mama.

'Oh dear, Mrs Rivers, I fear *I* am one of your husband's protégés,' said Paris. 'Does that mean you want to send me packing too?'

'Don't be ridiculous, Mr Walker,' said Mama, suddenly diverted. She actually smiled, forgetting all about Clover and Nurse Budd and Beth. 'I hope *your* New Year's resolution is to finish my portrait!'

'I don't need to do that, for it's very nearly finished already. No, my New Year's resolution is also to take more exercise. I very much enjoyed our ride, sir,' he said, nodding at Grandpapa. 'And it was very fortuitous that we met up with Lord Mackay and his guests.'

I stopped eating. The fish stayed in my mouth, damp and dead on my tongue.

'Was the stunning Miss Wentworth one of the party?' Rupert asked enviously.

'She was indeed,' said Paris. 'She's such an interesting girl. Did you know that she's doing a university degree at the new Royal Holloway College?'

I couldn't bear it. She was not only beautiful, she was highly intelligent too. Paris glowed as he talked of her. Then he turned to me.

'I'd like you to meet Miss Wentworth, Rose. She's so independent-minded and determined to make her mark on our patriarchal world. Let me tell you about the university magazine she has started with some other students,' he said.

The fish stuck in my throat. I heaved. 'Excuse me,' I mumbled, and stood up.

'Rose! Don't be so rude!' said Mama. 'Mr Walker is talking to you.'

'I'm not feeling very well,' I said, and ran out of the room.

I couldn't make it as far as the ladies' cloakroom. I hurtled into the gentlemen's and was very sick. Then I pulled the chain and leaned against the floral wallpaper, shuddering. The tendrils of honeysuckle seemed to reach out, as if seeking to wind themselves around me. I waited until the nausea had subsided a little, and then made my way shakily up to the amber room.

Beth and Clover were having their lunch with Nurse and the children in the nursery. I had the room to myself. I lay down on the truckle bed and put my hands over my ears, trying to shut out the sound of Paris's voice waxing lyrical about Miss Wentworth.

He wasn't being deliberately cruel. He had no idea how much he was hurting me. None of them seemed to feel the way I did. They didn't seem to understand what it was to love someone. Grandmama and Grandpapa had been married for forty years and were considered a perfect couple, but I'd never seen them share a single affectionate gesture. Mama and Papa might once have been in love, but they'd seemed on the brink of a shameful separation. Rupert was already carelessly toying with the feelings of every girl he came across. And Paris was just as bad – worse, really, because for all his fancy ways Rupert was still a child, whereas Paris was a grown man and knew what he was doing.

I heard footsteps coming along the corridor, steady masculine steps. I thought it must be Papa, and sat up quickly, trying to tidy my hair, hoping I didn't look too dreadful. Poor Papa – first a distraught wife, and now a despairing daughter.

There was a knock on the door.

'Rose? Is this your room?'

It wasn't Papa, it was Paris! I sat still, not knowing whether to answer or not. I didn't want to talk to him, not now. But when I heard the footsteps start up again, I found myself rushing to the door.

'Yes?' I said, flinging it open.

'There you are! Are you all right?' he asked anxiously.

'Yes, I just felt a little faint,' I said, not wanting to admit I'd been sick because it sounded so childish.

'Perhaps you were drinking wine last night?' Paris said. 'I know Rupert had several glasses.'

'Well, *I* didn't!' I said. 'Rupert might be my twin, but we behave very differently.'

'I'm sorry. I was only teasing you,' said Paris. 'Don't be cross with me, Rose. I've got something exciting to tell you!'

I turned away and went over to the window, staring out at the garden.

'Don't you want to hear what it is?' said Paris, coming into the room.

'Not particularly,' I said, resting my forehead on the cold windowpane.

'It's about Miss Wentworth, one of Lord Mackay's guests,' said Paris.

'I know who she is,' I mumbled.

'Rose? Are you still feeling faint?'

'Not at all,' I said, though the garden was a blur.

'Miss Wentworth was telling me all about her life at the Royal Holloway. It sounds as if she's having a marvellous time,' said Paris.

'Good for her,' I said flatly.

'She's started editing a student paper with a feminine perspective,' he went on. 'She showed me the latest issue this morning. You would love it, Rose.'

'I doubt it. I'm not the least bit interested in fashion or crochet patterns or romantic stories,' I said.

'Not *that* sort of women's paper, silly. Miss Wentworth's paper is satirical, very humorous and political. She's called it *Judy* – and she's had the wit to send a copy to the editor of *Punch*. Half of literary London is reading it now. Of course, it helps that her father is a well-known newspaper proprietor, and assists her with the distribution, but she's still done remarkably well to make such a mark,' Paris said enthusiastically. 'Rose? Aren't you interested now?'

'Not really,' I said, still with my back to him. I tried to sound bored, but I was struggling not to burst into jealous tears.

'Well, *I* was interested – because I thought it would be a splendid showcase for *your* work. I had your Christmas card in my pocket, so I showed it to her.'

I turned round and stared at Paris. 'You did *what*?' I gasped.

'I didn't think you'd mind. I thought you'd be pleased! Miss Wentworth was tremendously impressed by your

442

wit and style. She wanted to reproduce your card in *Judy*, but I thought that it was perhaps a little too personal. I didn't want to get you into trouble with your family! But, anyway, she'd love to see more of your work. Here's her address.' He put a scrap of paper on the empty amber cabinet. 'You *will* send her some drawings, won't you, Rose? Promise? I think this is your big chance!'

How could I have doubted him? He really *did* care about me after all!

'Oh, Paris!' I ran towards him, threw my arms round his neck and kissed him.

He laughed and hugged me back.

'*What on earth are you doing?*' Mama was standing in the doorway.

Paris let go of me, actually pushing me away from him. 'My dear Mrs Rivers, don't look so appalled! Rose is just very excited because I am the bearer of good news,' he said hastily.

Mama put her hand to her throat, shaking her head. She stared at us, blinking as if she couldn't quite believe what she'd seen.

'Tell your mama, Rose,' said Paris. 'Explain about your drawings!'

'Mama—' I began, but she wasn't listening.

'How *could* you?' she gasped.

I didn't know if she was addressing me or Paris or both of us. She turned and ran off down the corridor, her new navy dress billowing behind her.

'Oh my Lord,' Paris breathed. 'I'd better go after her and explain properly.'

I was left in the amber room, my heart thudding. I couldn't quite take it in. Everything had happened so quickly. I paced to and fro, my thoughts in a whirl. I stayed there for a long time. I heard the distant hum of voices, Mama's urgent and high-pitched, but I couldn't hear what she was saying. Then I heard Papa – and at last he came along the corridor and stood in the doorway. He looked incredibly weary now, and leaned against the door frame for support.

'Oh, Papa, please sit down, you look so dreadful,' I said, taking his hands and leading him to a chair.

He kept holding my hands. 'Dear goodness, I *feel* dreadful,' he said. 'So much has happened. There have been so many shocks. But this last is the worst. I simply can't believe it. Your mama is in a very nervous state, though she's made a heroic effort to gain control of herself. She's exhausted after her sleepless night. I think she must be deluded – but she says she came across you and Paris here in your room. Surely this can't be true!'

'You must let me explain, Papa. Mr Walker is helping me to get my drawing published! It's going to be in a college publication. The editor is that red-haired girl at the ball last night, Miss Wentworth. She likes my work, Papa, my comical style.'

I hoped that he would be impressed, but he was hardly listening.

'Rose, look at me. Please tell me the absolute truth.' He clasped my hands even more tightly, crushing my fingers. 'Did you actually invite Paris into your room?'

'No. Well, yes. You see, I suppose I was sulking at first, but when I heard him walking away I called him back,' I said.

'Surely you have enough sense to realize that a young girl should never invite a strange man into her bedroom!' Papa said.

'But he's not strange, he's Mr Walker, our friend. And this isn't really *my* bedroom, it's just a guest room. I don't see what all the fuss is about. The door was wide open anyway,' I said hurriedly.

'Yes. Your mama came up because she was concerned when you left the lunch table so abruptly – she says she saw you and Paris together,' Papa said. He lowered his voice to a whisper. 'She says she saw you embracing. Can that be true?'

'Well, yes, I hugged him because I was so happy about my drawing. He showed Miss Wentworth my Christmas card and—'

'Never mind your wretched drawing, Rose,' Papa said sharply.

I was so hurt. 'You don't care about it, do you, Papa? Just because you think it's silly scribbling you don't see that other people might find it amusing and interesting. But wait until it's published in *Judy* – do you see, it's a satirical feminist reply to *Punch*—'

'Did you kiss, you and Paris?'

I flinched, hating his tone. 'Papa, please. I don't know. Well, yes, I think we did kiss, but why is that so very dreadful?' I said.

Papa stared at me. 'Surely you understand, Rose! Was it just an innocent childish kiss? Please tell me that it meant nothing to you.'

I struggled. I had always been utterly truthful with Papa, and I wanted to be so now. 'Well, of course it meant something. I love Mr Walker,' I admitted.

'You love him as a child?' Papa asked, looking desperately hopeful. 'But you're becoming a young woman now and must never embrace a man like that, even a dear family friend. You're too young to understand why, but Mama will explain when you're older.'

But I already understood. I thought of those alarming depictions of the naked man and woman in Grandpapa's medical book, the unsettling explanatory text. I felt myself blushing a deep, painful red.

Papa stared at me and then dropped my hands. 'You *do* understand! Your mama is right. I can't believe it! My own dear little daughter!' he said brokenly, and he got up and left the room.

'Papa! I haven't done anything wrong, I promise. Please!' I ran out after him.

'Go back into your room and shut the door. I can't bear to look at you,' he said.

I did as I was told, trembling now. Papa was treating me as if I'd done something truly shameful – but it hadn't been like that at all. I hadn't planned to kiss Paris.

I'd just been so overjoyed that he hadn't cast me aside for Miss Wentworth. He'd talked to her about me, he'd tried to help me, he'd shown he cared about me. I had to make Papa understand. I rehearsed the words in my head, but I couldn't make them sound convincing, even to myself.

No one came near me all afternoon. Papa hadn't locked the door, but I didn't dare leave the room. I had my books, I had a sketchpad and pen and ink. I would normally have been happy to amuse myself, but now I couldn't settle to anything. I couldn't understand why Rupert or the children didn't come looking for me. Dear goodness, had Mama and Papa forbidden them to approach in case I contaminated them? And why hadn't Paris come to reassure me and help me explain what had happened?

I went to the window and looked out. I paced the room. I flung myself down on the truckle bed. I tried the four-poster, though I fancied it still smelled faintly of Nurse Budd's carbolic soap. I pulled the curtains together so that I could curl up in privacy, but they seemed to close in until I felt I was being smothered in yellow damask. When I flung the curtains wide, the walls themselves seemed nearer, and I wondered if I were going mad.

Some time later I heard Beth crying, and Clover's soft voice, but then there was silence. At teatime a maid brought me a glass of milk and a plate of bread and butter. No scone and jam, no cake – but at least they weren't starving me.

'What's happening?' I asked the maid. 'Are my parents very angry with me? Am I to stay here for the rest of the day?'

'I couldn't say, miss,' she said, looking worried. 'The mistress just said I had to bring this to your room.'

'The mistress? You mean my grandmother?'

'Yes, miss. She says she'll come to see you presently. I must go now, miss,' she said, and flew from the room.

I tried a few sips of milk and a mouthful of bread but couldn't manage any more, even though I'd had little to eat all day. The thought of seeing Grandmama was terrifying. I had no idea what 'presently' meant. In ten minutes? In a couple of hours? Would she slap me the way she'd slapped Mama?

I clenched my fists. She'd talked about grit. Well, I'd show her *I* had grit. I wouldn't howl and flail about the bed like Mama. I'd hold my head high to show her I'd done nothing wrong.

But when, half an hour later, Grandmama marched into the amber room without even knocking, I felt faint with fear.

'No wonder you look ashamed, Rose Rivers!' she said, her hands on her hips.

'I'm not ashamed,' I said defiantly.

'You brazen hussy,' said Grandmama. 'That dreadful nurse was right. She told me you'd set your cap at that ne'er-do-well, and I thought she was just making ludicrous suggestions. I thought your mother was bad enough, having her head turned when she was scarcely seventeen – but now here you are flaunting yourself at a grown man when you're still a child!'

'I didn't *flaunt*,' I said.

'Inviting that man into your room – my amber room – and behaving like a trollop!' said Grandmama.

'I didn't, I truly didn't!'

'Your mama told me in the strictest confidence that the night you arrived she caught you creeping along the attic corridor towards his room!' Grandmama whispered, speaking with such hissing emphasis that spittle gathered at the corners of her mouth.

'I wasn't!'

'So you're calling your own mother a liar?' Grandmama asked.

'No, she just misunderstood. I was trying to find Clover,' I said.

'Clover? The scruffy little nurserymaid? Why on earth would you be looking for her?'

'I was looking for her because she's my friend.'

'Have you no sense of shame? You want a servant girl for a friend? Dear goodness, I can't believe I have such a girl for a granddaughter. No wonder your mother was distraught.'

'That's not fair! She was upset because of Papa and that Louisa Mayhorne, it was nothing to do with me. I haven't done anything wrong, so why am I being blamed? Ask Mr Walker and he'll explain everything,' I cried.

'Lower your voice! How dare you talk to me in such a tone, missy! I wouldn't waste my breath talking to that degenerate, even if he were here,' said Grandmama.

'So where is he? Has he gone to Lord Mackay's?' I asked anxiously.

'I don't know and I don't care. He's certainly not welcome here. You're not welcome either, Rose. I can't believe that my own grandchild could behave in such a sly and disgusting manner. Still, I can hardly send you packing like a servant. So I'm asking you to stay in your room while we think what on earth to do with you,' said Grandmama, and she left the room.

I was so angry I kicked the end of the bed, and stubbed my toes painfully, but I didn't cry. I *wouldn't* cry. How dare they treat me like this! How could Grandmama talk to me with such contempt and refuse to listen to my explanations? Did she really believe Nurse Budd? And how could Mama be such a hypocrite, when she had been flirting with Paris herself? What had *she* been doing creeping around the attic bedrooms? How had she explained that to Grandmama? And did she really love Paris – or did she just want to get back at Papa?

Worst of all, Papa had said that he couldn't bear to look at me! I'd seen the way he'd looked at Louisa. I'd seen the way he'd painted her, his infatuation obvious in every stroke of his brush. He'd betrayed Mama. I hadn't betrayed anyone. I hadn't done anything bad with Paris anyway.

Had Paris really gone off and left me? Why hadn't he made them understand that nothing had happened between us? It was an innocent kiss. Or was it? I couldn't be sure. It had simply felt wonderful at the time. Even now I didn't wish it had never have happened.

There was a cautious knock on the door and someone whispered my name.

I ran and opened it. 'Rupert!'

'Ssh! We've been told not to go near you – even me! But they're all having their baths and getting ready for dinner so I thought I'd risk it. What on earth's been going on, old thing? What exactly have you *done*?'

'Oh, Rupe!' I said, and at last I burst into tears.

I sat on the edge of the truckle bed and Rupert sat beside me, his arm round my shoulders.

'There now. Have a good cry. Then you'd better mop your face and go and say sorry for whatever it is. They're being very fierce, so you'll need to look extra penitent. Even Papa refuses to talk about it,' he said. 'Come *on*, spill the beans!'

'I haven't done anything, Rupe. I just kissed Mr Walker and—'

'You did *what*?'

'Don't you go all stuffy on me – you told me you kissed Pamela!'

'Yes, but that was different. She's my age. I can't believe you had the nerve to kiss Mr Walker. So *that's* why he cleared off without saying goodbye to anyone. I just thought he'd had enough of us, especially Mama and her fit of hysterics. But whatever made you do such a thing! I knew you had a pash on him, but I never thought you could be so bold,' said Rupert.

'It was just a kiss. He's going to help get my drawings published. I was just so pleased that I threw my arms round his neck.'

'Where were you?'

'In here.'

'You're incredible! My little twin sister, so stern and studious – and there you are, inviting artists into your room!'

'I didn't! You're turning it into something horrid, just like the rest of them. Stop it! I'm not going to become one of your nasty stories. Mama and Papa are making a fuss about me, but what would they say if I told them about *you*?' I retorted.

Rupert sat up straight. He'd gone white. 'You won't, will you?'

'No, I won't tell, I wouldn't ever, you know I wouldn't, no matter what they did to me,' I said, furious that he could think that of me.

'Good old Rose,' he said. 'But I wonder what they *will* do to you? Oh well, at least you're a girl, so you won't get beaten. I dare say it will all blow over in a day or two. Only this morning it looked as if Mama and Papa were going to separate, but now they're united in their shock and horror over you – so you could say that you've done them a good turn.'

'Don't *joke* about it.'

'I'm just trying to cheer you up, that's all,' said Rupert. 'Oh well, I'd better go. They'll be furious if they find me here. At the moment I'm everybody's blue-eyed boy and I'd like to keep it that way.'

'You are such a devious monster, Rupert. I don't know how you can live with yourself,' I said.

'I manage very easily. Don't look so shocked. At least I'm not a hypocrite,' he said, and sauntered out of the room.

No one else came all evening, apart from the maid who brought me my dinner on a tray – clear soup and an unbuttered roll and a glass of water. It looked as if they were trying to purify me. I didn't really care. I wasn't in the least bit hungry.

However, I *did* mind when no one came to say goodnight. They were treating me like a leper! I'd hoped that Papa might relent and come to my door to make sure I was all right.

I found myself longing for Nurse to come and comfort me the way she used to when I'd been naughty. She'd tut at me, but when I'd had my cry she'd pick me up in her arms and hold me close. 'There, there,' she'd go. 'No need for any more tears. Nursie still loves you.'

But she clearly didn't love me any more, because she didn't come. I lay in bed, my head throbbing, aching with weariness but unable to sleep a wink. Some time after midnight my door opened and someone pattered across the floor.

'Rose?'

It was Clover!

'You shouldn't be here, Clover! If they catch you they'll send you away,' I whispered. 'Papa's so angry now he might do anything.'

'I don't care,' she said, climbing into my bed with difficulty. 'My goodness, this is a squeeze! Why aren't you sleeping in the big bed with the curtains?'

'I don't like it. It's where Nurse Budd slept.'

'I'm so glad she's gone!' Clover whispered. 'Poor Beth wants her back, but it's only because of that medicine. It's going to be weeks before she stops wanting it.'

'Don't you mind looking after her? You have to have so much patience. I've tried, but I'm useless with her.'

'I like trying to help her.'

'I wish you could help *me*, Clover,' I murmured, clinging to her. 'My whole family's turned against me.'

'The maids are saying that you did bad things with Mr Walker. *Did* you?'

'No, of course I didn't. I just kissed him because I was so grateful,' I said.

'Just kissed him! Then why are they making such a silly fuss? The girls in Cripps Alley do far more than that,' said Clover scornfully. 'Boys down the alley tried to kiss me, but I wasn't having it. I didn't want anyone slobbering over me.'

'Our kiss wasn't slobbery,' I said.

'Anyway, why were you grateful to him?' Clover asked.

I told her that he'd shown Miss Wentworth my card and she wanted to publish my work.

'That's wonderful! Your pictures will be in a proper paper!'

'Well, it's just a college paper, but lots of people read it. Of course, I don't know whether she *will* use any of my drawings,' I said.

'Of course she will,' said Clover. 'You'll be famous, Rose, you mark my words.'

'You're the one who'll be famous,' I said. 'You're a much better artist than me. Maybe one day, when we're both grown up, we could share a studio,' I suggested.

'You and me? That would be lovely!'

'What do you think's going to happen to me, Clover? Are they going to keep me cooped up in this room until we go home next week?' I asked her.

'We're going back tomorrow. Nurse and I have been packing the children's trunks. We're to get the ten-o'clock train. Didn't they tell you?'

'They haven't told me anything! They didn't even send a maid to help me pack *my* things,' I said indignantly.

'Well, I'll help you now if you like,' Clover offered.

'No, better not. We might make a noise opening and shutting cupboards. You'd better go back to your room now, just in case, though I'd give anything for you to stay. You're my only true friend in all the world, Clover. I thought Mr Walker was my friend, but he's just run away. I don't suppose he'll be Papa's friend any more either. I always counted Rupert as my best friend, but I don't think even he really cares about me.'

'Well, *I* care about you. Try to go to sleep now. Everything will be all right once we're back in London,' said Clover.

I tried to believe her. I lay awake long after she went, but eventually I fell fast asleep. I was woken by the maid coming into my room with a tray of tea and toast.

I sat up in bed and gulped my tea thirstily. 'Thank you. Can you tell me the time, please?'

'It's ten to nine, miss,' she said.

'What!' I started out of bed. 'But we'll have to leave soon to get the train! I haven't even packed! Can you have my trunk brought in, please?'

'Don't fret, miss. You're not getting the train.'

'So we're staying here for the rest of the holidays after all?' I asked.

'Well, *you're* staying, miss,' she said.

'What do you mean?'

'You'd better ask the mistress, miss.'

'Are the rest of my family going back to London?'

'Please, miss, I'll be in so much trouble if I tell you,' she said, nearly in tears.

'They're going without me? Not even saying goodbye?' I said, unable to believe it.

'*We're* coming to say goodbye, Miss Rose,' said Nurse, appearing in the doorway, Phoebe bundled in a shawl on her hip. 'Your mama said she didn't want any contact between you and your brothers and sisters, but it's too cruel. You're still a child, for all you've got yourself into

456

a pickle and brought disgrace on us.' She came forward and gave me a stiff little hug. I tried to hang onto her, but she eased herself away. 'You'll squash Baby,' she said. 'I'll fetch the other children.'

First Sebastian came running in, holding his mouse cage. He was already buttoned into his outdoor coat, his face very pink.

'Oh, Rose, I'm going to miss you so much,' he said. 'We don't know what you've done, except it's very bad, but I don't care, I still love you.'

'I love you too, Sebastian,' I said. 'I shall miss you so much too.'

'Will you be very lonely?' he asked. He went even pinker. 'Perhaps I'd better let you have Montmorency for company.'

'That's so sweet of you, but I think he'd pine away without you,' I said.

'Yes, I think you're right,' said Sebastian, mightily relieved.

I pushed back his soft white hair and whispered into his ear, 'Do you know where I'm going if I can't come home with you?'

He shook his head. 'They won't tell and Nurse says she doesn't know.'

Algie and Clarrie came in together, holding hands. Clarrie was crying, her face damp with tears as she pressed it against mine.

'Bye bye, Rose. Promise you'll come back to us soon?'

I promised, hoping against hope that I would.

'Crybaby!' Algie said scornfully to Clarrie – but when I gave him a hug he burst into tears himself. 'Don't go!' he begged, though he was the one going, not me.

Then Clover appeared, encouraging Beth to come with her. Beth started whimpering again when she saw the washstand. She touched the empty amber cabinet and shook her head sadly.

'Say goodbye to Rose,' Clover prompted her.

'Goodbye to Rose,' Beth repeated obediently.

But when she got to the door again she turned. 'Rose, Rose, Rose!' she wailed.

'Oh, Beth!' I cried. I tried to give her a hug but she shrank away.

'Goodbye, Rose,' Clover whispered. There were tears in her big green eyes.

I wasn't going to be thwarted again. I put my arms round her and gave her the longest, fiercest hug. 'Goodbye, my dearest friend,' I said.

Rupert was last. He shook his head. 'Oh dear Lord, this is like those child death scenes in sentimental books. It's as if little Rose is about to join the angels. Or devils, in your case, if the parents are to be believed.'

'Mr Rupert!' Nurse reprimanded him. 'Say goodbye to your sister and stop this nonsense. Come on, we've got to set off to the station.'

'Goodbye, Rose,' said Rupert, and then he dashed out of the room.

'That's a fine way for your brother to behave,' Nurse clucked, but I'd seen that Rupert's face was screwed up to stop himself crying.

'What about Mama and Papa, Nurse? They're coming to say goodbye, aren't they?' I asked.

She looked uncomfortable. 'I don't think so, dear. Perhaps they think it will be less upsetting,' she said.

'*Papa's* not coming to say goodbye?' I whispered.

'Perhaps he'll change his mind at the last minute,' she said. 'Goodbye, Miss Rose. Do try to be a good sensible girl now.'

She left the room so quickly I didn't get a chance to kiss my littlest sister goodbye.

The maid was hovering, near tears herself. 'Finish your breakfast and get yourself washed and dressed, miss,' she said. 'The mistress said you were to come downstairs at ten o'clock.'

I drank the rest of my tea, but my throat ached so much I couldn't swallow any toast. I washed and put on my best green frock, taking care to brush my hair properly.

As the grandfather clock struck ten, I walked downstairs, my head held high. A couple of young maids peeped at me from behind the green baize door, nudging each other, their eyes round.

I went into the drawing room. Grandmama was sitting bolt upright on a hard chair, her face stony. Grandpapa was drumming his fingers on the velvet cushions of the Chesterfield.

'There you are, Rose. At least you're prompt,' said Grandmama. She peered at me, frowning. 'Look at you, all got up as if you're about to go visiting! You don't seem even a wee bit ashamed of your conduct.'

'I can't seem to please you at all, Grandmama. If I'd come down in my nightgown you'd have told me off even more,' I said.

'You wee besom!' She heaved herself to her feet.

'So it's my turn for a good slapping?' I said, determined not to show her that I was frightened.

Grandmama snorted, and looked at Grandpapa. 'You deal with her, Angus. I can't bear to look at her any more.'

'That's what Papa said about me,' I murmured.

'Well, I never thought I'd have anything in common with that father of yours, but we are united on this matter,' said Grandmama. 'Please do your best to keep out of my way until you go, Rose.'

She walked out of the room with as much dignity as she could muster, though I noticed for the first time that she had started to move with an old woman's shuffle. Grandpapa looked very old, his white hair standing on end. He'd had a restless night too.

He sat silently watching me. I stood there, still as a statue.

'You can't fool me, Rose,' he said suddenly. 'You're in despair, aren't you, lassie?'

I nodded. 'Am I really to be kept away from my family?' I asked huskily.

'For a while. Sit yourself down now.'

It was as well he'd given me permission, for I'd have fallen down any second.

'If you ask me this is all a nonsense,' said Grandpapa. 'Everyone's nerves are fraught after the fiasco last night, with poor Jeannie getting in such a state and your father making a fool of himself over that wretched woman. I think you've been turned into a wee scapegoat, Rose. I don't think you were seriously carrying on with the artist. I'm sure that wicked nurse was telling lies – and your mama is simply deluded. It seems to me you're still an innocent little girl. However, if this artist chappie forced himself on you I'll have him horsewhipped.'

'It wasn't his fault. Or mine. I just hugged him because I was so happy. Mama misunderstood. Papa did too,' I said. 'Oh, Grandpapa, at last someone's on my side!'

'I wouldn't go so far as to say that, lass. You've behaved very stupidly – and taking that insolent attitude with your grandmother won't help. I can't wave a magic wand and make everything all right. I don't think you're old enough for true seduction, but I certainly think you're old enough to understand that you behaved very unwisely.'

'I promise I'll behave myself now, Grandpapa. I'll be as good as gold. But how long do I have to stay here?' I asked.

'You're not staying here, child! Your grandmother won't countenance it. You're being sent away as a punishment,' he said.

'Sent away!' The room seemed to spin around me. *Where* were they sending me? 'To an asylum?' I whispered.

461

Grandpapa stared at me and then burst out laughing. 'Dear heavens, child, what an idea! I have an institution in mind, certainly, but scarcely an asylum. I have written to Chadwick Hall – it's a girls' boarding school by the sea. The Master of the Hunt sends his three lassies there. I don't hold with schooling for girls, but I think you'd benefit, especially as you seem to like studying. It will give you a chance to forget all this unpleasantness. If the headmistress will take you, I'll get your grandmama or her maid to take you to Draffens department store to kit you out in the right uniform. You should be able to start at the beginning of term. What do you think, eh?'

What do I think? I'm going to school. It's what I've always longed for. I'd imagined intellectual teachers, lively girls, long talks about life and art and literature, fascinating new forays into science and maths and Latin and Greek. But I have to admit I'm scared. I have no idea what it will really be like. The other girls will all be Scottish, so I'll stand out with my English accent. I will probably be an odd one out anyway. All the girls I've met think I'm strange and don't really want to be friends. I suspect I'll be very lonely. I can't even box if the girls turn against me!

I must take courage. Show some grit, like Clover, like Hetty Feather. A girls' boarding school isn't a slum alley or a foundling hospital. I will get an education at last. Perhaps I will even go on to study for a degree like Miss Wentworth. I have her address tucked inside my sketchbook.

I am not going to think about Papa, though his coldness breaks my heart. I am not going to think about Mama. I am not going to think about my siblings, not even Rupert.

I can't help thinking about Paris.

He's sent me a letter. The maid slipped it to me, knowing that Grandmama would confiscate it if she saw it.

Dear Rose,

I am so sorry. I feel devastated that I've got you into trouble. Your father is very angry with me, perhaps with justification, so I thought it better to leave at once.

I very much hope you will contact Miss Wentworth and continue your brilliant satirical drawings. You truly have talent. You simply have to believe in yourself.

Perhaps we might meet some time in the future?

Your loving friend,
Paris

Perhaps, perhaps, perhaps . . .

Is he my loving friend? Does he really care for me?

I know Clover cares. *She* is my friend. I twist the silver bangle on my wrist. Hetty Feather is my friend too. I hope I have their courage. Perhaps I will make even more friends at school. Please wish me luck.

ABOUT THE ILLUSTRATOR

NICK SHARRATT has written and
illustrated many books for children and won
numerous awards for his picture books, including
the Children's Book Award and the Educational
Writers' Award. He has also enjoyed great success
illustrating Jacqueline Wilson's books.
Nick lives in Brighton.

VISIT JACQUELINE'S FANTASTIC WEBSITE!

There's a whole Jacqueline Wilson town to explore!
You can generate your own special username,
customize your online bedroom, test your knowledge
of Jacqueline's books with fun quizzes and puzzles,
and upload book reviews. There's lots of fun stuff
to discover, including competitions, book trailers,
and Jacqueline's scrapbook. And if you love writing,
visit the special storytelling area!

Plus, you can hear the latest news from Jacqueline
in her monthly diary, find out whether she's doing
events near you, read her fan-mail replies, and
chat to other fans on the message boards!

www.jacquelinewilson.co.uk

ALL ABOUT THE VICTORIANS

Rose Rivers' story takes place in London during the reign of Queen Victoria. Read on to find out more about this important period in history . . .

Queen Victoria ruled for sixty-three years from 1837 until her death in 1901. Born in 1819, she was only eighteen years old when she became queen!

✦

Queen Victoria married Prince Albert, and they had nine children together. Queen Victoria's descendants are still on the British throne today – Queen Elizabeth II is Queen Victoria's great-great-granddaughter.

✦

Like Clover Moon, many Victorians were born into extreme poverty. Children from very poor families wouldn't have gone to school; instead, they went to work in factories, mines, or as chimney sweeps or shoeblacks; or they might have sold items like matches or flowers on the streets. Many Victorians were so poor that they were forced into workhouses – factories where people worked in terrible conditions in exchange for scraps of food and a place to sleep.

✦

In contrast, other Victorians, like Rose Rivers' family, were extremely rich! Boys from wealthy families were sent to school and often to university. Wealthy girls, on the other hand, might have been sent to a 'finishing school' where they would learn to become a 'lady', taking lessons in French, singing and dancing, playing the piano – and even curtseying!

✦

The legacy of the Victorian era is very much still felt around the world today. It was a period of great human ingenuity – now called the Industrial Revolution – during which British scientists and engineers invented key technologies that have shaped the modern world. But it was also a time of great hardship and suffering for many poor people in Britain and around the world who were powerless in the face of the might of the British Empire.

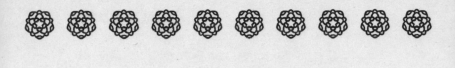

VICTORIAN ARTISTS

Art and artists were very important in the Victorian era. Painting in the early years of Victoria's reign was dominated by the Royal Academy of Arts and by the theories of its first president, Joshua Reynolds.

❖

Reynolds and the academy were strongly influenced by the Italian Renaissance painter Raphael,

and believed that it was the role of an artist to
make the subject of their work appear as noble
and idealized as possible.

✦

When Victoria came to the throne, the most famous
living British artist was J. M. W. Turner. He painted
landscape watercolours. He left behind over 2,000
paintings and 19,000 drawings and sketches.
He is sometimes referred to as 'the painter of light'
and is buried in St Paul's Cathedral, London.

✦

In 1848 three students at the Royal Academy,
William Holman Hunt, John Everett Millais and
Dante Gabriel Rossetti, formed the Pre-Raphaelite
Brotherhood. The PRB rejected the ideas of Joshua
Reynolds, and believed it was important to paint
from imagination to show things as they most
likely would have been, not in the way that
would appear most attractive.

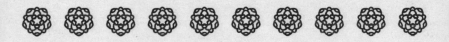

HOW TO MAKE A SILHOUETTE PORTRAIT

You will need:

✦ A photograph of your head and shoulders taken from the side (in profile)
✦ Pencil
✦ Black card
✦ White or coloured card for the background
✦ Glue
✦ Scissors
✦ Frame

1. Take a photograph from the side of your head and shoulders and print out the photo onto ordinary paper.

2. Using scissors, carefully cut around the person – you may need to ask a grown-up for help.

3. Place the cut-out onto some black paper or card and draw around it using the pencil.

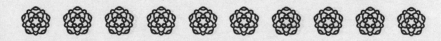

4. Cut the silhouette portrait out of the black card.

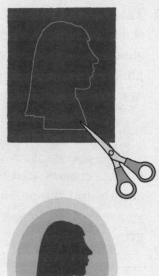

5. Cut a piece of coloured card in an oval shape so that the black cut-out fits comfortably in the centre and glue in place. You can glue this oval onto a slightly larger oval of a different colour if you like.

6. Cut a piece of white or coloured card to fit the frame and stick your portrait onto the centre of it.

7. Now frame your portrait! If you don't have a frame to use, you could make one out of card.

Jacqueline has written many other wonderful
stories inspired by the Victorian era –
have you read them all?

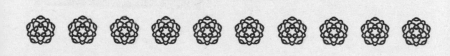